If the Walls Fall

Book One of the Ascend Trials
K. Malady

"I am no bird; and no net ensnares me: I am a free human being with an independent will."

Charlotte Brontë, *Jane Eyre*

For my favorites.

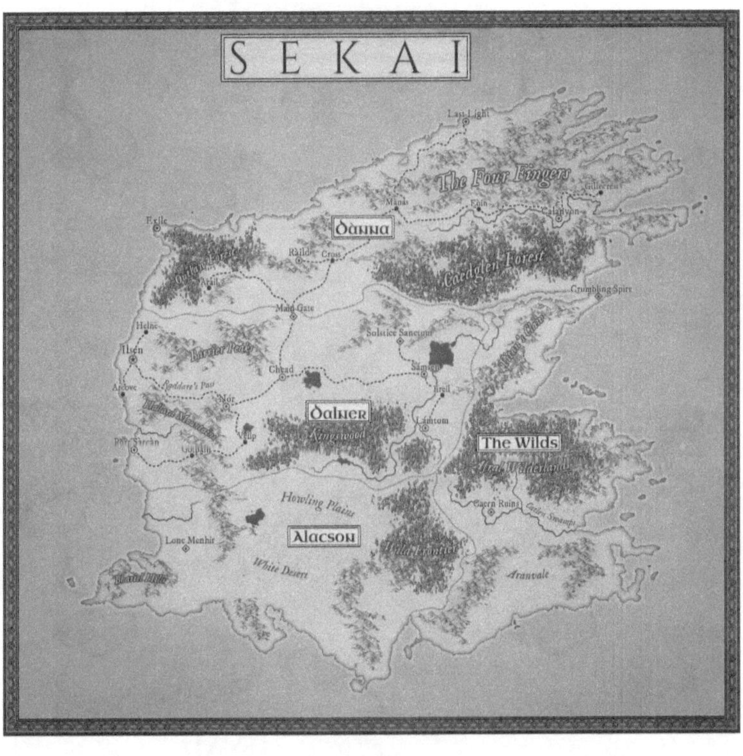
SEKAI
Last Light
The Four Fingers
Gillecreu
Manas
Eoin
Calanvon
Exile
Danna
Raild
Cross
Caedglen Forest
Outlaw Forest
Arail
Crumbling Spire
Main Gate
Helne
Solstice Sanctum
Ilsen
Barrier Peaks
Titan's Claw
Chead
Samhen
Arcove
Godderr's Pass
Breil
Nor
Malland Marshes
Dalner
Lantom
Velip
Kingswood
The Wilds
Port Sarean
Gorpath
Ural Wasteland
Howling Plains
Caern Ruins
Caden Swamps
Lone Menhir
Alacson
Wild Frontier
White Desert
Aranvale
Blasted Hills

Contents

CHAPTER 1

Tonight is Halloween, and I'm dressed as the 'girl who will get a date.' Assuming I can summon the bravery needed to ask. So far cowardice always wins.

"You didn't need to walk me home," I tell Dave when we arrive at the door to my dorm apartment, hoping to stall him for a few more minutes while I search for my courage.

This is a practiced dance. Each night when I leave the student union, Dave escorts me home. Most nights I wear my boxy work uniform that removes even the slightest hint of curves, my almond skin splattered in pizza grease. But not tonight. Tonight, I dressed in my favorite t-shirt and jeans, styled my unruly chocolate brown hair, and volunteered to spend my rare evening off manning the safe-sex table for the school's Halloween fair since I knew he was working.

"You know why I do," Dave says, his voice cracking as if he's the kid barely out of puberty instead of me. "And we get some real fanatics on campus that wouldn't appreciate what you're doing."

"You mean encouraging sex out of wedlock?" My cheeks heat as I gesture to the knapsack that holds the few leftover condoms and pamphlets from the fair. Unsaid is that I've never used them before, or that I stole the joke from a bodice ripper I read three weeks ago—one that gave me the confidence and idea to show Dave how worldly I am.

"Exactly," he says as his feet scuff the pavement. "Add in how young you are and it's not right, you walking alone all the time."

At seventeen years old, I'm not the youngest student on campus but am the youngest in my year, and the only one forced to live in campus housing until I turn eighteen as a condition of enrollment. Dave is the only guy I speak to regularly, and my feelings jump from infatuation to friendship and back each time I see him. When he learned how young I was, something I struggle to keep hidden, his chivalry kicked in and my chances for catching a boyfriend dwindled. But I'm armed with more than just condoms tonight. I've got a mind full of romance novels, and one of those plots has to work.

I've imagined a hundred scenarios for my first date, each carefully curated from whatever book I'm reading at the time. On tonight's walk, Dave doesn't have a bouquet of belladonna and I wasn't just released from confinement, but the base tropes can apply. We'll be friends to lovers. Or opposites attract, since I'm not quite what Dave does when he's not working security, or mentor/mentee because of the age difference—

"Do you have plans for tonight?"

My mind stalls as the list of plotlines spins away. I always assumed I'd need to ask someone out, once I mustered up the courage, since no one was lining up for me. I try not to swallow my tongue as my opportunity arises.

"Just finishing my book," I blurt, pulling my knapsack higher on my shoulders. "I'm completely free otherwise, just me. My roommate's not supposed to be home for—"

"Good, there's supposed to be a storm." He peers at the darkening sky.

"You could come over and we could watch a movie," I suggest, undeterred when he remains silent. I bat my hazel brown eyes like my roommate Julie does, pressing out my chest. She told me it was a "good way to emphasize your lacking assets, since your personality can be off putting." Julie's a jerk but with my flat chest and wide hips, I can use all the help I can get. Maybe I'll pretend to trip and fall into his arms. That seems to work no matter the book.

"My roommate's boyfriend left some horror films here," I add when his gaze remains on the sky. I can salvage this—this can still be my first date, a *pre-date*. Or even just a night with a new friend; I'm low on those too. I'd even take being his plucky sidekick. Anything over another night alone.

"I need to check the windows at my boyfriend's. But I'll see you after your next shift," Dave replies, giving me a strange look. "You be safe, kid."

A rock sinks in my gut as he yanks on the glass door of the building until it scrapes open. I slink inside, twisting my lips in defeat. After he checks that the door latched behind him, he waves goodbye and lopes away.

I stare at Dave's retreating back until he disappears before turning to the concrete stairwell. At least I managed to try this time. As my foot lifts to the first step, the world goes black.

Spots dance in the darkness until a long hallway appears. It feels like a dream, that hazy floaty feeling where nothing is *quite* real. There's a door at the end of the hallway, one that looks like the entrance to my Grandma's house at the nursing home where she died—dented blue steel, sad and forgotten.

Something tugs me towards the door, like a fishhook wrapped around my waist, which tightens and yanks.

I wake up, face down and prone. It isn't light behind my eyes or the feel of the earth below me that tells me something is amiss, but the smells. Instead of the normal dorm smell, it's fresh. There's no acrid scent wafting from the piles of dirty clothes in the corner. There's no lingering scent of cheap spearmint cologne that Julie sprays on her pillow each night before bed, her awful boyfriend's signature scent. Instead, it smells like earth and open air.

Blearily, I open my eyes and straighten the crick in my neck while trying to adjust to the bright light.

It must be a vivid dream—a continuation of the fishhook dream that haunted me only moments before. Maybe this dream is a gift for my solitary brain, one where I'm the protagonist and find my true love. The book I'm reading has a similar theme—a woman wakes in the desert, and her kidnapper is a mobster (as they often are) who she falls in love with (as one does).

I roll onto my back and sit up, dirt and dust kicking into the air, a bright sun shining above. There's no handsome pirate-kidnapper in my sight line. My head is also pounding, which removes the prospect of 'romance' from this possible dream. Grass stains my jeans, and my fleece windbreaker is ripped at the elbow;

dirt smudges my nails, and the ground is dewy beneath me. I'm outside, in a mossy green field, with nothing else in sight.

This can't be a dream. Unless my charming love-interest shows up in the next two minutes, I need to face facts. I've been kidnapped.

I live in my imagination most times, running through various silly scenarios, like the one in the book I'm reading, like the one I imagined with Dave last night. But I'm unprepared to live through any of those outlandish plots. I wrap my arms around my middle to self-soothe, something that helped me as a child when I was nervous, and lean my head on my knees, letting my dusty hair cover my eyes. Spots of worry invade my vision. I may have been uncharitable to those literary damsels in distress.

After taking a few deep breaths, a child's voice sounds inside my head, high pitched and lilting, with an accent I can't place. It tells me to **calm down** and **start moving**. It's reassuring but oddly reminiscent of that British slogan that made the rounds over the internet a few years ago. It must be *my* inner voice, that running internal monologue that constantly flits through my head, reverting to something more innocent to relax me.

I listen to myself—calm down and start moving—but my childlike guide gives me no help on which direction to go. There are no roads, only an emerald green field with rolling hills in all directions. The hills behind me grow into a forest green mountain range where a veil of mist shrouds the peaks. Aside from the gray mist hazing above me, I'm engulfed in green.

It's certainly more charming than the yellowed brick building of my dorm and the view of the trash-filled alley from my window. After living in a suburb of Chicago in school, and in and out of my father's apartment before that, this is the first time I've seen somewhere so... empty. There are no cities anywhere in sight, not even phone or utility lines.

Phone lines. *Phone!* my inner voice cries, back to its normal pitch and dialect (a Missourian twang). My cell phone should be in my canvas tote bag, the free one I received from a University bookstore promotion. I whip around until I find the bag on the ground a few feet away, crawling towards it with a giddiness caused by adrenaline and nerves. It still has my phone, wallet, pen, six pieces of chewing gum, a dog-eared romance novel that I found at the thrift store for less than a dollar, and a dozen extra condoms and pamphlets left over from the volunteering event. Whoever forced me here stole nothing but my dorm keys.

I shake off the agitation licking at the edges of my brain that demands I walk towards help. Instead, I pull out my battered flip-phone from my bag. The low battery light blinks but with shaking fingers, I put in the passcode, Mom's birthday, and call 911. The numbers stare back at me, remaining unchanged even after I mash the green 'phone' button until my thumb turns white. I peer closely at the top of the screen. Instead of a half pyramid of bars in the corner, a mean little exclamation mark greets me. I toss the phone to the bottom of the bag with more force than necessary.

I rest my chin on my crossed knees again. I'm in the middle of nowhere, with no communication and no way to get home. In short, I'm doomed.

Twenty minutes and lots of sniffling later, I trudge towards the mountains, praying a town emerges from the open field. The field has grasses taller than my knees that swish in the wind, but the wildlife, if any exist, remains eerily quiet.

Pain blooms in my legs after the start of hour three. When the strap of the tote bag digs into my shoulder, I ditch my excess weight: the pen, book, condoms, and pamphlets. I grimace at the litter trailing behind me but the condoms' phantom encouragement from the night before vanished when I woke on the ground.

Finally, an outcropping of trees rises from the hills, and behind them, buildings with shingle roofs. Beyond that, the smattering of white and gray mist recedes into the mountains. I break into a run until the buildings grow human sized.

The wooden shingle roofs connect to modest stucco houses patterned with wood strips in the shapes of crosses or squares, each crammed together in winding rows. It looks like a real-life fairy-tale village, one the younger me saw with my parents in Europe, seemingly unspoiled by technology until a closer look reveals the cell phone stuck to someone's ear. I stop the memory before it goes any further, banishing it to the recesses of my mind with other thoughts of Mom (back when Rick was Dad and not just father), because straying down that path brings tears. I focus on the town I've found, hope blossoming in my chest.

Close up, it resembles a strangely detailed Renaissance Fair. Ribbons and flags wave from the windows, sounds of people and bells trill in the air, and the smell of meat and hops is thick around me. The women wear jewel-toned dresses with white aprons, some smeared with grease and dirt, others crisp and clean. The men wear black or brown leggings and long jewel toned shirts belted with twine. I reconsider—not a Renaissance Faire, but a medieval fair where actors mill about, all in character as they go about their day. Except—I don't see any booths selling wares, instead it looks like the illustrations in one of my textbooks. There also isn't a ticket area or any form of security nearby. I ignore this, choosing to focus on the fact that there are people, there is food. Which means somewhere, there is a phone and some help.

I scan for someone, *anyone*, I can turn to for help, but the moment I catch someone's attention, they flee from my reach. I collide with the first person walking slow enough for me to accost, a pale woman about my age wearing an indigo shift dress loosely laced over her substantial bosom and gray apron. She meanders down a dirt road (aisle?), holding a basket filled with something sweet smelling. My stomach and my mouth groan in tandem as the scent wafts towards me and I clench my fists to keep from snatching something from inside.

"Hi," I say, wide eyed and struggling to control the shaking that I've pushed off all day. "I need help. I need a phone."

"Sásche tlóh chàkres," she says, lifting a single bushy eyebrow and trailing her gaze down my sweat-soaked and grimy clothes. I blink back at her, hope fading that she was a Faire actor overly committed to staying in character.

"Do—do you not speak English?" I haven't considered the possibility that I might be in a different country, assuming I woke up only a few hours after leaving Dave. A pressure blooms behind my eyes at the thought, the tears I'm holding back minutes from bursting out of me.

"I said, don't speak nonsense." She bares her crooked teeth, clutching her basket closer and inspecting me with more purpose this time.

The tiniest bit of relief replaces the panic oozing inside me.

"You *can* understand me. I need a phone." I cross my arms around my middle, keeping my traitorous hands from either grabbing her or the basket.

"A... phone? I told you, don't speak nonsense." She juts out her chin and turns away. The string on my self-control tightens and all the panic and fear I'm holding in threaten to erupt.

"Yes," I say, snagging her bell-shaped sleeves and holding her in place, but she shakes out of my grip. "A phone. Please. I need a phone. Or a ride to a hospital, something. I think I've been kidnapped."

As if I've said the magic word, her eyes flood with concern while her hands loosen on the basket in her arms. "Kidnapped?

My word, you poor dear," she tuts. "Follow me." Without touching me, she directs me down the road onto another street.

An unsettling feeling washes over me as I follow her. My festival impression of the town wanes—the doors we pass don't shake against the stucco like a moveable festival building would, and the outfits have a handmade quality rather than something mass produced. If this isn't a Faire, I've found myself in another country, one that speaks English as a second language and lives in technological isolation

"My husband," she calls out after stopping in front of a single-storied straw-thatched home with curved wood slats covering the outer walls. A giant man ducks under the doorway, but the woman keeps her eyes on me. He dresses as she does, in a grease smudged indigo shirt but with leggings and an unruly red beard covering half his face. He gazes down at her, clasping her hand and bringing it to his lips before narrowing his eyes in my direction.

"My husband," she repeats in a reverent tone. She gestures with a sharp shake of her head. "This dirty child speaks gibberish, but she bade me help."

The man looks me over as she had, stopping on my tight jeans for longer than is polite. Considering the woman in front of him could probably breastfeed without loosening a single lace, his preoccupation with my legs has me frowning and slumping over, using the windbreaker to cover my ample hips as best I can. One corner of his mouth ticks up when I do.

"Her attire causes me a different sort of alarm." He leers, his teeth as crooked as hers and yellowed. "She appears not as a child but as an Eósy sent to tempt the good husbands of Dalner. I recommend we call on the town council about a possible weakening in the walls near the Eastern Gate."

My limited self-preservation kicks in as I ignore the insult. I need help in whatever form, even if it's from the ogling creep.

"Yes—call someone. Anyone. I just need a phone… or take me to a security guard, even," I say, running dusty fingers through my sweat caked hair. The woman gingerly takes my hand and tsks out of the corner of her mouth.

"These are not the words of Dànna, my love," she tells her husband. "Merely the ramblings of a lost fool."

The string on my self control snaps. I rip my hand from hers while the emotions I've avoided all day force themselves to the surface.

"This isn't funny anymore, this isn't a joke. I don't care if you'll break character." I grab her by the shoulders and shake her hard, getting an eyeful of bare skin as her bodice opens in front of me. "Get me a phone, get me to customer service, get me a cop. I don't care, just do something!"

The street empties quicker than the condom jar did when the freshman seminar let out. While I bang on the door the two strangers ran through, someone speaks through the walls of a stucco building nearby.

"We should send word to the castle of a fool wreaking havoc near the Eastern Gate." Two other voices murmur agreements.

I wipe roughly at my eyes, dirt and sweat smudging my skin. With no other options, I trudge towards the mountains in search of this 'castle.'

My stomach gurgles as I pop the second piece of gum in my mouth. I press my palms to my empty stomach, huffing at the lost opportunity to fill my belly from that woman's basket. The mountains rise far in the distance, this castle most likely miles and miles away. In the distance, a veil of mist still clings to them, but dissipates and reforms to give me glimpses of their height. They're majestic, almost reaching the sun, and too far to contemplate. I sink to the ground. Someone will report my disappearance. Someone will find me. I can wait it out.

Get to the mountain, get to the mountain, get to the mountain, the childlike voice repeats, growling as I consider giving up and waiting to be found. The voice's tone intensifies until I shuffle to stand to stop the internal shouting.

That I'm arguing with my mind, a sign of my diminishing sanity, is something I'll handle when I'm saved.

"Get to the mountain, get to the mountain." I repeat out loud, in sync with the child's, until my voice cracks.

Hours go by, but the mountains look no closer and still there are no people or living things in sight. I finally reach a stream surging out of the valley between two emerald hills. While I have no survival skills, I know I won't last long without water. I'd read a book where the protagonist's first love died from a lack of water and the description was nauseating. The stream is less than three feet wide and mud colored, but dehydration isn't a viable alternative.

I scan overhead as the sun sheaths behind the mountains. It seems inevitable I'll spend another night out here without even a cricket for company. I sit at the edge of the stream bed and hold in a mewl.

Suddenly, something appears in the sky. My breath catches, comfort filling me in knowing that I'm not completely alone. I squint, watching its wingspan cast shadows in the dimming light as the comfort quickly fades. As the creature crests overhead, it looks as wide as a horse and twice as long, a serpentine being with black wings that flap with such fervor that causes the small stream to splash onto my ankles.

The small part not quaking from fear shames past-Grace for how I judged characters in books. I can no longer say I'll react differently, *better*, than the protagonists, or that I just needed the opportunity to show it. Because when the flying beast attempts to land, instead of reacting bravely or logically, I scream and pass out.

CHAPTER 2

"Diya thinks she's alright?" a male voice says when I regain consciousness. His voice has an accented lilt, from a location I can't pinpoint.

"I am unsure. The better question is how she arrived here," another voice says, also male with a cultured edge, similar to the childlike voice that made its home in my brain.

"We can't leave her here," a third voice says. Another man, his voice honey smooth. "It doesn't look as though she breached a wall, but..."

The second man hums.

"Do you thinks she's the—" the first says.

"After she fainted," the second voice says, which sounds like a statement and not a question. "Though you are aware of my theories on the subject. We cannot be too sure until we know more."

"Wait, she appears to be waking."

Three faces peer down at me when I open my eyes. I claw my fingers and kick outward, attempting a defensive position in case they approach closer. I flail to the side, my legs too exhausted from walking and the adrenaline crash from fainting. It takes two tries until I sit with my knees pressed into my chest, fists balling at my side.

All of them are male, and taller than me, though that isn't difficult. They resemble the Medieval cosplayers from the town, with earth toned blouses (tunics?), snug pants, leather vests, and shoes. They all have long silken hair and one has a trimmed beard. And they're far too attractive for this countryside setting.

"Easy," the first voice says. His big green eyes, the color of forest leaves, twinkle. He stands shorter than his companions with wavy apple-red hair worn loose down his back, his gem-colored eyes bright against ruddy freckled skin. His shirt looks frayed and yellowed either from age or stains. "We aren't here to hurt you. You lost?"

I blink rapidly, trying to force my brain into focusing before nodding.

The second voice, a blond, knickers at me as one would a wild animal. I try not to take offense, but I did just faint in their presence. He smiles disarmingly from a crooked mouth split by wide pink lips and framed by a dark goatee. Taller than the others by several inches and older by several years, his long blond hair is braided into a thick plait that ends at his hip. He wears a crisp cream tunic, not the yellowed color of the redhead's but something resembling whipped butter. He has wrinkles at the corner of his eyes and a deep crease in the middle of his forehead but, unlike the others, no callouses split his fingers. He grabs his friend, the third man, by the shoulder, keeping him from getting too close.

"She must be frightened. To awaken with strangers staring over her." The blond's voice is elegant, like he took elocution lessons in his formative years.

The third man leans over me, too close for my current comfort level, pushing against the arms of the blond holding him back. "She's not frightened. She's distracted by my winning smile and handsome face," he says.

I scowl at him as my cheeks heat. In a different scenario, I would be attracted to him because he's my idea of gorgeous. He's thinner than the others, thinner than me, but still toned, with wavy midnight black hair interspersed with a few small braids that trail past his shoulders. His bronze face is sharp but pretty, with high cheekbones and supple lips. With his looks, he should be leaning indolently against a wall or kicking his feet up on a desk. His outfit is as well made as the blond's, but dust covers the charcoal fabric. When he notices my appraisal, he stops shoving against the blond man and bows. He gives an exaggerated wink when he rises, his mahogany eyes smoldering.

"Enough. She is a child, not a threat," a new voice says from behind me. The three men above me jolt and slink away, giving me room to collect myself enough to stand. I only waver for a second, causing the blond to reach out to catch me, but I manage to swing myself upward and plant my feet.

"I'm not a child. But I do need help," I say, sounding much stronger than I feel, my temper rising to keep me from sniffling.

The three men eye each other and my legs again, muttering to themselves without responding.

I groan, putting my hands on my hips. "This again? *Excuse me yee old gentlemen, I beseech thee to tell me whaeth the hell is going on and to geteth me a phone.*" Bitter tears burn behind my eyes.

The fourth man stomps forward to stand a foot away. He is the broadest of the four and all muscle, covered by a sweeping fur coat that skims the ground. He looks younger than the blond but is obviously the leader, given his stance and the way the others defer to him. In his whisky brown hair are dozens of red and blue beads. A single silver bead rests at the point of a thin beard, which is peppered with gray. There is a hardness to him that isn't found in the others, one that must have prematurely aged his hair. While not the most handsome of the four, he commands attention and I almost lose my balance as his ice blue eyes stare down at me. If he wasn't scowling, I'd call him ruggedly beautiful.

I blink twice. This isn't the time for this. No matter what happens in the books, romance has no place in a real life kidnapping scenario.

"Calm yourself," he says in a deep and, I hate to admit, sultry baritone. "You've had an episode of hysteria. You need not exert yourself." The disdain from his words and his sneering expression wipe away anything pleasing about him. I bristle at his tone.

"Calm myself? *Calm* myself?" I bellow, my voice rising in pitch with every word. "Someone abandoned me in this open field. I was most likely drugged, possibly assaulted. And those stupid cosplayers refused to help me. I've been walking for hours and I'm exhausted. Oh! And I saw a flying monster!" The words tumble out of me faster than I mean them to, telling them more than I plan. It isn't until something warm rolls down my cheek that I realize I'm crying. The fourth man continues his appraisal but doesn't show any reaction to my outburst.

"We saw you faint in fear of the dragon. But you needn't do so. They are not dangerous unless provoked," he finally says.

I wipe the tears and almost giggle in frustration. Even kidnapped, I can't escape people who refuse to take me seriously. "A dragon? I'm trying to find help, figure out what the hell is happening to me, and you guys are messing with me."

The blond puts his palms out in a non-threatening manner. "Do you know where you are, Miss?" His soft voice and kind eyes almost make me weep again. His open expression reminds me of Dave, the only person nice to me back home, even if I learned last night that Dave's kindness came from politeness and not any interest in my friendship.

"Since it's rural, I was thinking this was Idaho or one of the Dakotas, maybe?" I churn my brain for other American locations empty of civilization and bursting with untouched nature but turn up empty. "Except—that doesn't explain all the hills. Where am I?"

The men look amongst themselves while the fourth, the leader, furrows his brow.

"You are in the Kingdom of Dalner," the leader answers. Although my knowledge of United States geography is limited, no kingdoms exist here.

"This schtick is getting old." I cross my arms about my middle as anger replaces my fear and worry. "Where are we? Montana? An incredibly elaborate VR studio? I couldn't have traveled too far since I was outside Chicago last night, unless someone got an unconscious girl on a plane."

The third man whispers, as if afraid I will faint again. "No, love. This is Dalner, free Kingdom under the reign of Raddare the Twenty-Fourth." He tumbles over the next words. "There is no Mount Ánnà or Chíck-à-gó here."

I gawk at them, starting to respond with a complaint, but stop when the dark-winged beast in the sky appears again. When it swoops back towards the water, I faint for the second time.

When I wake again, the four men loiter in my eyeline. The blond kneels closest, idling a few feet away. I'm more bothered by my third awakening on the ground than their proximity.

"As you said, Kórol, she isn't a threat," the handsome brunette murmurs to the leader. He's linked their arms and speaks in a soft tone, but with nothing but empty air around us, it's as if he's right beside me.

"She may not be Eósy, but could be something else," the redhead says.

"If she is, we should take her with us. That is the entire point," the blond argues, moving away from me to stand next to Kórol.

"You saw her with the dragon," Kórol says sharply, shaking his hair until the beads clack. The blond mutters something I don't catch, and Kórol exhales through his teeth. "I accept your counsel," he says, pulling from the pretty brunette's arm and lumbering a few yards away.

The other three give me tentative looks while I clear my throat and sit up, brushing away the dirt that showered me during my second unceremonious crumple to the ground. I can't imagine what they're thinking, watching me work through what they said. I'm not a threat (*yeah, no kidding*), but they're sticking with the 'this is a country with dragons' story.

The childlike inner voice scolds me, **they were speaking the truth, they will help**. I shake my head to clear those unwanted thoughts. Never would I consider my subconscious a gullible creature, but the voice in my head certainly is. The childlike voice again presses me, **trust these men, trust the voice**. I grind my jaw together so hard it aches.

"Let me confirm," I say, pulling my thoughts away from my mind's internal fight. "You're saying we're nowhere near Chicago?" All but the fourth man nods. "And we're in a place called Dalner?" Nods again. "What country is that?"

The redhead pipes up. "Dalner is the country."

My last geography module was three years ago, which I learned through an independent home school program. While I did all the classes by myself, I know I didn't forget an English-speaking country named Dalner in my studies.

Accept what they tell you, the child in my subconscious whispers. I swipe at my eyes while taking a wobbly breath. I refuse to faint a third time.

"Can you show it to me on a map?" Maps don't normally lie. While I stand, the blond rummages through a worn brown leather purse and produces a rolled piece of yellowed parchment. I reach for it carefully, afraid it might disintegrate beneath my fingers. When I unravel it, the parchment crinkles. Another country, another *land*, explains what happened in that town—the teeth, the outfits, and why 'phones' are a foreign concept.

I peer at the parchment, squinting over words I don't recognize. It shows a massive land mass, with mountains and rivers. Besides Dalner, other names scrawl across it. The shapes depict nothing recognizable. I tell them as much.

"Earth?" the blond man repeats. "This is Sekai. Dalner is the land of men, our home. The northernmost point is Dànna, the Kingdom of the divine. To the south is Alacson, and the east, the Wilds." He points at each location on the map as he describes them, and the crease in his forehead deepens. "Do you not know this?"

I fumble with the map, almost dropping it, but the third man catches it and rolls it up. None of the names the blond listed are familiar. It's highly unlikely there's a massive English-speaking landmass somewhere on Earth that doesn't show up on world maps. Although I enjoy conspiracy theories as much as any casual internet user, an entire continent can't be a secret.

"This is either the most annoyingly method LARP in the world, or I'm somewhere else."

The childlike inner voice huffs. ***It makes sense, does it not? The people from the town earlier, the lack of roads, the dragons***, my subconscious voice says.

Suddenly, I arrive at the most rational explanation. "It *is* a dream!"

This *must* be part of the fishhook dream. That's the only thing that makes sense. My normal dreams always depict things that wouldn't happen, but with a cast of my real life—like when my father pushes me off a cliff, or I'm chased by his third wife's dog. Those dreams never have fantastical elements, but boredom can create anything. There's no way I *actually* ended up in some magical land. My brain must have taken my one-and-only shot to find a boyfriend-slash-friend earlier that evening and produced a fake-Ireland with dragons and a cast of overly attractive potential romantic partners. And with the midterm in my Feminine Identity and Persecution in Medieval Europe class in two days, the setting solidified.

The four men stare as I amble closer. "That clears everything up. You should introduce yourself, then. I've got a lot of plot lines to go through before I wake." I pause. "Or am I supposed to introduce you? Which one of you is the love interest? This'll be fun! I've never dreamed about that before."

The handsome brunette beams and starts towards me, but the blond digs his fingers into his shoulders and holds him back.

"Excuse you?" the last man, Kórol maybe, says, brows almost reaching the widow's peak below his scalp.

"Kórol, if she comes to us from another realm—" the blond says, trailing off with wide eyes.

"Kórol isn't a name I'd think up," I tell the group with a wrinkled nose. "Al maybe, or Sam. But, fine—Kórol it is."

"Not the Sìnnách," the redhead mutters. "A confused girl."

"No need to be hasty, Sáven," the blond says. That's another name I can't believe came from my brain. "We've no idea if the Sìnnách is an Eósy, or even from Dànna. Her appearance is still something of importance."

"Her appearance is what interests me," the pretty one says, his caramel eyes winking at me. The blond's fingers squeeze tighter on his shoulders until he winces.

I snap my fingers twice. "Main character of the dream here, boys. Stop with the nonsense talk and let's get this dream going. I don't think waking from a fake hike is going to leave me well rested in the morning."

"*We're* talking nonsense," the redhead, Sáven, says, though it sounds like a question.

"How do you convince someone they aren't dreaming?" the pretty brunette asks, fingering a long braid near his left ear.

"That *is* an interesting question," says the blond. "One of our philosophers—"

"Fates, forget I asked," the brunette groans.

"Take her with us," Kórol announces. "We'll take her as far as Chead and leave her with a mind healer."

CHAPTER 3

I'm not much of a hostage. The four men don't tie me up and toss me over their shoulders. Apparently, it's not *that* kind of dream. Kórol and the blond march ahead of us, while Sáven and the pretty brunette flank me like too overly friendly guards. Sáven has a long bow crossing his chest and over his shoulder, but I don't get the impression it's supposed to threaten me, especially since a worn canvas-style backpack covers it.

I pinch myself for the first twenty minutes while the two watch me silently.

"What're you doing?" Sáven finally asks, tightening his hands on the bow.

"Trying to wake myself up. You seem great, but this is missing the romance I'd expect from a dream, and a hike isn't my idea of fun." The skin on my forearm darkens and stings. "But it's not working. Maybe I won't wake up until I complete some goal."

Or I fell down the stairs and am stuck in a coma. I don't dwell on that idea for long.

"It's not a dream," Sáven says under his breath.

"I'll help clear things up," the brunette says, grabbing my hand to kiss the palm, the skin warming at his touch. "I am Tansr, my friends call me Tans. The less attractive but much more distinguished brunette is Kórol. The blond chaperone is Fílga. And the young one next to you is Sáven," he continues. Sáven squeaks and jabs Tansr with the edge of his bow while I barely duck out of the way. Fílga turns to watch from in front of us.

"It is like corralling children," Fílga mutters. "How Tansr leads—" Kórol holds up a hand and Fílga goes silent.

When they finish jostling each other, they switch sides, Tansr now on my right with the setting sun behind him, Sáven on my left.

"You failed to provide your name, lovely," Tansr says, winking.

"Grace." The blush rises on my cheeks involuntarily. Maybe it *is* that kind of dream.

"And how did the lovely Miss Grace come to join us?"

"Do you mean in the dream? Or what I was doing before the dream?"

"I meant to us, but I am desperate to hear whatever you may say." He bats his long lashes.

He's the love interest, I think. The child in my head scoffs.

"I started this direction because some villagers mentioned reporting me to the castle because I was too close to a gate, or something. The logic of this dream still confuses me."

Both he and Sáven stumble but Tansr recovers first. "Although I am thrilled you are, as I would not get to gaze upon you otherwise—why do you travel to the castle?"

I shrug. "Until I realized this wasn't real, I assumed that meant I'll find someone to help me there, or at least a phone or cop."

"No phone or cop," Sáven says, stumbling over the words. "But come the Winter Solstice—"

"The Great Matron will arrive, that is their meaning," Tansr finishes in a rush.

"What's a Great Matron?"

"She is a carrier of magic, one of our virtuous beings." Tansr explains. "We tithe to her, and she bestows a blessing on our King every Winter Solstice."

"Like a fairy godmother," I say. Maybe I'm Dorothy and need to find the 'Wizard' to go 'home' and wake up.

"She's nothing like a children's tale," Tansr says, crinkling his nose as if I'm a child who can't tell reality from fantasy, ironic considering this is my dream. "An actual creation of magic, an Eósy, who arrives through the main gate that separates us from Eósy lands of Dànna. She is the remaining leader of the Light Eósy, and our people's first defense from the Dark."

"When do I meet her?" I ask.

Kórol slows and turns to watch us, involuntarily drawing my eyes. He commands the space without saying a word.

"Do you expect to?" Tansr's expression is grave.

I shrug. "I assume she's the reason I'm here."

They remain quiet the rest of the day.

Kórol stops us a few hours later after we trudge through a small copse of trees when the moon gleams high overhead.

"We make camp here," he declares, gesturing to the small opening between the trees. After Kórol gives his order, Tansr directs the others where to set up while Kórol stalks away. I sink to the ground and watch them interact, wincing at the twinges that course through my muscles as I do. I wish I could lucidly dream, to imagine a bed instead of another night of the ground.

You don't get hurt in dreams, my subconscious says, but I ignore it.

Sáven and Fílga give Tansr a compact bundle of sticks, and he places them in the middle of the opening to build a fire. He glances in my direction a few times to confirm I'm watching as his hands fluidly pass over the bundle, brushing them with the tips of his fingers. After a few seconds, they light.

Magic, my subconscious provides. I struggle to restrain a grimace. Fantasy is one of my least favorite genres, second only to period pieces, and I can't fathom why I've dreamed this up.

It isn't a dream, my inner voice argues. ***Or a coma***.

"Alright, Butterfly?" Tansr asks. He flicks his fingers towards the low embers and the fire grows.

I mimic his movement twice, then snap and point at the fire when flicking doesn't work. "How do you do that?"

"Surely our visitor has magic in her homeland?"

Defeated, I switch my attention to kneading the back of my neck, trying to work out the knot that my mind connected to a day's walk. "There's no magic *in this land* either, but I'm curious to know how you'll explain it when my brain can't."

"So you say." He brings the fingers of his left hand to his lips and licks them. My eyes narrow as he edges closer and I cover my neck protectively. I find him incredibly attractive, and he is the probable love interest in this dream, but even dream-me has too many hygiene instincts to let a stranger touch me with saliva slick fingers.

"Have faith in me," he says, pouting until I allow his hand to replace mine on my neck. A low thrum of heat seeps from his fingers and the ache fades. I stroke the skin with tentative fingers. The spot tingles with residual heat but the knot vanished. "That was my magic," he says. He gestures to the fire and his hands. "Heat and a bit of healing."

I motion to the others. "Does everyone have magic?"

"Not *now*," he says. "Everyone in this world did before the world split. Some stayed here in Dalner, the rest live in Dànna. But after generations, those in Dalner changed into regular men, normal people. With each generation born, magic dims." He makes two small flames materialize on his index fingers. "My mother's gifts are greater than mine, her father's greater than hers. My children's children may lack gifts entirely." Tansr extinguishes the finger flames and turns back to me. "As you've now seen two demonstrations of magic, do you agree this isn't a dream?"

"It's all in my head, meaning magic would work as long as I thought it would work."

He sends me a pitying look. "You are exasperating," he groans. "It's a self-fulfilling prophecy, darling. No matter what happens, you will assume you are dreaming. You'll convince yourself otherwise."

"Unless I actually get hurt," I say. He fixes his gaze on my neck. "*Really* hurt, like near death experience hurt. I learned about it in a correspondence course in high school—actual pain wakes you up, since it's not compatible with REM sleep. That's why I was pinching myself, but it wasn't enough pain."

"Do you mean to tell me you'll remain convinced this is a dream unless you're critically hurt?" He sighs dramatically, dropping his head to his chest. "Which we wouldn't allow to happen, anyway. It's a predicament you've put us in, dearest."

"I've made you a bit of a caricature," I say, watching Tansr lift his head to run his fingers through his silky hair.

Fílga huffs from the other side of the clearing. "That is the nicest way to say your personality is off putting."

"Off putting!" Tansr stops grooming and glowers.

"You're overly flirtatious, as if you're playing a role to rile me up or something," I explain. "It's too unrealistic for even a fantasy dream."

Tansr smirks and leans closer. "Do you mean it is only fantasy that you would find yourself in the company of a charming man whose looks are only outmatched by his wit?"

"You describe Sáven well. I can only imagine how you'll describe yourself," Fílga says. Sáven barks out a laugh as he finishes laying out his bedroll on the other side of Fílga.

"Yes, yes, you think you're so funny, Fíl." Tansr flicks an ember at Fílga's feet but misses.

"It's playing out more like a story than a dream," I say. "My dreams don't have made up characters and they're usually based on my life. I don't know why I've created you all."

Fílga's eyes tighten but Tansr gives him a scathing look, and he turns away. When Tansr looks back at me, he's still smirking but there are cracks in it.

"You must play the role of my voice of reason," I tell Fílga, who remains silent.

"If this is a story, it is a boring one," Tansr whines. "Can't you dream up another dragon and show us you can fly?"

I shrug. "Most of my dreams are boring, sorry. But if I get to choose... I'm more into romances. The super tropey ones with slow burns, enemies to lovers, mistaken identity, fake dating, bed sharing, huddling for warmth. Anything that ends in a happily ever after."

Fílga clears his throat. "I believe we should sleep, Miss. We have a long walk ahead of us." Fílga looks pointedly at Tansr. Tansr rolls his eyes and winks in my direction before turning away and setting up his bedroll.

The men, minus Kórol, whisper together until one by one they quiet. Not long after, the gentle snuffles of sleep fill the opening.

This is an odd dream. If the point is to show me a parody of friendships, something I have limited experience with in real life, I could understand it. But why add dragons and magic?

It's not a dream, that childlike inner voice whispers. I ignore it, wrapping my arms around my middle and bowing my head. If I don't wake up in my dorm, hopefully tomorrow I'll dream up a coat.

Before dawn, a child's laughter echoes from behind me, startling me awake. But I'm still in the dream, curled in a ball on the ground. Waking in dreams doesn't seem possible. Maybe this *is* *a* coma. A pressure in my head forces me to shuffle up and lean against a nearby tree trunk.

"Grace, you need to wake up." It's the whisper sound of a child. Except for the sleeping bodies, the opening is empty but now a low mist undulates around my feet.

"Who's there?" Coma or no, I'm in no mood for my mind to introduce a new character.

"Fates, this will be exhausting," the child mutters. ***You are not in a coma. Listen to me so I can tell you about your ability to return home***, they continue, this time inside my mind. I release a shaky breath, dropping my head to the tree trunk.

"That was you?" I speak softly to avoid waking the others, which seems silly since it's my coma-dream, but social niceties are hard to avoid.

"You are not a coma. But yes." The childlike lilt that comforted my inner thoughts sounds stilted and horrifying out loud.

"Are you supposed to help me wake up?" I whisper as my eyes scan the opening, seeking a body that belongs to the voice but finding none. Their voice must come from a speaker plugged directly into my ears.

They pause, the only sound rising from the breaths of the slumbering men. "I am to guide you through your purpose here."

Of course, my brain couldn't just *let* me wake up. The one non-traumatizing dream I get, and it isn't even the tropey romance I want. "What's my purpose then?"

They giggle, vibrating the air near my cheeks. "I cannot tell you everything yet. For now, I simply ask that you continue towards the mountains and arrive at the castle, as quickly as you can."

I sit up straighter. This may not be a coma, but there's no good reason for my subconscious to have a secret. "Why?"

They trade the demented giggles for a more somber tone. "She is coming, Grace. She is coming for you and She will want to hurt you. But with my aid, you can defeat Her."

I groan. "No romance, but some action dream?"

A soft wind blows through the opening and the mist clears. **You must destroy Her. Before She destroys you and everything you care for.**

And everything quiets.

I startle awake the second time to the sounds of the men chatting softly. Although the sun has barely risen, all but Kórol lounge around a spit. The opening looks bigger in the daylight, wide enough that I can see the mountains looming through the leaves. No mist covers them today and the peaks stretch into the morning blue sky.

At least I have a goal to wake up in real life now, though why my dream-body needs sleep pings something in my mind I'd rather not touch. I rub my eyes, blinking at my new imaginary traveling companions in the new day's light. Tansr reclines with his feet in Fílga's lap and Fílga's placed a map over Tansr's shins. Sáven keeps his eyes half on Fílga and half on the charred piece of meat he roasts.

"Morning, love," Tansr says, gesturing to the empty seat beside him. Fílga grabs hold of his ankles when they wiggle and grouses under his breath.

"I thought we talked about toning it down." I slump down next to him.

"Good morning, *Butterfly*," he amends, one hand idling on a braid next to his cheek as he smirks.

The chill seeping through my ripped windbreaker takes my attention from Tansr's manufactured flirting. I wish this dream didn't have to feel this *lifelike*. "How long until we get to the castle?"

Fílga doesn't look up from the map on Tansr's shins. "If we keep pace, twenty days."

Depending on how lifelike this dream will feel, that's almost a month away. "Can we get their quicker?"

Fílga gives me a sidelong glance. "Do you have another method of travel in mind?"

I tick off the options on my fingers. "Planes, trains, automobiles. A blimp. We could sprout magical wings for all I care. Anything but walking for a month straight."

"What're those first words?" Sáven asks from across the fire pit.

My nose scrunches as I consider how to explain it to another facet of myself. "A giant passenger flying machine, a giant passenger road machine, a smaller road machine, a flying ship made of air."

All noises stop while Fílga raises his eyebrows and clicks his tongue against his teeth. "Do you *fly* on the backs of any of them?"

"Inside them, but yes," I say, twisting my lips at his wary expression.

An actual smile replaces the wariness, blooming pink on his golden skin. "You *fly* in your Kingdom. How interesting." He scans overhead again before resting his gaze back on the map.

Sáven finishes cooking and offers me a leg of unknown meat. I snatch it, ignoring its mystery meat status, because nothing in dreams can hurt me. The way I gnaw at the meat isn't ladylike, it's barely humanlike, but my dream-self is starving.

I stop midbite. "Why didn't I find any food during the earlier part of the dream?"

"It is unlikely you would have located any meat," Tansr says from beside me, smirking as he hands me a handkerchief to wipe my mouth. They've clearly decided not to quibble with my (correct) conclusion that this is a dream.

"Wildlife only comes at dawn and dusk," Sáven explains.

I wrinkle my nose. "So, they're crepuscular. That means—"

"We know what it means, darling," Tansr says, rolling his eyes.

"Aye, only your nonsense words need translating," says Sáven.

Tansr leers. "But have no fear, I would rescue you from any beasty. As my reward, I would only ask for a kiss. In fact, did we not save you from the dragons yesterday? I believe payment is already due—" He waggles his eyebrows.

I blush at the brazenness of my imagination while Fílga and Sáven groan. Tansr must be a subconscious manifestation of my loneliness and dismal love life.

"To avoid arriving at Ilsen in *twenty-one* or more days, we must leave now," Kórol interrupts from behind Sáven. He clenches his fists under the cuffs of his heavy fur coat. Looking anywhere but me, he continues, "Tansr, with me."

CHAPTER 4

I'm even less of a hostage now, walking by myself with the four in front of me. But that makes sense, since the Voice (as I'm calling them since they didn't introduce themselves otherwise) led me to them. I'm not tempted to leave them since my goal is to defeat the villain at the castle, but I wish we *could* fly.

We continue on foot throughout the morning. The four of them don't speak to me but the words "tame" and "snatch" float back to my ears. When the sun is high overhead, Sáven escorts me, handing off small pieces of meat for lunch.

"Will you tell us how you came here?"

"Before the dream?" He pauses just long enough for me to notice, but then nods. Tansr slows down to hear. "I can't remember everything. Dave walked me home after passing out condoms at the Union. And then the dream started."

"Who's Dave?" Sáven asks.

"Are these yours then?" Tansr speaks over Sáven and holds up a handful of multicolored condom wrappers. "Naughty girl. Were you taught not to litter where you come from?" I leap for his hand, but he snatches them away while jeering, running a few feet ahead of me. "I think not. They are mine now. I have many uses for them."

"You're being a caricature again!" I call as he dances around us.

"He won't explain what they are," Sáven complains, his green eyes flashing the same shade as the surrounding hills. "Only opened one behind my back giggling, then hid them away."

"I'll tell you when you're older, my sweet Sáv," Tansr says as he tosses an arm over Sáven's shoulder.

Sáven growls, his voice low. "I've six months on you."

"Or I could ask Fíl to tell you." Tansr flashes his teeth.

"Hurchá," Sáven snarls, knocking off Tansr's arm. Tansr snickers and saunters beside me, out of range of Sáven's hands.

Scowling, Sáven gives me another piece of meat. After I finish that one and he produces a third, he returns to our conversation. "I know you think this is a dream. But say it's not. Why might you come here, especially near the Sanctum?"

I chew thoughtfully, unsure how much to tell them. They're figments of my imagination, yes, but distinct parts of my brain might have ideas about what should happen in the dream. I read something similar once, and clearly one part of my brain is keeping secrets from others, or else the Voice would have explained everything the night before. "I *might* have an idea why this world, but not why here exactly."

"Should we guess?" Tansr leans in conspiratorially, immersing me in his pleasant and smoky smell. It isn't sour like cigarettes, but a heady scent evoking images of a manly campfire. "You caught the eye of an Eósy who wishes to marry you and make you his own for eternity."

"That's not my kind of romance," I say, rolling my eyes and tamping down the hormones. Those stories rarely end up in the thrift store book bin. The library maybe, but I'm too nervous for the staff to see me check them out. Buying a bucket load of historical romances written before I was born from a bored high school student was easier somehow. And the homeschool curriculum I foisted on my father had a few fantasy options, tamer stories than I liked and ones I trudged through for the completion grade only.

"Or you're a magical being in your own right, having somehow breached the wall, and seek to destroy the restraints keeping you from Dalner." Tansr watches me from his periphery before looking at the path. "No, no, no. Something supernatural wouldn't faint so often."

"Twice isn't *often*," I grumble. His lips twitch at one corner.

"My mistake." He steals a look through his full lashes. "Not to destroy us, but to save us then, love?"

An incredulous look blooms on my face until I remember the Voice's hints. Only in a dream would I be the key player, destined to save the world from some evil. "Sure, yes. Something brought me here to save everyone."

His bronze cheeks nearly glow as he smiles. "As I suspected, Butterfly."

When I sleep that night under the stars again, no trees blanket the autumn wind that whips my hair and stings my skin under my thin clothes. While I still want to wake in my dorm the next morning, I don't want to lose the feeling of friendship from today.

When I open my eyes before dawn, a thick fur coat covers me. I snuggle back into the warmth. *Dreaming this a little longer won't hurt.*

Time stretches like the elastic on my favorite sweatpants, the ones I wish I could dream-wear. I've traveled with these men for a week, going at only half pace because even in a dream my muscles weren't prepared for significant use. The mountains and the castle nestled within them are no closer, making this the longest and most detailed dream I've ever had. There were moments where I thought—this *must* be real, no way would I think this up, who would willingly dream about using the bathroom outside—but the Pack, what they call themselves, is too accommodating for that to be true.

"Primed for the hunt today, Miss?" Sáven asks one afternoon, holding an enormous bow in one hand and a knife in the other.

I squint at Sáven, moving a hand in front of my eyes to block the setting sun. An uneven tan clings to my almond skin. If today is like the prior days, it will freckle into a sunburn Tans heals during the evenings (no matter that sunburns shouldn't exist in dreams, no matter how authentic this dream feels). Tans hooks his chin on my shoulder.

"It's your turn, love," Tans answers. I elbow his taut stomach, and he releases me, rubbing the spot I jabbed in mock pain. "Violent woman, we want you to feel a part of us. That means giving you a task. We're going to attempt hunting."

Each man has a specific purpose within the group. I've figured them all out except Tans—Kórol is the leader, Sáven hunts and cooks, Fílga guides us and analyses the map. Tans' only uses seem to be having private conversations with Kórol and flirting with me.

Tans grins, as if he hears my internal designation of his role, though he *might* be a mind-reader since I still remain unclear on the magical rules of the dream. Our friendship, the imaginary one, grows every day. He's overly familiar with me, but he's the same with the others. He never 'hits on' me, content to tease me and make me blush. I'm struggling to stifle the romantic urges I have toward the synapses in my mind.

"I've never killed anything. I don't think I can, even in a dream," I say, returning to the present conversation and hoping they'll attribute the flush on my cheeks to the sun.

"You have nothing to fear," says Fílga, approaching us from behind.

"Let me remind you of the horrors my brain created that Sáv had to cook up. Deer whose shark sized mouths are at finger-biting level, ducks with more heads than I have hands, a snake with poison darts on its tail." I turn to Sáv and point sharply at a welt on his lip Tans didn't see in time to heal. "And we should eat dirt before leeching the poison out of those again. I don't know how I came up with that monstrosity."

Fílga's skin pinks as he scowls at Tans. "You may think you're dreaming, but dirt won't sate your hunger long."

Kórol joins us and watches with heavy set eyes. I shift to stare at the moss below our feet. "Giving me a weapon is a terrible idea anyway. I'm more likely to shoot one of you than catch anything."

Tans' face contorts as he twists his lips. "One of us, but not yourself?"

I shrug. "Probably both, but I'll respawn. I'm not sure about you guys."

"Respawn?" Tans mouths the word to Sáv, who shakes his head.

"You have no experience with weaponry?" Kórol asks, furrowing his brows.

"None." I have no enhanced dream skills either. A few days prior, I ran and jumped and tried to shoot lasers from my fingers, but everything remained the same. I'm as unskilled in the dream as I am in real life. The only real change is that my mind has slimmed down the extra weight on my hips and toned my thighs.

Kórol gestures to Tans with two fingers and they march away, leaving Sáven, Fílga, and me alone. Sáv looks disappointed at my refusal and Fílga upset.

"It's not that I don't want to help. I do. But killing something isn't my way to do it."

Sáven shakes his head. "Don't think of it as killing. Think of it as a sacrifice. The beasts' time in Dalner is fleeting. We must appreciate their worth and kill to feed, not harm."

I can't hold in a grimace. "I get that. I'm sure we'll inhale whatever you catch, snakes included. It's just a step too far for me, even in a dream. I'm sorry, Sáv."

Sáven and Fílga exchange glances as Kórol and Tans rejoin us. All four men have a secret conversation with just their eyes, which ends with Kórol clearing his throat and shaking his head. Sáv pads off into the sunset with his weapons.

"I *am* sorry," I tell the remaining three. Fílga waves me off, making an expression I can't decipher while neither Tans nor Kórol meet my eyes.

"Think nothing of it. We will find some way you can help us," Fílga says.

Kórol's gaze snaps to mine, casting his eyes down to my neck, as if studying me. I flush when his gaze dips below the collar of my dirty t-shirt. After a few more seconds traversing my skin with his eyes, he ticks up one corner of his mouth in a facsimile of a smile. "You may have already," Kórol murmurs.

The long hours and days may be mere seconds to my sleeping body back in my dorm, but I wish I had a fast-forward button, not because I want to leave my pretend-friends but to avoid all the walking. I have several ideas on how to find Her, but the Voice has been absent and I can't end the dream on my own.

They visit again a week after I refused to hunt.

"It is imperative that you increase your friendship with Kórol," the lilting childlike Voice says, as a dense mist shrouds the surrounding ground.

I roll to my back and stare at the stars. "I thought you'd never show up again. Do you know how weird it is to know you're dreaming and wake up *inside* the dream? There must be some way to end the dream sooner rather than later. I've got some ideas on how to meet Her but there's been no opportunity to use them yet." My stomach sours at the thought of leaving but I dutifully withdraw the parchment I got from Fíl that I store inside the pocket of my windbreaker. My thoughts are written in blocky text, ranging from a pretend ritual to changing routes and traveling to Her home in Dànna.

"You're not prepared for Her yet." Their childlike voice is sibilant. "But with my help you will be. I urge you to connect with Kórol, as his friendship will aid you more than the others. You should open yourself to him." they say, softer.

I roll over on to my side to watch the men sleeping several feet away. I make a note on the parchment as an excuse to stop observing them. "I'm opening up. I *am* open. They're in *my* brain."

"You can do more. Do you not enjoy your newfound friend-ships?"

Of course, I do. I have friends now. But they're only synapses firing—or something, my homeschool curriculum didn't em-phasize hard sciences—not flesh and blood people. These men respond and interact how my brain decides they should. I don't want to think about the devastation I'll feel when I wake up. It'll be like Mom all over again.

"I can't let myself get any deeper with them," I say, speak-ing candidly to the dream guide extension of my mind. I shove the parchment back in my pocket, disturbing the mist swirling around my prone form. "It's almost worse the longer the dream goes on, because I know how wrecked I'm going to be when I'm back in my dorm come morning."

"You still believe this is a—Fates, you're certainly more accommodating but—and then when I consider the risks of failure—" The Voice seems exasperated but isn't speaking to me, like I'm eavesdropping on someone else's phone conversation.

"What?"

The Voice exhales. "Keep towards the castle. Befriend Kórol, and the others, I suppose. I will speak with you again soon. I've plans to make."

CHAPTER 5

Three weeks in, I'm no closer to waking, but I don't know that I want to as every day my friendships deepen. Though the dream doesn't work that way, I feel like I could fly because of it.

That morning, I almost do, when the most alluring sight in Dalner greets me. "A lake," I shout, taking off running. I don't know why my dream created this vision, but I don't care.

The liquid beauty in front of me is bigger than a football field and deep enough for me to submerge fully. The pool rests at the bottom of a valley which rises into rolling hill that meets the lush forest mountain range ahead of it. Trees surround it and brilliant green lichen covers the shore. It looks like a postcard, with shining water reflecting the sun from a clear sky.

Tans, who still travels beside me more than the others, laughs and follows, beating me to the edge of the water. He grabs my waist and plants his feet, as if he thinks I'll leap in fully clothed. "Would the lovely lady care to explain why this is an exciting find?"

"I haven't bathed in *weeks*. Even in dreams, baths are a necessity." Washing in the trickling streams or foot-deep ponds we've come across never seems to remove the ever-present layer of dirt and sweat. The dreck must be reset each morning when I 'wake.'

Tans drops my waist in feigned disgust and shudders. "Butterfly, I know you are not of Dalner, but one would hope cleanliness transcended realms."

"That's not what I meant!" I cackle, punching him in the shoulder, but he deftly avoids it. He grabs my fist before I make contact and presses a kiss on my wrist. Butterflies swoop in my stomach but I play along, as I have the past weeks, because he's not real. That thought makes my lips tick down.

"I'm teasing, love. Don't fret. Let me speak with Kórol about setting up camp here. A day of rest wouldn't be remiss. Sáven would certainly prefer to butcher and clean this morning's kill before nightfall. I'm told it was a rather ample one this sunrise and I, for one, don't want to help him carry it." He holds tight to my hand and presses another kiss on my wrist, dragging his lips upward and gazing at me with a flirtatious smirk. "Will you permit me to wash your back?"

I pull away and slug him again, which he lets connect with his toned chest. He chuckles, kisses my cheek, and bounds off to the other three.

Once naked, I submerge under the water, spreading out my fingers and floating my legs on the surface as the water holds me aloft. In my dorm, I took a bath almost every night, the steaming water and bubbles melting away the daily worries and stress. Those worries involved whether I could find someone to go to the latest movie opening with me (unlikely), whether I'll be able to afford the books next semester without contacting my father (probably), or whether Julie's boyfriend would act like a jerk (definitely). Dream-me has no worries, until I wake up and lose my only friends.

Disheartened by the reminder, I paddle back to shore soon after entering the lake. When I redress and toss a smattering of the water on my face, something black and inky appears under my reflection.

I didn't see the animal when I bathed, but I'm not so unobservant that I wouldn't notice it splashing around with me. I watch in confused fascination as the black form slithers towards my place on the shore, faster than I've seen any fish or water creature on Earth. With a guttural howl, it shoots from the water, uncovering mange-dark skin stretched tight on its eel-like body, a mouth full of sharp teeth, and eyeless sockets.

I don't know if it can leave the water, but I'm not waiting to discover what my brain decides. As it propels itself towards the shore, scraping deep gouges in the mossy embankment, I scamper away. I make it back to the encampment hearing no telltale signs that the thing pursued me. But if the rules of the dream have changed, I need to find the others. Instead, I find a dead fire, the lonely spit sitting atop it, and an empty clearing.

Something crunches in the woods behind me in the opposite direction of the lake. I turn towards it as two more branches snap. It sounds like heavy footsteps made from something wild. I'm not afraid, knowing that a dream protects me from any genuine danger, but the memory of the eyeless monster stays with me.

Between the trees, two luminescent green eyes emerge. Whatever those eyes belong to lumbers forward, exposing a beast larger than a lion, more vulturine than a wolf. On all fours, it stands as tall as my shoulders, with apple-red fur freckled with beige spots. The creature lazily plods towards me, not noticing or caring about my presence yet. A dead deer hangs limply in its mammoth jaw, the corpse clean and prepared for butchery. A few drops of blood drip from the beast's fangs.

Suddenly, the beast sees me, and recognition floods its bottle-green eyes. It growls before a flash of light blinds me, one that forces my eyes closed. When the spots behind my eyes disappear, the creature has vanished and Sáven replaces it, clutching the dead deer in his thin arms. His skin reddens to the same color as his hair, and his Adam's apple bobs. My mouth drops open—he's a shapeshifter.

His voice pulls me from my shock. "Miss! I didn't expect you back this soon." He dumps the deer on the dirt and wrings his hands together. "I was cleaning the sunrise hunt. It's easier to carry when I'm... not quite myself."

His embarrassment keeps me from commenting on his newly revealed shapeshifter status. "I—I saw something in the lake. I figured you'd want to know since it's after sunrise, which seemed important. I'd say you can catch it for dinner, but you seem to have that handled," I joke.

His shoulders slump as he stops wringing his hands. Without asking for more explanation, he lopes towards the water.

I force away the curiosity at this newly revealed piece of magic my mind created. Instead, I search for the others to tell them my new discoveries. Harsh voices guide me to Fílga and Tans, who face each other between two trees. Fílga's mouth is pursed and red blotches erupt over his high cheekbones. Tans holds two of his raven black braids like tiny reigns. Both men don't notice me approach.

"We should try harder," Fílga says. His voice is strained.

Tans flexes his fingers and runs his hands through his sleek hair. "It will happen when it happens. There's no harm in it now."

"You only say that because you benefit from it. Those lingering touches will disappear when—"

"It's real for me. I mean them. Not at first, Kórol and I decided I should attempt it to gain information. Don't scowl at me Fíl, we use every arrow in our quiver."

Fíl huffs. "At the expense of—"

"They're sincere now!"

"What's sincere?" I ask when I reach them.

"Me, of course," Tans says, darting his eyes to me and the grass while sauntering away from Fílga's narrowed gaze. When he reaches me, he touches my low back and guides me back to camp and away from Fíl. "How was your bath?"

I roll my eyes at his antics, even though the attention pleases me, dream or no. "Fine, but let's go find Sáven."

"Find him for what? I have no interest in seeing *him* in the bath." He looks behind him and smirks. "Although if he needs an audience—"

"A caricature," I say, pointing at the space between his eyes. He catches my hand and kisses it, creating a tiny spark of heat where his lips brush.

"I will stop, Butterfly. Why do we need Sáven?"

"I saw something in the water, and I told Sáven about it. He's going to catch it, but he'll need help as it was massive. And I'm confused that it showed up outside sunrise and—"

"You saw something," he repeats flatly, as if he doesn't know how to react. His hands creep to my shoulders, and he squeezes them gently, but no magic flares from his touch. "Describe it."

"A giant eel with a lot of legs. It was underwater but I'm betting it goes on land too."

Blood leeches from his expression before he grabs Sáven's bow and dashes towards the water, unknowingly following Sáven's footsteps. "Stay here," he calls behind him.

But the whole point was for us to go together. I groan as I take off after him.

When I arrive, Sáven shapeshifted back into his lion form and has his jaws clamped around the back half of the eel-creature, the two thrashing on the banks of the water. The eel's slithering torso struggles in Sáv's grasp, its gaping maw curling to snap at his flanks. Before it can break his skin, Tans nocks the bow and aims, hitting the eel in one of the eyeless sockets. It roars as an arc of red bursts from the air, its body undulating against Sáven's teeth trying to drag it from the water towards the lichen bank.

The arrow snaps off, an inch of wood still sprouting from its socket when the eel finally connects with one of Sáv's legs. Blood dyes the water surrounding their bodies as Sáv releases the eel to screech. Tans withdraws a knife from his boot and leaps closer to the eel, but knocks into Sáven instead, their bodies breaking below the surface of the water.

I scream and rush towards the waterline. This is *my* dream. I must be able to control it somehow. I wade into my knees, but my jeans restrict the movement.

"Stop it! Get away from them!" My voice is shrill, but it doesn't matter—I'm in control and the eel *will* listen.

Tans and Sáv burst from the water a dozen feet from me. Sáv has his animal-mouth around the neck of the eel while Tans slices whatever he can reach. It's not good enough. There's too much red and I don't know if they'll reset if they die in the dream. I trudge further past the shallows, my eyes narrowing as I focus all my attention on diverting the dream-beast from my friends. Its eyeless sockets find me as if we're the only beings in the lake. *Good.*

It vaults from the water towards me, dragging my two friends with it, until it shakes off Sáven's bite and knocks Tans back under the water. I howl as its teeth connect with my hip, pain blossoming somewhere below the water's surface. The water's color deepens as I kick but it slashes again and again. Tans roars something, but its garbled over the sound the screaming and splashing.

"Stop it! Stop it!" I scream. "This isn't how this is supposed to go—you're supposed to listen to me!" There's more yowling, something high pitched, as my vision blackens at the edges. It could be from me or the eel, I can't tell.

Sáven grabs ahold of its neck again and bites until blood paints the sky. Tans surges between me and the eel, dragging me from the water and leaving me on the banks as my eyes pinch closed.

There's one last squeal from the depths before the only sound comes from my pained breaths and the ringing in my ears.

Someone shakes me. Tans is there, hissing something but I can't hear the words. His face is the last thing I see before my eyes close again. Then, I'm dreaming—a dream within a dream, my first while in Dalner.

I'm the eel-creature now, watching myself and my tree trunk brown eyes, through the empty holes in its skull. Or I'm watching the eel-creature watch me. The dream isn't clear.

Something, something the eel can only describe as a flower—what looks like a purple pansy with black veins—told it to—to watch and hurt. I—we—the eel doesn't know who, but the demand is strong and oily.

I feel the eel's need to bite and scratch, its desire to kill until my tree trunk eyes close forever. It can't decide which hunger to sate. It attempts both, waiting until my tree trunk eyes peer into its watery nest. It scratches my arms, nips at my legs, bites my middle. The tree trunks narrow and vanish.

Leaf green eyes—Sáven—interrupts its meal with sharp teeth and claws. Acorn brown eyes—Tans—has sharp teeth attached to its hands and bites, piercing the eel's flesh.

Then red, only red. Acorn takes tree trunks while leaf watches. Leaf gets smaller and pinker but still waits. I—we—the eel dies.

I wake slowly but the pain seeps into me all at once. I'm lying on the ground, not my dorm room. I'm still in the dream of Dalner. I blink my eyes at the sunlight blinding above me, pain and relief battling for dominance over my mind.

"It was well past sunrise, Kórol," Tansr says from a few feet away, his voice tinted with panic.

"There is nothing in the texts that account for its appearance except for a breach in one of the walls," Fílga adds.

"An increased rift would explain it," says Kórol slowly.

"You know that if one opens, the others follow like a kindled fire. We would see more than a single creature. I worry that there is a slow leak we cannot account for, or some direct influence we don't know about," Tans retorts.

"Check the scout's reports in the next town, Tans. One Eósy cryptid is no cause for alarm yet. I only worry for Miss Grace," says Kórol.

"We should have tried to convince her the truth earlier. All her chatter of being untouchable led to this. I hope you're satisfied," Fílga says curtly, but I can't tell who he's talking to.

"Cease the infighting," Kórol says. "Sáven may need help to dress the last of his wounds, I suggest you join him. Tans will stay with me." Fílga's footsteps die away before Kórol speaks again, his voice hard. "This confirms we need the Sìnnách's hope more than ever."

"Have you come to a conclusion about—?" Tans sounds worried.

"It's too soon to say. I feel something, but she is not what I expected."

I try to roll over without alerting them, but a pained wheeze forces its way out of my throat. In an instant, Tans is in my sightline.

"Don't move, darling." His caramel eyes are bright and red rimmed. His long hair looks like that of a hair-spray happy 80s rock star, the braids messy and half-done.

"What happened?" My voice is hoarse.

"You thought to take on a dobhà with your bare hands, unsuccessfully," Kórol answers. He stands above me, peering down with an inscrutable expression. "Given your alleged unfamiliarity with weapons *and* your desire not to kill another living being, I find myself curious why you would attempt to try."

"Kórol, not now," Tans snaps.

"I didn't—" I start.

"No, now is the time." Kórol kneels next to me and caresses my cheek. My skin burns where our skin connects, and he drops his hand as if he feels the burn too. I touch my cheek and it comes away wet.

"She reopened one of her wounds," Tans says. He roughly elbows Kórol out of the way to heal me. His touch lessens the pain in my cheek like heat on ice-frozen skin. "Whyever you did it, it was a silly decision," he mutters.

"I wanted to help," I say. "I didn't think Sáven could do it on his own."

"That help could have killed you," says Kórol. "Special though you may be, even immortals bleed."

Tans rolls me to my other side and grazes the skin under the hem of my shirt. The shirt isn't mine, too big and smelling of mint and lemon. "Your blouse is fine, simply muddy," he says, pinching his lips together. "But I need to check your bandages to make sure you haven't bled through them." At my nod, he reveals my waist up to my ratty bralette and busies himself pulling a wad of cloth off my left hip.

Kórol still kneels next to me, unblinking. "Do you have any explanation?"

"I—I thought I'd—be fine, that I could control it." Kórol's ashen expression and Tans' reddened eyes show how wrong I must be. "I can't get hurt in a dream."

Tans' hands fumble on my hip and I hiss from the pain. He mouths inaudible apologies and heat extends from his fingers into my skin.

"You jest," says Kórol, thick brows raising. "You are surely not that stubborn."

"Kórol, stop, she's in pain," Tans scolds, hands shaking. "You'll lose control again and hurt her."

"Speak for yourself. You're closer to burning than I, and you've got hands on her. She must dispense with these absurdities. We have pandered to this for far too long. You, my friend, have pandered to it for too long."

"At your direction, always."

Kórol scoffs. "Not since the beginning."

Tans releases me to run trembling and bloodstained fingers through his mussed hair. He doesn't look me in the eye.

Kórol does, his pale eyes pensive as he rhythmically clenches and releases his fists. "Miss Grace, you need to quit this delusion immediately. While we believed there was no harm in indulging you, we were wrong on that count. Although none of us could have imagined indulging you would require Tans to pack your guts back in your body." He drops his gaze. "You're not dreaming. If anything, I have been dreaming."

My head shakes until pain forces me to stop. "No. You're *supposed* to say all that, since you're a manifestation of my mind."

Tans pets my knee. Tension in the muscles release with his touch. His eyes are still too bright, like he's holding back tears, but he attempts a smile. "It's a self-fulfilling prophecy, remember? You'll assume nothing is real. Until—"

"Until I get seriously hurt," I finish for him. Tans ducks his head while I press my hands against my gaping mouth. I—all the signs, they—the panic I felt when I woke in the dream (*not a dream, not a dream*) is nothing compared to now.

"She's hyperventilating," one of them says, sounding like they're underwater, like I'm the eel again.

It goes black.

CHAPTER 6

Night fell before I woke. The clearing is quiet, except for a rolling mist on the ground. I'm revisiting waking in Dalner the first time, as the same hysteria and fear seep into my pores. It takes me several minutes to pull to a seated position, but none of the slumbering men stir from the noise. Tans and Kórol sleep closest on the bare earth with arms reaching towards me.

My hands shake as I claw through my dirty hair. I can't tell how long ago I bathed, but the comfort and cleanliness from the water deserted me. Brown smudges of mud or rusty blood are stuck to my arms and lodged under my fingernails. The otherworldly dream I experienced while unconscious must have described the truth.

With trembling hands, I stifle a sob. It's all real, all of it—every day, each minute of what I thought was a dream, I've *been* here. I can't say a coma would have been better, not after what Mom suffered, but the mental anguish might have been less.

"You finally know," the Voice whispers into the still air.

I shudder at the intrusion, aggravating the damage to my hip as a thunderous thought strikes me. I've followed that Voice, listened to them, made choices based on their confirmation that they were here to help me.

"You need not panic," they console. "Your reality may have changed but I have not. I still aided you."

"How do I get home?" I hiss into the night. The Voice hums thoughtfully.

"You can't, at least not now. But do you truly want to? What about your friends, the ones I brought you to?"

I can't call them friends anymore. Our relationship is based on me behaving as if there were no consequences to my actions. I spoke without considering the implications, acted without paying attention to social codes. They must think I'm a nutcase, spouting on about dreams, or *completely* self-absorbed, suggesting that I created their personalities and that their decisions were manifestations of my mind. Those friendships are over. Getting home is my only option. At least there the lacking relationships aren't wholly due to my own irrational behavior.

I sniffle wetly. "That changes nothing. You lied to me and let me act like a fool."

"You weren't reacting rationally to your situation. All evidence pointed to this being real, but you ignored it. Letting you believe it was a dream was my best option, and all humans have a 'little voice inside them' to guide them. I never lied—I am here to guide you."

I roughly wipe the frustrated tears from my eyes. "What do you want?"

"I want what I told you originally—that has also not changed. I will guide you through your purpose here."

I lay back down on the pallet made from Tans and Kórol's packs. The idea of fighting a phantom stranger to end the dream seemed reasonable, but not anymore. Not when *I'm* the champion. "Defeating some woman, you mean."

"Precisely."

I shake my head hard enough to rattle my jaw, ignoring the spasms of pain clawing up my side as I do. "I'm not doing that. Maybe when I thought this was a dream and I was battling synapses of my brain—but we're all well aware now that I'm not untouchable. I'm a nobody who can't manage to avoid tripping over my own feet. I'm not putting myself in danger just because some mindreading child tells me so."

"You cannot avoid your purpose," they admonish, pitch rising in irritation. The mist rolls closer, brushing against my skin. Tans twitches in his sleep nearby. "You were brought here for a purpose: to defeat Her. If not, you make that decision at the expense of your new friends' safety."

I bite my lip hard enough to break the skin, hearing the unsaid threat. The knowledge that my failing to defeat this Woman will hurt my *actually-existing* friends drops a lead rock deep in my stomach. The Voice continues, avoiding or ignoring my inner conflict.

"I will still be there for you, whether you agree willingly. And I promised you more advice. Now that you've abandoned your delusion, it might become helpful: Deception will be your armor. You will need fire and ice to succeed."

I spit out a gasping laugh, one that's thin and wet. "Riddles. After all the lies and games, you have riddles?"

"I can't give away everything, as much as I want to," they say. "I've too many limitations. But there are things in the works. Keep an eye out, Grace."

"What's in the works? Wait—what about fire and ice?"

But I'm alone, hissing my questions to the empty air, my voice fading into the stillness of the night.

We're still at the clearing by the lake. The others watch me warily, like they're afraid I'm going to crack. To be fair, it's not an inconceivable thought. I've barely spoken with them, only enough to confirm that 'yes, I'm still in pain; no, I'm not hungry; yes, I promise to sleep; no, I don't know how to get me home either.' The combination of 'must engage in battle to the death to save my friends' and 'I acted overly familiar with said friends and now I'm too embarrassed to speak with them' makes for a confusing mindscape.

I spend my time at the shore of the lake where my reality shattered, sitting silently on the spongy lichen, though no other animals claw from the depths. I stare at the waterlogged parchment I used for notes. The notes are nonsensical ramblings now, but no more outrageous than the idea that *I'm* a savior. I should have listened better, and I furiously write what I remember—there's someone (Her) coming, that She is probably a Dark Eósy; something about fire and ice and deception. The notes look no less bizarre now.

"How are you tonight, love?" Tans says on the third night when he invades my bubble of loneliness. He's something I took for granted, and I don't know how to react to him. My face flares in memory of the times I teased him and held his hands. He sits beside me on the shore, as close as he has for the last four weeks, but I flinch. He notices and exhales heavily.

"Fine." I can't look at him or I'll turn into a bruised tomato.

"Your wounds are healing quicker than we expected. I expect we'll be able to restart the trek in another sun-cycle," he says.

"Great."

We sit silently for another few minutes before he bursts. "Tell me what I did so I may fix it!" He sounds devastated and I forget

I'm ignoring him to gawk, but he doesn't wait for me to answer. "I've attempted to determine exactly what I did to make you pull from me. Should I have kept you from coming to the lake, protected you better? Was it not trying harder to convince you of this reality?"

He nods, as if he figured something out, dragging his hands back into his feathery hair. "That's it. It must be. It—it was easier in the beginning, to let you assume it was a dream. You were more open that way and we could gain better information. I don't speak only speak for myself when I admit we stopped caring about figuring you out because we wanted to know you instead. You were the puzzle piece we didn't know we were missing, and you fit well in that open space. Yes, you were an oddly shaped one, what with your silly comments about dreams, but the instant familiarity you displayed was infectious. I was justifiably afraid it would cease when you—"

"That's not it," I blurt, cutting off his rambling confession. Only a small part of me wants to fume at them using my mistake to gain information, but the rest sees how sensible it was. They *tried* to convince me, and he admitted they started liking me for me and not for the mystery I was. They're the first ones who ever cared. It's muscle memory that has me grab his hands.

He trails his gaze over the thin scab on my cheek and a small spark flashes within the amber of his eyes. "Then what is it?"

I cringe and attempt to pull my hands away, but he tightens his grip. "I—It's this," I gesture, shaking our clasped hands.

He slumps but doesn't release me. "It *is* me then. I was overly familiar, taking advantage of your friendship when you thought I was imagined."

"No!" I'm quick to reassure him. "It's me. *I'm* too much. I thought I made you up, and I treated you that way! I've been acting like an absolute narcissist, thinking this was all a dream."

Regular Grace never got me anywhere on Earth, and that was when I kept a film of control over my behavior—don't try too hard, don't ask for too much, don't assume someone wants to keep talking to me because their eyes will glaze over soon enough.

"But I like this you," says Tans, his eyes crinkling in the corners.

I finally force my hands from his and intertwine them in my lap. "But it's not me though. I don't—I don't *act* like this, all overly familiar and—"

"I'll wager it is the *most* you, if you weren't afraid of the consequences," he says, ducking his head until I'm forced to meet his sincere gaze. "We all wear masks. You had the opportunity to go without one for a time, behaving without fear of judgment. That was you, Grace."

The weight into my stomach rises until it evaporates. He's right—I've been embarrassed for acting like me, and they *like* the authentic Grace. Even my own father didn't like her. Without thought, I leap into his arms, inhaling his smoky scent. He catches me and chuckles, burying his face in my hair.

"I have missed the affection, but you're still healing. You must not further injure yourself."

"It's fine," I breathe into his neck, though I struggle to hide the twinge in my side. "You'll just fix me up again."

"She realizes magic is real, and suddenly I'm nothing but a servant," he teases, waggling his sculpted brows. After a beat, though the lighthearted tone remains, he says, "I *am* sorry I didn't try harder to convince you this wasn't a dream."

"It's okay. I wouldn't have believed you."

"At least being in my presence is dream enough."

"No, you're more like a nightmare," I say.

He mock-pouts before a grin trickles back onto his face. "I'm only now realizing all the fun I've missed out on. Yes, we indulged your delusions, but we never took advantage. The things I could have convinced you to try, since you believed them all in your head."

I yank on a braid. "I was dreaming, not delusional."

He pokes my waist on the unharmed side. "For you, that may be the same—"

"Am I interrupting something?" Neither of us notice Kórol standing behind us until he speaks. Tans peels me off his lap.

"Merely discussing our little Butterfly, and her metamorphosis from dreamland to reality," Tans says, moving to kneel beside me.

I roll my eyes but can't stop the smile from forming. "That analogy doesn't even make sense."

"May I speak with you, Miss?" Kórol rocks on his feet as he stares down at us.

I shrug silently as Kórol pulls Tans up.

Still holding his arm, Tans whispers in Kórol's ear. "Kórol, as your second, I must--"

"I know what I'm doing, Tans," he says, scowling.

"Do you? Because your singlemindedness has not always served you."

Kórol clenches his fists. "Leave."

With a lingering look and a less-than-reassuring wink at me, Tans saunters back to the fire. Kórol sits a foot away and picks up a rock. He skips it across the lake and we both watch it make two jumps before it falls below the surface. He hands me a smooth speckled rock and stares my hand while I take it, his gray-blue irises almost eclipsing the dark pupils.

"We are only a day away from Chead," he finally says. "Do you intend to seek your own way home?"

I've thought about that over the last few days too. I have no way to get home, and my reconciliation with Tans is fresh in my mind. A world with possible supernatural foes but friends might edge out Earth with neither. "I—I think I'll stay. For now, at least. You guys are here and I wouldn't even know where to start on how to leave."

He rubs the nape of his neck and observes me from the corner of his gaze. "I know you are eager to arrive at Ilsen. Will you tell me why?"

I hesitate. Going from 'this is all a dream' to 'the disembodied voice of a child told me I'm to save you from danger and I haven't decided what to do yet' doesn't scream stability, no matter that Tans says they like me for who I am. And I still haven't wrapped my mind around the purpose the Voice seems to think I must fulfill. "I need—It's where I need to be."

"I understand duty," he says, straightening. He reaches for the rock, our skin brushing before he tosses it into the water. It skims across the entire lake, wind suddenly emerging and carrying it until it falls with a small plunk near the far edge. Perhaps he controls air much like Tans masters fire and Sáven shapeshifts. "You may continue traveling with us until and after Ilsen," he offers. "But your injuries must pain you. Let me escort you back to the fire."

He bows when he takes me to my sleeping spot. I ball my gritty windbreaker under my head for a pillow and Kórol covers me with his coat. I doze lightly until the others finally sleep and the encampment is silent again.

"Your relationship with Kórol is progressing as I hoped," the Voice whispers. I jolt, not expecting their presence so soon, catching a dense mist shrouding the surrounding ground. "You should have admitted something brought you here to remove an enemy of the Kingdom. Your path would be much simpler if you did."

"I'm not talking with you right now," I hiss. *And stop listening to my thoughts.*

"You must speak with me. I am your only help in defeating Her."

Whether or not I battle Her, I have zero intention of doing so simply because the supernatural child told me to. This isn't a book where the plucky nerd turns out to be the hero because some higher power deemed it. In this story, *I'm* the plucky nerd and more than ever, I'm aware of my own limitations. The thin lines Tans healed on my cheek, stomach, and leg are nothing compared to the deep gauge in my hip. I'm not waking up if I fail, meaning my 'purpose' better come with detailed instructions and a guaranteed happy ending.

"Go away." They were thankfully absent while I recovered, and I yearn for the silence.

"If you must know, I gave you space to reacquaint yourself with reality. But we must work together."

I scowl and wrap my arms around my waist, one hand pressing against the healing wound. "Working together implies trust, and for me to *trust* you, you'd need a time machine."

"You need to trust me, and trust that I want you to succeed in your endeavor here. As a... compromise, I will not read your thoughts unless necessary."

I hug myself tighter, disturbing some of the mist swirling around my prone form. "*Unless necessary*, which is a decision you make on your own I assume? What a *great* way to build trust and create a genial working relationship."

"I forgot how much you humans employ sarcasm. No matter. I have given you my word, and I can offer no more."

"Fine. Then, are you going to guide me on this visit, or just rile me up? If you're reading my thoughts, you know I need something better than riddles," I grumble into the still night.

"Go to sleep, love," Tans mutters from a few feet away. "I need my beauty sleep."

Let me not keep you from healing, the Voice says in my mind. **Remember this: Deception will be your armor. You will need fire and ice to succeed. She is coming**.

CHAPTER 7

C head is a day away, but we take three. While I'm lucky to have several superficial cuts from the encounter with the dobhà, the wound on my hip doesn't fully heal and pulls when I walk.

"I've explained to Miss Grace that she will travel with us after Chead," Kórol says when we linger a mile from town. He gathered us in one of the many green valleys that divot the path. The grass in the hollow is still dewy, and I lean into Tans' side to keep from slipping. "Until certain things are confirmed, we need to be on high alert and behave without suspicion."

"Confirm what? What suspicion?" I didn't pay enough attention to their running commentary earlier in the trek to understand the significance of what they're saying. Perhaps that would explain what they're talking about now. They all look solemn, like this is a meeting of extreme importance. Kórol's the most serious I've seen him, which is saying something because his normal expression makes a block of marble look soft.

"We split up," Tans says. The lines of his body tighten as his muscles tense against my own.

"Is everything okay?" I ask, but they ignore me. I tug on the soft sleeve of Tans' tunic. His eyes flit down but return to the others without acknowledgement. In protest, I stand without his support, crossing my arms and clearing my throat. They continue ignoring me and my hip pinches for my trouble.

"Pairs are out of the question," Kórol says, his brows furrowing. "We will split into thirds. I will walk alone."

Tansr sputters and his muscles shake from the pressure of clenching them. "Without significant preparation, it is better to let me, and you trek with Sáven or Fílga."

"Do we have reason to worry?"

Tans' mouth ticks downward. "Not any more than usual, hence my usual concern."

"Very well. Fílga and Miss Grace will take the lead. Tansr, you will go second, then myself and Sáven. One hour each," Kórol suggests.

The others busy themselves distributing our baggage. Sáven normally carries all the food, but they split it between their four backpacks. I only have my windbreaker and canvas tote, which Tans started carrying inside his bag the second day I traveled with them. It's empty except for my dead cell phone and wallet, rolled up into a four-inch-wide cylinder bundle Tans hasn't ever unfurled.

Part of me is annoyed they're keeping secrets and not explaining what's going on, but the distress he's broadcasting tamps down my impulse to bother him about it. With a sigh, I ask, "Anything I can do?"

He hoists the pack on his slim back. It's heavier now, bulging out on the sides, but he doesn't struggle with the added weight. He smiles down at me. It isn't as wide, or sincere, as his normal grins but I don't call him on it. "Your presence is all we need."

"Seriously—should I be worried?"

He runs his hands through his long hair, catching on his braids and wincing. "For yourself? Of course not."

"Should I worry for *you*?"

He forces the smile back on his face, one that's tense in the corners. "Everything is fine. Fílga will take good care of you. I even imagine you can convince him to explain a little. I need to stay focused on Kórol, or I'd do the same. Now, go forth, little Butterfly, and spread your wings in town."

"Still a caricature," I mutter. If my voice is less teasing than normal, he doesn't call me on it either.

When it's time to leave, the other three congregate in the hollow. Kórol and Tans mutter together while Tans makes large gesturing motions with his hands. Sáven appears only half listening, his attention on me and Fílga. He fidgets with the hem of his stained tunic when we leave.

Fílga and I pop out of the valley onto a worn path to Chead. I hold on to his arm, proposing that our story, if anyone asks, is as father/daughter pair on a shopping trip. Fílga grouses, the crease on his forehead deepening. "I appear younger than thirty years, barely a decade older than Sá—" He coughs. "I look but a decade older than all but Kórol, and his twenty years look grayer than any of mine. Although subterfuge has its merits. We shall be siblings."

"Why the need for subterfuge anyway?" I ask when the wood-shingled roofs grow and Chead's principal thoroughfare draws near. The town seems larger than the first one, but I spent little time gazing at the sights to make a complete comparison. Though, unlike the first town's festival-like atmosphere, Chead is an amusement park recreation of medieval life. It reminds me of an authentic version of Disney World's Fantasyland from our last family vacation before Mom died. I kill the memory of my last pleasant family encounter before it has time to fester.

"I forget this information is unknown to you," Fílga says, dragging me from my thoughts. "You have ingratiated yourself so well into our company. Even when—" He cuts himself off to purse his lips. "Even when you thought things were in your head, you still behaved as a working member, inability to hunt notwithstanding."

"Don't remind me," I groan, my face warming with tandem feelings of belonging and embarrassment. "Let me just take the compliment that you all like me, without discussing the weeks where I thought I was the center of the universe."

"It wasn't rational but responding to trauma rarely is. I can only assume I would cling to something that made sense if I woke up alone in your world. A dream isn't the worst choice you could make." He watches me from his periphery and his pale cheeks pink. "I wanted to apologize for my part in indulging your delusions. I should have tried harder to convince you."

"It's fine. Tans kind of explained why." He looks up sharply at that. "Honestly, I'd rather ignore it and quit talking about it. And don't think you can distract me from my questions," I say, tugging on his long braid.

He snorts. "You're as bullheaded as Tans sometimes."

"There's another compliment because Tans is awesome. And *he* already told me I'll convince you to tell me."

"Worse than Tansr," he says under his breath. "Very well. You have heard us call our group a Pack, correct?"

I shrug. It's vaguely familiar, something I overheard and discounted when I assumed this was a dream.

"That has special significance to the Sàrkany. We are a symbolic search party for the Sìnnách, the dragon-rider, our long-lost gift from the Great Matron, one of the leaders of the Light Eósy."

Those words I do remember—the Great Matron as a non-fairy godmother who might get me home, the Sìnnách as someone who they whisper about when they think I can't hear. I wish I could pull out my notes but they're safe with Tans right now. "The Sìnnách is a person who rides dragons?"

"Among other things. Dragon-rider, dragon-tamer. Legends say they can control the beasts enough to ride them, a magic rarely seen. Early interpretations have named them dragon-riders or dragon-tamers interchangeably."

"Didn't Kórol say that dragons weren't dangerous unless provoked?" I have another vague recollection of that from my our first meeting. "Couldn't we all ride one?"

Fíl jostles next me, suppressing a chuckle. "That's the literal interpretation. Do you believe that straddling the neck of a dragon would not provoke it?"

"Right," I say, flushing. "So, one of the consecrated magical Eósy gave you a dragon-rider and you symbolically search for her every year?"

He drops my arm and looks skyward, as if seeing the riders in his memory. "Our history says dragon-riders act as protectors for the Kingdom and will usher in an era of happiness and bounty after the dark time that forced the erection of the walls. The Great Matron brought Packs into existence hundreds of years ago. She demanded that the crown construct a temple, in the high fields, the Solstice Sanctum. The dragon-riders were lost to us, but every other year, a Pack makes pilgrimage to the temple and pays homage to the dragon-riders of the past, hoping another one would return."

"This is a *spiritual* quest?"

"We have mentioned giving blessings and our continued pilgrimage before. I don't know how this should surprise you," Fíl says dryly.

"No offense, but you four don't strike me as devout journeymen." The day three weeks ago when Tans convinced Sáven to walk backwards for six hours runs through my mind.

"We are an unconventional group, I'll give you. This is my fifth trek. I joined the pilgrimage when I came to the castle to apprentice under the prior Historian. This is Kórol's second, though he has—involved himself in the pilgrimage much longer because of his family." He pauses to slide shifting eyes in my direction. "Kórol achieved a higher rank at Ilsen three years ago and recently promoted Tansr to a higher position when he turned seventeen, meaning both were required to walk this year."

"They're both high ranking at the castle?" Kórol radiates both power and prestige, what with his determinism and appearance, but not Tans.

"Both, yes. You can see the weight Kórol carries, surely. Kórol promoting Tansr, which was warranted no matter Tans' playful demeanor, did no favors for him, thus he behaves even more absurdly to spite his naysayers. People underestimate Tansr, given his age and temperament, but he is a gift to Dalner."

"What about Sáven?"

He clears his throat and brings one hand up to fiddle with his braid. "Packs are always groups of four. Our usual fourth was unavailable for the forty day journey. Sáven grew up at the castle, not high-ranking mind you, but in the kitchens and knows the others well. Tansr suggested he join us this year. He's a wonderful addition, an incredibly gifted cook and hunter."

"You don't have to convince me," I tell him, squeezing his arm lightly. "Forty days of pilgrimage, that's a big commitment."

"It is actually longer. We leave on the equinox and travel at half-pace for forty days. The pilgrimage ends once we give blessings and turn back towards Ilsen, which would usually only be a twenty day trek back. This time, that was the day we encountered you."

A violent feeling runs down my spine at the coincidence. If something brought me here to eradicate an enemy of the country, if that enemy was the Woman the Voice mentioned, and I arrived at the tail end of their pilgrimage—it's another thought digging into my subconscious that I forcefully bury. I clear my throat. "Why did the dragon-riders leave?"

"I am unsure how much I can share without Kórol's leave. And no, you can't convince me otherwise. You must bat your eyes in his direction not mine." I elbow him in the stomach. "I did not mean it as an insult. I was teasing."

"Leave the teasing to Tans," I grumble. "What *can* you tell me then?"

He rolls his eyes skyward again. "Perhaps—yes. A thousand years ago, a poor King banished the dragon-riders and removed any chance we had at receiving the Matron's bounty."

"And—and you've been asking for another one ever since?"

"Do you see any anywhere?" he asks, archly.

"Absolutely not." The words force their way out of me before I think them, but they're true. "Sorry. So, you didn't find the dragon-riders and you don't want people to know you're looking, is that about the gist?"

He covers my hand with his as we crossed into a small lane on the outskirts of town, lugging me out of the way of an incoming man on a horse with wide antlers. "It announces something we are not yet prepared to announce. It wouldn't be a leap in judgment if someone saw a group of four, during the month after the pilgrimage, with a woman. Particularly one who dresses as *you* do, in trousers and non-Sàrkany clothing. Someone might suspect you to be a rider, an outsider to Dalner."

My voice catches in my throat, and I cough to clear it. "Surely the Great Matron, or *whoever*, wouldn't just—drop the dragon-rider here. There'd need to be lots of fanfare, women flying in the sky, fireworks, loud chorale music, that sort of thing."

Fílga's nose wrinkles. "We know little about how the Sìnnách returns. We have had false Candidates in the past but how they arrived in the Kingdom was irrelevant. What mattered was whether they were true. Hence the subterfuge."

The deeper implication—that I'm a potential Sìnnách—sends pinpricks of dread through my bones. "But they'd know if they *were* one though. I mean, it's not like it would be a surprise to them—"

"We do not know. The possibility exists that they don't know their status until they are confirmed. They might also hide their magic, voluntarily or otherwise. The records that remain tell us the Sìnnách returns, but not whether it is by their own design or at the direction of the Great Matron. The Eósy cannot directly interfere with the lives of the Sàrkany. With the wall intact, they can only provide guidance unless one of us expressly invites them across, but the extent of their *indirect* interference is unknown.

It is possible the Great Matron could create the circumstances that allow the Sìnnách to return."

"Fílga," I say as the town grows around us. "Could one of those Eósy interfere with the lives of a *non*-Sàrkany—like bring them here for some unknown purpose?"

Fílga rubs his hand over my arm in a soothing rhythm but his expression is grave. "With proper magic and the right bit of wordplay, there are no limitations to what an Eósy can do." With his pursed lips and pinched eyes, I can almost hear him finish the sentence with '*to you*.'

After Fílga's bombshell, he pulls me down a crowded street that lacks privacy enough for us to continue our conversation at even a whisper. I'm tongue-tied anyway and doubt I could formulate the questions rolling around in my brain. That I was brought here at all is implausible. That it's because I, a seventeen-year-old middling student with no discernable skills, am supposed to destroy some Woman before she shows up is already incredibly farfetched. Adding that I'm a prophesied savior too? I may not know fantasy, but I know when something is too convenient. The fact that I hit the fairy tale tropes for protagonists—loner with a dead parent—isn't enough. There's no way I'm special enough for otherworldly heroine status. I can't even create a generic romance out of my normal life, much less fulfill some fantasy plot.

Fílga doesn't notice my internal freak-out as his attention turns to chasing off overly familiar townspeople. Several approach and graze my tight denim jeans, which are painted onto my skin after weeks of sweat embedding into the fabric. When the fifth person in a row points in my direction and whispers, Fílga suggests we go down the merchants' alley and find Sàrkany clothes.

I immediately protest. I can't ask him for new clothes as I refused to be indebted to anyone the moment I moved out of my father's house. But Fílga negligently waves off my protestations that I can't take his money. I only accept when he explains how important it is to the Pack to avoid questions about me, and that if I fit in, the rumors of my being the Sìnnách will lessen.

That convinces me. Anything I can do to stop that rumor spreading, even among strangers, is worthwhile.

When we round the corner into the merchants' alley, my senses are overwhelmed. It's the height of the business day and all around people shout noisily. Even Tans at his most emphatic, and the other three reacting to him, is quieter than the din of shopkeepers and their customers. It's like the mall on Black Friday, except instead of stores, piles of products teeter on wooden tables or small stalls. People chatter excitedly, and the loud noises block out the terror of my own thoughts, a distraction from the confusing revelations and questioning stares.

It takes more than an hour to find a merchant who sells pre-made clothing. Most of what I find are stacks of wool and tanned hides, ready for a talented seamstress to create clothing from scratch. Since the nights are colder, I also search for my own fur coat. Although Kórol leaves his every night, I don't want to rely on his generosity because it will, inevitably, end. But his coat is the only fur in sight.

I dig through the piles in a simulacrum of my methods at the local thrift shops, searching for a good deal to cover me on a meager budget. I find my prize: the simplest and (I hope) cheapest tunic there. With a string around my waist, I can bunch it together like a short dress. It won't keep me warm, but I'll avoid notice.

After I show him the garment, Fílga gestures for me to wait beside him. "Much like the many bandits hiding on the road we travel, these sellers will rob you blind, or worse, if you aren't careful."

I debate asking him to let me haggle for him, betting I'm the more experienced of the two of us. Fílga still looks like he's never spent a day sleeping outside; his bright braided hair lays flat without a single strand out of place, his leather shoes and vest gleam without the streaks of dirt that cling to the other men's outfits. I doubt he's ever bought anything from a wooden stall, or anything that isn't handmade to his specifications. But Fílga makes a shooing motion before holding the tunic with the tips of his fingers.

"Five coppers," says the overweight and ruddy colored merchant.

"I'll give you one."

The merchant rubs his nose with the back of his calloused hand anwineucks. "You'll give me five or you'll leave."

Fílga obviously expects the man to fold, or at least negotiate. The bored expression falls as his eyes narrow and indignation forms a frown. "That is robbery! We will offer no more than two."

"You give me five." The merchant bares his teeth. A glint of metal flashes from his hand as he places his palms on the table. "Or you find yourself worse than robbed. 's a long alley and there are plenty of dark places. For you and the pixie with you."

"Fíl, it's fine. I don't need it, or I can pick something else. Let's just go." I place a placating hand on his arm and try to drag him away. Fíl is at least a foot taller than me and built of solid, tensing, muscles, meaning he doesn't budge. He stands his ground and glares at the man, shrugging off my touch.

"Are you threatening us?" Fílga's voice sharpens to a point.

"'s a promise, but someone too dumb to pay value like you wouldn't get that."

I can't speak for Fíl, but I have no intention to brawl over a scrap of cloth.

"Fílga, sir." I step between both men and shakily pat their shoulders. *I can do this.* Except for the venue, goods, and that the merchants carry knives, it's almost like being back home. "What's your name?" I ask the surly merchant.

He scowls at me as his muscles tense. "Saal," he mutters.

I remove my hands and awkwardly curtsy. Fíl send me a curious look but remains silent, watching Saal with wary eyes.

"Saal. How wonderful to meet you. My name is Grace."

Feats of strength won't work with this guy, neither will intimidation, not that I'm skilled in either. If I'm right, and merchant's alley can be compared to the weekend flea markets I trolled back home, my haggling skills will transfer. This might be my chance to give back to the friends who give so freely, by reducing my burden on them. I smile until my cheeks pinch my eyes closed. Saal crosses his arms and grunts.

"I see why you might want five coppers," I tell him, batting my eyes twice. I spare only a thought to the knowledge of what my professors back home would think about me exploiting sexism for personal gain. But they aren't here and home is gone. And the tactic is surprisingly effective considering this world's main deity and savior are women. "This craftsmanship must take you an enormous amount of time, you'd have to focus solely on this to the detriment of your other work."

He flushes, his ruddy skin mottling a deeper burgundy and crosses his arms around his portly chest. "It ain't that hard."

I grab the tunic and hold it up to the sunlight, squinting. "But all that sewing must be difficult."

"Ain't nothing. Mam's magic is in textiles."

"Right, how silly of me." Fílga's gaze turns from wary to amused as I speak. "I'm sure the cloth cost quite a bit. Probably a seller who didn't haggle, forcing you to pay unreasonable prices."

Saal puffs out his chest. "I got the whole bolt for a song," he boasts. "Bartered the man down to almost nothing."

A smile melts onto my face. "So then—if it cost you nothing, and took little effort, why won't you take our two coppers?"

He stammers, but no words emerge. "Man's gotta eat," he finally grunts.

"I know what it's like to pinch pennies—err—coppers. I wouldn't want you to starve. What about three?" I grin wider. "Would that be a fair price?"

His mouth pinches as he uncrosses his arms. After a long moment he slumps his shoulders. "That'd be fine."

With an astonished expression, Fílga pays him and drags me aside. "Where did you learn to do that?"

"Do what? Haggle?"

"That." He motions behind us, his eyes wide. "Make that man do your bidding."

I snort. "That's just bargain-hunting mixed with luck and a smidge of sexism."

"I do not think so." The amused look is back. "Magic exists everywhere. And *that* was magic, Miss Grace, tamer of Sàrkany merchants."

I change in an abandoned doorway right beyond the market. As I straighten the hem, an arm snakes around my waist and pulls me down another alley. The telltale campfire scent of Tans is missing. I let out a squawk and kick the shins and elbow the stomach of my possible captor. They release me with a growl, and I spin to stare into familiar steely blue-gray eyes.

"I suppose I should be content you have some sense of self-preservation, though it feels as if a rabbit accosted me rather than a girl," Kórol grunts.

I blow loose hair out of my eyes before tucking the unruly strands behind my ears. "Rabbits are both adorable and fast, so thank you."

"Not here they aren't." He stares at my legs until he clears his throat and stares above my head. "What are you wearing?"

"A dress," I gesture down at myself in irritation at his presence and tone. *Not irritation*, something tries to convince me, *intrigue*. It feels foreign, like the Voice but subtler. I shake it off.

Kórol's gaze flits back to my bare legs before he looks skyward. "I'd call it a child's shift before naming *that* a dress."

I look down at the outfit. My wide hips pull the garment higher than I expected, but it covers everything important. Although it presses tight against my thick thighs, meaning I should have purchased pants too. Apparently, I have less magic than Fílga thinks.

"It was cheap." I cross my arms around my middle, which only causes the dress to inch up higher. I drop them to my sides.

"Did Fílga tell you where payment for this clothing came from? Did he only allow you to purchase that?" He flaps a hand in my direction but ends up gesturing to the doorway three feet to the left of me.

"No. But I didn't know what the budget was and wanted to be respectful."

He closes his eyes and rubs the back of his neck, whisky locks swaying and beads clacking together against his cobalt tunic, the fur conspicuously absent. "I did not think of that," he says, tucking my clothes away. He holds out his hand after he slips the bag over his shoulders. "May we continue?"

I smooth down the dress again and take his hand. "I thought you were walking with Sáven and I was with Fíl."

"Your shopping trip put you behind us. Fílga walks with Sáven while Tans has business to attend to in town. They are to meet us outside Chead. We will travel together instead, so we may speak."

"What business would Tans have in town?"

"Meetings for the crown," he says gruffly without further explanation. It must be related to the promotion Fíl mentioned. Kórol's arm tenses where it meets mine. "Fílga tells me he indulged your curiosity in some of our history."

He says it casually, but expectation hides behind it, and Fíl's revelations batter the sides of my head. There's a thought shouting that the reason he mentions it isn't to make conversation, but to connect dots I prefer remain separate. I peek at him from the corner of my eye as he directs us out of the alley.

"Dragons are scary!" The words bubble out of my mouth outside my control. Kórol falters in his steps while I force my eyes closed and hold back a wince at my delivery. The so-called soft touch with the merchant abandoned me and I'm left with unintelligible thoughts. I've already proved I'm not the Sìnnách: no famous dragon-rider would be as awkward as me. After taking a deep breath, I barrel onward, ignoring the rising flush on my cheeks.

"Yes, Fíl told me about your history, but not as much as I wanted. He got me thinking about dragons, and how—scary they are. Uncontrollable, *untamable* even, at least by me. I fainted twice because of them, remember."

"What prompted you to make this confession today?" he asks while his jaw ticks in time with my heartbeat.

"No reason. Just on my mind."

"Fílga also reported you earned a new nickname: Tamer of Sàrkany Merchants." He arches a single brow. "Does that mean anything to you, Miss?"

I hold in a snort. "No—only that you guys don't spend your weekends at flea markets like I do."

His hand tightens. "I cannot say that we do."

We wander further into town, amounting to a few blocks, until we arrive at a fountain in the middle of a small square, one decorated with tiny figures on lizards. While Kórol splashes water on his face, I peer down at the lizards chiseled into the stone. Up close, they have wings.

"Are these supposed to be," I squint my eyes and imagine them life-size, "dragons?"

Kórol inspects it with twisted lips. "It appears to be. Fear not, they are too small to terrorize you."

A man passes peddling overripe turnips, and a small girl toddles up. I grin down at her as she reaches for the hem of my dress.

"The Sìnnách!" Her little voice squeaks as she points at the tiny riders.

"Those are the dragon-riders, right?" I ask. She ignores me, attention lost and wanders back to a nearby woman. I run my fingers over the stonework. Although chiseled crudely, the design shows people flying on dragons. It's more literal than I would have expected after Fíl's explanation, though I suppose the name 'dragon-rider' should give it away. Even shoddily done, the figures resemble warriors. Two of them hold swords over their heads, another has a bow. *That can't be me.* My only talent, according to Fíl, is haggling. I'm certainly not a fighter.

"What did you say?" Kórol stands behind me. I must have spoken out loud.

"Just that Sìnnách is a cool name. For cool women who—who aren't terrified of dragons."

He shows no expression. "I was unaware one could determine the temperature a word may invoke. Though, if I had to choose, cold is my temperature of choice."

The peddler stops a few feet away and pulls a root vegetable from his pocket. He sniffs then brandishes it, his fingernails black with dirt and the turnip littered with scratch marks.

"Someone tellin' you stories about the women's return, eh? Sìnnách, dragon-riders. 'f you believe that, let me sell you this apple." He waves the turnip in my direction. I shuffle closer to Kórol and hold in a cough from the vegetable's potent smell. "She should stay away. They put up the wall for a reason. If magic ain't coming back for all of us, then the King don't deserve his own magic whore."

Kórol shoves past me and his eyes flash silver. "You do not know what you speak. The Sìnnách was to be a savior ushering in prosperity for the entire Kingdom. She is not simply for the King, she was a friend to the entire kingdom."

The peddler spits onto the ground. "Any dragon-riders, these women, left us. They left us because of the King and it ain't rightly fair that this new King get rewarded because of his family's mistake."

Kórol looms over the peddler as the autumn temperature plummets. "We need none of your animal feed." He and the peddler stand toe-to-toe until Kórol directs him away with a flick of his wrist. With bared teeth, the peddler shoves the turnip back into his pocket and ambles towards another set of potential customers.

"Wait. What—?"

"Ignore him. He lies, intent on discrediting the Kingdom and the sacrifices our forefathers made. That is all." He starts down the street, but I yank on his arm.

"Hang on—are you okay?"

The corded muscle of his forearm tenses and releases as he avoids eye contact. "I will leave the tales of our history to Fílga. He will explain better than I."

"I don't see how a history lesson will explain your freak-out, but fine. Keep your secrets *again*," I say through gritted teeth. We walk in silence for another minute before I reach out again. I exhale heavily. It's not as if I'm the poster child for rational responses to stressors. "I'm sorry. That wasn't fair."

He holds out his hand, interlacing our fingers when I take it. I don't pull away, though it's a move I expect from Tans, not Kórol. "Thank you for attempting to keep me tame," he murmurs.

CHAPTER 8

"Tell me more about the Sìnnách."

It's the day after Chead and Kórol's permission, that Fílga could answer my questions, is fresh in my mind. I filled an entire page of notes on what Fílga told me the day before. While I can't be the Sìnnách, the coincidence of me arriving here to destroy some evil Woman while the Sàrkany are waiting for a female savior digs at something under my skin.

Fílga fusses for a few seconds but doesn't outwardly complain about my questions. "I should not have questioned your ability to convince Kórol to share more of our history. Perhaps your name should simply be the Tamer of the Sàrkany."

I huff out a laugh, but no one else thinks it's funny, sharing weighted looks.

Fílga finally begins his lecture. "First, you must know why the Sìnnách appeared. Now, it begins—"

"Once upon a time, you mean," I say, attempting to add levity to a conversation I don't think will go well for me. Kórol and Tansr's heads cock in my direction. "If you're telling a story, you have to tell it right."

Fílga rolls his eyes but still gives me a patient, if somewhat disapproving, smile. "Fine, from one bibliophile to another—once upon a time, four hundred years after the separation, the Third of the Raddare line came into power."

"The separation," I repeat. "What's that?"

"Do you want to know why the dragon-riders left or learn about the evolution of Sàrkany man from Eósy?"

"Both, if possible." Fílga glares at me until I clasp my hands together in what I hope looks conciliatory. "I mean—please continue with the current story with no interruptions from me."

"That is what I thought. Now, the first Raddare King, known as the Second in honor of his late father, ruled alone on this side of the wall, uninterested in the pure magic the Eósy have. After certain… tragedy and strife, his father closed off the connection to the Eósy and to the now ancient home of Dànna through barriers, what we call the walls, with only the Gates allowing magical beings to move between sides. And with the walls, the magic of the Eósy vanished. The first line of Raddare Kings believed they should rule humanity alone, with no advisors or magic to aid them. The King's will and his will alone commanded Dalner. There would be no counseling him and no second guessing him."

"Seems a bit despotic," I interject. Tans coughs in front of me while I wait for the reprimand from Fílga for interrupting, but instead he ticks his head to the side.

"It was a turbulent time. He believed he was doing what was best for his people. Factions arose from the chaos creating the wall, those of us that followed him to Dalner, and those who became voluntary and involuntary citizens of Dànna. But without a magical consort, or even advisors, the Kingdom suffered. Magic lessened, which was… expected, given it was the goal of the barrier. But the Sàrkany lost the protection of the Light faction of the Eósy, and the skills that were innate in our blood." He slows, letting more space slip between us and the other three, and lowers his voice. "As generations passed, all former knowledge was lost. We knew that some innate senses would be lost as the magic left, but we were illiterate in the ways of the world and forced to create our civilization anew. Crops died without proper care, laws were forgotten, craft works ignored, many died.

Raddare the Third understood we could not avoid our past but should embrace it. He put his life in his hands and appealed to one of the Light Eósy to descend."

"What does that mean?"

"Much as the Sàrkany cannot cross the walls, the Eósy are locked behind them and cannot descend to our realm through any of the Gates without an explicit invitation. Eósy can indirectly influence minds, by invitation or force. He opened his mind and invited them across the wall, risking the wrong Eósy hearing and taking advantage of the rift."

I think of the Voice, and of the Woman I'm supposed to defeat. "What's the *wrong* Eósy?"

He doesn't reprimand me for my multiple questions. "The third faction. The Dark Eósy would kill you for sport and force you to thank them for the pleasure. The Light Eósy—even they can be tricky and interacting with them requires a delicate hand. They cannot lie to you, none of the Eósy can, but they are not fully mortal and do not understand certain aspects of humanity, meaning their gifts and counsel can appear—warped. But the Light understand we are all kin. Dalner worships the remaining leader of the Light for all the benefits she provides."

"The Great Matron?"

"The very same. When Raddare the Third opened his mind and begged her to descend, she arrived in a fit of magic, something not seen for centuries. It made the King fall to his knees, so moved was he by her power." His eyes shine when he continues.

"She bid him stand, placing her hands on his shoulders. She told Raddare the Third that he should not rule alone. That a man left by himself to rule without the pure magic of the Eósy would only cause ruin. She offered him a gift: the Sìnnách, the dragon-riders, those who tamed and rode the beasts."

"How could they help?" I ask. "I mean, you say you lost knowledge, magic diminished. How could a woman on a dragon fix that?"

He's no longer whispering, but reporting facts like they happened last year, not centuries ago. "The Sìnnách acts as the King's advisor, his connection to man's divine history, to rid him of his hubris and offer magic he lacked. The first Sìnnách was like a goddess herself, one who commanded the dragons. With her, famine, sloth, greed, all of man's sins forgotten. There only was her. She was their hope, their queen."

A twinge of something unpleasant slides down my back but I'm not sure why. I squeeze my eyes shut before shaking my head to clear the feeling. "And another King banished her?"

"Greed and power are heavenly temptations. Raddare the Eleventh suspected he knew better than his forefathers, that the original Raddare had it right in locking away all Eósy and magic. He raved that the Sìnnách was corrupt, only there to exert control over the Kingdom, control the Eósy ceded when we constructed the wall. He banished the Sìnnách, forcing her out of the Kingdom and out of rule."

"What happened after she left?"

The other three pause as we catch up. Fílga's gaze darts to Kórol, who watches us with ice-sharp eyes. "Things were satisfactory, at first. The knowledge and hope the Sìnnách brought lasted throughout Raddare the Eleventh's reign. Only when his grandson, the Thirteenth, came into power, did man again desire for the touch of the divine. But by then, the people lost hope. Worse, they lost faith in their King and in his ability to rule and to act as their salvation. The return of the Sìnnách would bring about a new era, one of light, not marred by the mistakes of the past."

"I can't believe the King was so selfish. I mean, we have *a lot* of issues where I'm from, but to screw over the entire country forever just because you don't want to share power? That's—well, more than despotic, definitely."

Fílga purses his lips while fidgeting with the end of his braid. "That is an interesting way to explain it."

Kórol stands in front of me with his hands at his side, his fingers twitching. His eyes glaze over, a milky film almost covering the crystal blue irises. "Do not impugn the King."

"No, I'm—I'm not. It's like that street vendor said. Maybe the *way* he said it wasn't great but the conclusion is the same. Seriously, you wouldn't be out on this bi-yearly hike if a long-dead King hadn't made a mistake."

Kórol looms closer and growls. "How typical to think it your place, your *right*, to express your opinion on things you know nothing about."

I hold up my hands in what I hope is a cross-universal disarming gesture. "I'm on your side. I'm not trying to be rude, or disrespectful. I'm upset for you guys."

"Were that true, you would stop treating the knowledge of my people's history, their trials and successes, as your entertainment. My people are not a substitute for the foolish fables of love you lack."

Shocked, I turn to the others, but they aren't my allies against Kórol. Fíl's expression is blank, while Sáv glares at the ground. Only Tans ping-pongs his focus between us. It feels like it's four against one, and over something as silly as a history lesson. "That's not what's happening," I grind out. "*You* were the one who said I should hear this."

"These stories are sacred, and Fílga was honoring you by sharing them." He presses his fist against his chest. "I was honoring you, as a friend to the Kingdom. I presumed you understood that, that you could understand why this knowledge is important to us."

"I appreciate that—"

Kórol speaks through gritted teeth. "We were wrong to expect an outsider to recognize their worth. I was wrong to see you as anything but a silly little girl."

"Kórol, that's—" Tans starts, but Kórol holds up his hand.

Fílga hasn't taken a breath for a minute or more. Sáven now conspicuously stares at his fingers as if they were the most fascinating things he's ever seen. Tans finally tears his eyes between the two of us and pinches them closed. I'm missing something important, but I can't figure out what, too focused on stopping the tears threatening to fall. Not since my last conversation with my father has someone spoken that harshly to me and I'm afraid I'll react the same way—to run.

"If you have no respect for our Kingdom, then the Great Matron will be of no help and the castle will provide you no aid. You are but a selfish mortal little thing and I no longer wish to gaze upon you."

With permission given, I flee from his sight.

Roughly wiping at my eyes, I stumble down a worn path a few hundred yards from our campsite into a dense thicket of trees. When the sun barely peeks through the leaves above me, I slump to the ground, pulling my knees up to my chin and kicking up a thin layer of mist that curls around my feet. With a wet exhale, I rest my cheek on my crusty jean-covered knees.

A rush of pressure builds inside my head, something I attribute to the Voice.

Who could have guessed you'd make an enemy out of Kórol?

"Leave me alone," I rasp, bitterness coating the back of my throat.

They giggle, sounding shriller than the last time. ***Do not fear, Grace, it will only make the reconciliation much more satisfying.***

"Like you'd know, you deranged five-year-old," I sniff, rubbing at my nose.

And the being who is your best hope of succeeding here.

"Oh, screw you. I'm not in the mood. Unless you have something helpful to say, like how to get home, go away."

And then my mind is full of my thoughts alone.

Pressing the back of my hands to my cheeks, I stop sniffling and stand. I stumble back the direction I came to get my bag and figure out my next move. Home isn't possible, but somewhere else maybe. Leaves crunch and grass flattens under the stomp of my feet, the rattle of my steps the only thing keeping me from slumping to the ground in self pity.

In the distance, footsteps sound ahead of me and the heaviness in my chest releases. "Tans, is that you?"

The footsteps turn into a figure shuffling forward, features obscured by shadow. I squint to identify him. Long loose hair trails down his back, which means it can only be Tans. But the gait is off, and I falter. We're only a day from Chead, and I remember Fíl's admonitions about bandits too late. With an uncoordinated shake, I bolt. The figure is faster, and he blocks off one direction. I shoot off in another, but he whistles loudly and suddenly, a dozen or more men surround me. I shuffle my feet, peering for an opening to escape and finding none.

The tallest man saunters forward until I'm pressed into the man behind me, the one with greasy dark hair that I mistook for Tans. He runs a finger down his stained indigo tunic and bares his blackened teeth. In the dim light, he looks ill—his skin both sallow and sunburned red, a blotchy coloring that does nothing to lessen the danger he presents. With surprising speed, he brandishes a heavy knife and raises it before I can flinch, slamming the hilt down.

CHAPTER 9

Time passes without my knowledge.

When I wake, the surrounding woods are dark, lit only by torches the men hold. My hands are bound, my head is throbbing, and I've been tossed over a man's shoulder. It isn't the man with the knife, but another from the circle. The acrid smell of sweat and bile lingers in my nose, but I can't blame it for the watering of my eyes—that belongs to the absence of my former friends, who'd have shown up if they planned to. When the man carrying me walks over a fallen tree trunk, I use the jolt to wipe my dripping nose. No one is coming.

But I'm not alone, I realize. The Voice constantly haunts the edge of my subconscious. They want me to succeed and being murdered by bandits removes that possibility. If anyone can help me, it's the Voice. I focus as best I can, calling silently for aid. *Where are you? Come back! Please! Anyone!* The man jostles me again, leaping over a thicket of underbrush, his hands groping my thighs to keep me in place. My concentration slips, but it's no use—I'm begging into an empty space. I'm still alone.

And worse off than before as we breach the forest and enter a pock-marked field. A large tent sits in the middle and I worry that if I enter it, my dim hope of escaping is scuttled. My transporter tosses me onto the ground a few yards from the tent's canvas flap and I land directly on my still-sore hip. My palms scratch the gritty dirt as I struggle to plan my way out of here. The romance plots in my head give me few options—to lay limply until the hero arrives to release my bindings, spit out sarcastic quips until someone lets me go, *or* to engage my only-just-revealed ninja skills. None of those ideas are helpful. If I ever home, I'm only reading survivalist guides, or *at least* books where romance is a subgenre.

The man who carried me kneels beside my stomach before running the dull end of dagger down the side of my face. "You promise to be good and I'll untie you. If you're good, you can stay unbound all night." He leers, and half his teeth are missing.

I say nothing to the man. If he unties me, I might outrun him. Even with my damaged hip, I've spent the last month walking miles each day. But—he has a knife, while all I have was an invisible mind-reading five-year-old throwing a tantrum and a head full of book plots. He smacks me with the hilt of his weapon, the jewels pressing into my temple while I'm thinking through a plan.

"Did ya hear me?" I nod, feeling a dull ache bloom from the spot where he hit me. "And will you be good?" I nod again. "Good girl."

I tense my leg muscles while he cut the ropes. As soon as my arms are free, another man grabs my legs, thwarting my possible getaway. When the ropes fall to the ground, he grips my ankles and hoists me upward, half upside down. The man holding my arms grabs my waist as if he's going to toss me backward over his shoulder, but chucks me to another man, who passes me to another and another. I squirm as blood rushes to my head and I grow woozy. Their big hands haul me inside the tent until I'm forced right side up on the lap of the tall man, who sits in a wide chair in the center of the tent. I perch precariously on his lap as he wraps a possessive arm around my waist. Up close and in the bright candlelight, grease and grime cover his skin, the sallow complexion not evidence of sickness but of his appalling hygiene. His expression is glazed, his eyes a watery blue, and he sways as he stares around the tent. It's a medieval version of a meeting room, with three men sitting on pallets of straw facing the leader.

A dozen men enter, positioning themselves near their comrades and next to the leader. My chances of escape without harm were slim, but now they're nonexistent. The leader's hand jostles my breasts and pinches, as if confirming they're there under my crusty t-shirt, making me thankful I'm not wearing the dress purchased yesterday.

"The girl may wear a man's clothes, but she's all woman," he announces. His men whoop and jeer while I try to stay still, like a deer staring down an approaching car.

His thumb and fingers trace my body until he gropes the juncture between my hip and thigh. I try to disassociate from what's happening and the knowledge that his hands are the first to touch me. Those are Tans' hands, Kórol's, the hero from the mafia book I ditched when I landed here, *anyone* whose touch I might choose. But I can't help shuddering in revulsion, and he can't tell it isn't desire. "And she wants it!" His voice booms as his rheumy eyes drag over me.

Motionless, I watch my captor drag his hands down to my thigh, winking at his men. His eyes are glassier now. Someone hands him a sizable skein of something, and the smell that wafts towards me identical to the scent of my dorm when I came home from a late-night shift. He guzzles it, letting it dribble off his lips and down his chin.

The Voice's riddles play in my head. *Something about deception.* I don't have my notes, not that I could look at them now but combining the riddle with my love of fiction, and the outlandish plots I've read—the traces of a plan form. My captor takes another guzzle of alcohol. The liquid drips from his chin and down onto my denim-clad hip, and he closes his mouth with a wet smack. The plan takes root.

In a bout of misplaced courage, I grab the skein from his hands and take a swig, pretending to swallow more while my eyes stay trained on his. Only a teaspoon of the liquid makes it down my throat, but it still burns.

My captor smirks at my brazenness and slaps my thigh, his dull eyes warm but unfocused, like he knows I'm there but can't quite find me. He peers intently, his hands catching my chin and holding my face in front of his until a slight burst of cognizance surfaces.

"Want to enjoy it too, pet?" I hold back the bile that rises in my throat and simper in what I hope looks demure and maidenly, like I did with Saal. I slide my finger from his wine-soaked chin down to the middle of his stomach, where my body presses against his, suppressing a dry-heave.

"More wine," I suggest shakily, whispering in his ear. It's a crude deception, probably not all what the Voice has in mind, but it's the best I've got while I'm on my own, something I read in one of those romance novels. I'm gambling that he'll drink himself into a stupor before my body pays the price my mouth bid, and gambling he isn't a violent drunk. Tears build at my eyes and I attempt to dissociate again. *This is normal. I chose this. I can do this.* He calls for more wine.

And more wine.

And more wine.

His hands get heavier, his voice louder, but he doesn't appear any drunker. His eyes have the same dazed expression it did when he first placed me on his lap. His friends loll about, struggling to keep up with their leader, before each leave the tent or sag into sleep. He still paws at me and I pretend to snuggle into him, hoping I can get his guard down. I need it low enough to put him at ease, but high enough that he won't toss me over his shoulder. His hands rub over my cheeks roughly, like he's trying to keep track of where I am, his eyes half-lidded and filled with want rather than inebriation. I press my eyes closed and scream inwardly. Unsurprisingly, silence meets me, the only mental sound is my own frantic thoughts. I can't disassociate anymore.

With one hand on the skein, he draws the fingers of his free hand across my throat. Suddenly, wet lips brush against my neck and his tongue licks down to my collarbone. I stiffen and grab the skein from him. My last plan, the plan I should have thought of originally—hit hard and run, no matter that someone will recapture me—suddenly seems much better than helping him along. At least now, most of the room is too drunk to chase me. As I lift the skein, he bares his teeth and bites down at the juncture between my neck and collarbone, sucking and tearing at my skin. I rip backward, dropping the skein from the shock and blossoming pain. There's bright blood on his chapped lips that he licks off. His eyes clear, the dullness vanishes as he licks his lips a second time.

It's as if he finally *sees* me and he leers, running his tongue over his teeth from canine to canine. As a last resort, I snag the skein and shove the opening back to his mouth. The skin on my neck burns, as blood traces down the valley between my breasts under the collar of my grimy shirt. He takes the skein, licking the nozzle in a lewd simulacrum of *something*, but I've no actual experience to understand what. He misses half the nozzle; I must be near the end of my plan. Undeterred, he bites down on it with his yellow teeth and waggles his eyebrows. I choke back bile again when he surges forward with his tongue and licks the blood from my skin. He leans on my shoulder, slurring that I'm "his pet, only his to do what he desired," before slurping from the skein. I pat his sallow cheeks while eyeing the skeins he's ingested, hoping he drinks his last.

I count the seconds until he finally sleeps. The wine consumed, he drops the empty skein and grasps me loosely. The remaining three men in the tent snore. They rightfully don't think I'm much of a threat. I take a few deep breaths and run my fingers over the spot on my collarbone where he's bitten me. Blood has pooled in the bite marks and they sting. I rip a corner from my shirt to press against the skin. If Tans were here—but I smother the thought, not wanting to add more tears to the stains on my shirt.

My kidnapper stirs, and I freeze. When he lets out a soft snore, I ease myself off his lap, wrapping his fingers around the leather skein. The three sleepers are easy to sneak past, but I can't account for the other ten or more. I slip out of the tent on my knees, keeping low to the ground. Luck is with me as the multiple prone forms illuminated by the moonlight are all asleep. I take off running, refusing to stop until I'm deep within the trees. I trip through the underbrush and over roots until I slump against a trunk and rub panicked tears away.

Suddenly, my head pounds, not from the fear but from a barrage of images accosting my mind. It's like a waking dream, like the eel dream but I'm still conscious. I'm not the protagonist but I can tell I'm the focus while an omniscient narrator tells a story about my life.

First is only blackness, something as dark as night, but with no stars for light. The black recedes until neon purple blinds me. When my eyes clear, I'm watching the leader of the bandits, as if seeing through his eyes.

The same day I arrive in Dalner, he sits alone in the tent I just ran from. He's not religious, but he prays at the conclusion of the crown's biannual pilgrimage because his men like it. It's a rote benediction at the celebration, one some of his men take seriously while the others use it as a reason to seriously drink. He misspeaks, slurring the usual prayer but thinks nothing of it. He doesn't believe the Eósy truly care about Sàrkany. In fact, he's as dangerous as any so-called immortal.

The scene shifts. While I'm walking through Chead, he's murmuring under his breath, repeating the words given to him. He twists the point of his jeweled dagger into the meat of his palm. When the blood wells up enough to drip to the ground, he wipes it

*on his opposite thumb and paints a bloody 'X' on his forehead. He
mutters something, but I can't make it out.*

*The scene shifts. When I fight with Kórol, the bandit leader sits
around his men in the same formation as they had been when I
was with him. He sends them out to find me.*

I shudder as the images vanish. I'm still leaning against the
trunk. I wasn't transported anywhere, to the past or elsewhere,
no matter how it felt. Maybe it was my mind trying to make sense
of why I was taken, to give meaning to my experience because
they had a nefarious purpose *just* for me, and not because I
was a victim of circumstances. That's the rational thought. The
irrational thought remembers the coincidences, Dalner's magic,
the Voice, and my supposed purpose here.

I slide down to the earth and hug my knees. I don't have time
for another panic attack. While I'm out of danger, the bandits
have the advantage in the woods. Maybe if I run the opposite
way, I'll find where the Pack slept the night before. That's assuming I didn't get turned around when I was knocked unconscious.
Without a better idea, I trudge towards the Pack's last campsite.

Footsteps thunder nearby and the bottom drops from my
stomach. I'm too tired, too *demoralized*, to have any hope of
outrunning the bandits. The best I can do is to attempt to injure
one. Sucking in a wobbly breath, I blast towards the noise, barreling into a gangly body. They grunt and reach out, but I pivot
away with my hands positioned into claws. Rough hands catch
me as I flail, jabbing the hands clutching my stomach. I bite into
the palm that snakes over my mouth when—

"Quit it, Miss!" the man groans, voice low. I crane my neck
and find familiar bright green eyes framed by curling red hair.

"Sáven?" I mumble against his hand. He releases my mouth.

"Aye, now shut your trap and quit hitting me. We're trying to
save you." He shakes his hand. "Biting your saviors, honestly."

Relief seeps into me as I melt to the ground. I'm not alone. They haven't left me.

Tansr materializes on my other side and the two men gently drag me through the woods to the campsite. Black and silver juts of color char the grass around the camp, but it's otherwise identical to how it was hours earlier. My tiny bag sits where I've left it, flanked by the belongings of my companions. I fall to the ground in front of the fire and let the heat wash over me as Tans places a light kiss on my forehead.

"Watch her," he orders Sáven. "I must return to Kórol."

"For what?" I ask as Tans dashes into the dark woods.

Sáven massages the back of his neck where I pinched it earlier. "Handle the situation."

I don't register his meaning, too focused on the pain from the bite on my neck. I lean over the fire again, taking comfort in the soothing heat. My hands grasp the ground below me, struggling to keep a foothold on my emotions, fixating on the solid earth to stop the adrenaline eager to burst out of me in a wail. The feel of the dirt and grass momentarily distracts me. It's ash, pitch black that crumbles into dust on one side of me and shiny slivers of ice that crushes the dirt into sand on the other. I gaze bewildered at Sáven who mumbles something about how strong emotions lead to lack of control over one's gifts. *Tansr then*. A second kind of warmth suffuses me, knowing he cares that much. I could probably guess where the ice came from. But as the adrenaline fades, so too does my curiosity and interest.

It's not until much later when the fire barely illuminates the small tree-lined encampment and the rest of the Pack returns that I calm down. Tans flies to me, crushing me like he can't trust I'm there.

He keeps his hands on me, kissing my hair and nuzzling into my neck. With an audible sniff, he leans away just enough to look at the bite on my neck. He licks his fingers and presses them to the wound. I shiver, not from the healing, but from how close he is, and my face blooms with color. Now I understand why all the stories I read devolve into a sex scene after a high-stress situation.

Sáv calls out from the other side of the fire. "She need anything?"

Tans turns my head back and forth and I hold back the desire to lean into him and replace the memory of the bandit's hands. "We have no pain relief," he murmurs, his amber eyes shining and bronze skin glowing in the light of the fire. "Would a relaxant help?" I shake my head, and he shouts back to Sáv. "We are fine. Although—pass me some birchweed."

He leans away to catch a bundle of greenery Sáv tosses to him. While he does, Kórol stalks back to the opening and sits on my other side. Tans unwraps his arms from around me to pinch out a portion of whatever Sáv threw.

"Are you truly alright?" Kórol asks, reaching over to grab the plant from Tans. He acts as though he didn't throw a hissy fit and banish me from the Pack. Though I'm distracted by what happened to me, I still know what led to it.

I nod, prompting Kórol's thick fingers to clasp my chin as he angles my head to see the bite. It's an identical to Tans' appraisal but feels uncomfortably intimate. I flinch and Tans strokes my thigh, leaving a soothing heat in its place. He leans into my side, but doesn't wrap his arms around me again, instead talking with Sáv and Fílga, who joined the circle with Kórol.

With the others distracted, Kórol trails his fingers down my neck, avoiding the bite and finding his way to my ribcage, tracing down my uninjured side. Now, it's oddly similar to what the bandit did, but I hold in the flinch as best I can. Kórol presses his forehead into my neck and his breath cools the heat of the bite.

The desire that trickled in with Tans' presence pools into the pit of my stomach. It's more instinctual, *chemical*, than anything else, by being in the presence of two attractive men. My closest connection to the opposite sex is Tans, who placed me in the 'friend' category early on. Kórol's an anomaly—attractive and aloof, the brooding romance archetype who should stand by rain-splattered windows sighing. His attention pricks at me, like I'm something wanted and cherished. His hands knead into my skin under the hem of my shirt.

I lean back to gaze into those ice blue eyes, which are pearly in the light. If I lean in just an inch more, I'd kiss him, my first real kiss. My stomach curls miserably at the thought. This isn't one of my 'foolish fables of love.' This isn't the time for teenage hormones threatening to overtake my sense, especially considering my last conversation with Kórol. Adrenaline won't be the reason for any poor decisions tonight.

I clear my throat wetly. "Kórol, about earlier—"

He stiffens, but he doesn't release me, instead resting his chin on the crown of my head. "I should not have pushed you away. I cannot even understand why I would. The moment you left, it was as if my thoughts cleared and I knew we needed to reconcile."

Concerned, I pull back to see his eyes glaze but he shakes them clear again. Before I can ask what he means, Fílga shouts across the flames.

"It is gratifying to see you well," Fílga says as Kórol releases me, giving Tans the opportunity to tuck me back into his side. "Tansr says you escaped on your own."

"Tamer of the bandits," Tans calls. The other three echo him, with the deep baritone timbre of Kórol the loudest. I raise my hand in a mock salute, releasing all the tension and weird feelings the day inspired.

"How'd you get free anyway?" Sáv asks after a comfortable silence grows between us.

Over the course of an hour, I tell them, downplaying the potential risk to my skin and avoiding any mention of my unanswered call for the Voice.

"What if it hadn't worked?" Tansr runs a shaking hand through his glossy hair. His other tightens around my shoulders, heating the thin material of my shirt.

Without warning, Kórol vaults away from the fire and juts his finger at the remains of the healing bitemark on my neck. "It was completely irresponsible and shortsighted. Look at the damage you wrought. You are needed at the castle and you cannot put your life in jeopardy in that manner." The other three shuffle tellingly at that. "You should have waited for my men to rescue you."

Embarrassment speckles my skin as I leave Tans' arms and hug myself. I know it could have gone poorly. I know that more than anyone else sitting around that damned fire.

"Kórol, don't push—" Tans starts.

"Luck and the blessings of the Eósy alone kept you safe." Kórol seethes, his fists clenching until the skin pales. He's not wrong, but it was his mercurial attitude that made me leave. I twist my lips in preparation for a second fight. A wind picks up and goosebumps ripple on my skin.

"It was not a well-thought-out plan, but I understand it," says Fílga before I can mount my verbal attack. Fíl sighs at the outraged noises that echo from the others. "Do not look as if I sprouted another head. Tans, ignore your fear for her for a moment. What other chance does a single, unarmed, woman have against a dozen bandits? She played to their weaknesses. They underestimated her, leaving her unrestrained. She plied them with alcohol to lower their inhibitions and made quite a neat getaway. I have read of similar plans in Sàrkany's history."

Tans makes a pained noise while Kórol scoffs and stalks away from the fire. "One might even say she tamed them," Fílga calls over to him. Kórol falters but doesn't turn around.

"And it worked, that's what matters," I say. It sounds much better the way Fílga explains it, and not the hackneyed idea it was. "It was the best thing I could think of. It's not like I knew you were coming for me."

Tansr looks like I slapped him. "Why would you think we wouldn't retrieve you?"

The three men stare at me. Kórol even turns, watching out of his periphery. "I—we were fighting. Kórol told me to leave. I thought it meant forever. It had been hours, and I figured you'd left."

Kórol's shoulders tense as he marches farther from the fire. Tansr grabs my hand and presses it to his heart. My eyes track Kórol before Tans commands my attention.

"We'd never leave you behind." Tans sniffles and attempts a smirk, but it's wobbly. "We can't afford it. Without you, the level of attractiveness in the group would plummet. I cannot manage that burden alone."

CHAPTER 10

I wake early the next morning to a darkened camp. A hand runs through my mussed hair, gently teasing out the tangles.

"Go back to sleep," Tans whispers.

The sun barely peeks out from the clouds. "Don't we need to make up for lost time yesterday?"

He shakes his head. "It is early yet, and you must rest. You went through an ordeal yesterday, emotionally and physically, and we want you to recover."

"It wasn't an *ordeal*," I mutter, pivoting to squint up at him in the dim light. His lips thin.

"As your personal healer, I demand you rest."

I roll my eyes and curl back to my side. Kórol didn't drop off the coat, our fight clearly ongoing. "I don't need to be taken care of," I say to the ground.

"You may not need our protection, but you are our friend, and we will care for you accordingly. You're one of us."

I bite my lip to keep from expressing the pre-teen giddiness rushing through me at the continued confirmation that I have friends. Although Fílga said the same recently, it feels different when Tans says it, especially after last night. When my face smooths, I roll flat on my back to see him kneeling above me. "Fílga said something similar."

"He'd call you sister if you gave him leave, just as he calls us brothers. Except Sáv, though I don't think he realizes that yet. Another two years, perhaps," he finishes with a chuckle.

"Do you *all* think of me that way?"

He looks to the ground beside my head. "I already have sisters, what is one more?"

It isn't the answer I'm looking for, but it's one I should have expected. I stifle the surge of disappointment that accompanies it. "Let me guess—you're the youngest and you terrorized them."

"I am the youngest, yes." He smiles wistfully and rubs down his braids. "It has been some time since I have seen them as I remain the heir and they married into other houses. But I have more than enough siblings of my heart to make up for it."

"Lucky us." It sounds more bitter than I planned.

"Don't disparage such a gift," he says. "It takes a special person to win our trust, and you did it handily. This should be no surprise, we wouldn't have stomached that dream talk otherwise." His thumb grazes the back of my hand, creating an itch in my chest. "Dreamy though I may be."

"You've used that line already."

He exaggerates a wink. "I have never claimed to be creative. My clever witticisms are deserving of repetition, Butterfly."

"Caricature," I groan.

"You've used that before," he repeats in a high-pitched voice, a poor impression of me. He presses a kiss onto his index finger and then runs it from my forehead down the bridge of my nose.

Instantly, the pull of sleep and calm washes over me. "Sleep well, Grace."

Not much later, I hear Tans' voice whispering above me. One eye opens, ready to tease him about letting me sleep.

"You cannot go on like this, Kórol," he says, still brushing his hand through my hair. Kórol grunts and I feign sleep. "We nearly lost her."

"She would not abandon her destiny because we fought," Kórol grumbles. I can't tell if they know about the Voice, or this is more of the coincidences surrounding the so-called Sìnnách.

"Destiny is inevitable. It is in the very definition. While you have more schooling than I, even I know that means we cannot change it. If she is what we hope, it happens no matter your choices. Why then wouldn't you choose paths that allow us to keep her friendship? If your quest continues to blind you, you don't deserve even that." A heat begins in my stomach and rises upward to my cheeks. I pray Tans can't see it.

Kórol lets out a growl. "Deserve her?" As if remembering my presence nearby, his voice drops low, and I strain to catch his last words. "None of us deserve her. She will be our salvation."

"What if she isn't what you think? Isn't it worth it to know her as herself?"

"There are far too many coincidences for that, Tans. Her arrival, the Pack being the first people she finds, the merchant, the bandits, my own feelings."

"And what are those feelings?" Tans' voice tightens with an intensity I've not heard from him before.

"As you say, I am—intrigued. I see visions of strings under our left ribs connecting us, of little birds. I am physically drawn to her, almost against my will. I wish to know her more," Kórol says, his voice low. "You know my mind, Tans, sometimes better than I do. There is something odd there. All the circumstances add up."

Tans' fingers pause on my scalp, and he exhales. When he speaks again, the tightness vanishes. "Maybe they do, maybe they don't. If they do, subterfuge does nothing to help us. We should be honest with her about your thoughts. You cannot spring this on a person."

"My legacy will arise by presenting the *real* woman, not a false Candidate. We hold until I feel sure of it."

"Kórol," Tans murmurs, as if attempting to soothe a skittish animal. "You are hunting a miracle. Miracles are given, not taken—"

"My decisions are my own." Kórol must walk away, as leaves crunch in time with his plodding steps.

"But they affect us all," Tans says in a whisper.

The next time I wake, the sun is high overhead, meaning they've let me sleep in much later than normal. Tansr braids his hair while speaking with Kórol. Fílga pours over some parchment as Sáven pulls feathers from a foot-long pigeon. When the men notice my movements, they watch me warily. There is a palpable tension with the four of them that I can't explain and don't know how to dispel, one that grew overnight. From the conversation I overheard this morning, there are unexplained expectations for me to be their Sìnnách, adding another millstone around my neck.

I ignore them and the tension that is a fifth member of the Pack. Instead, I rummage through my tote bag, dumping everything onto the dirt and seeking my last remaining piece of gum. If ever there's a time to use it and experience some comfort, it's now.

Tans silently perches beside me and helps gather the meager items from my bag. I snatch up the notes before he can, leaving the phone for him. When his skin grazes the plastic, sparks and a burst of smoke shoot outward. With a yelp, he dumps the phone in my tote bag and rubs his sparking hand on his tunic.

The smoke billows off his hand and he stares at it with an amazed expression, waving it and making crude shapes in the air like a smoker blowing rings. "Should've guessed you were a fire starter too," he says, laughing.

"It's never done that when I touched it." I grimace at his charred flesh. Even dead, the phone must have some mechanism incompatible with these non-technological people.

"She can replace you, Tans," Sáv calls out. Tans makes a crude hand gesture half hidden in smoke and Sáv throws a feather at him. Fíl rolls his eyes skyward and mumbles something about traveling with children. Immediately, red blooms onto his cheeks and Sáv stares back nervously. The tension no longer focuses on me, but on the energy between Fíl and Sáven.

Fílga sidesteps Sáv's wandering gaze and helps me stand. His stoic composure is ruined by the faint sheen of sweat on his brow. "Perhaps when we get to Ilsen, you'll let me study that piece? Human articles would be a welcome addition to our historical accounts."

I brush off the back of my jeans and take the subject change, just as happy to ignore the tension surrounding me as he is to ignore the tension surrounding him. "What's mine is yours. And the sooner we get there, the sooner you can. Are we heading out soon?"

Sáven, Fílga, and Tansr watch Kórol, who says nothing.

"We thought we may need to rest this day," Fílga finally explains. Kórol turns to the map Fíl left while the other two conspicuously look elsewhere. They aren't a subtle bunch.

"Why? I'm fine, we're all here. I've already put us behind with my first stupid injury. And don't we need to keep moving so the bandits won't find us?"

"There is no need to worry about that," says Fílga with an enigmatic smile.

"What does that mean?"

"It means none of those men will hurt anyone ever again, nor will any of their comrades."

I wrap my arms around my waist. "How can you be so sure?"

Fílga's eyes flit to Kórol, who stares back at us with a flat expression.

"We killed them," Kórol says before cocking an eyebrow at Fíl and gesturing at the parchment he was reading, beads clacking as he does.

My mouth falls open in surprise. "*All* of them?"

"We couldn't leave even one with your memories," Tans says from beside me. His hand no longer sparks, allowing him to grab my wrist and lead me back to the kindling.

More for my notes. I stumble over the underbrush and slump to sit. "How would they have my memories?"

He takes my hands in his and I suppress a pleased wiggle as his heat races through me. "There is much you don't know. Do you remember when I told you we have different forms of magic here? The Sàrkany are a people with a long history of aggression. All had limited mind magic to aid in their battles that existed before the creation of the wall. We remain at peace now, but the weakened Eósy mind magic still lives within us when we fight. When Sàrkany feud, through combat or any physical altercation, the champion gains the defeated's memories of what led to the failure. It's a reward for the winner to relive the victory and learn how to repeat the success should they meet that enemy again."

That explains the movie reel of images I experienced after escaping. At least it wasn't a sign of my fading sanity. The invisible child in my head has make me wonder. "And I repeat—how would they have my memories? I got away from them, I won."

"But they took you. They bested you by kidnapping you. They would have whatever memories led to that point, most notably, your argument with Kórol."

"No," I counter. "I *bested* them. I think I got the leader's memories of it too."

He twists his lips like he doesn't believe me. "What did you see?"

"It felt like I was watching a movie, but inside his head while it happened. I knew when he was thinking about me. When he put that 'X' on his head, it's like I understood he was doing it for me."

"That seems to be the mind magic of battle memories. But as a non-magical being, you shouldn't have experienced them." He squeezes my fingers. "I am sorry, but I don't believe you escaping him would count as besting him. I believe you beheld the echo, which occurs when the loser of the battle receives memories. They receive the memories of the victor that led to their defeats. They are less clear, but poignant nonetheless."

"That's lame. Why would the loser get a peek in the winner's head?" I pull my hand away and yank on one of his braids. "And I did *so* best that guy."

He ignores my teasing. "We are a combat friendly people. It serves as a lesson for the loser to learn from the mistakes they made and do better in the future, and as a punishment to experience both the humiliation and the memories that led to their downfall."

"I think you're wrong," I say with a sniff. "It wasn't an echo but the real thing. It was crisp, like I was watching through his eyes."

"Not that you would know the difference," he mutters under his breath. I poke him in the stomach, and he chuckles. "Not so hard, your nails are sharp. I am not trying to disparage you.

I've not heard of a non-Sàrkany experiencing the swell of battle memories."

"Hung out with a lot of Earth people then?" I poke him again. He doesn't acknowledge me the second time, as he turns to lock eyes with Kórol, who stopped reading and listens intently to our conversation.

"If it wasn't an echo, it could mean you have dormant magic in you, weakened like the Sàrkany or—"

I roll my eyes. I can't escape the comments on me being something special here, even from Tans.

"For all we know, there's ambient magic in the land, or the 'swell' happens as long as someone in the fight has magic. There are lots of explanations." I stand and brush invisible dirt from my jeans again. "But it's getting late. By Fíl's last count, we're still almost a week from the castle, and I, for one, am tired of sleeping on grass and bathing in streams."

"Take the day, darling," Tans says, pulling me back to sit with him. "One extra night on the ground won't kill you." He covers my mouth when I fuss. I hold back the impulse to lick his palm. "I say this as your personal healer. And you have plans today that don't involve walking."

Kórol stands above us and clears his throat. He motions for me to accompany him but I refuse, turning back to Tans. Tans is uncomplicated, doesn't keep secrets, and doesn't run hot-and-cold. Tans didn't tell me to leave. Kórol hisses through his teeth.

"We shouldn't have argued," he bites out. "Neither yesterday before your kidnapping nor after when you'd returned."

I peer up at him. "Was that an apology?"

Kórol kneads the back of his neck and sighs. "Perhaps."

Tans pulls me to stand, which I allow under silent protest. I follow Kórol's stomping steps, my grumbling remarks hitting his back.

He directs me a few yards from the campsite in the opposite direction of the woods that hold my terrible memories, instead to an small glen where the bright midday sun illuminates us. Even with his scowl, Kórol is still striking, his whisky hair gleaming burnt gold and the powerful muscles in his back rippling below his tunic with each step. But the man is the human equivalent of a moody grapefruit: something that *looks* delicious and sweet but is sharp and sour. I cross my arms and plant myself in front of him.

"This is my compromise—I came over here *even* though you didn't apologize, but in return, you'll answer my questions without vanishing or yelling."

He considers it for a minute, eyes dilated and unfocused, before he nods once.

"Last night, when you were angry about how I escaped the bandits, you say I was needed at the castle. What did you mean by that?" *And what do you think I'm supposed to be doing here?*

"They were words said without thought. I can give you no answer right now." I squawk a complaint, and he holds up a hand. "I will give you my answer when I confirm my thoughts. Know this—there is something at work here that none of us understand. If I announce something substantive now, it could affect the conclusions, inadvertently compelling you to behave differently. It will benefit no one if I make premature proclamations."

It's not a satisfying answer, but I can't force it out of him. Kórol buttons up his thoughts tight, and only in the last few days did he even allow them to tell me why they were out here. But I can't shake the feeling his 'conclusions' have something to do with the Voice, and the Sìnnách.

"Fine. So long as you promise you'll tell me when you know."

"I do. And now, for the purpose of our meeting," he says, pulling out a six-inch blade from its scabbard on his right hip and handing it to me, hilt-side out.

I don't take it. "What am I supposed to do with this?"

"You are to keep it on your person to protect you should another attack occur."

I nervously tuck my hands into the waistband of my pants. "Giving me a weapon is a bad idea, remember?"

"You may not have the option to tame men with your words or your—" Kórol pauses, his eyes trailing down my body and snapping back up like a broken rubber band.

"And the solution to that is to—what? Carry a knife? Something I'll stab myself with first?"

He frowns and flips the knife so he's no longer holding the blade. "Very well, little skeptic. If you will not carry a weapon, at least learn how to keep one from being used against you." He beckons me towards him. Swallowing my concerns, I shuffle towards him at a snail's pace while he points the knife at my chest.

"Grab my wrist," he directs, before sighing. "No, the one with the knife."

With a brief hesitation, I switch, squeezing the taut muscles of his wrist under my fingers. "Now disarm me," he says. I struggle against him for a second, trying to wrestle the knife from his hand before he turns me around, trapping me between the hand with his knife and his chest.

"Yeah, this is much better," I groan.

"Think of how you can disengage from me. Similar to your actions in Chead—but effectively."

"Got you to let me go last time," I say under my breath. He huffs, pressing his broad chest snug against my back. If I ignore the knife lightly resting against my sternum, it's a scene from one of my stories. My muscles tense as I focus on his arms around me and not the knife inches from my neck.

"You must do something. Injure me, hurt me, or distract me and flee," he whispers. "A true foe would not wait for you."

I elbow him in the abdomen, but his muscles don't even ripple from my attempt. I rest my head on his forearm. "They'll have to," I whine into his skin. "I can't even fight a statue."

"Maybe not. Next time avoid the elbow to the chest and instead punch the soft area above the hips, the inner thigh, the groin. All have the possibility of incapacitating your captor, assuming they are male. For now, your wit will continue to tame your enemies." He hands me the knife after releasing me. "But for the sake of the Pack, try not to get captured again."

CHAPTER 11

"**B**ut why would Lady Melanie be unfaithful to Jason after courting so long?" Fílga asks, puzzled. "If she truly wishes to marry him, she would not dally about with this cattle farmer."

After the fight that led to my kidnapping and knowing that Kórol would explain everything to me eventually, I spend our free time on the walk to the castle entertaining Fílga and Tans with stories of my own, mostly of the bodice rippers I read back home. Although Sáven's too shy for my stories and Kórol acts like they're beneath him, they still crane their necks to listen. I avoid any books that have heavy subtext, ones where the happily ever after wasn't guaranteed, the kind Mom loved, where only at the conclusion of the novel the readers realize it was about class and gender oppression. Those are to be read for graded purposes only and only revisited under duress.

"Because Cowboy Lucas is her true love and even though she moved to the big city, she's a country girl at heart."

Fíl purses his lips. "That is *quite* rude to Jason."

"I'm bored with this one, Butterfly. Tell us another. The one about the woman who dressed as a man and married the brother of her betrothed," Tansr says, batting his eyes at me playfully.

I yank on one of his braids. "I told you that one yesterday."

"I never complained when Fílga made you repeat the story about that prostitute."

"Escort," Fílga corrects. Sáven dips his head in front of us.

"Escort, fine. The only interesting part was the fire. I demand you reconcile my grievance by recounting the better tale again," Tans says.

"But does Jason find someone better for him than the inconstant Lady Melanie?" Fílga asks.

"After I finish *Hunting Season*, Tans. And Jason's not the main character, Fíl. I don't—"

Kórol abruptly stops a few feet in front of me and I unknowingly smack into his back. He turns and inspects me with a raised brow while I claw beaded strands of his hair from my mouth.

"We're coming to the fork," he says, dragging his gaze towards the others. "Tans and I have already determined that we cannot travel through the high hills as we would normally."

Fílga shifts seamlessly to his stoic state, reaching for his bag and pulling out the yellowed map. "It is early enough in the season that the low hills are still passable," Fílga declares, as if he wasn't spellbound by Melanie and Lucas' story only minutes before. "The low hills will take a few more days but would be less—dangerous."

The sun sets while shapes resembling dragons fly overhead, and small bat-creatures flutter around their feet. I gesture to Tans and point, and he twists his lips.

"Imagine—a Pack wandering through the low hills with her? Might start a riot," Sáven says.

I cross my arms. This is about the Sìnnách again, I'm sure. "No one would think anything of me. I'm just another woman around here, wearing Sàrkany-ish clothes even—not anything special. And I promise not to say or do *anything* that might make me seem out of place."

The four men give me sidelong glances but don't acknowledge my proposal.

"There is merit to traveling separately again," Tans says, tearing his eyes away from me.

Fíl agrees. "The reasons for spitting up in Chead have grown exponentially."

"We don't all need to take the low hills, only one of us must escort Grace. I volunteer," Tans offers.

"No," Kórol quickly argues. "We need your skills in the high hills. I will take her." All but Kórol exchange glances that time.

"I would argue my skills make me the obvious choice to remain with Grace, while you remain flanked by the rest of us," Tans says.

"It is settled then," Kórol announces, as if Tans hadn't spoken. "I will take her through the low hills. The rest, our usual route. We will rendezvous at Raddare's Pass in three sunrises."

We plan to separate the next morning. I don't mind separating if it's safest, but they can't have it both ways—either I'm capable of making my own decisions or I'm not. Either they trust me or they don't.

After making camp for the evening, Tans wraps an arm around my waist and rubs soothing circles on my injured hip as we sit beside our bedrolls. "I know you'll miss me terribly, but it is safest for us to separate." While no magic emerges from his caress, it comforts me all the same.

"It's not that. I just wish I had a say in it," I huff, leaning onto his shoulder. While I'm talking only about splitting up, the sentiment applies to everything happening. "You all talk about how I'm important to you, that I've gained your trust, that I'm an important member of the group, but I don't even get a vote."

Tans rests his head on mine. "I cannot answer for—for Kórol. But we follow his command and if he decrees, we must separate. None of us, even our most precious newcomer, can change that."

"But why?" I'm only slightly ashamed of the whine in my tone.

"I am bound to keep certain things private but, no don't give me that look. Come back here!" He growls and tries to yank me back when I withdraw. When he's wrapped me back up into his arms, and we both ignore the reddening in my cheeks, he whispers into my ear. It's hard for me to keep thinking that it's *only* friendly, but Tans cuddles with everyone.

"The high hills have bandits," he explains, "more like those who captured you. But they're less crowded, allowing us to avoid people and their questioning eyes, which is why it is the ideal path for the Pack to take. The low hills are safer from outward dangers, but busier. There's even a town for you to practice your taming skills."

"It's more of the same from Chead, then. You all think people will ask questions if we stay together."

"Exactly."

I cross my arms around my chest, dislodging from his lap. It still makes little sense—we could travel together in shifts. It's the same excuse they had for splitting up in Chead, and I traipsed around that town with multiple Pack members for hours.

A cleared throat sounds behind us, and we both turn to see Kórol with his arms crossed and his face expressionless. "We have a long day tomorrow. When you finish toying with each other, I recommend you sleep."

"I've room for you on the other knee," Tans says, winking and patting his empty lap. Kórol cocks a bushy eyebrow until Tans wilts. "Sulking doesn't go with your eyes," Tans mutters. Kórol remains silent.

After Kórol stalks away, Tans smacks his hands on his knees. "You heard the man, love, time for bed. Separately, of course, although Fates know I'd join you if I could."

I roll my eyes, not because of Tans' over-the-top and insincere attempt at a come-on, but because Kórol's moodiness is apparently catching. I turn to continue my complaints about being excluded while Tans leans in to give me his customary goodnight kiss on the cheek. Like something out of one of my favorite cheesy romance novels, our lips brush.

It isn't *much* of a kiss, but a grazing of skin to skin, lips to lips. Neither of us move. Neither of us *breathe*.

After what feels like minutes, Tans responds, adjusting his head to meet my lips lightly, pillowing them against mine. Butterflies take flight in my stomach, creating a fluttery sensation that floats upward. It's my first kiss and it's less sure on both our accounts than I expected but I've read enough books to mimic what I'm supposed to do. I slide my lips to catch the soft skin of his until he repeats the motion. His lips are warm against mine, echoing the blaze that threatens to light up my skin. How odd that something so warm can make me feel like shivering. He breaks the connection with a gasp but stays close, resting his lips against my cheek, right at the cleft of my eye. They both flutter closed as his breath fans the flames the kiss ignited.

He groans before digging his nails into his knees and leaning away. I suck in my lips to revisit the heat left there while Tans draws a ragged breath, keeping his eyes tightly closed.

"That was—unexpected." A rasp replaces the honey in his voice.

My stomach plummets. 'Effusive praise' may be too lofty a goal for a girl's first kiss, but something other than confusion and surprise would have been nice. It's nothing I shouldn't expect after he called me a sister yesterday. It was silly of me to hope, silly of me to expect anything else from him. Disappointment and embarrassment hit me like a punch to the gut. If I'm lucky, the ground will open and swallow me whole. Maybe, in a world with dragons and magic, there's a real chance of it happening.

"And then there is Kórol," Tans murmurs to himself. "Let us forget about this until you return, after which we will have a long *long* discussion about everything."

I nod, ducking my head to wipe my eyes. He catches my fingers, a move that would have excited me yesterday, and transfers little zings of heat from where we connect. In my embarrassment, the jolts aren't comforting but a reminder of my foolish and unrequited feelings.

By the next morning, I've sufficiently shamed myself after spending hours tossing and turning on the ground, unable to sleep as my mind kept revisiting the kiss. The first viewings were to remember, knowing it would never happen again, and add it to my daydreams—the safe kind that involve an unrequited crush and an unthreatened friendship. Later, more exhausted, viewings dissected the kiss and each piece that might have disgusted Tans and destroyed one of the best relationships I've ever had. He called me a sister, and I manhandled him, taking advantage of his warmth. I can't forget, even stuck in this fantasy world where someone thinks I'm the protagonist, that life isn't a romance novel—love doesn't follow plotlines, as much as I want it to. There's always unpredictability and unhappy endings, no matter how I try to avoid them.

It's lucky that Kórol and I leave for the low hills right after breakfast. Sáven takes the beads from Kórol's hair with some ceremony while Tans silently retakes my canvas tote. We don't speak, and I can only hope the days apart will cool the awkwardness between us.

Before we leave, I toss off the sulk in my expression, trying to remind myself that Kórol isn't the cause of my sour mood.

The low hills aren't hills, but pathways on the side of the mountains interspersed with thin trees and brambly bushes. On the northern side, the mountains; the southern, more fields that rise into another distant mountain range. The land is still a shocking green, and the many lumps look like mossy pockmarks from a distance.

We speak little the first day. Kórol doesn't seem to mind, but he rarely speaks anyway. The coat returns that night, and the lingering glances double. I don't read anything into them; I did that with Tans and that only caused heartache.

By the second afternoon, I'm embroiled in cataloging my own neuroses, debating whether age or inexperience is my problem. At almost eighteen and independent, should I know how to behave with boys, with friends, with my own life? While Fíl implied he's under thirty, Tans and Sáv are my age, and Kórol's only twenty. The Pack is sure of themselves while I bumble around in the metaphorical dark, accidentally kissing my first real friend, trying to trick grown men into releasing me by getting them drunk. What about that description leads someone to believe *my* purpose is to defeat Her—or act as a Sàrkanian savior?

You are young, but youth does not necessarily linger. Experiences ages you faster than the skin on your face. These are things you are gaining every day to prepare for Her.

I stumble when the Voice speaks mentally, kicking up the mist that unfurls by our feet. Kórol catches my elbow and doesn't release me. I still don't read into it but smile up at him gratefully.

Your definition of 'need to listen to my thoughts' and mine are quite different, I say inwardly.

Suddenly, a warmth suffuses my brain, like they're pleased with me. It's unnerving. **You left yourself open, and the need was apparent. You are avoiding my counsel and behaving recklessly. To allow yourself to be captured, to toy with** *your friends—it is certainly a novel method in keeping them close.*

I blush, sure that blotchy spots of red flare on my cheeks. I keep my eyes on the ground to avoid Kórol seeing. He towers over me, so the possibility is slim. *I'm doing my best. I'm just not good enough. You need to put your hopes for dealing with this Woman in someone else.*

You are in a new place, Grace. There are no set guidelines for you to follow. You have made missteps, but I expect you can still complete your goal. Indeed, while I do not condone the need for it, your tack with your captors was inspired.

I cringe, my stomach roiling at the reminder, remembering how upset the Pack was when they realized how cavalier I was with my safety. I sneak a look at Kórol, who still has his arm hooked through mine. *I called for you,* I think. *After I told you to leave, I called, but you left me alone. If you were looking for a time when I needed you to read my thoughts,* that *was it.*

I'm more sensitive to the Voice's intrusions now and I can tell they feel hesitant. **I was—unable to answer your call. Outside circumstances kept me from interceding. But you did well enough. If nothing else, it was excellent practice for when She arrives.**

Aren't you supposed to be my guardian angel or something? It could have been—

Did my counsel not provide useful information regardless of my absence from your mind? Did you not decide to deceive them based on my guidance?

Yes, but—

Deception comes in all forms, Grace. You deceived him well. I have the utmost confidence in you that when She arrives, you will thwart her plans with all forms of deception.

I trip on an exposed tree root, too focused on the mental conversation to watch my feet. With Kórol holding me up, it shifts me closer to his chest. He inspects me but I stare the flattened grass below us.

My mind quiets, but I can still feel the Voice at its edges. *What would that entail, exactly?*

You'll know when She arrives.

That's not an answer!

They scoff. **I'm to guide you, not make decisions for you. You have steps to undertake first.**

You're the least helpful magical guide I know.

They giggle. **Take heed that you are doing well. You are nurturing your relationships as I advised. You're attracting attention, which is necessary. The path will show itself to you soon, within days, if I'm right. And I usually am.** They exhale, the sound echoing around my brain. **I may be able to answer a few questions for you. Choose them well.**

I involuntarily clutch Kórol's arm to keep from gasping and play it off as fatigue when he inspects me again. When he refocuses on the path in front of us, I ask my first question. *You keep saying I will defeat Her. Does that mean you* know *I'll be successful? I mean, will I honestly be able to defeat Her?*

I do not know the future, but I expect you will. You possess something no one else in this world has. Heed these words—everyone bleeds in the end. The pressure in my head dissipates like the surrounding mist. **With your questions answered, I bid you and Kórol a pleasant evening.**

I trip again, falling into Kórol muscular chest, who catches me with raised eyebrows. I ignore the expectant look he gives me and shout silently. *Wait! That was one question! Am I the Sìnnách? Can you at least tell me that?*

There's another laugh and then silence.

CHAPTER 12

After I've swallowed the frustration leftover from my conversation with the Voice, we approach the town Tans mentioned the day before. It's massive even from a distance. The tan and nut-colored buildings crawl halfway up the mountain, layered on top of each other like little cakes. As we pass the threshold of the outermost rickety wooden construction, Kórol tenses. He rarely responds outwardly to anything, meaning the 'concern' Tans mentioned about people questioning them is a visceral fear for Kórol.

This unnamed village makes Chead look like a one stoplight town in comparison. The buildings are made of stone carved directly from the elements, with only the second stories constructed of thick wood. The only way through the town is by traveling each layer, going up four streets until we can cycle to the lower levels that open into a pathway through the mountains. The sun sets as we rise farther into the town, but Kórol pushes us into the darkness, refusing to stop until we reach the other side. Although his unease is palpable, I hesitate at the end of a street near the top level. Kórol cuts through a side alley and bends to hop one level lower to the wider street below. When he sees I'm not behind him, he beckons me forward.

"We must continue if we are to reach the Pass on schedule," he says.

"We need to sleep sometime," I wheedle. "We won't be suspicious, just two travelers, not the Pack. No one will care or even focus on us."

He studies the area with wary eyes. Only one other person is on the street with us, but Kórol shakes his head. "We can sleep when we make it through town."

"How long will that be?"

"It may not be safe." He scans the dark buildings around us as if someone will appear without warning.

"Or it will be fine. We'll make up some story, act all stealthy and discreet, and we'll get a hot meal and soft bed."

He tears his gaze from our surroundings and stares deeply into my eyes. I'm not sure what he looks for or whether he'll find it, but he offers his arm again with a heavy sigh. "Against my better judgment, we will stop, so long as you follow my lead."

At that moment, I'd agree to almost anything if it meant I could sleep on a mattress. Arm in arm, he takes us to an inn in one of the middle levels. It's the biggest building nearby, boasting two stories with paneless windows and double doors with the words "Dobra e Kàdora" crudely cut above the threshold. I blink and the words "Stag and Hawker" flash in their place. While the changing sign might intrigue me, my continued exhaustion and hunger removes any collected curiosity.

Inside, we're met with a packed room filled with people who've never heard the term 'personal hygiene.' Crinkling my nose, I bite back the disappointment that there won't be room for us, as even a musky bed is better than no bed at all. While my body sags to prepare for another night on the ground, Kórol's stiffens at the sight of that many people. I only notice because his grip on me tightens. I pat his forearm placatingly, knowing he's putting himself through this stress, irrational though it may be, for my sake.

"S'cuse me, sir," the innkeeper calls out to us as we shove past several sleeping drunks curled around a thick wooden table. The man is portly, with rosy cheeks and a comforting smile, and wearing heavily stained clothing. "We're glad to have your patronage." He gestures to Kórol before he flicks a finger in my direction, his ruddy face sweaty and pinched. "But the tavern doors are closed to unmarried women, whores, and the like."

I straighten my back at his implied insult while Kórol wraps his arm around my waist. "Understood, but this dear maiden is my wife. We only recently married but lost our betrothal tokens during our travels." He glances around the room and a muscle ticks in his jaw. "Please celebrate with us and allow me to buy your patrons a drink."

"Newlyweds! Then cheers to that," the innkeeper roars, his rosy cheeks brightening.

"Bring us your finest bottle of port, and a game hen for my bride," Kórol says before he drags me to an open table near one of the back walls. The stone is covered in intricate etchings of stags. "I apologize for the subterfuge. But a falsehood about your marital status was necessary to keep any harm from befalling you here."

I wave him off while letting my annoyance fade, murmuring though the din of the room hides our words. "It's fine, thought I shouldn't be surprised by the sexism. *This* I understand more than anything. Fake dating, fake marriage I guess, to further some goal. Although buying everyone drinks isn't exactly cutting a low profile, it falls in line with the usual trope."

The left side of his mouth twitches upward. "Ah, yes. From one of your stories."

A heavy set and well-endowed bar-maiden struts towards us, and I whisper to avoid her overhearing. "Being mistaken for a whore isn't the usual plot, but two strangers pretending to be married is."

"I would hope we are more than strangers now." He leans forward and smirks, stealing an expression from Tans' repertoire. It doesn't fit on Kórol's face but still my cheeks heat without my permission.

The server brings our order directly to Kórol. She slams down a pitcher of an amber liquid, a single mug, and a platter with a double-necked hen. There are no utensils or personal plates in sight. I snag the hen before Kórol moves, the last few weeks on the road having changed my eating habits. (The most important lesson I learned: she who eats slowly eats the least.)

The server loiters by our table, twirling a strand of her coarse blond hair in her fingers, her mousey eyes fastened on Kórol. I squint at her while gnawing on a large bird leg, though I understand why she stays. Even without his braids and beads, Kórol's an intense man who commands attention without trying. But her persistence in lingering near a supposedly married man creates a different sort of crescendo of feelings in me. I cough and drape my arm over Kórol's muscular shoulders, tangling my clean hand in his loose whisky brown hair. When that doesn't work, I simper and bat my eyes cartoonishly until she finally leaves.

"Subtlety is not a skill you possess," Kórol says, raising an eyebrow as I remove my hand.

"I wasn't going for subtle. She shouldn't gawk at married men. And a good wife would mark her territory." I ignore the feeling of foreign want that thought gave me, the idea of marking my territory in other ways, and stab the game hen with my thumb instead. "Why can't Sáven find one of these on the road?"

Kórol tenses in his seat again when I groan in delight, his right hand clenching while the other takes a long sip from the cup. "I was unaware you had such strong opinions on food."

I swallow a considerable bite and wash it down with a drink from his cup. It burns pleasantly, like mulled cider at Christmas and not hard liquor. "You know what they say, the way to a woman's heart is through the stomach."

"Who says that?" He reaches for the cup and runs his fingers over the part of the rim I sipped from.

"It's a quote. Although they say it about men, but I think that's gender normativity," I say, licking at my fingers when I've finished my portion. I still needed two courses to finish that minor, but I've given up that goal, as I assume there's no Dalner university for me to transfer my credits to.

Kórol furrows his brows, hands still tracing the rim of the cup. "I assumed literary allusions were the way to your heart, not food."

"Maybe? I've never dated anyone, so I can't say anything definitively." I think of Dave, whose kindness I mistook as interest. I think of Tans, where I did the same. "What about you?"

He shifts and inspects the half-eaten bird in front of him. "Ask me in a month," he murmurs, his voice taut.

The server's re-appearance interrupts my opportunity to ask him more. Bypassing me, she refills the cup between us, pressing her ample cleavage against Kórol's shoulder and neck. I grab his forearm again, moving my hand upward until it's between him and her half-clothed breasts. She maneuvers towards a nearby table with a knowing smirk. Kórol raises his eyebrow at me and I shrug in response.

"I'm possessive of my husband *and* the food," I say, checking the plate for any last crumbs as an excuse to avoid his eye.

Kórol leans forward. "Little wife, perhaps I will make your happiness with excellent food and matrimony." Something in that phrase pings within me, but he doesn't give me time to think about it. "Although perhaps Tansr will compete for your hand. He certainly kisses it enough."

I struggle to ignore the last encounter with Tans' lips while my face flushes. "It isn't kissing. It's—it's healing."

A smirk graces his bearded mouth. "Is it?"

"Yes! He licks his fingers and then—" I stop when I Kórol raises an eyebrow. "Fine. That's not the point—Tans isn't competing for me. In this inn, my hand belongs to you, remember, *little* husband?"

His eyebrow falls and his hands flex against the table's woodgrain. "I should not jest on such a subject, knowing Tans as I do.

He has not taken a measure of his own actions with you. While he is a loyal man, he will flounder when the games end."

The continued confirmation that Tans is nothing but a flirt pricks, but only a little. "And you wouldn't?"

"I suspect not," he says. His face flickers with something I can't define, something sharp and troubled. He finishes the pitcher in one gulp. "Now, little wife, shall we retire to our rooms?"

I nod, letting my heartbeat slow as the odd tension between us eases. We leave the table and Kórol flags down the innkeeper. But we've caught the attention of the other patrons, the ones whose mead Kórol paid for and which clearly ran out.

"Give him a kiss!" "Plant one on your lucky lady!" The shouts buzz from all around the room.

"It seems your taunting didn't go unnoticed," Kórol mutters. He releases something that sounds almost like a laugh as he stands close enough to lean his head against mine. "We do not need to prove anything to them," he whispers, gripping my waist. "But something tells me to attempt it."

"It's part of the story, right?" I say tremulously. "Newly married, we can't keep our hands off each other."

He leans down. Birds claw at my stomach while I chase the vision of doing the same thing to Tans before I press my lips to Kórol's. It's faint at first, skin scarcely brushing, the parallel to my kiss with Tans. It veers off immediately as Kórol's lips become pliant against mine and he deepens the connection. One of his large hands shakes as it pets my low back, the other awkwardly clenches the base of my neck. The patrons of the inn howl but I break us apart seconds later to surreptitiously wipe my mouth.

It's not a *bad* kiss. From what I've read, it's textbook perfect—no bumping of noses, no teeth clacking together, the littlest bit of tongue (which was a surprise) sweeping into my mouth. With Kórol's long hair and broad physique coupled with my Sàrkany dress, we could grace the cover of one of my favorite romance novels. But—the kiss felt off, like kissing a stranger. Exciting, but missing the connection I had with Tans. Even so, the dazed look in Kórol's eyes gives me a hot feeling of want and power, just like the books described. He shudders; maybe he's feeling as off-kilter as me.

The innkeeper clasps Kórol on his free shoulder, while I duck under his arm. "Let's get these two to their room."

Kórol wraps his arms around me as I hide further into him, my heart still hammering in my chest. "Was that better than your stories, little bird?" he whispers into my hair.

I take my own unsteady breath, willing myself to act normally. *It's different*, I want to tell him, *not bad but not quite right*. But I can't, he's as lighthearted as I've ever seen him, and I don't want to bring on his grim mood. Kórol doesn't care that I don't answer, content to wink at our captive audience and waggle his brows. He and Tans clearly underwent a personality transplant.

The same server unhooks us, taking Kórol's arm in one hand and mine in the other. I no longer need to 'stake my claim' with her. The proud smile Kórol offers the crowd, coupled with his dazed expression show more than my over-the-top expressions ever could.

She drags us upstairs, directing us to a room right above the bar area. She winks, smacks Kórol's behind, and pushes us in the dark room. The door closes behind her, weighed with the expectations of the inhabitants downstairs.

It's a sparse room, furnished with a small wooden table and chairs in one corner and a single bed in the middle covered in a pilled cotton comforter. *Of course, there's only one bed.*

Kórol lights a candle in the far corner and stares back at me with an eager expression, eyes flashing white. Like the one he showed downstairs, it doesn't fit on his face. Aggressive friendship is my only weapon against the new connection between us, one I'm flattered to experience but don't truly want. His isn't the 'friends to lovers' relationship I sought.

Because being myself earned their friendship in the first place, I hope it saves this one. I leap onto the bed, dust showering the room when I land.

"I missed beds," I say, ignoring the elephant in the room for more pleasant thoughts like a mattress. The high-intensity up-down/push-pull I felt kissing Kórol seeps out as I melt into the thin pallet. Likewise, color bleeds back into his eyes and the anticipatory expression fades.

When pale blue is all that remains in his irises, Kórol's expression turns amused. "I did not realize traveling with the Pack had been that difficult for you." He trails over my body, almost too quickly for me to notice but I'm keyed up enough to catch it. It isn't predatory, more cataloguing.

"I didn't say that. I love the Pack. Now, hop up and let's go to sleep," I chirp. I scoot over and pat the spot next to me, presenting a friendly, and possibly manic, expression. "You've been sleeping outside longer than I have." He drags his gaze from the space next to me and back, slower this time. His eyes narrow, and he shivers.

"I have another idea," he tells me, stomping towards the bed. "I think I know something you may prefer more than sleeping." To my relief, instead of joining me, he veers to left and exits the room, his long hair the last thing to disappear into the hallway.

He stalks back inside before I can guess what he's up to. Keeping the door open, he motions to someone outside. Their backside appears first, displaying beige pants belted with string. The stranger's head pops past the threshold, face straining as he drags something into the room. Finally, his quarry appears—a large copper-colored bathtub. He yanks it just past the door frame, angling it next to the bed. He bows low and exits before reappearing minutes later with four men behind him, each carrying a pitcher of steaming water. Between the five of them, they fill the copper tub in under ten minutes. Kórol's expression is solemn while he scrutinizes them, more like the sedate man I'm used to.

When the other men leave, Kórol turns around for my privacy. I waste no time in stripping myself of my dusty traveling clothes and dip into the water.

Kórol doesn't turn from his spot facing away from me, only shifting his feet slightly when I submerge. I lean back on the rim of the tub and flutter my eyes shut. A phantom pain twinges in my hip as I try not to think of the last time I bathed. "Thank you, Kórol. This is one of the nicest things someone's done for me in years."

"It was the least I could, given what you are doing for us." That startles me. After the weirdness downstairs, I'd momentarily forgotten why we traveled separately from the others—the secret they keep from me, all rolled up in the legend of the Sìnnách. He continues when I don't answer. "I'm also told every wife should expect a gift on her wedding night."

I sink lower into the tub. The reminders prevent me from enjoying the bath as I might have otherwise. I hastily scrub myself and shake off the leftover water clinging to my skin before getting back into my musky traveling clothes.

Kórol turns back when I signal him. He eyes the steam still curling above the water. "Did you not enjoy it?"

I hop back on the bed, unwilling to start a conversation when heavy expectations scent the air between us. "Take my selflessness for what it is and enjoy half of my bath. Husband and wives share, you know."

He expression is inscrutable while he removes his tunic. I squeak and drag the light coverlet over my head for privacy.

"The Sàrkany do not share your kind's modesty, you know," he says as he plunks into the water.

"Oh, I am intimately aware. I could sculpt you all from memory by now." Traveling for more than a month with men, even respectable *gentle*men, means seeing a lot more of the male form than even the internet showed me. I avert my eyes whenever I'm presented with a surprise peek at someone's anatomy, something they don't understand considering how often they inspect each other to avoid infections from scratches and blisters. After an hour-long argument when my make-shift pad leaked that ended with me shouting 'no, that blood is none of your business, read a book if you have questions about the reproductive cycle,' they lessened their focus on me and learned to turn away when I was exposed. But they still drop their pants at whim.

I doze, startling awake when Kórol grunts as he exits the tub and turning to avoid seeing the water rippling down his back and buttocks. A small part of me wants to watch, the same foreign part that pushed me to act flirtatiously downstairs. But I keep my eyes firmly on the opposite wall, going so far as to pretend to sleep as he lies on the floor.

We stay silent, quiet enough that echoes of the ruckus down-stairs wafts through the floorboards. I twist back and forth be-fore finally bunching the small coverlet down to my feet and stretching out like a starfish.

"I thought you were asleep," Kórol murmurs, his voice barely traveling the distance to my ears.

"Room's too hot," I lie. It's the trace feelings from the kiss with Kórol and the implied rejection from Tans that distract me. Kissing Kórol was strange, like I kissed someone else's husband, or played spin the bottle with my boss. But I've never had a boyfriend; maybe I'm too picky. Or, the more rational part of me thinks, *maybe I should ignore* anything *romantic in light of the Voice's enigmatic quest*. I kick my legs out in frustration.

"Does nothing please you, Miss?" The irony of his words tears me from my thoughts.

"Ignore me."

He laughs a little. "Woe that I could."

"Sorry." I roll away from him, reaching to cover myself with the coverlet again.

"You do not need to—in fact, it is I—" The words die on his lips. I peek over the bed to where he lays but stay out of his eyeline. He's a dark shape on the floor but the candle flickers over the lines of his body, illuminating the thickness of his calves, the strength in his waist. He's kept his tunic off, displaying the dark hairs on his pale, muscular, chest and a small scar under his heart. I've seen him half undressed, but I've never *looked* at him that way before.

"Raddare the Eleventh was—misguided. He put himself above the needs of his people." The first words whisper out of him, then build to a deep baritone crescendo, as if he found a foothold to grasp.

"That's—that's good to know," I say after a few seconds of quiet.

"It was also misguided of me to react so strongly to you questioning his character."

"I wasn't trying to question his character," I murmur. "But I'm sorry if it came out that way."

"As I told you, you do not need to apologize. It is I who should. And I am." His head pops into my eyeline, a faint smile playing on his lips. He leans onto his elbow and I do the same. His skin looks supple in the low light as he unknowingly mimics a cover of a sensual book. "Would you care to hear the rest of the story?"

I assent and lay back down, visions of his skin scalding the space behind my eyes. I forcefully erase them; he's my friend and I won't disrespect him that way.

"Once the Thirteenth Raddare King came into power, he realized the error in his great-grandfather's ways. He sat in penance, beseeching the Great Matron to return, offering his adoration." The gentle baritone lulls my troubled thoughts.

"Did she?"

He clears his throat. "She did. And he, mirroring his forefather, fell to his knees in front of her, in the wake of her power and might. But she could not bring back the Sìnnách. They needed to return on their own, after we paid suitable penance."

"Fíl told me about that part—that you four take this trip as a spiritual quest."

"It is more than spiritual," he reveals. "It is a burden upon us, one I hope to ease. Each time we beg that we are worthy. Each time we hope the Sìnnách will return. And each time for so many hundreds, they have yet to return to us. My lasting hope is that I see one in my lifetime."

"I hope you do too," I say. I mean it. I also know he can't find the Sìnnách in me.

CHAPTER 13

A knock on the door wakes us both the next morning. I'm surprised Kórol isn't already awake, but maybe the darkness of the room let him sleep longer too. The door opens from the outside before we answer and Kórol hops upright into a fighting stance. A server, a different one from last night, peeks her head around the door, biting her lip when she sees Kórol's naked torso. He flexes his strong back when he slips to my side, disturbing the silken strands of hair clinging wildly to his skin. I have a strange urge to slide my fingers through them and brush them back into place.

"Morning, sir," she says breathlessly, her hand tracing her collarbone as she stares at him. I'm too tired to put on any 'jealous spouse act.' Sleeping in separate locations kills the alibi anyway. "The innkeeper wishes to discuss the added cost of the bath with you before you depart this morning." With a lingering look over his body, she shuts the door.

"Stay here, Lady." Kórol pulls his tunic over his broad shoulders. "I'll deal with the cost and then we'll depart."

I get up as he leaves. On a whim, I stick a finger in the leftover bathwater. The water is frozen, and icicles crawl up the sides of the copper.

Minutes tick by while I wait alone in the room. The prepared food from last night leaves a stale and acrid taste on my tongue. I smooth down my tunic and lounge on the bed, wishing I had a toothbrush, or any remaining gum.

The door opens. "Do you guys chew on mint or something here?" I say, turning towards the man who enters, assuming it's Kórol. "Because that's something I miss—toothpaste. And while your breath was lovely last—" My voice drowns in my throat.

It isn't Kórol returning after settling the bill, but a hulking man. There's a rust colored smudge on his forehead, almost unnoticeable against the tawny color of his skin. He slams the door closed with a thick knee and lumbers towards me drunkenly. I freeze, my pulse racing but my body sluggish to respond. *This,* the delay in reaction, is why I'm not meant to be a savior. My head finally convinces my hands to curl into fists and my body obeys, right as he reaches towards me with grasping hands.

I knee his crotch, but it does nothing. As his arm slithers toward my neck, I flail, kicking groin and scratching his face but neither slow him. His palm comes down hard on my neck. Then blackness.

When I wake, I don't know how long has passed. I'm sitting in a dank windowless room. The only light comes from two stubby candles which illuminate the mold crawling up the walls. I'm not bound, but I'm woozy. Losing consciousness makes my head heavy and my body slow. Kórol will kill me for getting kidnapped again. Tans too, if I see him again.

I need a punch card for the number of times I black out or faint while in Dalner. *Five unconscious events, free concussion!*

It's a small blessing that I still have my humor.

A figure rummages through boxes in the corner on their knees. I slump back down, pretending to be unconscious. With my messy hair covering my shifting eyes, I search the room for an exit. It's dark enough that I can't see anything but moldy stone. The figure shuffles farther away, uncovering a line of light on the floor. Hazily, I recognize it as where the floor meets the bottom of a door. I need to get around him and get out of this room, but no grand plan emerges from my leaden head.

Planning on helping this time? I sluggishly whisper the words to the Voice, but I know I'm alone. There's no rush of pressure from the Voice, just my own grousing thoughts. Assuming I escape, I'll find a second punch card for the number of times my psychic guide ignores me when they're needed.

The form stands, and I pinch my eyes closed. They stumble towards me and their thick fingers jerk my chin upward. I open my eyes slowly, trying to keep the ruse that I'm waking up. As expected, the drunk who wrenched his way into our room stands in front of me. At least he's alone.

His eyes are a washed-out brown color, as if a gauzy film rests over his irises. He acts drugged, not drunk, like he's not completely in command of his movements, although the type of inebriation doesn't matter so long as I overpower him. I clench my fists, ruing my past self for not taking Kórol's self-defense lessons more seriously.

The man still holds my chin while his other hand raises to my neck. Something glints off the flickering candles and my body stiffens. Curling my fists, I lift my legs, preparing to slam my knees into his groin and crash my fisted hands into his throat before the knife strikes me. It didn't work before, but I have no hope to get out otherwise. I repeatedly chastise my past self for never reading anything *helpful* in emergency scenarios.

But he doesn't angle the knife towards me. Instead, he releases my chin and slices open his own wrist. Blood gushes onto his forearm and he presses the wound onto my forehead. I stifle a shudder of revulsion, losing the advantage in forcing my way out because of the unexpectedness of it.

He speaks as his wrist remains against my skin, blood leaking down my face and narrowly avoiding my eyes. "I do as I'm told, no thought do I hold. Driven to obey; never to betray." His tongue seems too big for his mouth. On the last syllable, he presses hard enough to knock my head backward.

"You will report to the Keep. Repeat," he garbles. His drugged eyes cloud until they become a marbled gray. He repeats himself, this time with some urgency. "You will report to the Keep. Repeat." I squint to keep his blood from running into my eyes, but I can still see the outline of the door to the left of me. He lumbers towards the doorway, the knife slipping through his fingers and a bloody hand wrenching the door open. He pivots and points at the hallway beyond the door. "You will report to the Keep. Repeat."

I nod cautiously, my body finally catching up with my brain and seeing my opportunity to escape. I ignore how unsanitary it is, and open my mouth, letting a few drops of blood spill inward. "I will report to the Keep," I say, suppressing a gag. He steps aside and lean against the wall, blood from his wrist pooling to the floor.

"I will report to the Keep," I say, spitting out the blood. I stand, my knees locking together as I drag myself to the door, my captor now slumping on the ground. "I will report to the Keep," I repeat, my body shaking as I stumble out the door and into the dark hallway. "I will report to the Keep." I ascend the rickety ladder at the end of the hallway. "I will report to the Keep." I open the heavy door at the top of the stairs. I rise from a cellar on one of the higher levels of town. And then I run.

I run until my lungs scream and my legs buckle under me. The streets are empty, and no one stops me, even when I slam onto my knees several streets down onto the stone road. I heave, spitting out nothing but stomach acid, but the taste of man's blood remains.

I find a nearby fountain and crawl to it, leaning against carved stone. I rinse my face and gargle a palmful of water when the swell of memories hits me.

There's a flash of blond hair, and plump red lips against pale skin. Before I arrive in Dalner, my kidnapper prays at a small altar in the house I ran from. He brings alms of dried bread and honey twice a week. Each time he prays to her. He's careful with his words, even good Eósy are slippery and opening himself up to direct interference is a risk no Sàrkany will take. He tells the Great Matron how he loves her and wishes she could be with him.

The scene shifts. When Kórol and I split from the Pack, the kidnapper is tired and not so careful. It's been a dreadful week, he lost two jobs and split his chisel. He prays, and a single misspoken word grants Her full access to his mind. With that opening in place, he sees violet at the edges of his vision and hears Her in his mind. At Her behest, he twists the ragged chisel in his palm, pressing the blood onto his forehead. He mutters something unintelligible and lingers in town for me.

The waking dream ends and I'm still hugging the stone fountain. It *was* the swell of mind magic. Triumph overtakes the panic as I now know that I was right and Tans was wrong.

The disorientation in receiving someone else's memories remains but is less unnerving than the last time I experienced it. With the memories fresh in my mind, I recognize the similarities in the two kidnappings—both involved men speaking to a woman who must be Her, something definitively supernatural, who used mental magic to convince them to attack me.

I can't think about what that means until I get to the castle, where the Voice says more will be explained. I sprint through the town, tripping and scrambling down the levels until I pop out into a valley between two mountains. There is nothing recognizable, now only mountains surrounding me. I search the sky like Fíl did, but nothing in the morning light explains whether I picked the right direction when I exited the town. With no other options, I start hiking, praying I travel towards Raddare's Pass, rather than back the way I came.

I stop at what must be midday, moving off the path and situating between two colossal rocks at the base of an emerald hill that grows out of the mountains. The space between them is small enough for me to wedge myself into and hide. My stomach rumbles as I shove my hands under my chin, slumping me head onto my palms. A few tears leak out and I roughly brush them away. With a substantial sniffle, I close my eyes and will myself to rest for a minute.

The sound of thunder wakes me from my accidental nap. A startled shriek bursts from my throat but I kill it when a figure stomps in my direction. The flash of lighting and another roar of thunder cover my blunder. The sun is missing, cloaked in deep gray clouds, and I don't know how long I dozed on the side of the road. The gray sky hazily illuminates the figure coming towards. Whisky colored hair trails down the back of a stocky and muscular body. The figure's hands are clenched and its strides long as it storms towards my hiding place.

"Kórol?" I speak no louder than a whisper and only someone listening would hear me over the crashing thunder. The figure whirls around and stalks towards me, silver eyes glinting in the light. He yanks me from my hiding spot into a gruff hug, pressing his face into my neck.

"Are you safe?" The words are quiet around us, but loud against my skin.

I nod. He releases his grip and cups my cheeks in his large hands. He searches my face and neck to check for injuries. "Are you wounded?"

I must have missed some of the kidnapper's blood. "Not mine," I whisper back. He presses a kiss into the space above my ear and a shiver sweeps through me. His hands encircle me, and he ghosts his fingers over my spine. There's nothing romantic in the touch, but my hormones still try to make an appearance. I force them down.

I lean into his chest. "Don't say 'I told you so.' You said it was safer not to stay the night, and that I should know how to better defend myself. Just—don't rub it in."

The sound he makes comes from deep within his throat, a gurgling laugh that tinges towards hysteria, as his arms tighten around me. "The perils of bending to your will, my Lady."

CHAPTER 14

Kórol expects several more hours of walking before we rest for the night as we're already half a day late to meet the rest of the Pack at Raddare's Pass. My feelings are torn—on the one hand, I'm eager to get back to the Pack and finish this lengthy journey; on the other, Raddare's Pass is a straight shot to the castle where I'll hop into a probable death match with a supernatural being. But being alone with a slightly clingy Kórol makes my skin tighten in ways that aren't pleasant.

When we move again, he questions me on what happened with the man who kidnapped me. I don't mention that She may have sent him; I'm not prepared to deal with the questions (and probable conclusions) it will create. I tell him an edited version of the events, making a special note to repeat the words the man said exactly.

"He let you walk of your own volition and be free." he says, eyes darkening. It isn't a question, but I answer anyway.

"He told me I needed to report to the 'Keep,' whatever that meant, and I escaped when he thought I was going there. He couldn't tell I was faking. Does that mean anything to you?"

"No. I know of no keeps in Dalner. I will ask Fílga to look into any records from Alacson or the Wilds when we return to the castle."

"What about in Eósy land?"

"In Dànna? That is possible. Although someone demanding you breach a Gate is a serious concern. Did the echo give you anything else?"

I suppress a scowl. "It wasn't an echo, it was the real—never mind. He didn't."

"I should not have left you alone. You are mine to protect."

"It wasn't your fault, Kórol. It wasn't anyone's fault, except the guy who kidnapped me. And I don't need your protection."

Kórol frowns. "I worry for you. I know you have removed yourself from two difficult situations twice, but I should have been there to protect you. It is my job as your consort."

There's a flash of lightning in the distance. It echoes the shot of heat in my gut.

"What do you mean *consort*?" If intentionally kissing Kórol means I'm somehow betrothed to him, I'll amend all my prior statements about this not being a romance novel.

His eyes cross slightly, his fists clench by his sides. "The King's consort," he says, fumbling.

"What does that mean?"

He doesn't look at me, staring at his fists as if they hold the secret to this conversation. "I have spent the past several weeks thinking about your purpose here. No matter how you jest, one of the Eósy plucked you from the sky and brought you to us for a reason."

I think about the Voice again and the notes burning a hole in my bra. "Whatever the reason, it definitely wasn't to be someone's *consort*."

He slows us to a halt, idling by the worn path as his eyes search mine from a few feet away. The thunder closes in, louder and roiling like the feeling in my stomach.

"There is something I considered a few weeks prior but—" He presses his fist to his chest. "Destiny brought you to us, arriving when you did. Fate allowed you to charm so many of my people, and to walk free from perilous circumstances where luck was against you. Both explain my feelings."

My teeth grind while he makes his declaration. When he stops, he's breathing heavy with his expression more emotional than I've ever seen. "What—what are you saying?"

"You have bewitched me, angel." His voice is missing that urgency now but has a ragged quality like he scaled the mountains around us. "You needn't respond. I will not—cannot—act on those feelings until you are confirmed. But it is because of these feelings I know why you came here—to be our savior. Our Sìnnách."

My stomach twists uncomfortably. "I'm not—"

The sky opens, cutting off my denial.

He grabs my hands before I can refuse and yanks me down the path. "We must stop!" he yells, scarcely audible over the rumble of thunder. The wind whips his hair forward like a wet mask.

"Can we try to make it?" I shout back. I can't spend another night alone with him after this odd confession. The wind takes his answer, but he keeps pressing forward and I use his stocky body to hide me from the wind and rain. He veers off; I follow only because I'm clinging to his back He shifts us into the side of the mountain, ushering us into an opening that only he sees.

"We didn't need to take cov—" I start.

"The Eósy have taken our choices from us with this storm. We will make camp here tonight." He uses his commanding voice and I don't argue. "Although we will not have the benefit of a fire."

I scan the opening he pulled us into and slump my shoulders. The space is narrow, naturally carved out of the stone mountain. There isn't enough room for two people to lie down comfortably, much less start a fire. Aggressive friendship is still all I have, and I refuse to comment on his wild accusations.

"This is the first rainstorm I've seen since landing here," I start before going silent. Anything else I say is pointless chatter to bring back normalcy after the bomb he dropped.

"The storms are a gift from the Eósy," he says, answering my unasked question. He wrings his hair free of raindrops near the entrance. The opening feels more confining than when we crashed inside minutes earlier. The crisp timbre of his voice echoes in the small space.

"Perhaps a nearby villager has that gift, or an Eósy itself deemed it time for a cleansing rain." He watches me shiver and leans towards me before pulling off his tunic. "We need to get out of these wet clothes to avoid freezing."

I spin towards the opposite rock wall, forcing any butterflies from clawing my stomach open. I'm *definitely* in a romance novel because real life couldn't invent this cliché. It's a multi-genre one, with a comedy-adventure component I didn't sign up for either. I peel off my tunic-dress and jeans hesitantly. My hands cover my soft stomach while my ratty bralette and graying underwear protect the rest of me.

Sufficiently shielded, I twist to ask Kórol for an extra shirt, finding him rummaging naked through his canvas bag. He looks better than he did at the inn. Each flash of lighting that glints off the stone shows a still image of a broad back, a strobe light effect of flesh rippling against firm muscles. My eyes briefly travel over his backside and down his stocky legs. Like Tans, he could be the perfect model for a chiseled statue. None of the slender Michelangelos, but stocky warriors built only for battle. He stands and I stare at a clump of dirt on the ground.

"Here," he says, tossing over a piece of cloth. I snatch it as he turns around, brandishing his naked form. Comparing him to a creation of one of the master artists is accurate—his broad shoulders, his muscular arms, his chest with the small scar under his heart, his thick legs, his hanging sex—all combine to create a perfect vision of masculinity. It's nothing I haven't seen before, but the charge in the air makes everything different. All the color leaches from my face as my brain short-circuits. In a romance novel, I'd—but *no*. The hormones can't win.

This vision of a man may be attracted to me, but only because he thinks I'm the Sìnnách, something I can't be. I'm not the right person to deal with Her, much less some fated heroine. I clear my throat and drag the tunic over me, inhaling the cloying scent of spearmint and lemons. "Thanks," I say, staring at the opening that narrows to a point fifteen feet above us. Kórol rubs the back of his neck with his hand, his shadow leaning back as if to try to catch what holds my focus. "This is a *cliched* romance novel," I mumble, "stuck in the rain, needing to get naked to dry off, only body heat for warmth—"

"We should try to sleep. Although, you are right about body heat." He hesitates. "I will not take liberties but given the lack of fire and your inability to withstand the cold, we will need to embrace for warmth."

He looks more uncomfortable than I expect for someone who thinks he wants me. I should be the distressed one between the two of us. *Aggressive friendship*, I remind myself.

Summoning all the bravery I possess, I plunk down to the floor and lay on my side, tugging on the hem of Kórol's tunic to cover my hips. He silently lumbers up behind me and lays down, leaving scant centimeters between us. Literary characters in this position describe feeling anticipation rather than anxiety, which is the only feeling cresting through me at his proximity.

Kórol's hand hovers above my waist. "I apologize, Lady, that we are in this position," he whispers behind me. The temperature in the crevice drops.

"It doesn't need to mean anything, just two people avoiding hyperthermia." His hand grazes the cloth covering my hip bone. I grab his hand and yank his arm around me, pressing it into the space just below my breasts. His hand freezes my skin through the cloth, and I shuffle back into his chest, curling my legs to fit next to his like puzzle pieces. His breath stutters against my back.

"I cannot believe *this* doesn't mean something," he confesses. "Even if I cannot act on my feelings." Ice crystals form on the surrounding walls.

"You've got it all wrong. What you're feeling is circumstantial because we're almost naked. It has nothing to do with me being—" A chill skitters through me and I squirm closer to him, ruining the point I'm trying to make. "You've just never experienced it before. That's all," I finish. First crushes are always all-consuming. Mine ruined the second half of sixth grade, when Jake said I was stupid.

He clenches his jaw hard enough to crack against his teeth. "The depth of my feelings goes beyond what any man could feel for another without divine influence. Were it to occur naturally, it would have before now. I have never felt this before, and I know I will never feel it again. I have read the records of my forefathers—they tell me these feelings spring from the Sìnnách. From you."

I shiver again. "I'm not what you think. I'm not your savior. I—I have a reason to be here but it's—"

"I know what you are. You will not convince me otherwise." His voice is harder than steel. "Sleep, my angel, my little bird."

With another shiver running through me, this one from unease and not the cold, I try again, "Kórol—"

"I said sleep," he growls.

When morning comes, an unfamiliar weight presses against me. It takes me a minute to remember Kórol's naked body embraces mine as his breath kisses my neck. He stirs and I feign sleeping.

"Good morning," he murmurs into my scalp. I shift away from him as casually as I can. He doesn't notice, instead humming while passing over my clothes that dried during the night. I dress while he does the same.

Last night, I spent several restless hours working through how to approach Kórol. He's already shown to have a hairpin trigger, but I hope a discussion when we're both clothed and things are less tense will give us closure on the 'Grace is a Sìnnách' story he invented yesterday.

"Kórol, we need to talk about the Sìnnách. You wouldn't listen last night and—" Before I finish speaking, he brackets me against one of the rough stone walls. He kisses my forehead lightly and his eyes practically sparkle, like the sun reflecting off a gray lake in fog.

"I promised to provide you answers when we reach the castle, and that promise remains, but we are already several days behind schedule. We must meet my men at Raddare's Pass."

"And we will," I shift away from him, but he keeps me in his cage. "But we still need to talk. Not just about the Sìnnách, but about this Voice and how I feel. I'm sorry but—"

He rests his chin on top of my head. It's nothing Tans hasn't done before, but the expectation in it unnerves me. How do I convince someone I'm not interested without ruining the friendship? Maybe I should let Tans do the same and take notes.

"You have brought me hope, Lady. I will not let you tear it from me without explaining the entire story." His voice deepens, and he clings to me. "It is my promise that everything will be explained. But for now, know that you brought me hope. That is all I can give you now."

After more internal debate, I let him snuggle into me. I'll figure out a way to let him down easily before this goes too far. But he's still my friend. I don't have enough of those to throw them away for a little discomfort. With my arms limp at my sides, I let him hug me for the count of twenty, then wriggle away.

Raddare's Pass is a valley dug out of two vast mountains that acts as a path to the castle. The castle spills up and out of a third peak, a grander mimicry of the town we visited a night prior. Small buildings and streets lay at the base, and the castle looms over it. It looks nothing like the Earth castles I've seen, but a vertical fortress of a dozen tall shards of stone jutting into the sky like broken glass. It's a tar black and chilling version of the Sagrada Familia.

Our three friends wait on the path and stand when we approach. Kórol hasn't touched me since we left the cave that morning, for which I'm grateful, but when the Pack is in view, he increases the distance between us. Tans breaks into a run when we're a few yards away, hugging Kórol before lifting me and spinning me in a circle.

"Glad you're back in one piece," he whispers in my ear. Fílga and Sáven stand behind him and take turns greeting us.

Kórol immediately pulls them into a group huddle while I wait nearby. Although I can't hear him, I know he's telling them what he told me yesterday. I see it in Tans' jittery movements, Fíl's contented sigh, and Sáv's wide eyed gaze.

As soon as he finishes ruining my morning, Kórol sets off at a whirlwind pace. Tans trails after, offering a '1-minute' sign to me and a blown kiss. The awkwardness with Kórol overshadows my relief that Tans and my friendship must be back to normal. I follow numbly behind them.

"Are you alright?" Fílga asks as the small town at the base of the castle grows to full height. Sáven walks beside him and their hands dance near each other, barely touching. "You've been quite silent since rejoining us this morning."

"I'm fine," I lie.

Fílga sighs. "I cannot believe I'm bemoaning your silence. Do not fear for the castle, Miss. After the King's confirmation, you'll have plenty of time to rest and relax and enjoy your time in Ilsen as our honored guest."

"Honestly, Fíl, tell me you don't believe this Sìnnách thing too? Hang on—the *King* knows about me?" Kórol mentioned being the King's consort, but I thought I had time before Kórol gave his opinion to anyone official. The stakes against me increase tenfold.

Tans bounds up beside me, his eyes shining like an excited puppy. "We are only an hour from the castle, but you three will keep us walking another day at this pace. Fíl's delay I understand, given his increased age and fragility, but not you two," he tells Sáv and I. He stares at the bemused expression on Fíl's face and the horrified one on mine. "What happened?"

"Miss Grace wonders whether the King knows about her," says Fílga.

Tans grins mischievously, something that isn't a good sign. "That he does."

I scowl and barely refrain from punching them both in the arm. "What are you talking about?"

The words are lost to a tremble of feet. Tans slips from me with a wink to stand beside Kórol, who stops a few yards ahead of us. The noise surges as thirty soldiers hurtle forward in a marching formation. They each wear black armor with silver grommets connected by red stitching. It must be leather, given the embroidery sprawling over their chests and arms. Beneath the leather, dark indigo fabric, the color of a moonlit sky, peeks through. They halt in front of Kórol and kneel. After he tilts his head, they stand in unison with their hands clasped behind their back and face Tans. He still grins but mimics the soldiers' poses.

"At ease," Tans calls out. The men relax as one, no longer locking their knees and letting their hands swing by their sides. "Third Commander Faburth, you may address your King," he says, looking back at me and winking.

A short man about Fílga's age, dressed identically to the others, approaches Kórol, and bows. When the tips of his sparsely braided hair skim the ground, he pops back up like a spring. "King Kórol the Twenty-Fourth of the Raddare line, we welcome you back from your pilgrimage," he says, thumping his chest.

My jaw falls open. Kórol clasps Faburth on the shoulder and addresses the group. He motions me to join him, but I stay frozen in place until Fílga pushes me a few feet and Tans drags me the rest of the way. Tans narrowly avoids a jab to his side from my grasping hands as Kórol gestures towards me. "Men, behold your Sìnnách."

CHAPTER 15

Fílga immediately ushers us into the castle, meaning I can't panic with an audience, or yell at Kórol for his announcement, or kick them all for hiding Kórol's royal status.

He then escorts me to a guest room, something high and off to the side of one the spindle-like spires. A "solar" he calls it, with thick stone walls and two thin floor-to-ceiling windows that display the ocean to the west. The room is larger than my dorm *and* the room where Kórol and I stayed two nights prior (where everything went wrong), but not by much.

A canopy bed with heavy red draperies and an overwhelming amount of brocade pillows commands the space. It's nicest looking bed I've seen in years. Shoved between one wall and the bed is a side table with two carved chairs and a small dresser. Fílga explains I'll appreciate the distance from the castle's inhabitants, given that an overwhelming number of visitors and guards will crowd Ilsen, not only those who live in the castle but those who will arrive to meet the new Sìnnách. I only just stop myself from growling at him for the reminder before he leaves, shutting the heavy wooden door behind him.

I toss myself onto my bed and press my palms against my eyes until white spots dance behind my lids. The freak-out that's been simmering under my skin, the one that began when I learned this wasn't a dream, bubbles out against my will.

Everything that's happened—being in another world, one with friends who think I'm a mythological dragon-riding warrior, and one of them might love me because of it—makes me want to hide under my bed. If this is a book, I don't want to be the protagonist anymore. And if any additional Eósy are listening to my thoughts, I suggest they make me the sidekick.

I scrub my hands down my face. I should have convinced Kórol when he brought up the Sìnnách thing yesterday or stopped the innuendo when Fílga hinted at it in Chead. But *no*, I ignored the problem, thinking it would go away on its own. I ignored it to avoid losing one of my few friends, which will happen when I explain that his crush doesn't have a secondary meaning.

Now I might lose all of them. Maybe there's a way to get home before it's too late, no matter that the thought makes my skin itch.

I pull out the notes I wrote on the trek, my chunky handwriting spiraling all over the pages. Six months ago, if someone told me I'd be transported to a magical world and act as that society's savior, I'd have snorted at their imagination. If they maintained the fiction, I'd direct them to the ER to pump their stomachs of the massive dose of drugs they'd taken.

I let out a wet laugh. If not for the mangled scar on my hip, I'd still think this was a dream.

Someone knocks on the door. "Come in," I call out in a warbly voice, stuffing the notes back into the tattered remains of my bralette. Tansr's dark head peeks around the wooden threshold. He bathed recently as his wet hair curls at the ends and several new braids hang by his ears. He's no longer in a musty tunic from the trek but wears a leather outfit like the soldiers outside. His is inverted—the leather armor a midnight blue and the clothing below it black. Instead of the silver grommets and red stitching making a geometric pattern over his entire chest, a small dragon symbol is embroidered in silver right above his heart.

"I wanted to check-in on you, Butterfly." He sees my tears and sits on the bed. His bronze skin, black hair, and supple dark leather armor are a beautiful complement to the opulent bedding and gilded curtains. "What's wrong?"

I roll onto my stomach and shove my head under a pillow without answering.

"Surely hiding Kórol's family line did not cause this reaction. If so, I'll remain tight lipped about mine forever." He rolls me over and drags me to a seated position, placing his arms loosely around my waist. "Tell me what is wrong."

I lean into him heavily. The memory of the last time we were close—when I kissed him, and he rejected me—digs into the edges of my mind. I'm thankful our friendship survived it. I can only hope the same happens with Kórol. "E—everything," I hiccup.

Tansr rests his head atop mine and brushes his fingers down my spine as I burrow closer to him. "That can't be true. I can think of three good things right now. One, we're finished pilgrimaging forever. Two, you'll no longer be sleeping on the ground. Three, I'm here."

"That doesn't outweigh the bad. There's this other thing I don't want to do, but now I think I have to. And when Kórol finds out I'm not what he thinks I am—"

He hums noncommittally. When the leaking tears dry, he dips his head to stare into my eyes. "You are not a Sìnnách then?"

"Are you kidding? Have you met me? I can't tame a dragon."

He smiles. "You may not need to."

Tans takes me the castle library, where we should find Fílga. The library is in one of the southern spires, several floors and corkscrew towers away from my own distant sleeping quarters. When Tans opens the door, I'm transported to a fairy tale. Bookshelves upon bookshelves of leather-bound paper span as far as I can see. Light streams through thin floor-length windows, creating pockets of sunshine. Dust kicks up from unseen corners and the smell of parchment scents the air. Had I seen Ilsen *and* dragons on the same day, I would have realized this wasn't a dream earlier, because no way could my brain make up something this striking.

When we find Fílga in one corner, he's not alone. He and Sáven cluster together at a long wooden table covered with books. The title are obscured, but the ones I can see involve the Sìnnách. Sáven's ruddy complexion blanches as he listens to Fílga whisper. They both jolt when they see us.

"Lady," Fílga calls out, clearing his throat and leaning away from Sáven, who slides down a chair and looks at the woodgrain on the table. "We thought you'd be resting. It will be a busy night tonight."

Tansr settles me in a chair across the table from the other two. "We need to discuss the Sìnnách."

Fílga's eyes flit between me and Tansr while Sáven fiddles with his hands. "Would it not be better to delay until tonight?"

"No," I stress. "I need to figure out how to explain to Kórol that I'm not the Sìnnách before he tells anyone else."

Sáven looks up at that. "How'd you know?" he asks. He speaks more to Fílga than to me. "People can learn lots of new things about themselves." Fíl keeps his gaze fixed on the windows. His hands twitch as he reaches for his braid before aborting the moment and clenching them at his side.

I groan. "Not you too, Sáv. I'm no dragon-rider, tamer, whatever."

Tans places his hands on my shoulders and lets soothing bursts of heat trickle down my back. He speaks to Fílga. "Tell Grace about the interpretations you mentioned before."

Fílga strides to one wall lined with books. His fingers graze several rows before resting on a wooden covered book held together with twine, which he plucks from its place and brings back to the table, sidestepping Sáv completely. He carefully opens it to a page near the end of the book.

"We have lost most of our early writings on the Sìnnách, but this one of the few we have remaining. It tells us that Sìnnách came and tamed the dragon, bending them to her will and riding them like a docile pet."

"And?" I shove the book away from me with shaking fingers. "I knew that already. I just said I can't ride dragons."

He closes the book. "And many of my predecessors speculate that taming and riding the dragon is a metaphor. What we can cobble together is that there existed dragon-riders, someone who tamed the dragons and was the right hand of the King. Some scholars believe that these texts refer to a skillful queen, one who tamed the King, bent the Kingdom to her will and protected the people from the Dark, as the official emissary between the Sàrkany and the ruling Light."

"So, you're saying anyone could be the Sìnnách, assuming they somehow tame Kórol and protect the Kingdom?"

"Not that *anyone* could. Only someone who can make Kórol submit to her."

"And outwit bandits with only her wits." Tans choruses.

"And subdue a greedy merchant," Fíl finishes.

Stunned, I sputter in confusion. "That's insane. There are actual dragons here! Why would the word *dragon-rider* be a metaphor?"

Fílga replaces the book. "Directly translated, Sàrkany means the dragon people. You've tamed many since you arrived in the high hills. What proof to you have that you are *not* a Sìnnách?"

Because I'm not from here; because I'm nothing special; because life isn't a storybook and not every little girl is a hero. I stay silent.

Tans sits on the table and puts a finger under my chin. As usual, it feels like he's reading my mind. "I don't know if you are the Sìnnách. But you *are* something special. If anyone would be a Candidate, it would be you."

I look between them, bewildered. Sáven is the only one who hasn't spoken yet. "What do you think?"

He taps his fingers on the table and shrugs. "Ladies don't fall from the sky."

"But I'm a human girl, not an Eósy warrior-woman."

"What's it hurt to try?" he asks as he glares at Fíl, who keeps his back to us.

Tans grabs my shoulders, looking back at his two companions. "Grace. You are a butterfly, no mere caterpillar. You cannot live as a caterpillar, always looking at the sky from your place on the ground and waiting for metamorphosis. You must take that chance and get in that cocoon. Will you?"

They're wrong, but I can't help but grin at their confidence in me.

"Caricature," I mumble. Only Tans smiles back.

The three pointedly suggest I go back to my room to rest for tonight. With a wide eyed gaze, I let them direct me to my bed and tuck me in. I'm flustered and don't think to ask what might happen tonight.

Several hours later, a pressure forces into my head. "Grace," the Voice whispers, their childish voice tickling my ear. "Welcome to Ilsen. Are you prepared for your next steps?"

I bolt upright. "It's time? She's here?" This is too much for one day.

They giggle shrilly. "Not yet. Does that mean you've accepted your purpose here?"

I stare down at my hands, blood and dirt still stuck under my fingernails. "I don't have a choice, do I? If I don't, she'll hurt me and my friends."

"Have faith, little Grace. I do not expect Her until you've undertaken several trials first. Your presence and actions at Ilsen will draw Her to you, like a predator to prey."

"That's reassuring."

"It is not meant to be. She will underestimate you; that is the entire point."

"Do you have anything useful to say?" I slump back onto the bed and scowl at the dark canopy above me. "So far I can sum up your 'guidance' as 'She's coming; defeat Her, Grace or She'll destroy you and your friends. I won't tell you how or when, but I will toss out nonsensical riddles and then giggle creepily without giving any practical help when you need it, like during your *two* kidnapping attempts.'"

"I cannot do more, else I would. With the walls in place, you know why."

I do, or at least I think I do. The conclusion circles the back of my mind. "Whatever."

"What a delightful diversion you are, Grace. Until we speak again."

"Wait!" My tantrum isn't worth missing out on answers I need. A small sigh reverberates in my brain and I risk asking the question I've wanted to ask it for the past week. "At least make this visit somewhat useful. Tell me—am I the Sìnnách?"

There's a knock at the door. **You'll see**, the Voice says. And then my mind is my own.

I roll out of bed and stomp to the door, already angry at whoever stands on the other side and kept me from my answer.

Kórol greets me. He's cleaned up too, something I should have done during my brief respite but was too frustrated to attempt. He wears a red leather vest, a midnight blue tunic, and black leather greaves over his black pants. He's exchanged the fur coat for a fur cape, and fur covers the tops of his heavy boots. He looks powerful, regal even, like something out of a painting.

"Should I bow?" I mutter. He either doesn't hear me or ignores me, instead pulling me out of the room. I plant my feet at the doorway.

"No, no no," I snap. While I still worry about losing his friendship, the sooner this is handled the better. "You said we could talk at the castle and we're at the castle. While I'm flattered you like me, it doesn't make me the—"

"I told you all would be explained, and that promise remains." He places a chilled hand on my low back. "Join me and you shall see."

Rolling my eyes and holding in a scream, I let him drag me downstairs. Once we reach the ground floor, he takes us down a long hallway. We stop in front of a wide wooden door inscribed with intricate designs. It's an overlapping pattern, and most depict larger versions of the stitched dragon on Tans' leather chest plate. Without letting me do more than scan the carvings, Kórol intertwines our hands and lugs me inside.

We enter the back of a long stone room. Stained-glass windows the size of doorways that start six feet above us and rise ten feet high reflect the setting sun. People of all ages and dress pack into the room, standing near the entrance we arrive through and spilling towards the front. Most people have braids and beads in their hair and wear elegant jewel toned tunics. A few near the back look like they haven't washed their clothes in years. Some examine me with fascination, some with derision. I can catch a few words here and there ("her?", "not what I expected", "finally"). Out of the entire crowd, I only recognize Tansr, who stands near the other end of the room next to a bulky wooden throne on a stone platform. More carvings of the same dragon motif cover the throne and precious metals adorn the crest of the seat, casting complementary colored shadows from the reflected window light.

Kórol drags me to the front of the room and people instinctively move out of his way. "You look as though you belong there, Lady," he murmurs to me when we reach the throne.

It's as big a lie as the 'Grace is the Sìnnách' declaration, given I still wear the clothes I woke up in that morning, the rain-dried tunic-dress and my faded jeans, and I'm sure there's dirt on my cheeks and in my hair. I surreptitiously finger-comb my hair and rub my face. With my luck, I'm probably just spreading the dirt around.

Turning back to the crowd, he raises our clenched hands. "People of Dalner," he announces, his booming voice cutting through the chatter. Everyone quiets. "We have endured her absence patiently for many years. We have given alms for centuries. We have asked that we be worthy. And now, our prayers have been answered." He gestures towards me triumphantly. "A Candidate has arrived. Though her confirmation is scheduled for the Winter Solstice, when we open our doors to the Great Matron, I have faith that the Sìnnách stands before you."

Nausea churns in my stomach as the crowd starts screaming. The cacophony is deafening, but the noises are more joyful than outraged.

"Would you care to address your people?" Kórol asks. I decline, concentrating on not regurgitating the dried meat Sáven served earlier.

Tansr emerges from behind the throne. He whispers something to Kórol, who makes a dismissive gesture. Kórol speaks to the audience again, but the loud ringing in my ears blocks out whatever he says. Once Tans drags me back into the hallway, I double over to wheeze.

"You were splendid, Grace." Tans tells me, rubbing my back. I glare at him. "You didn't faint, I consider that a success."

"That's the 'tonight' you were talking about, then. A more *detailed* warning would have been nice," I complain, crossing my arms around the waist of my crumpled tunic-dress.

Before he can respond, Kórol opens the door and clasps my shoulder with one hand, gesturing for Tans to go back inside with the other. I shake my head and reach for Tans, but he chuckles and dances away from my grip.

"Rat," I hiss at his retreating back. When Tans reenters the throne room, Kórol slides his hand down my arm until he can make lazy circles on my palm with his thumb.

"Do you understand now?" His eyes glaze as if he's not truly looking at *me* but something within or beyond me. "This is why you came. This is who you are. You are the Sìnnách."

"Kórol," I say, wrenching my hand away. "That wasn't an explanation, or a discussion. That was an ambush."

"You are right, and I am sorry, Lady." He clenches his fists. "I cannot explain it because everything you have done has built upon the last, until those stones formed a castle in my soul, you at the center atop a dragon."

That's a worrying image. "But that doesn't *tell* me anything, just that you think I'm something I'm not. I told you before—you've probably never had a crush on anyone before, so you're confusing your feelings. And, I'm sorry, but I don't feel—"

He cuts me off with a wave of his hand and the temperature in the hallway drops. "Again, you are right. I have explained my feelings but not what they mean. It is because I am King that I know you are the Sìnnách. The stories say the Sìnnách will bewitch the King and they will remain connected more deeply than marriage. And you have bewitched my soul." He grabs my shoulders as I blanch. "I need you because you are my Sìnnách. You are my Sìnnách because I need you. Make my happiness by accepting what you are, and I will make yours."

CHAPTER 16

I don't see Kórol again for several days. He must have lots to do, particularly since he was gone from the castle for several months, but it makes my ability to 'let him down easy' impossible. He failed to listen the night of my announcement until I finally gave up and demanded he let me go back to my room.

The confirmation ceremony will occur on the Winter Solstice, giving me two weeks to convince everyone I'm a normal girl who can't be their people's hope or Kórol's ladylove. Preparing for Her to protect the people I care for, and figuring out how to get home, assuming I even *want* to, is overwhelming enough. Anything Sìnnách related would probably break me.

The 'minutiae of confirmation,' Fílga explains when I ask the morning after Kórol's official announcement, is nothing to concern myself with, and involves reading texts, consulting with those loyal to the crown, and, ultimately, begging for a sign from the Great Matron. Dalner hasn't had a Candidate in a century, and no one knows what I need to be doing.

Fíl also says that the Sìnnách was the King's consort, so Kórol was right on that count. I ask Fíl whether the feelings need to be two-sided, but he says that only the devotion of the King for the Sìnnách matters and there's no evidence the Sìnnách needs to return the King's feelings. It's another tally in the negative column of my life.

The Voice doesn't return, and I grow increasingly nervous about what I should be doing, so much so that on the fourth day here Tans drags me outside and forces me to spill my secrets.

The castle towers over the town below, but several grass and floral balconies spaces were built between spires.

"Are you still fretting about your Candidacy, Butterfly?" he asks as he directs me to a flat stone bench outside on the ground floor of the castle. Several hundred plants burst from the ground in front of us, and just behind them I can see the tips of wooden rooftops. He sits and pulls me next to him.

"How can I not be?" I frown. "Everyone has all these expectations for me."

He slips his hand around my waist. "In all I know about the Sìnnách, if you are confirmed there is little you must do. You simply are."

I jerk away from him with a shudder. "Along with apparently being married to Kórol."

Tans draws a startled breath, his fingers twitching. "Only should you desire to do so. Our histories tell us the King had a depth of feeling for the Sìnnách, but not that it *must* be romantic. The prior Kings had wives."

"Really?" I ask, looking at him hopefully. Fíl didn't mention that, and I'm skeptical given Kórol's grand pronouncements.

"A Sìnnách is a *consort* to the King and guiding light to the Kingdom. Not necessarily his wife. Was that what was troubling you, love?"

He reaches out to drag his thumb over my cheek while waiting for me to answer. Telling Tans takes trust—that he'll believe me, that he won't be angry I kept it from him.

"There is a reason I'm here," I admit. His hand leaves my cheek. "It isn't being the Sìnnách. An enemy is coming, and I'm supposed to stop Her. If I don't, She'll hurt those I care about."

I pause for an outburst from him or a joke but instead he flattens his lips. "How can I help you?"

"That's it? You don't have questions?"

"Of course, I do, but I trust you. We all have secrets, and you've hinted you have other objectives. You will tell me what you need me to know and I must content myself with that."

I dig into the bodice of my borrowed dress and hand over the notes I've worried several tears into. "I've been visited by—something. One of your Eósy, maybe. I think they're the one who brought me here, or they know who did."

He hastily reads over my sparse notes, eyes widening at a few phrases. "I believe Fílga explained how Eósy can be Light or Dark. Are you sure this being isn't attempting to harm you in some fashion, and to force open a rift to allow them to descend?"

"I don't *think* so. I don't even know how to invite them here. They've been slightly rude and definitely intrusive, but they're trying to help me. They gave me a few riddles that helped me escape from the bandits that first time. And they led me to the Pack."

"For that, I will thank them. Do these pages contain the riddles of which you speak?"

I point the words on the parchment as I explain. "Something about needing fire and ice to survive. And 'deception being my armor.' They say other things, but they repeated those phrases a lot."

He returns the notes which I slip back down my dress. "I need to think about these 'riddles,' as you called them. Would that be acceptable?"

A weight lifts off my shoulders; so long as She doesn't arrive, he can have all the time he wants. "Whatever you need. I know I can't do this alone. Well, as alone as I've been with a disembodied Voice giving me advice."

"I will do whatever I can to help you thwart this enemy and protect those you care about." He watches me with an inscrutable expression. "Should I assume I am one of those at risk?"

I put my hands on my hips in mock annoyance. "What do you think? You four are the most important people here! Also, the only people I know."

"High praise, love. But I have an even bigger reason to help you succeed," he says, chuckling. "Do you have any other information on this enemy and how to defeat Her?"

"Except that she's apparently a Dark Eósy? Only that She's on her way and I need to be ready for Her."

"Not to imitate Fílga, but perhaps we should review any available books on probable enemies of the Kingdom and the Dark Eósy."

"That's a great idea!" I can always find solace and guidance in books. I don't know why I didn't think of it before, but I'll blame the distraction of the last few days. It might give me ideas on how to get home too, though a knot forms in my throat at the possibility.

"It can't hurt. Perhaps you can learn more about what it might mean to be a Sìnnách as well." He cradles me in his arms and breathes into the skin behind my ear. "We will figure this out, Butterfly."

With Fíl's approval, I work in the library. Since I'm one of the few castle visitors who can read and write *and* has free time, he allows me to read what I want, provided I spend a little time each day recopying parts of certain decaying texts. I consider telling him about Her too and using his knowledge, but restrain myself. Fíl seems more 'adult-like' than the others but I can't shake that he seems me as a little girl who can play 'Sìnnách' but can't handle anything else.

On the first day, I discretely checked for books on realm hopping but found none because of the confusing filing system. And I couldn't ask Fíl, not without dealing with unwanted conversations. Something I didn't know was clenched released at the realization that there may be no options for returning home. Sìnnách or no, I could be meaningful here, with these people who needed me, *wanted* me here. Tans convinced me of that every day. Earth didn't have that.

On the sixth day after I arrived in Ilsen, with barely more than a week until the Solstice, I find a leather-bound journal engraved with a sun at the top of the stack Fílga laid out for me. Although not dated or signed, it must be important, or else it wouldn't be in the stack. It's ancient, the parchment crinkling like dead leaves as I open it.

> Mother says I must chronicle my days because my thoughts may become important someday when I ascend. I told her it was a complete waste of time but then Father acted as her muscle. Fine, *Mother.* Let Father fight your battles. (And if you read this, Mother, you cannot complain because that would be a breach of trust, would it not?) Today bored me. And journaling is a worthless endeavor...

I don't think Fílga will find anything I desperately needed to recopy there, and I put it near the bottom of my stack of books to transcribe. I start on the next book, an actual text, that lays out the history of the royal family.

> The Thirteenth King of the Raddare line understood his forefather's mistake, and that the Sìnnách was a blessing, something squandered. He sat in penance for a week, then a month, then a year,

hoping to draw the Great Matron back to his Kingdom. Each day he begged she descend.

I finish copying the paragraph and blow on the ink, wanting it to dry lest I smudge all my work. When that happened on the first day, Fílga made me rewrite pages from the most boring guidebook on how to farm 'dergen,' some starchy fruit that didn't exist on Earth. I refuse to make that mistake again.

"Fíl?" I call to the pile of records next to me, the man himself hidden by his work.

"Yes?" His voice sounds muffled.

"I skipped one of the books. It was some kid's diary." He remains silent. "But you never told me Raddare the Thirteenth waited for a full year before the Great Matron descended."

Fílga rustles behind the books before his head pops in my eyeline. "I take it you haven't finished rewriting that history yet?"

I squint my eyes in suspicion. "No, I have not."

"I suggest you continue reading," he says as he vanishes again. A few minutes later, Tans bounds through the door for our daily walk. Even though I busy myself in the library, he still visits me every day and forces me outside. He tells me the gossip of the Kingdom that day, and I share what I've learned about Her. When we separate until dinner, he kisses me on the cheek and tells me how much he enjoys my friendship. If my massive crush wasn't one-sided, they'd be perfect medieval life dates.

"Ready for our outing, love?"

"Not yet. I need to finish this passage because Fílga isn't being helpful." I cast a dirty look at the books obscuring the Historian from my glare. Tans smirks and leans against a bookshelf.

But still the Great Matron did not descend. He sat
in penance for two decades until the birth of his
son, the Fourteenth of the Raddare line...

"Twenty years?" I shout. As if attacked, Tans leaps from the bookshelf. But instead of fear, he shakes to smother a chuckle.

"Shh!" Fílga reprimands from his seat hidden by books, emphatically whispering at me while Tans stifles his laughter at my outburst. "This is a library!"

"Do they not teach you manners on Earth?" Tans says, giggling as he looks around the empty room. I toss a nib of ink at him and he squawks to avoid it.

I rise from my chair and make a hole in the piles to peer at Fíl. "Twenty years? I could be waiting for her to decide if I'm a Sìnnách for *twenty* years?" My life flashes before my eyes. Twenty years of library work; twenty years of Kórol declaring he loves me and then hiding. Actually, except for the latter part, it doesn't sound so bad. If She can wait too, I'll have lots of time to prepare. Would my home on Earth still even exist then?

"To get her here originally. She returns every winter now, as you know."

"But she made him wait twenty years. And you all are—were—waiting hundreds for the Sìnnách."

"Does this mean you finally believe you could be the Sìnnách?" Tans asks. I throw another ink nib at him, but he catches that one and tosses it back at me. Fíl's intent on his reading now, or he'd reprimand us for misbehaving.

"That is part of having faith," says Fíl. "We have faith that the Great Matron knows what she's doing."

I slump back down in the chair, daring to speak the thought that plagues my mind. "Fílga, what will happen to me if the Great Matron arrives and I'm *not* the Sìnnách?"

He tilts his head and his brows knit together. Tans leans back against a bookshelf and pretends not to hear our discussion. "I am unsure," he says after too long a pause.

"I won't—there aren't repercussions for failing the Candidacy, right?"

Fílga comes around his books and leans on the table in front of me. He pats my shoulders in what he must believe is a reassuring manner. "I do not yet know. But I can tell you that no matter what happens, each day you are here is necessary to further your path."

"Which means?"

"Destiny cannot be stopped. Now keep copying or leave."

CHAPTER 17

Only a day later, Fílga finishes his research on Candidate confirmations.

My day starts by waking up to Tansr on my bed, peering down at me. "Kórol instructed me to awaken you and tell you that you must dress for the day," he says when my eyes blink open.

"Not yet, creep," I say, stretching away the sleep from my muscles.

His expression darkens before a flash of something concerned run over his eyes. "What do you mean creep?"

I shut my eyes and throw my arm over my face. "Creeping in here to wake me up. That makes you a creep." I pull him down next to me with my free hand, rolling over so my arm pins him to the bed. "Now let me close my eyes for a few more minutes." I shut my eyes and burrow deeper into the blankets, enjoying the (absolutely platonic) feeling of him that close. He tenses under my arm.

"We need," his voice cracks. He clears his throat and begins again, voice soft but firm. "We need to awaken." I peek one eye at him. He isn't looking at me but staring deliberately ahead.

"I need my beauty sleep," I whine. "You of all people should understand that."

"You could stay awake for a month and still have beauty to spare," he says, his eyes meeting mine.

"Flatterer," I mumble, hiding the pleased smile in my pillow.

"Good morning," another voice echoes off the stone walls. Tansr leaps from the bed and leans against the wall while Kórol stomps to my bed.

"Why is my room the new clubhouse?" I sit up and cross my arms. "If we're choosing, I pick Fílga's, just because that angry eye twitch of his is hilarious and he needs to remember being nearly thirty isn't that old. Me, on the other hand—"

"You need to arise, Lady," Kórol murmurs, stomping to the bed and smiling at me with ice-bright eyes. "Today starts your Trials." The capitalization is apparent.

"Trial? What trial?"

He reaches out and smooths a bed rumpled clump of hair, tucking it behind my ear. "Your first test as a Candidate for the Sìnnách begins today."

I bat his hand away. "I didn't realize there would be tests. Fílga said—"

Fílga peeks through the door. "Oh good, you're awake."

"Hardly," Kórol grunts. Tans, now standing by the door, huffs.

"This is still my bedroom!" I throw the covers over my head.

"Be in the throne room in ten minutes," Kórol demands. Seconds later, all three men leave, latching the door behind them.

Nine minutes later, I slink down to the throne room. I took my time dressing, deciding my favorite (and only) pair of worn jeans might bring luck for whatever test they've concocted.

The room sounds as boisterous as it did when Kórol announced my candidacy, but instead of being packed with people, the noises are animalistic. When I open the heavy wooden door and peer inside, I immediately heave it closed. Fílga must have seen me as he yanks open the door from the other side and drags me over the threshold.

I was only partly right—the sounds come from a growling and scowling dragon. It's as black as tar, with tiny scales that wrap around its body and wings. The only color it has is found in its bright red eyes. Up close, it fills the corner of the room, about double the size of an Earth horse. When it rears, it stands taller than the windows behind it, with black skin stretched tight over its skeletal wings and a sinuous neck that flares from side to side. I remember why I fainted the first time I saw one.

In the opposite corner cower four men in black leather, all stockier than Kórol and taller than Fílga, each whimpering noisily. Tansr tilts his head in my direction as a greeting and turns back to inspecting one of the men, with two women in white beside him.

"What are the odds that's one of Sáven's lesser-known forms?" I joke nervously. Fílga doesn't react, whether because he's ignoring my lame attempt at humor, or he's too focused on the danger in the back corner.

He drags me closer to it. "They managed to corral it inside the castle through a series of ropes and back passages, thank Fates, though I do not believe any of those men will rush to accept a request from the King anytime soon," he explains in hushed tones. "The rest is up to you."

I whip my head back to him so fast my neck cracks. "I thought dragon riding was a metaphor," I hiss, watching the beast from the corner of my eye. Fílga lifts one shoulder elegantly, too casually for what he demands I do.

"We shall find out," he says. The dragon roars.

"You have got to be kidding me!" I squeal, hiding behind him and pulling on his tunic. "I've learned my lesson after the dobhà. Hell, I have the scar from it. And I fainted the first time a dragon came near me! You cannot expect me to *ride* it."

Fílga steps out of the way and forcibly unfurls my fingers from his clothing. He spares a minute to straighten the tunic I crumpled before pushing me towards the dragon. "We have faith in you." He gestures to the opposite corner where a red leonine creature with green eyes sits on his haunches next to an ochre wolflike creature, flanked by six men in black leather. "And insurance in multiple forms."

With a final deep breath, I shuffle towards the dragon. I grouse the entire way, specifically about why in the hell they chose the throne room for this, because thinking about my inevitable demise isn't a pastime I enjoy. There are surely plenty of other rooms in this place, with a dozen or more spires and levels. *Or, novel idea, outside!*

I stop halfway towards the dragon, doing anything I can to delay the Trial, and study the stained-glass windows, the ones I didn't have the desire to inspect the day of Kórol's announcement. I take my time now because the alternative is an immediate Grace Bar-be-que, though I should have confirmed whether dragons here can breathe fire. One windowpane stands out, red and yellow reflect light brilliantly and abut black panes, showing a dragon sitting on its haunches behind a feminine figure in black and red, wind whipping her long dark hair as her outstretched hand presses against the dragon's snout. It reminds me of a long-suppressed memory of a movie I saw with Mom.

I meander closer to the reptile, extending my arm like the woman in the window, silently cursing everyone in that room. If this works, I will probably pass out. If this doesn't work and the dragon takes a bite out of me, I will *definitely* pass out. The dragon watches my outstretched hand, cautiously prowling forward. Murmurs sound behind me.

"Hi, dragon. There's a good dragon," I call in the sweetest and lowest voice I can muster. I'd laugh at myself if I wasn't inches from being eaten. The dragon's red eyes focus on mine as my hand grazes the skin of its nose, right between the nostrils. It feels softer than I expect, less like a snake and more like expensive suede.

It allows my touch longer than I expected, before it finally vaults over me to make its escape. I crouch to avoid it, but its long tail whips into my hand, slicing the backs of three fingers.

Someone behind me throws open the wider of the two throne room doors and it shrieks before becoming lifting off and flying out. Sáv, the wolf-being, and a half dozen soldiers chase after it. There had better be an easy exit to the outside or the castle's inhabitants are in for a big surprise.

My three remaining friends surround me. Tansr grabs my hand as blood drips onto the dark stone, but I'm too wired to feel the pain. Kórol looks jubilant, better than I expect considering I failed the trial.

"She was wonderful," Kórol says, eyes shining.

"What the hell are you talking about? It didn't let me tame *or* ride it," I snap.

Fílga fidgets with the end of his long braid. "No one has drawn so near a dragon in centuries. This will be recorded as a success in the annals of our history."

"But I touched it and it fully freaked out!"

Kórol speaks directly to Fíl, his voice loud enough to echo around the empty room. "As I expected. Continue your research on the remaining Trials, as we have less than a week before the Solstice." He leaves the throne room in a blur without saying goodbye or checking to see if I'm alright. I suppose I should be thankful he isn't declaring his love again, but I only feel cold.

Frustrated, I stare down at my hand and watch Tansr kiss the closing cuts until the skin heals and the blood vanishes. My lips curl but before I can utter a word, he releases me and sprints after Kórol.

Fílga mumbles unintelligibly, making notes. When he finishes, he hides the book in a pocket. "While it may be a metaphor, it was a good show, nonetheless. I cannot wait to see the next one."

Like someone pulled a plug on my emotions, all the adrenaline masking my fear drains out. I whirl towards Fílga, realizing how close this one came to a bad ending. If the remaining Trials are anything like this one, I'm doomed.

"What the hell, Fíl!" I smack him in the shoulder. "Why didn't you mention the Trials before?"

"We have not had a Candidate in so long," he begins, his fingers knitting together at his stomach. "I had forgotten but was guided to a book I'd not catalogued in the library previously. It described the relevant rituals. In prior centuries, we had so many false Candidates who wanted fame and power that the King fashioned the Trials to root out false Candidates"

"The *King* came up with these?"

His eyes glaze over in thought before he uncrosses his arms. "Yes, a past King, although I know not which one."

"You can't keep stuff like this from me again. I'm not good at surprises, especially when they involve dragons!"

"I planned to explain, but we had a burst of good luck catching a dragon this morning, leaving no time to provide notice." He looks to the windows as if searching his memory. "There will be four trials in total. The Trial of the Beast, the Trial of the Feast, the Trial of the Will, the Trial of the Skill. If you succeed, you are presented to the Great Matron on the Winter Solstice where she will bless you."

This isn't the first time I've heard rhymes before. The thought slithers back into my mind—that man, the second one who kidnapped me. "More rhymes," I groan.

Fílga cocks his head, the glazed look gone and the curious researcher face in its place. "Rhymes have power, magic even. Do you have experience with them?" I'm not feeling generous with information and remain silent. His lips purse but he continues. "Well, you've passed the Trial of the Beast. Your next Trial will be tomorrow."

"Which is that?"

"Trial of the Feast, of course. The next in the rhyming pair." He pulls us towards the door before abruptly stopping a foot away. "I almost forgot—we intend to celebrate your success this evening. Sáven has already directed the kitchen staff to prepare a delicious dinner. You should get changed." He exits through the grand wooden door.

Before Fíl can disappear down a hallway, a thought slips in and I call out to him. "What happens if I don't finish the Trials?"

His face is half in shadow, but the grimace is there all the same. "You should not concern yourself with that.

"Fíl, come on. What about the *other* Candidates, those that weren't Sìnnách?"

His spares me a glance for the briefest of seconds. "They died."

CHAPTER 18

I immediately search for Tans. A man wearing a black armor directs me to one of the beautiful green spaces in Ilsen. I find him in a floral garden balcony, one that spans the width of the throne room as the stained-glass windows act as one side of the square garden. I scowl at the windows as I trudge towards Tans.

"Did you know about the Trials?" I growl, poking him in the chest when I get near enough.

"Kórol—Kórol told me this morning," he stammers. "Had I known you were unaware, I would have told you when you awoke."

"When did Fílga know? Kórol?" Tansr says nothing. "Why didn't they tell me? Warn me?" My voice catches in my throat.

Even though we're alone in the garden, Tansr keeps his voice low. "I don't know what Kórol knew, love. But you shouldn't worry."

"Not worry?" I hiss. "Fílga said the Candidates who failed *died*. I'm a little worried!"

"That will not happen to you. Those Candidates came to the Kingdom as false saviors, to take from us. You didn't, you have said it yourself. You didn't ask to be tested. They did, and the Trials stole their lives as consequence. You gave no claim and asked for nothing. If you fail, no harm will become you." He shakes his head hard enough to dislodge the two small braids he tucked behind his ears. "I will not—my King will let nothing hurt you."

"That isn't *that* reassuring." There's no guarantee Kórol won't overreact when he realizes he's infatuated with a normal person and not the Sìnnách. There's no guarantee the Great Matron won't bring down justice when she discovers the mistake. I find myself longing for the early days when I thought this was a dream, or the weeks during the pilgrimage when foot callouses and worrying about my feelings for Tansr were my only problems.

He stares at me, eyes intent with a frown on his handsome face. Silently, he holds out his hand and I let him direct us down a row of delicate mauve irises. After we turn to the next row, he speaks. "I see the torment within your eyes. The nutty color appears bruised, like a wilted autumn leaf."

"Thanks a lot," I grumble.

He smirks and stops to smell a sunny yellow daffodil. "As you see, I have a vested interest in cheering you up. You are much more pleasing to look at when you remain in high spirits." I'm in no mood for false assurances and turn to go back inside with a sigh. He grasps both hands in his and rubs them. "I jest, Butterfly. Please. Let me hold your worries for you. Surely the Trials did not cause you this much misery."

I close my eyes to avoid the sincerity on his face. "It's too much—the Candidacy and Trials and trying to prepare for Her." And I can't do any of it.

"Shall I tell you the story of the caterpillar?"

With a snort, I pop my eyes open. "Again, with the butterflies and caterpillars? Did you have a butterfly garden as a kid or something?"

He pats my arm placatingly, little jolts of heat spilling over into my skin before directing us down the next row. "I am nothing if not consistent in my metaphors, love. Now, the caterpillar knows not what will happen when it begins its cocoon. Perhaps it feels scared. Maybe it is angry it had no warning of the impending change. Or it's confused about what may yet happen. But it does it all the same. "

"I'm pretty sure it's a biological requirement for it to get into a cocoon, at least on Earth. And I don't think caterpillars have emotions."

We stop midway down the row, rich gold marigolds to my left, winter white poppies to my right. "Hush. The sentiment is the same. It takes that chance, not knowing whether it will transform into a butterfly, not knowing what may yet happen to it when it enters or emerges from that cocoon. But it does it anyway."

"And what if I don't turn into a butterfly? What if I'm only a moth?"

He chucks me under the chin, amber eyes blazing. "Both still fly, dearest."

I lean against his shoulder and sniffle. "Your analogies could use a little work. But I appreciate you trying."

He exhales, heat physically rolling off him as he chuckles. "I will do my best for you, as long as I can." He plucks a purple lilac and tucks it behind my ear. "With that settled, will you join me tonight after the feast? I would like to speak with you privately."

I scan the empty garden. "More private than now?"

He bumps my shoulder. "A different private."

I think about our mistaken kiss, the many non-dates we've been on, and that he's one of the few good things in my life. And still I say, "I'd love to."

Tans escorts me to the opening feast several hours later, taking me to a wing slotted between two southern spires, where another large windowless stone room waits for us.

This one is filled with long tables of food and wine and lit by colossal candelabras hanging from the stone ceiling many stories above us. The ceiling tapers upward, meaning we must be inside one of the spires we strolled past, and the candles create shapes in the flickering shadows around us. In a corner, a small quartet of musicians thrums folksy music. When we arrive at our seats, Tansr sits on one side of me with Kórol on the other. Kórol doesn't greet me, and I don't acknowledge him.

"You look lovely tonight," Tans murmurs and I grin back at him.

Over the past week, someone provided me more dresses to wear. Most resemble more luxurious versions of the simple dresses worn in Chead, the only difference being color and fabric choice. A few are more ornate, with delicate black and silver stitching on red or blue cloth. Tonight, I wear a blood red gown that cinches at the waist, something powerful and bold. The bodice cups my lacking curves, giving me a bust to go with my solid thighs and hips. The neckline dips low and would be indecent if I had any cleavage. Instead, it makes me look taller and leaner, a formal replica the figure in glass in the throne room. I added two small braids by my ears as an homage to Tans. I have nothing to use to tie the braids, meaning my waves will undo them by the night's end.

I lower my head to my chest while imagining how they might unravel, assuming Tans wants to speak with me privately about what I think, *hope*, he does. Anything to keep my mind off the Trials. Romance is safe, something I've read enough about, and I rehearse what Tans might say and how I'll respond. All those hours spent putting myself in the protagonist's place of every book I read, and *finally*, it will be real.

People pass platters full of all kinds of meats and plant dishes, but I accept few of the offerings. I have little appetite, but I pick at my plate to support Sáv's efforts. After servants clear the food, the music plays a lively jig and couples edge into the open space between the tables. When the space is half-full of dancers, Tans looks down at me through full lashes and motions to the dancers. Flushing, I follow him to the dance.

"I have been thinking more about your *secondary* purpose here," he murmurs, taking my hands. "I would like to speak with you more, if you are amenable."

My heart preemptively constricts in disappointment as I consider *that* is the topic he wanted to discuss. It's asking too much for two men to decide they're madly in love with me. But I need to be sure— "Is that what you wanted to talk about in private?"

He shakes his head and winks. "That's an entirely different subject."

I bite my lip around a smile and focus on the dance, watching his feet bounce in a rhythm I can't follow. *Will he ask to speak to me privately later? Will he take me to his room? Walk me to mine?* While I run our potential romance through my head, I falter and step on his foot.

"There's no need for you to worry about the steps, my love. You could lie down on the floor and pretend to be a fish, and no one would comment. In fact, let us do that," he teases, pulling my wrist downward.

I laugh, freeing myself from his grip. "Tans!"

Smirking, he puts his arms back around my waist. While watching the others dancing, my feet tap in a pattern of my own. Frustrated and forcing down the amorous thoughts for now, I try repeatedly as Tans watches my steps. After the fourth time, he mimics my nonsensical movement instead of following the steps.

"There you go. See? You can do no wrong in their eyes."

I falter and stumble over one of my feet at the reminder. "Only because they think I'm the Sìnnách," I say glumly.

"Because you're *you*. Do we honestly need to talk about the caterpillar again? Even *I* feel I have overused that analogy today." His hands, still holding mine, warm my skin.

"Why do you have so much faith in me?" I ask, still looking at my feet to avoid tripping again. He pulls my chin upward to look into my eyes. The sincerity is blinding.

"Because I can feel it. I feel it under my skin and behind my eyes. I feel it in my bones and blood. Sìnnách or no, I know you are important."

My face heats involuntarily and I duck to avoid him seeing my blush. I don't believe him, but the thought is nice. "You sound like Kórol."

"A welcome comparison," he says, but he sounds upset. As if he hears his name, Kórol stalks towards us, causing Tansr to release my hands like they scald him. He tips his head as Kórol takes his place, but my eyes track Tans who leaves the room. I frown at Kórol's interruption.

Kórol doesn't follow the steps either but sways, a move that feels awkward with the lively fiddle music surrounding us. I shift his hands from my low back up to my hips. "You resemble a goddess incarnate, angel," he rumbles, raking his pale eyes over me. "Would that I could pay you the tribute you deserve."

"Kórol—we need to talk," I say, keeping my voice softer than the music, hopeful that the phrase has the same connotations as Earth. Given he stares back at me with a simpering smile, it doesn't. I continue, more forcefully this time. "All the love talk needs to stop. I'm—I'm sorry, but I don't feel that way about you."

His brow furrows, and his eyes glaze for an instant before clearing and returning to their striking blue. "Am I hideous?

I glance at the other dancers before answering quietly. "No, but that's not the point."

"Must we have this discussion now?" When I frown again, he eyes the room, and I parrot his actions. Reassured that no one watches, he directs me out of the banquet hall. The stone hall chills me but is quiet as only a low rumble from the musicians and revelry follows us. Silently, he leads me down a series of stairways and passages until we stand before the throne room.

"This is my favorite place to be during the still of the night," he explains as he opens the door.

I can see why. There's a weighted tranquility to the room that was absent during my prior visits; our footsteps echo off the stonework and our shadows play on the walls. He gestures to the stained-glass windows illuminated by the night sky behind them. "These are the stories of my people. This is our history, and who you will be protecting." He points out the glass dragon with its Sìnnách master. He shows me the shards of glass, of red, blue, and green were of the three elements: fire, ice, and air and their meaning. The last pane is of a man, woman, and child. The woman poses in white, her dark eyes crinkling at the corners and blond hair haloing around her head, as her hands rest on the shoulders of the child. The man stands beside her wearing dark blue. Joy radiates from the adults' faces. Only the child, decked in purple robes and sitting at their feet, frowns. Above the three, an inscribed motto, "Bound by our history, led to our future."

Kórol stands under the last window, pressing a hand to his heart as torment bleeds into his expression. "This is my favorite scene. When I was a child, I sat under this window and prayed the Great Matron found me worthy enough to bring the Sìnnách to my people."

Something about how vulnerable he looks forces away my irritation. He's acting irrationally, but his family searched for the Sìnnách for centuries. If I were in his position, I might make hasty and unfounded conclusions too. Didn't I do the same when I thought this place was a dream? I grabbed the closest, easiest, explanation and ran with it. If I'm the first person he's been attracted to, and I showed up at the end of the pilgrimage, it's not a surprise he'd connect the wrong dots. He's still my friend and I want to support him.

I stand beside him and pat him on the shoulder. Taking the opportunity I unintentionally presented, he spins and grabs my hips. He drags me closer until our chests graze together, and chills scratch down my spine. My hands go to his shoulders to force distance between us.

"Kórol, I'm incredibly flattered that you're interested in me, but I only care about you as a friend."

The door behind us bursts open and Tans' voice calls from behind us. "Kórol, have you seen Grace? I wished to speak with her when your business concluded."

Kórol pulls me closer. I shove at him, but he holds me close as he peers over me to look at Tans, tightening grip on my hips. "She is here. My Sìnnách, my love." He kisses my cheek while I wriggle in protest. When his arms loosen, I shoot away from him and smack him on the arm.

"Stop that," I bark before shuffling towards Tans.

Kórol winks, an action that looks unnatural on him. "I apologize for taking liberties in front of Tansr," he says.

"But you would have taken such liberties alone?" Tansr's question seems teasing but the glare on his face says otherwise.

Kórol ducks his head. "I cannot deny my feelings for the Sìnnách. You may speak with her."

Tans bows and leaves the room.

"You're not in charge of me and we're going to finish this conversation about you not listening to me," I call back to Kórol while I exit the room to follow Tans.

Tans doesn't stop so I break into a run, tripping on the dress and stumbling after him. I grab his sleeve before he can turn down another hall. "Hey, I thought we were going to talk?"

"I didn't mean to interrupt you and Kórol," he says, eyes focused on the stone wall behind me and shaking off my touch.

I groan. "*Don't* get me started on that mess. We need to talk about this 'being in love' thing. But I don't want to talk about Kórol. I want to hear whatever you had to say and finish the conversation you wanted to start outside earlier." Tans shifts farther from me and clears his throat. "What's wrong?"

"Grace—don't make me do this."

I reach for him again, but he sidesteps away. "Don't make you do what? I thought we were getting along, and maybe—"

"Kórol is a good man. He's my friend and my King. Don't make me convince you, I could not bear it."

"What are you talking about?"

He shakes his head and pivots away from me. "I have had too much mead. Perhaps we may speak another time."

He abandons me in the hallway.

CHAPTER 19

T rial of the Feast arrives the next morning, leaving no time to mope about whatever's wrong with Tans or the rejection I felt for the second time.

It's Fílga who drags me to the test, not Tans, and I try not to show how discouraged I am by that fact. Before he lets me leave the room, Fíl presses one of the day dresses into my arms, a thick black fabric that drapes past my tennis shoes and covers my arms.

After I'm dressed and we descend the spire, Fíl stops us at castle gates, where Kórol waits with a grave expression. A frisson of dread unfurls in my chest. Whatever will happen today can't be good.

"Trial of the Feast requires the Candidate to prove what bounty, what value she could bring to the Kingdom," Fíl explains, not looking me in the eye.

My sense of humor and general presence isn't enough, Fíl clarifies, after I suggest it. "You must bring us something precious and rare, Lady. I have consulted the texts, and the King demands you bring him a sprite."

"A sprite?"

Fílga and Kórol dip their heads as one. "It is one of the few pure beings left in our world," Fíl says. "They are magic, born of the Eósy unlike most other beasts that visit us through the rift."

"Sure, of course. A land of dragons and magic must have sprites." I peer beyond the gates, suspicious of how easy it sounds. "Where do I find one?"

Kórol follows my eyeline and points to the left of the town. "They live on the edge of our land and the sea, just north of one of the smaller Gates. No more than a half day's journey east. You should arrive before sunset if you are quick."

The long dress seems bizarre for a hike to the ocean, but maybe I'll need to convince the sprite to visit and resembling a Sàrkany woman will help. "Better than the dragon. I'll find a sprite, invite it to a feast and see you tonight."

"No," Fíl says solemnly. "You will find it and bring back its corpse for the feast."

"You want me to—to *kill* something you just told me was precious and rare. You know I can't kill anything."

Fílga and Kórol murmur amongst themselves for a minute before Fílga finally pats me on the shoulder. "It is meant to test you, Lady. That is the purpose of these Trials—to prove you are worthy as our guide or—" He doesn't finish his explanation and I don't need the audible reminder.

They leave me just inside the castle gates where I loiter for several minutes. As I scuff the ground in irritation, I consider turning right around and telling them they could go to wherever amounts to Hell in this realm. But the threat of what might happen if I don't go through with the Trial weighs on me—not death, this Trial can't kill me, but the disappointment that I've let my friends down. Failing the Trial is one thing, the Pack could forgive that, but ignoring it completely? That's a step too far. And I can't ignore the tiniest part of me that wants them to be right and show that I *am* something special.

When I finally convince myself to move, feeling sorrier for myself than I have a right to considering I plan to kill another being, persistent footsteps thump behind me. Tans and Sáven are scurrying in my direction. Our missed connection from the night before settles in under my skin as I catch the muted look on his face.

"I thought you should speak with Sáv before leaving," Tans mumbles, cuffing Sáv on the shoulder.

I can't look him in the eyes. "I take it you know what they want me to do?"

Sáven sniffs, his fingers fidgeting with his stained tunic. "Aye, I do."

"I know this is the Trial and this—this is your culture. But I don't like the idea of killing something, especially something that's pure and innocent."

"Remember what I said—'s not a killing but a sacrifice for the kingdom."

I twist my lips. It's one sacrifice in the place of another. "Do you think I should go through with it?"

He looks at the gates and speaks more gravely than I've ever heard from him. "Sometimes we do difficult things, not because we want to, but because we need to." He looks back at me. "Whatever you choose—be prepared for the consequences."

Tans clears his throat. "I also thought you might need this," he says, handing over the dagger Kórol gave me when he fruitlessly attempted to teach me self-defense, something I left in my chambers. I take the knife and thank him for being there, but my words hit his back as he slips away.

Sáven points me to the northwest, and I start on my half day's journey. The town at the base of the castle is bustling with business and life. In my dark dress, I look no different than the many women wandering the dusty streets. The anonymity hides me as I shuffle towards the sea.

The salty spray reaches my nose before the waves pierce my ears. It reminds me of visiting my grandmother after Mom died, and, for a moment, I pretend this is a cherished memory with her. I'm here to spread my toes in the water while Grandma asked me about boys or the latest book I read before she died and left me more alone.

As the sun slips into the horizon, I toss myself down onto the soft sand, flinging the knife in my pocket away while I wait for sunset. I bring my knees to my chest and lay my head against them. Too late I realize I don't know what a sprite looks like. Water licks up the hem of the black and dusty dress. I should have tried harder to find a way home, instead of gambling so much on the *possibility* of being someone important.

The waning sun glistens off the waves as the wind flaps the damp hem of my dress against my ankles. The water twinkles in the dim light. When a wave crests, diamond droplets glitter brighter until a single little diamond leaves the water, balancing about a foot above the spray.

The little diamond flies towards me, a genderless figure with wings. They are less than three inches tall, with spiky white hair, black eyes, and a naked, milky white body. They land in the sand a few feet in front of me, their light glinting a bright green. Their hair stays white, but their body is a shock of neon.

"Hello, human." Their voice is melodious, not the childish tone I'd expect from something that petite but full and radiating sensuality.

"Hi, sprite." I cringe. I'm not the most socially adept in the best of times and have no idea how to carry on a conversation with something I'm supposed to kill.

"You watch us in the water," they say curiously, tipping their head to one side and slowly blinking their black eyes.

"Well—the sea's beautiful."

"But it makes you sad." The light flickers, the green fading.

I can't explain my reason for being out here, not when the choice I plan to make involves snuffing out the diamond in front of me. "It reminds me of my grandmother," I finally say. "And I miss her."

"True. But there is more." Their surrounding light turns yellow, a duller and less bright glimmer, and they narrow their little eyes. "Tell me why you approach."

I wrap my arms around my waist. "I'd—I'd rather not say."

The light flares, turning sparking orange. "If you do not tell, we cannot help you."

"I guarantee you *don't* want to help me, no matter what reason I give you."

"Why not?"

Huffing bitterly, I scrub a hand over my face. "Because I came to kill one of you. Because I'm choosing my own life over yours."

The light fades from orange back to brilliant white before returning to neon. They hum and fly to stand on my bent knees, feeling no heavier than a feather. They give off a warm glow that seeps into the skin beneath my black dress, like a more condensed version of Tan's comforting heat.

"This I knew before I left the water. Others kill us to hide their true selves. You wish to kill us to reveal something. I see that you must prove yourself worthy, but I do not understand why."

"Because it's a test," I explain, wishing Sáv was here. "I have to bring back something special to show I'm a savior for the people of Dalner."

The sun sets while we speak, and the sprite blinks a dazzling white in the darkness. "I am special. I see why I am prized. Why are *you* special?"

What a loaded question. I groan and slump until my forehead grazes my knees, dislodging them and they hover a foot away. "I'm not. It's all coincidence and circumstance anyway. I should've tried harder to get out of this at the beginning."

The light flashes red and they give off sparks. The sprite crosses their arms and scoffs. "Lie."

I scowl back, choosing anger at them over anger at myself for killing something when I don't believe I'll succeed in the Trials. "You don't know that."

The light fades to pink and then white. "I do. I carry that gift."

"Then why'd you—" I straighten to stare directly in their doll black eyes. "You—you can tell I'm special, that I'm the Sìn-nách?"

They cock their head to the side again. "Future-speak is not my gift. I see something chose you especially, but not why." They trill softly. "I will give my light to the special Grace."

"You mean you'll—"

"You may take my light until it fades. Split my throat to take my light. I will accept death for you."

There's too much to unpack in its declaration that I'm 'special,' it could be they speak of my purpose with Her and nothing to do with the Sìnnách, but I won't deny the gift they give me. Bile rises in my throat as I force myself to reach the knife.

"Thank you," I say shakily. I don't have the words to say more.

They sit back on my folded knees and shine a brilliant white, lifting their head high and staring at the stars above us. I carefully make a small slash at the juncture between their chest and neck. The light blazes and I desperately want to look away before it blinds me, but I don't. *Honor the death you take*, Sáv told me once; *accept the consequences*, he'd said that morning.

It takes twenty minutes for the light to fade, leaving only a tiny body resembling a child's toy in my lap. I hold them in my cupped hands and hope their gift was true. If I'm not the Sìnnách, I may never forgive myself.

The wet slap of my dress on the earth marks my long trek home. I arrive in Ilsen when the castle is quiet, the moon sitting high overhead and Kórol and Fílga lingering by the gates. Blinking away tears, I open my cupped palms and show them the sprite. They both peer into my hands as one.

"The Trial of the Feast is successful," Fílga announces. "We will hold the Feast on another day, when you are less—fraught."

Fraught with what is still in question. "What do I do now?" I ask softly.

Kórol reaches to take the body. "We bury it."

My hands snap closed, and I protect the sprite against my chest. "What?"

"You completed the Trial," Kórol says. "Now we bury the body."

As if hearing my thoughts, Fílga pats my shoulder. "It was not in vain. The sprite helped continue your path as a Candidate. Now we honor it with a burial."

"I'll do it. It's my consequence to handle."

Kórol and Fílga exchange glances before pointing to a small area beside the entrance wall.

"I am proud of you," Kórol says as Fíl leaves to find a shovel.

"Don't talk to me. I don't like you much right now," I hiss, my frustration and heartache cracking through any civility I might otherwise muster. "You don't get to feel good about what you're making me do. You didn't even have the decency to warn me about the Trials or what happens if I fail. You don't care about *me*, just what I can do. If you did, you'd *listen* when I talk to you."

"Do not chastise me, dearest, when every atom of your flesh is as dear to me as my own," he whispers, his eyes, nearly white, darting around my face. That phrase pings something within me. I've heard it before, or read it before. He continues, "The intensity of my feelings—"

"Oh, screw your feelings!" I snap. Anger breaks through his obstinance as he staggers back as if I slapped him. I close my eyes and sniffle. "I—I need to finish this, honor their death. Then we'll talk again. Okay?"

He remains silent until Fíl arrives and then he lumbers back inside. Fílga stands beside me like a sentry while I dig the hole myself.

CHAPTER 20

I wake early the next morning, head aching and eyes sore. The sprite said I was special, and I need to believe them to get through the next few days. Everything else—the obsessive infatuation from Kórol, the odd behavior from Tans, the continued deterioration of my mental health—must be set aside until the Trials end. No one arrives by midmorning, meaning my day is my own.

Begrudgingly, I spend it in the library researching the Woman, another topic I tried to avoid.

I push the stack of books left to transcribe to the edge of my worktable and search for books on Dark Eósy. Prior Historians organized the contents of the library by year, and Fíl maintained the system, meaning finding helpful books is difficult. After some grumbling, but less than I expect, he brings me several books on the topic.

He piles a dozen books in front of me, having already warned me that none of them may be helpful, as a fire started in the library many centuries prior and destroyed older tomes. Before leaving, he fiddles with the pile, lining up the corners of the wooden and leather spines.

"Have you spoken to Sáven recently?" he asks, keeping his eyes on the table.

"Yesterday. Why?"

"No reason," he says. I peer up at him and he has an overly casual expression on his face. I expect him to whistle nonchalantly next. "How was he?"

"He seemed okay. He gave some great advice about making hard decisions but being prepared for the consequences. He's an angel."

Fíl furrows his brows. "What is an 'a-n-jel'?"

"You don't know what—never mind. Maybe you should talk to him yourself?"

Fíl sighs and shakes his head. "Thank you, Lady. I must return to my writings." He abruptly spins and bounds to the other end of the long table. Soon, walls of books surround his workspace, physically hiding from my gaze.

With a sigh, and because I'm in no place to help with someone *else's* relationship, I start reading.

> The main Gate remains closed, though the Dark have sought to breach it and its sisters since the wall's erection. Without the wall and Gates keeping them in, their magical reign would inhale everything in their path. It is the Light that aids us in the Gates' defenses...

Some of it is interesting from a historical perspective, but not helpful. Of the books Fíl found, most are nightmare fodder, bleak fairy tales that explain why Sàrkany seem tough (though that could also be the Medievalist lifestyle). A few of the stories may be about Her or others like Her, but none explain how to defeat Her.

"Hey, Fíl," I call after I finish skimming the books he set out.

He murmurs something unintelligible from across the room, sounding distracted.

"I can't remember. How do you tell the difference between a Light Eósy and a Dark Eósy?"

The scratch of a quill on parchment stops. "You cannot. It's an ideological difference, not a physical one."

"So, it's just a guess whether the Eósy you're interacting with is Dark or Light?"

"It is an act of trust and faith," he counters. "In an ideal situation, one can ask them a direct question as to their positions, and their inability to lie will out them as Dark or Light. But such direct answers may be considered interference, meaning you may not receive the proof you desire. Regardless, there is little risk of harm unless you inadvertently invite them into your mind."

I think of the two kidnappers whose memories still spin around in my head. "Can a Dark Eósy *make* someone do something?"

"Yes," Fíl says, the words sounding forced from him. "But that ability belongs to any Eósy with the gift in their bloodline, not simply the Dark. If you call for them specifically, you lose the protection from their full influence and, if they have the magic for it, they can spell you do to all manner of things. If they wiggle into your mind, they can only indirectly influence you through soft persuasion or manipulation, and only those families who have the skills." His head pops up above the wall of books and he purses his lips at my empty workspace. "Are you finished with your independent research yet? Sìnnách or not, those texts won't transcribe themselves."

I convince Fíl that a feast after the Trial of the Feast is both redundant and in poor taste. Before dinner, he leaves to make sure no one prepares a lavish meal, stammering about needing to visit the kitchen specifically.

After scarfing down a delivered dinner standing in the corner, I finish the evening in the library. I revisit all my notes about the desires of the Eósy and how to tell the difference, of which there are few and none tell me anything useful about Her.

When I prepare to leave after sunset, a buzzing sound echoes around my work space. If I weren't sitting in a magical world not my own, I'd assume my cell phone was ringing, but that piece of worthless plastic is sitting in my room with my few other possessions. I search the table for the source of the noise but find nothing.

The buzzing repeats when I head towards the exit, combining with a stinging in my temple. I lean against the stone wall nearest the door, pressing my fingers to my eyes to stave off the pain. When it vanishes, I stagger closer to the door until another bolt of pain strikes. This one hits harder, and I stumble backward several feet. I lean forward on the table, waiting for it to recede, accidentally jostling one of the Dark Eósy books I read earlier and the pain increases. Groaning, I slide back, hitting the pile of books in my queue for transcription. They topple like dominoes, more than half of them battering against me and leaving aches in their wake.

Only two books remain on the table after my accident and I'm loath to touch either in case they injure me again. But I can't leave the library a mess, no matter the sudden migraine plaguing me. I grab both books, one in each hand. The one in the left stings, but the one on the right feels normal. When I run my fingers over the burned-in sun on the front cover, the remaining pain vanishes. I put it aside while I stack up the remaining books, all which create a stinging in my hand that travels to my head. It's a painful version of the 'hot or cold' game where someone or something wants me to read the journal again.

I scan a section in the middle.

> I am to choose a bride soon. They are all immensely beautiful, but I feel no spark. Our histories tell me when I find her, I will feel whole. I've chased the

sentiment and found satisfaction of flesh but felt nothing but the exquisite release. Fat chance of one of these simpering fools managing that.

Nothing about it seems helpful or worthwhile, including the sexist rant. Dropping the journal, I start for the door again, and the pain has me doubled over.

"You win," I say between the spikes stabbing my brain. I slip the book into the satchel tied around my waist, because like medieval Europe, women's clothing in Dalner have no attached pockets.

When I arrive at my room, I take out my notes and the journal and toss them on my side table. I've learned little, miss my best friend, and am days away from possible death at the Solstice. I just want to sleep.

When I pull on my tunic from Chead and get under the covers, the buzzing starts again. With a growl, I grab the journal and read another entry, hoping to placate it enough to let me rest.

I am amazed I still write in these bound sheets, but Mother's wheedling hit its mark. I find myself wanting to write and knowing that these words will mean something someday. Is that odd? (And have I gone demented by asking my question to a crisp piece of parchment that can never answer?) On the chance I am not writing into the abyss but am doing so for future generations as Mother suggests, take heed. Terrible things will occur when I ascend.

The words swim on the page. Its importance eludes me, but even drops of water can crack a stone. Something in this journal must be significant or it wouldn't demand attention.

"Finally," a child's voice shouts from the corners of my room. I fall backward in bed, tossing the journal to the side and covering my eyes.

"I did not need that with this migraine. Finally, *what*?"

The Voice giggles. "If you know what I am, then you know telling you is too near true influence. If you don't know, after all that studying, you're less observant than I thought. A shame, considering my expectations of you were low to begin with."

"Alright, that's enough. You think highly enough of me to assume I can destroy Her, whoever she is. That says something more about *you* than me," I say, crossing my arms. "Maybe I should focus on sealing up the damn Gates to keep Her from coming, instead of wild goose chases in the library. I'm betting it would kick you out too," I grumble.

"You lack the knowledge to undertake such a feat," they say absently. "But you are in much higher spirits than I expected. I thought I would find you wailing like a fishwife over the Trials, not behaving so ungraciously about my counsel."

I groan. "Fourteen hours. I went fourteen hours without thinking about them." I lean back on my elbows and scowl at the top of my canopy. "And couldn't you haven't given me a hint or something?"

"Almost everything I say is a hint," they protest. "I even warned you there would be trials."

I reach for my notes and run through my memories of our encounters, finding a single scribbled line from my first day in Ilsen. "Oh my god. I thought you meant trials like difficulty, because, you know, I'm trying to stop a supernatural being. Not *the* Trials, you jerk."

"And now you know what I meant. It was an excellent piece of wordplay, getting around my constraints. I cannot be faulted for your lacking mind."

I raise my middle finger to the ceiling, but the impact lessens as the Voice is neither present nor do they know what that gesture means. "More explicit hints in the future, if you would. I suppose I should take your refusing to answer whether I'm the Sìnnách as a hint too."

"Perhaps," they giggle. "She approaches, Grace. Heed my prior counsel. Deception will be your armor. You must have fire and ice to succeed. And remember: everyone bleeds in the end."

The next morning I'm painstakingly taking notes from the journal when I get a slight reprieve in the form of the next Trial. The journal is both dry *and* whiny, a boring historical autobiography of a spoiled kid. I avoid those genres, which is the only reason I don't complain when Kórol arrives.

He stays eerily quiet as he takes me to the library which signals that the demand today may be worse than the last trial.

Fílga opens the door before Kórol can knock, sporting an expression that's identical to the somber pity he exuded during the Trial of the Feast. I warily let him take my arm and lead me to the center of the room while he speaks under his breath. "The requirements of the Trial of the Will should be obvious to you."

Tansr enters and the sorrow on Fíl's face doubles. "Although we all recognize you have sufficiently passed this Trial already, traditions are traditions," Fílga continues once Tans leans against the closed door. "Part of being a Sìnnách, being our *warrior* and guide, means understanding that sacrifices must be made, and a single person's needs cannot overtake the whole. Sometimes that means forcing someone to do something undesirable for the good of the Sàrkany people."

I swallow thickly, only imaging what horror they might re-quire of me. "Didn't I already do that by having to kill the sprite?"

"Although *you* may have felt forced, that was not the purpose of the Trial of the Feast. This Trial is an outward imposition of such pressure," he reveals, frowning. "The Trial of the Will involves convincing Tansr to betray Kórol."

I cross my arms around my waist. "That's impossible. Aren't they best friends?"

"Which is why it is your task. You must convince him to do something that would be tantamount to ruining their friend-ship. Given Tansr is the general of Kórol's army, such a betrayal would likewise have the potential of hindering any trust between them professionally."

"That's not a helpful way to explain it," I hiss.

"My goal is not to be helpful, but to impress on you, *all* of you, what the Trial of the Will truly is. We are accepting this risk in the hope that your confirmation as Sìnnách will seal these metaphorical breaches." Fíl snags Tans by the shoulders and pushes him towards Kórol until they stand in front of me in a two-person line.

I scowl at both dark-haired men. Tans stands stiffly closest to me, avoiding eye contact and hardly blinking. The light from a window bisects him, half in shadow and half in light. Kórol is parallel to him, all in shadow with clenched fists.

I desperately throw out tolerable options. Even though both have annoyed me recently, no one deserves betrayal. "What if we all play a game, and Tans cheats? Or Tans steals something special? Or tells me one of Kórol's secrets?"

Kórol shifts in place, knocking lightly into Tans who guiltily leaps nearly a foot away. The movement blinds me to Kórol's face, and his pale eyes look white in the light. "None of those would fulfill the task."

"Tans and I will think something up, Kórol," I promise. Perhaps the betrayal is that I don't do anything, that I fake the Trial. "You don't worry about it, and we'll talk to you—"

"The only true betrayal Tans could commit is by becoming intimate with Lady Grace," Kórol announces.

A flustered cackle bursts from me. That isn't a betrayal, particularly since I'm not interested in Kórol, something I've explained to him at least twice. Unless 'bros before hoes' has a Sàrkanian equivalent. Before I can summon a response, Tans yelps.

"We will never be intimate in that manner," Tans cries. "I would not disrespect Kórol in such a way!"

Off flies the remaining hope I have of kindling a romantic relationship with Tans. "Then we won't do the Trial. Fíl, you said I'd already passed it. Maybe we can double count—wait, why would it disrespect *Kórol*?"

By the door, Fíl purses his lips in thought. "As Kórol's beloved, that would surely meet the needs of the Trial."

"I'm not Kórol's—"

"It must be done," Kórol says hoarsely.

"Fílga, surely there is another test," Tans pleads.

"No, but Kórol and I aren't—"

"It pains me to cause such strife," Fíl says. He opens the door and gestures for Kórol to follow. "Let me impress upon you that these feelings are exactly the point of the Trial of the Will. Everyone in this room should be thankful Lady Grace does not need to convince someone to kill themselves."

Kórol throws me one final frown before stomping out of the room. Tans attempts to follow but Fíl shuts the door in his face.

"I did that yesterday," I snap at the closed door.

Tansr leans against the door and knocks his forehead into the wood twice as my stomach clenches.

What counts as intimate anyway? Books would demand something tantamount to sex at the very least, and Tans is a snuggly guy. Maybe I can get by with kissing him again, but it's intolerable when he doesn't want me that way. I sink into a tufted arm chair several feet away. Tans presses his back into the door and stares at the high ceiling above us. "I don't think you can melt through it you know," I tell him miserably.

"I suppose not," he murmurs before pulling himself to sit next to me, close enough that our knees almost touch.

"We could *say* we did. We tell everyone we were intimate, or whatever, and the real betrayal is me convincing you to ditch the Trial."

"That wouldn't count."

"It should. It's a pointless test. I could do *anything* and Kórol would be ecstatic since it's for the Trial. It can't be a real betrayal if he's the one making us do it." I slump, elbows on my knees. *This* is why I'm not the Sìnnách; a real warrior would have *real* tests and would accept them with grace. Except for the Trial of the Beast, none of these are physically challenging—it's all emotional warfare that I still don't have the strength to handle.

"He would care, anyone would care if this happened to them," Tans growls, his face pulled tight and a shadow behind his eyes. It's the most upset I've seen him. "If you were mine and—" He clenches his jaw.

I brush our knees together. "Look, I'm sorry to come between you and Kórol."

He reaches out, something the Tans of two days ago would have done without thought, but lets his hands fall back to his side. "I have not been a good friend to either him or you."

I twist my lips and take one of his hands in mine. "It's okay."

"No, I have been ignoring you and avoiding an important conversation that we must have."

I resist the urge to give myself a one-armed hug. Doubt and tension rush through me like floodwaters. I'm in no mood for Tans to preemptively reject me before we have to be 'intimate.' "Are you sure you want to talk about this? Right now?"

A wan smile replaces his frown. "I believe we must before we complete the Trial. Will you begin?"

I summon up the aborted confession from two nights earlier, but all my pre-planning fails me. "I was—I wanted to talk about you. And our—*relationship*." My bravery fails too, as I choke on the rest of the words. It's ironic that, even with the cheesy romance tropes running around in my head, I can only imply my feelings. It was easier with Dave, when the thought of rejection didn't squeeze my lungs together.

"Say nothing further. You are my dearest friend and will always be." His eyes flash amber while he squeezes my hand. "But I thought you wanted to discuss *Kórol* that night."

There's my answer. I swallow the disappointment, snatching the subject change and vowing to lick my wounds in private later. "Right. Kórol. Well, that's a mess. I still get the idea he wants to marry me and that's—"

My hand burns against Tans' fingers. I whimper and yank it back to my chest, catching a deep pink mark in the shape of Tans' fingers imprinted into my palm.

Quick as a whip, he snatches the burned appendage. "I am terribly sorry," he exclaims, kissing the mark away.

"What the hell happened? If you didn't want to talk about it, you should have said!"

He leans forward to keep hold of my still-injured hand. Both knees rest between mine and he lightly kisses over my palm. If it didn't sting, the butterflies taking flight in my stomach would be overwhelming. Maybe *this* can count as being intimate. "Heightened distress causes us to lose control over our gifts. That is the true reason I left you alone in the hall two nights ago—I was afraid I would accidentally harm you. It appears my fears were warranted. Please forgive me, Grace."

"This Trial is already too uncomfortable without adding spontaneous flames," I grouse, hiding a blush.

His hand trembles in mine. "Let me try again, please. You can tell me anything and I will maintain my control. I am your friend and will support you in every way I can. And my King," he adds.

"Support me right to the hospital," I murmur, leaning forward to hug him tightly and rest my head against his shoulder. He huffs a laugh against my ear as I breathe in his smoky scent and shut my eyes. No matter the rejection, he's my best friend—a flirty, charming, kind, and handsome best friend that I still want to make out with. But that's okay—being in my life is enough.

Our embrace shifts me to almost straddle him. It isn't a new position, as he's hauled me into his lap many times before, but never after I admitted my one-sided crush, and not when we both know Kórol will misinterpret it. Even so, I can't stop a frisson of desire trickling down my spine.

Tans seems equally affected, but from discomfort not attraction. He stiffens against me and his fingers twitch on my hips. I'm a terrible friend for enjoying this awkward situation, one he didn't want and was forced into by demand of others. "Is this intimate enough?" I ask softly, gently, staring into his sparking brown eyes.

He clenches and releases his jaw. "Perhaps," he whispers, breath ghosting over my lips. "Although perhaps we need more?" He trembles as he places my hand over his heart. It's a jackrabbit beat under my palm.

I lean forward as he tilts his head, brushing my lips against his. He whines in the back of his throat as his eyes drift closed. I try to remember that he doesn't want this and that I'd be a monster to enjoy it. But without warning, he grabs my hips and yanks me to straddle him fully. His lips firmly latch onto mine and a tremor runs through me as his hands inch to my low back and neck. His mouth drags along the space behind my ear and then down my neck. The heat in the room rises until I feel like I can't breathe.

Too soon, he tears us apart, gasping and shaking his head. He closes his eyes with a wince as he springs from his seat, knocking me and the chair we share to the ground.

"Congratulations on your success," he says, rubbing his lips with his fingers before barreling through the door.

Fílga and Kórol stand waiting on the other side. Fíl helps me right myself and the chair while Kórol takes rough breaths in the doorway.

"As you bewitched me," Kórol rumbles, his voice gruff and hoarse, "You will bewitch the Kingdom, my Sìnnách."

CHAPTER 21

I hide in the library rest of the day, penitent as I sit where I took advantage of the Trial's demand and forced my best friend into a situation he doesn't want.

My wrinkly notes are the fan to cool my cheeks, flushed from embarrassment, misery, and a pinch of remembered pleasure. Even with the third Trial behind me, I feel no more like the Sìnnách. A Sìnnách is supposed to be the hope for the Kingdom, a friend to all but my actions only break up friendships, my own included. Perhaps when the fourth Trial is over, I can make it up to my friends by defeating Her. At least then I won't be a complete screw up; I'll show I have some value.

Three books on the Dark Eósy remain from those Fíl pulled for me. While the Voice implies the journal will aid me more, I can't slog through another entry from the snotty and self-righteous author, not when I'm behaving similarly. But the Eósy books, like the others, are scrubbed of anything that could explain how to fight the Eósy, or whether She even *was* a Dark Eósy.

When Fílga slips out, I pull the journal from my pocket, unable to avoid it any longer. I spread out my few notes on one of the library's long wooden tables and force myself to read.

Lum nochlms tri...

I rub my eyes roughly. When I stare back at the aging parchment, the words are back in English.

Father took control today as Grandfather nears death. Mother says I should weep for the loss of our patriarch. But I cannot weep, especially for a man I did not know. I have no memories of him, none when he wasn't with Her. Even before Grandmother passed, he kept that Woman by his side. He remained guarded and regularly checked with Her before speaking, as if this Woman was the genuine power and he was merely Her mouthpiece. It is shameful! Father says it is tradition and when he ascends, the Woman will stand by his side as well. Mother will not admit her concerns, but I sense a wariness in her. I cannot blame her.

I almost stop breathing and drop the book loudly on the table in my shock, two pages falling from the binding. After stuffing the ripped entries back inside, I scratch my fingernail down the cover, tracing the sun a few times. If the author writes of my Woman, perhaps it *is* as helpful as the Voice thinks.

The next fifteen pages provide no more useful information, and the bubble of hope that arose at his first mention of the Woman leaks slowly. My eyes nearly bleed while the author complains about a robe fitting and whether one of the bakers had scales under her shift. (Spoilers, she didn't.) But then:

That Woman has me on high alert. I can no longer speak with Father. Even if She remains silent, the words emerging from his are Hers. He is more guarded, as Grandfather was. The Woman watches us closely, Her blood red nails (ghastly things) constantly clicking as if warning. The thought enrages me but there is nothing I can do. Father has made it

clear that he trusts Her unconditionally. To speak
against Her is treasonous. I rue the day someone let
Her through.

My heart thumps out of my chest as I consider what this
means. If it's Her, I have a hint at what She looks like; blood red
nails aren't standard Sàrkany attributes. I flip to the last few pages
of the journal, fingers skipping over entries and disintegrating
corners of the aged parchment, searching for more information
on Her.

"Got any other part I need to read? Help me out here. Don't
consider it influence, but targeted advice." I don't know if I'm
speaking to the journal or the Voice.

"Are you talking to that book?" Fílga stands behind me, his
tone both bemused and suspicious. I slam the journal closed and
shove it into my pocket.

"I get immersed in what I'm reading," I say, gesturing to the
pile of books on the table.

He smiles thinly. "Distractions are helpful during trying
times. I do not mean to interrupt your reading, but the Feast
nears."

Minutes later, he drops me off at my room, patting me on the
shoulder and saying, "Do not let yourself feel troubled. He will
forgive you."

I slump onto my bed as he closes the door behind him. Fíl
doesn't understand whose forgiveness I need—it's not Kórol's.

I dress in another outfit left in my rooms, something simpler
than the bold red dress I wore for the first Feast. I'm finishing
braiding my hair when there's a knock at the door. Tans waits in
the hallway, wearing breeches and an emerald open-necked tunic
that billows at the arms. For the first time since arriving in Ilsen,
he's not in his armor, and I'm not sure what that means. He
doesn't meet my eyes, his gaze not straying far from the ground.

"The Feast," he murmurs.

He remains silent as he leads me down the spiral staircase and across the main floor that will take us to the spire on the other side of the castle. At one point, his hand slides to the small of my back, sending soft waves of heat but as quickly as he does, he pulls away and tucks his hands into his pockets.

Kórol watches as we enter the room, his pale eyes judging the distance between Tans and I. Tans vanishes the moment we breach the large wooden doorway, and Kórol smiles triumphantly.

I'm on display at the head table again, Kórol on my left and some stranger in black armor on my right. After the servants clear a meal that I have no memory eating, the band starts playing. The main table, for all its grandeur, is stifling and I leave the second the ogling eyes turn from me to the dancers.

But Tans is nowhere to be found. I slip into a small room near the back where servers bustle empty trays and goblets, searching for Tans or someone to help me locate him. Sáv's there with a plump redheaded woman, one who resembles him except her face is rounder than his and she stands at my shoulder or shorter. They're in the middle of a conversation and I wait for my opening.

"I've spoken to Ramá's mother's cousin. She works in laundry, you'll remember. She says Ramá's keen to know you," the woman says. Sáv cringes.

"Ma, I don't want to meet Ramá."

Sáven's mother puts her hands on her hips. "Why not? You'll be twenty before you know it. You're not getting any younger. *I'm* not getting any younger."

"I told you, I'm not interested in any of the girls 'round here," he mumbles.

She smacks him on the shoulder, leaving handprints of jam (or blood?) on Sáv's dirty shift. The same handprints are smudged at her waist. "I know that! Thinking I don't know my boy, that I don't listen. Ramá's a strapping lad, big arms. He's an apprentice metalsmith in town. I know you like the wiry ones, but unless that librarian gets his head out of his ar—"

"Miss!" Sáven squeaks when he spies me standing in the doorway. His face is as red as his hair, but his expression bleeds relief. Sáv's mother sees me and flushes too, bringing trembling berry (I hope) stained fingers to her mouth. Sáv sneaks from her side to mine. "You need me?" He widens his eyes expectantly.

"I was looking for Tans." I slide my gaze back to his mother, who stays silent.

"Let me help!" He takes off his apron and tosses it into a corner. "Sorry, Ma. Grace needs me."

His mother returns from her daze to narrow her eyes. "You'll not be leaving me in charge of clean-up."

Sáv makes a face I'd expect on Tans, mischievous and suave as he assures her that he won't while lugging me back through another door. When we arrive in the hallway, he exhales heavily. "Thank you. I'm not prepared for her matchmaking right now. I only confessed before the pilgrimage to keep her from introducing me to some laundress or milkmaid one of her friends' sister's cousin's wives know. Thought I'd be fighting off her matches for months before she accepted."

"It's good she's accepting. And the *librarian*?"

He picks at a dried stain on his tunic. "Not everyone's accepting."

"He'll come around. He's been asking about you. I thought maybe you'd figured things out."

He ducks his head, but pleased expression emerges under his curling hair. When he looks back up, it's gone. "Enough about me, don't want to discuss it. You can't find Tans?"

I slump against the cold stone walls. "He's avoiding me."

Sáv leans next to me, our shoulders brushing, and fiddles with the hem of his shift. "Tans is born to be a general. Good at strategy and when there's battles to fight; he's the first to jump. Gives brilliant advice too, best friend I could have. But for himself? He hates conflict." He peers down the empty hallway and lowers his voice. "Saw him run from a girl once. Tiny little thing, worked in the kitchens with me a few seasons. She gave him a friendly kiss one day when he came to visit, like the kind he offers us all. He turned gray and bolted." He snorts at the memory. "Made me think we might had a little something in common, if you understand. We didn't, but he ran from me for months until I cornered him."

At my raised eyebrows, Sáv laughs again. "He's a people pleaser, and would do anything for his friends if he could. He thought I wanted him but couldn't tell me 'no' for fear of hurting my feelings. Took me forcing the conversation to get us normal again. The Trial, what I heard of it, is messing him up good."

I groan and knock my head against the stone. Sáv sidles closer until he embraces me with one arm. It's nice to experience the contact without the thought that it could mean something else.

"Let me find him," he suggests. "I can scrounge him up before tomorrow's Trial. I'll bring him 'round and lock him in. Good way to corner him, what with no exits."

That's the best I can do, I suppose. "Thanks, Sáv," I say kicking off the wall and extricating from his grip.

"Kórol understands too, he'll know how to handle him. Their friendship's iron-strong. Woman's never come between them."

I flush uncomfortably. "It's not like that with me and—"

"Kórol's feelings are true," Sáv says before I decide whether to finish with 'Kórol' or 'Tans.' "Never seen him with a girl before. Or a boy," he adds. "Twenty years and nothing. Thought maybe he wasn't interested at that kind of thing, 'til you."

That's not reassuring, no matter how many times it's repeated. "I don't know what to do, Sáv. I keep trying to tell him I don't feel the—"

"Sáven, we need you in the kitchen. Begging your pardon, Lady." His mother peers out of from the door to the staging room, but her eyes stay on the floor. "Fàleg dropped something and I need the hands," she explains. Sáv clasps me on the shoulder before joining his mother.

Scrubbing my hand down my face, I return to my room. One more Trial and I can put all the drama with Kórol and Tans behind me. One more day closer to Her. One more day until I can put the claim that I'm the Sìnnách to rest.

CHAPTER 22

I'm awake at dawn, pacing around my small room and waiting for Sáv to show up with Tans. After I wear a line of my footprints in the stone floor, I accept he's not coming. I read the journal only to pass the time until the Trial, though I take in little of what I read.

Skimming to the end doesn't help, as the author wrote about how much he missed his Father but that he was better off, and it isn't clear whether he missed his Father due to some nefarious purpose or because She was still around. I skip several years' worth of entries, instead concentrating on when the author got increasingly paranoid, talking about his father's ascension and Her and what She had done.

No matter that no one believes me—I know Father changed when he ascended. No one else remembers how he was before Her voice took over his.

> Mother will not admit it, but I believe it is only fear that keeps her silent. Else She has bewitched Mother too. Her voice already snaked into Father's; I fear She will overtake Mother too. I secret away to the library as often as I dare. She surely watches me, but Her target remains on my Father. His spirit and personality leave him every day.

That sounds familiar, but I'm too distracted to do more than jot it down. I mechanically read the next entry in the journal.

> Our records of the Dark Eósy are missing, burned in a sudden fire that coincided with Father's ascension. Luck delivered me a single remaining text that I spirited from the library only a day before the fire. It describes an Eósy woman that reminded me of Her—a being of untold beauty who seeks the love of us mortals. Their continued obedience and fealty sustain her. As for Father, I fear that where obedience and worship is not given freely, she takes it.

I make a single note on my parchment about the destroyed records before tossing the journal to the side. Nothing I read today will stick as the Trial is too present in my mind.

Today's Trial should show whether I can survive when the odds are stacked against me. As a non-magical human in Dalner who has no special skills to speak of, no matter what the Pack thinks, the odds are *always* stacked against me. That fact, plus the fact that I *can't* be the Sìnnách, suggests today won't go well.

A knock at the door saves me from turning further into my head, and a flutter of hope takes flight. Fixing my friendship with Tans can only make today better.

It isn't Tans but Sáv, who sheepishly explains that he can't find Tans anywhere. Although the hope plummets, my motivation to finish the Trials heightens.

Sáven leads me to an open balcony-style space behind the castle, somewhere I explored with Tansr before he decided he didn't want my brand of friendship, the clingy kind that goes romantic instead of platonic.

The opening measures only twenty feet in diameter with sets of bleachers on two conjoining sides and a fence separating them from the Trial-area. People are already seated and appear to be taking bets. The stone of the castle acts as a wall, and a bulky wooden fence, spanning twenty feet to the sky, the other. It's a cage—of people, stone, and wood.

December in Dalner is colder than Chicago, and I can't fathom why this test is outside when they let a dragon in the throne room. I try not to shiver while I wait for instructions, tucking my numb hands into my pockets. I've worn my jeans and Earth shirt for luck, but I'll need that and more to succeed in this Trial, whatever it is.

Fílga approaches as I stand next to the wooden fence-wall. It's perfectly smooth with no notches or imperfections. His expression is ashen and the line in his forehead creases. "You must survive in the arena for twenty minutes," he reveals as the ground begins to shake. The sound is rhythmic like someone stomping towards the cage. "No weapons, no rules," Fíl finishes.

Something massive breaks through the crowd, and a seven-foot creature, all muscle and taut flesh, lumbers into the cage. It's a nightmare parody of a man, a towering statue made real. Patchy hair covers his leathery skin, the Frankenstein-esque lines of sewn flesh implying he stole the skin rather than grew it himself, all combining into one hulking beast. Given his monstrous and animal like body, I'm surprised to see intelligence in his eyes. They appear cunning as they surveil the opening for whatever threat (or prey?) he might find. When he sees me, his lips curl back to reveal sharp canines.

Fíl speaks from the corner of his crooked mouth. "That is a dobdehìà. There is a colony near the wall a few hours to the north, and we persuaded one to help when we approached at sunrise. It is a being of aggression and skill."

Again, Fíl's not as helpful as he thinks he is.

He clasps my shoulder and leans down. "You may die," he whispers in my ear. "May the Fates be with you and bless you."

Before Fíl can abandon me to my fate, I ask if we can get any outside help. Fílga's face is blank when he explains that no one can willingly provide help or willingly intervene. My eyes narrow and I restrain myself from slugging him. *So much for 'no rules.'*

With a twisted grin, Fíl ducks back into the veranda area, where Kórol sits ramrod stiff in the front row. Kórol's expression pivots from dazed to excited to nauseous. I can't see Tans anywhere.

A bell rings as my twenty minutes begin. My opponent, the Brute (I call him instead of his proper name) doesn't budge, giving me the chance to size him up while he stares me down. There's dim recognition in his eyes, most likely that I'm not worth his time. With warriors like him, I can't fathom why Dalner needed the Sìnnách, especially if that Sìnnách is me. I smile wanly in his direction.

Smiling is a terrible idea. As if something breaks within him, he snaps to attention, bones cracking as he straightens his back. I can read in his ghastly expression that he sees me as something *wrong*. All color bleeds from my face—I can die in this cage, and no one would save me.

A brief life full of lackluster achievements and loneliness flashes through my eyes. My one moment of glory is my arrival in Dalner, and no one will ever even know. Panting like the cornered animal I am, I search the cage, seeing no place to hide and run out the clock.

But there—there's Tans sitting in the front of the other set of bleachers, his body tense, hands clutching at his braids and his eyes tracking the Brute's every move. *No help*, Fílga told me. *No willing help.* But someone not willing—someone forced to do something against their will, against their own desires—like that damned Trial of the Will, *again*.

The sky darkens while my mind races, and something crackles. Thunder, then lighting zig zag above Tans' head. Finally, the pitter-patter of rain begins, each drop landing harder than the last. The weather is another foe as it stings my skin and restricts my eyesight. Either someone in the audience wants a more interesting Trial, one where the Brute drowns me in the puddles forming, or an Eósy knows I'm not the Sìnnách and wants to punish me for trying. The former makes less sense than the latter, as the Eósy must be tired of the continued deceit of what I am and what I'm not.

Deception will be your armor. The thought hits me like the punch I hope to avoid from the Brute. The Voice's poorly worded riddle against Her could apply again. It almost worked before, distracting my kidnappers. My mind flies towards a terrible conclusion. Tans said heightened emotions caused the Sàrkany to lose control of their gifts. And whenever I mention Kórol, Tans reacts.

Rain hammers down while the plan forms, one of my worst. My opponent reacts to the rain by lifting his hands skyward. That's my opening. I run towards Tansr, my clothing starting to soak. My voice is lost to the beating of the rain, but he leans forward, his amber eyes wide and wild. "Tansr," I shout, but my voice can't overtake the thunder booming around us. "I need to tell you about Kórol."

He shakes his head as his lips form the word "not now," but his eyes never leave mine. His hands clutch the fence between us. If I can figure out what about Kórol will affect him most, this will work.

The Brute shuffles behind me, which I feel more than hear. Sáv told me Tans was a people pleaser, who'd do anything for his friends, and how much betrayal hurts him. There's a part of me that rails against what I'm about to do, but I hope Tans will understand my choices are limited.

"Kórol will never forgive you for being intimate with me." I force the words out behind clenched teeth as the Brute trudges behind me. Tans doesn't react how I expect, instead staring silent and slack jawed at me.

The Brute wraps his arms around my stomach and pulls me as I ratchet up my barrage of abuse. I spit out word after word, but none cause him to lose control. I finally say the words that someone should be shouting at me. "There's a reason you're alone. You break everything you touch. You don't deserve friendships."

As I speak those final damning words, Tans' hands tighten, and he releases his fire into my stomach, right where the Brute's hands clutch me. Tans rears back, whimpering while the Brute drops me to howl as flames lick up his arms.

The Brute growls and charges at me. Even through the sticky mud, he slams me ten feet back into the wall. The scar on my hip screams and blood drips down my ear where my temple connected with his long fingernails. I scrape my own fingers on the wood behind me, blindly searching for a way to climb or escape from the man-made cage. The burns on the Brute's arm blaze an angry red as he punches his fist into my stomach. I grunt and bite my tongue, doubling over until my head meets the ground and my hair mingles with the mud. The Brute raises his arm back to attack me again, but I claw frantically at the space above me, catching his forearms and leaving long red welts over the burns that drip dark sludging blood. He roars from the pain and stumbles backward. It's small, but enough of an opening to get out from under him and scramble back towards the veranda where Tansr gazes back at me with suffering in his eyes. I don't know if Tans grieves over what I said or at my pain. Knowing him, and how good he is, the latter.

But the Trial isn't over and time keeps ticking. Ignoring the pain blossoming in too many places to categorize, I slide towards the other bleachers where Kórol watches intently. The wooden wall is behind me as I skitter to him and the fence that keeps us apart. I don't know Kórol's exact gift, but I have an idea—it's something offensive rather than defensive, like Tans', like Sáven's. I hope it's enough.

I lean backward against the fence separating us and face the Brute who lumbers towards me. He gets caught in the dreck the rain created, slowing him down. He either doesn't have the dexterity to muddle through it or doesn't care enough to leap after me.

"Kórol," I hiss, turning slightly to keep one eye on the Brute.

"You can do this, Lady," he says.

"You don't get to talk to me right now. Not after what you've done to me. Not after forcing me into the situation where I will die."

He makes a strangled noise in his throat. "You will not. You cannot."

The words flow much easier than they did with Tans, because it's easier to lie to others than to yourself or because I'm *that* terrible of a person. "If you're wrong, then you're as bad as your ancestor. No—you're worse. Because you let yourself get bewitched by a pretender, by a faker." The Brute is eight feet away.

"No," he denies.

"You will be another in a long line of disgraces." Six feet.

"No," he repeats.

"Then how will you prove them wrong after I'm dead?" Three feet.

"I don't know," he says anxiously.

"You're just another disappointment in the long line of Rad-dares, *King*." And then I duck.

He cracks, springing to his feet and letting shards of ice splay forward from his hands. "No!" he bellows as the ice slams into the wooden wall behind me like arrows at a target. The Brute covers himself, but none hit him.

It's not what I expected to happen, but it's good enough. I stagger around the Brute before he realizes what I'm doing. The shards aren't perfect, but they give me a foothold to climb and stay out of range while I run down the clock. The Brute pursues me, making his stumbling trek back the way he came.

The rain melts the ice, but not enough to keep me from attempting to escape the Brute's range. My hands burn as I grab two jagged icicles and propel myself upward, my feet sliding down the wood as I climb. There aren't enough ice footholds, but I rake my fingernails into the wall, splitting them and splintering the wood enough to dig in. My hair claws at my vision but I can't let it slow me. Adrenaline lets me momentarily ignore the spiking pain, the flowing blood hidden by the splatter of rain. I force myself higher and higher, until the last icicles Kórol created, nubs now, rest under my feet. I stare at the top of the wall, five feet above my reach. The Brute is almost to me, and my feet are still within his reaching range. If he jumps, his long arms could pull me down even at fifteen feet in the air. I swallow deeply and will myself to be brave, to do something for once, to be the damn protagonist that succeeds when things are bad. Then I jump.

I spring off the icicle nubs, scraping and crawling my way up, trying desperately to reach the top and get a single finger over the edge. One hand makes it while the rest of my body swings freely, slamming into the wood and knocking the wind out of me. The Brute tries to grab my foot but misses. I haul myself upward, wrapping both hands around the edge of the wood, my nails and palms bleeding, my knees bruised. Using all the energy I have left, I crawl to a seated position at the top edge of the wall.

Then I wait.

The next ten minutes are both brutal and boring, as the rain hides the tears I can't stop from falling, born of pain, of anger. The Brute lazily jumps for me, but he misses each time. Hand-eye coordination was clearly sacrificed in favor of his bulk and brawn. The onlookers watch, disinterested, and finally the rain abates. I count the minutes until it's over, and ignore that both Kórol and Tans, two men I treated abominably, are key to defeating Her. And the realization that I'm minutes from completing the Trials and proving I'm the Sìnnách makes me sick to my stomach.

I wanted to be special, but at what cost? Being the hero was the only way to save my friends. Now, I've lost at least one, maybe more.

The twenty minutes end and Fílga announces the end of the Trial. He reaches up to help me down, and with only a second's hesitation, I land with a thud in his arms.

"No willing help indeed," he says, eyes flicking behind him to the bleachers. I flush with shame as Tansr slips into the departing crowd. Fíl chucks me under the chin. "He'll understand. What-ever you told him, he'll understand the need for it."

I'm not so sure, and I smile thinly at him in response. It stings; I must have split my lips while scaling the wall. Fílga clucks and checks my injuries with brusque hands. "Perhaps you can speak with him while he heals your wounds," Fílga suggests as he waves away two women in white tiptoeing towards me.

"We both have people to talk to," I say pointedly. To his credit, Fíl doesn't pretend to misunderstand me. But the subject drops when Kórol stalks to my side, his eyes sharpened like a hunter on its prey. Before I can stop him, Kórol crushes me into a hug that presses uncomfortably against my battered body.

"Brilliant. I knew my feelings were true," he says when he releases me. Up close, his ice blue irises are bleached and dilated.

"I'm sorry, Kórol." The words come out through clenched teeth.

"You were perfect, little bird," he says, slapping a hand on my shoulder and almost buckling my knees. I blink away the sprouted tears of agony and frustration to limp inside.

"I hope to see you tonight at the final feast," Kórol says to my back. I don't respond.

People avoid me as I stagger back into the castle proper, stepping aside when I stagger by and tilting their gaze to the ground. I'm not proud of how I finished the Trials, and my head hangs like everyone else's. A skittish courier, while staying in a bow so deep that his hair skims the ground, gives me directions to Tans' room, only a floor below my own in the same distant spire.

The swell of memories hits me on the spiral staircase. It isn't as strong or coherent as the last few times, maybe because the Brute doesn't have a humanlike mind or memories function differently. It isn't as vivid as the eel either.

While I'm pacing in my room, I get a flash of an underground dirt burrow. It feels warm and comforting. There's a flicker of something bitter like annoyance as he scents four weaklings too close to the comfort-place, his home. I recognize the weaklings (as the Brute thinks of them) as four Sàrkany soldiers. The scent of Sàrkany is of death and lemons. One weakling projects mind-pictures. It asks help-fight food-gift. The Sàrkany bargain with food to convince the Brute to spar with me. The Brute agrees to 'much-food' and asks 'death-win?' The Sàrkany agree—the fight is to the death.

The barrage of foreign memories leaves, and I'm leaning against a wall in the spiral staircase that leads to both my and Tans' rooms. I shudder; at least the Trials are over.

When I knock on Tans' door, a light scuffling sounds behind the door. Something thumps twice, his head against the wall most likely, before he opens the door and beckons me in. He's in dry clothes but his hair is still wet and crinkles at the ends. His eyes, though, are hollow and deeply set, the color of deadened wood.

His rooms are larger than mine, but cozy and lived in. The room I enter must be the living area, furnished with two spacious wooden benches backed with overstuffed bold brocade pillows, a wooden chest, and a large table with two chairs upholstered in blue. Two doors lead to other rooms. Candles cover every surface, in varying sizes but all partly or fully melted. Reams of parchment fill what little space the candles don't occupy. I can just make out his flourishing handwriting on the top of the page nearest me that says "Her" and "Grace" and "fire and ice." There's a pang in my gut that isn't from the Brute's punch.

Tans shifts a stack from a bench and motions for me to sit. He inspects me clinically, sweeping soothing fingers over my face and neck. I try not to lean into the touch; I don't deserve that.

"I cannot tell what else is injured and what isn't," he murmurs after he finishes checking me over. He holds up his hand to keep me from speaking, though no words were coming anyway. "You need to bathe to remove the mud. Then I can heal what injuries remain."

I limp after him into one of the two other rooms.

The bathroom he takes me to is larger than the one on my floor, windowless and with pipes that bring in water, and an actual soaking tub. Silver paint covers the walls and reflects the light from the candles in each corner. There's a large mirror on one wall and I catch sight of myself. I can't recognize the girl who stares back. Muck and gore cover me, and under the streaks of dirt is a bruise blossoming on my lip and spreading to my left cheekbone. Rain and blood mat down my hair, my jeans are ripped, and my t-shirt sticks to my skin. I've defeated the Trials but look like they defeated me. I lean against the wall and hold in a whimper. *They did.*

Tans fills the bathtub and adds some pink concoction from a small basket by the floor. When I turn away to undress, he hesitates by the tub. "I understand your Earthen customs of modesty, but I am uncomfortable leaving you alone for fear you may slip," he says.

"I trust you," I assure him. Of the two of us, I'm the one that takes advantage, that pushes too far, not him. He takes a deep breath, casting his eyes to the stone ceiling above us. I'm tired but not embarrassed as I tug off my jeans and underthings, things destined for the trashcan rather than back in my wardrobe.

I slip into the water with a hiss. The temperature is perfect, warm enough to soothe my aching muscles, better than my last bath before things got overcomplicated. The dirt and blood sluice off as I scrub myself clean, rubbing my skin raw. The bite of pain helps my guilt.

"I didn't mean anything I said at the Trial," I say to the water. "You're the best kind of friend, you're my best friend."

He winces and remains silent, watching diligently as I scrub. The look isn't sexual, but keenly focused on cataloguing injuries through the murky water, imitating what the Pack did constantly on the trek to Ilsen. When the water is a dull and dirty color, I step out into the towel he hands me.

Once I'm dry, he heals everything he missed on the first pass, pressing his fingers to his lips then grazing them over my skin. Bruises on my legs vanish. Scrapes on my stomach, hips, arms, and head seal closed. He delicately kisses the pads of my fingers, the inside of my palms. I'm metaphorically and literally bare before him and I shiver even with the heat of his hands on me. At the movement, his eyes snap to mine, and the flicker of tenderness, if I even saw one, in his gaze fades. His expression is blank as he leans close and kisses my cheek and grazes his lips against mine. A soft sigh escapes my lips as the pain vanishes.

"Tansr, I am sorry."

He pinches his eyes closed before leaving the bathroom. I dress quickly and follow, finding him standing against the open door to the hallway.

"Did you need anything else from me?" He doesn't speak to me but to the wall behind me.

"You know none of it was true. Kórol understands. It's not as if the stupid Trial was a betrayal anyway. You can't betray someone if there's no loyalty there in the first place," I blurt. He looks up with narrowed eyes and I flush. "That came out wrong. Not—not that I'm not loyal to Kórol, but not in that way. You're the only one I—"

"Don't you dare." He bursts through the doorway and escapes into the hallway, hands smoking at his side.

CHAPTER 23

E ven with the demands of the Trials behind me, the Feast that night is worse than the last. I wear a sparkling blue dress that I found folded in front of my room when I stumbled upstairs to my room after Tans left. The dress is a shimmering gauzy fabric, glittering like the sprites who danced in the water. It isn't a welcome reminder.

The room is set for a hundred guests but less than thirty appear, looking like a gloomy wedding no one attended. It's less of a party as it lacks dancing or music, and more of an awards ceremony. Kórol announces each attendee, a monotonal recitation of their long titles and adding a fun fact about them. Mine is obvious, though it isn't the one I'd choose. I'd pick something about reading or being the youngest ever enrolled at my liberal arts college. I sink low into my seat. Only the Pack even *knows* what college is; no one else would care.

Fíl is the youngest Historian Dalner has ever had, a fact that apparently still rankles some guests, who grumble under their breath when Kórol thanks Fíl for his service and loyalty. Sáv gets a brief shoutout too, as a member of the Pack who 'brought home the Sìnnách,' but with his wrinkled and ill-fitting green tunic, one identical to what Tans wore at the last feast, it's clear he's not a regular or expected guest at these events.

Kórol drags Tans to the head table, who looks as though he sparred after abandoning me, his leather armor muddy and braids half-done. Kórol cuffs him on the shoulder and beams as he extols the good work Tans does for Dalner. Tans whispers in Kórol's ears and Kórol's grin widens.

When the announcements are over, people mingle in small clumps. Kórol and Fíl stand with me while the other guests stare with uncomfortable interest, like they expect me to swallow a sword. No one approaches until Sáv drags Tans to us, one hand gripping Tans' leather cuff. Kórol raises an eyebrow.

"I thought you would be off with your new lady," Kórol says.

At the revelation, Fílga and Sáven practically clap their hands while the color drains from my face. "Have you found someone?" Fílga asks.

Tans peeks at me before responding. A weight falls into the pit of my stomach and I might throw up. "When haven't I?" he says, with a facsimile of a leer. The others chuckle.

"This afternoon, Tansr asked for my introduction to one of the ladies who traveled in for the feasts," Kórol explains.

"About time you began your search," says Sáv.

Fíl purses his lips. "Will you remain a general after taking up your seat?"

I can't understand the conversation, whether because of the topic or the ringing in my ears. Tans fiddles with his mussed braids and shrugs. "I will leave that decision up to the lady fate provides, whoever she may be."

"Not everyone can be as lucky in love as the Sìnnách and I." Kórol wraps an arm around me. Fíl and Sáv lean away from each other.

I wriggle out of his grip, feeling Tans' eyes on me like a physical touch. "We're not—"

"I can only hope the rest of you receive this gift." Kórol squeezes the back of my neck. It's on the edge of too hard, and I can't slip away. Tans watches with pursed lips and his hands stop twitching.

"I must be off," Tans says abruptly. "Much to do, swooning women to catch and the like. Good night." He bows to Kórol and nods to the others, his eyes lingering on me before he shakes his head.

When Tans leaves the room, Kórol releases me. Scowling, I smack his arm and stand closer to Sáv. Kórol furrows his brows and projects his voice around the large room. "You must excuse the Sìnnách and I. We have much to discuss before her Confirmation Ceremony."

The guests mutter their goodbyes while he grabs my hand, forcefully interlacing our fingers, and drags me out of the room. He's moving too fast, and my hip twinges. Even with the superficial healing Tans did, my bones ache and I can't match his pace.

"Slow down," I beg when we breach the hallway. He ignores my request, forcing us into another spire.

I'm wheezing by the time we arrive at the spire that holds the throne room. I finally rip away from him and plant my feet, crossing my arms around my chest. A chill caresses the walls as his eyes dilate and he bares his teeth. King Kórol, the one I supposedly bewitched and who spouts declarations of love, isn't standing in front of me—this is the Kórol from the trip, the man whose temper forced me wander off in the woods.

"You were acting inappropriate, mooning over Tansr in such a manner," he bites out.

"I wasn't mooning," I say, jabbing a blunt fingernail against his hard chest. "And I don't answer to you."

"I forbid you to see him and forbid him from seeing you. Your friendship is improper, particularly given he will be betrothed to another and you are mine."

"I'm not yours!" I yank my hands through my hair, nearly pulling out the frizzy locks. "Why does no one listen to me when I say that? I'm not something you can claim or conquer."

Kórol's eyes cloud, the pale color dilating until the black pupil is nothing but a speck. "Have I not wooed you? When you desired slow courtship, I left you my coat. When you wished for strife and wanted passion from an antagonist, I riled you. When you desired storybook romance, I behaved thusly. I even learned the phrases of love from your books." He leans down, his breath cool against my cheeks as I scowl up at him. "Am I hideous to you? When you are nothing but my good angel?"

"What—you've said that before." I peer into his white irises. *Am I hideous?* and *you always were.* And *I'm not an angel,* and *I will be myself,* the responding phrase leaks into my brain, in Mom's voice. It's been years, something I buried deep, but—

"Every atom of your flesh is as dear to me as my own," he croons.

"No, shut up. I'm thinking. Fíl—Fíl didn't know what an angel was." I grab his face as horror overtakes my frustration. "Kórol—your eyes, they're not *pale*, they look dazed, or drugged—did you say atoms?"

"Every atom of your flesh is as dear to me as my own," he repeats in a lilting voice.

"Every atom of your flesh, you've said that before too," I say absently, more to myself than to Kórol, who still stares down at me with an overly sweet smile on his face, all the steel in his gaze replaced with something loopy and soft. "'Am I hideous,' and 'good angel.' I know those. That's—that's from Jane Eyre. I—I've never told you guys about Jane Eyre."

He wraps me in his arms and presses a kiss to my forehead. "I know no Jane, you are the unearthly creature who captured my heart and caged me."

Those are quotes. I press my hands to my eyes, forcing space between us. It's been too long but I can almost hear Mom reading those words. I refused to touch the book after she died. I read romances in her honor, but ones that avoid deep trauma and thematic emotional growth, ones that would remind me of her. I chose ones with basic repeated tropes, happy endings and, usually, gratuitous amounts of smut—the slow burn, enemies to lovers, fake dating.

I gasp, but the sound is swallowed by my hands. The slow burn, the coat; enemies to lovers, our big fight; a 'story book romance,' when he pretended we were married, where we huddled for warmth, and he declared his love. Kórol followed the tropes I told them about on the pilgrimage. But—the thought rings around my head—*how could he quote Jane Eyre?*

My hands fall. "There's no science in Dalner, Kórol. What are atoms?"

He peers down at me, eyes still dilated and milky. He doesn't shrug but furrows his brow as color seeps back into his irises. As quickly as the color came, it vanishes, and he stares vacantly back, his fingers caressing the curve of my neck. "I need no knowledge except that you are my Sìnnách."

I convince Kórol to wait inside the throne room. He does without complaint once I promise to return to him and let him kiss my forehead a second time. I race back to the banquet hall as nausea churns in my stomach. Something (Her?) spelled Kórol—that's the only explanation. *But why?*

Perhaps it is a hint.

The Voice's interruption almost has me tumble down the stairs. I lean against the wall and take several stuttering breaths. There's no one in the staircase, and I chance speaking aloud.

"Did *you* do this? You can read thoughts," I hiss wetly. "Can you manipulate them too?"

I promised I would not read your thoughts unless necessary.

"That's not an answer."

Any Eósy can learn to read open thoughts, but only some can manipulate them, comes their placid response. *And any of us can breach the realms to learn of your people's history and literature should we so desire.*

Footsteps creak below me, and I stomp upwards again, whispering through clenched teeth. "And Kórol's thoughts?"

He leaves himself open to indirect intervention, the manipulation of which you speak. He invites my kind to sweep into his mind and influence him.

"But *why* make Kórol behave like that?"

Think, Grace. Why would Kórol's attention on you be beneficial?

My feet thump on the flagstone as I approach the banquet hall. "To bother me," I say mulishly, remembering how annoying his behavior has been. "It doesn't make any sense. It's not like Kórol being in love with me—damn it!" If Kórol didn't believe I 'bewitched' him, he wouldn't have pushed as hard to test me as the Sìnnách.

Indeed. Why not build you up to tear you down from greater heights? It is a clever way to destroy someone. The Voice almost seems proud. I don't let myself linger on the conclusion battering around in my brain, that I'd been right all along.

"And Jane Eyre?" That Jane Eyre is the last book Mom read to me is a form of psychological torment I didn't expect.

Even more clever. Is it not a tale about manipulation?

"No need to be chipper about it," I growl as I limp towards the banquet hall. "I figured out he's the ice I'm supposed to use, lest you forget your own cryptic riddles. How do I fix him?"

They hesitate. *I am bound by the limitations of my interference. But I can confirm the enchantment will break when She is dead.*

That's not good enough.

I burst into the banquet hall, which is empty except for several servants cleaning tables. One of them directs me to the staging room where she says I'll find Sáv. I only see the back of Fíl when I enter, bent over with one hand braced against the wall above his head.

"Fíl, thank God, I just found out—"

"Lady!" Fíl spins around, clutching his hands over his heart and backing into the wall. Someone squawks and Sáv shuffles out from behind him. Both avoid eye contact with me and each other, but Sáv's lips look bitten red.

We're quiet a moment too long before Fíl clears his throat. "Can we help you?"

"Right," I say, my own cheeks heated. Their romance can't distract me when I've got my own manipulated one to deal with. "We've got an enormous problem. Something is coming, and She spelled—"

"You are quite eager, our new Sìnnách. The Great Matron will arrive in a mere few days to bless your Confirmation." Fíl radiates stoicism, all evidence of his romantic interlude disappeared except for a few mussed hairs by his ears.

"That's not who I'm talking about. There's someone else, and She bewitched—"

"It's easy to see you bewitched him," Sáv agrees, resting his hand on Fíl's arm. Fíl looks down at him and their expressions soften. If not for the anxiety roiling through my insides, I'd spare a moment to comment on how cute they look together. But it is, so I don't.

"You're not listening! Kórol's been sp—"

"You make quite the pair," Fíl says.

They won't let you tell them, the Voice whispers mentally. **The enchantment weaved its web into their minds too**.

I back up against the door I came through and slide down to the floor, bringing my knees to my chest. "But how?" I say shrilly.

"Surely your connection cannot be a surprise," says Fíl, tracing his fingers down Sáv's arm until he intertwines them.

It takes but a word, misspoken or said in jest, to invite such influence.

"Are you alright?" Sáv asks, his bottle-green eyes wide with concern. "You've been sitting there looking dazed for a minute or more."

The irony is almost too much for me. Exhaling a groan, I pull myself up. "Where's Tans?"

"You were present when he left for his rooms," Fíl says, pursing his lips and reaching out a hand to help me stand. "Perhaps you are ill."

I windmill into the wall to avoid his help, muttering, "I'm fine," when they stagger towards me. Kórol's been convinced to love me by someone. Fíl and Sáv *can't* believe me because of the same influence. It's almost too much, how much control I've lost, and—another thought hits me.

"Fíl," I say, hands shaking. "Where did you say you came up with the ideas for the Trials?"

The lines on his forehead deepen. "I studied the few texts in our possession and asked for guidance from the Eósy behind the wall in crafting then."

I don't remember how I arrive at the spire that holds my and Tans' rooms, but at some point, I break into a wobbly run when I reach his floor.

How do you know he is not equally spelled? The Voice sounds as frantic as I feel.

I skid to a stop in front of his door, chest heaving from the combined panic and exertion. "I don't," I whimper between wheezing breaths. "But I have to try."

I bang on the wooden door with my open palm. Tans opens it, half dressed and still pulling one of his arms through the sleeve of a mustard yellow tunic. He blinks at me in confusion, amber eyes glinting against the few lit candles in the hall.

"What are you doing here?" He keeps the door half open and flits his gaze behind him.

"Did I interrupt something?" I wince; that isn't what I planned to say but jealousy never knows its place.

He opens the door wider, exposing the cluttered, but empty, room. Stacks of papers are scattered around the floor with a small opening in the middle, large enough for someone to sit. "I was working on the riddles you provided."

I slump against the door frame, doubly relieved. "You're still doing that, after everything?"

"Of course. I promised. But it's near midnight. Why are you here rather than with Kórol?"

His eyes aren't milky or glazed but the same soulful brown, ones that darken from amber to burnished mahogany while I study him. He's not wary or confused, but placidly waiting for my direction. "It's about Her."

His face pinches into a frown but before he can speak, a bell tings behind him. "That is the emergency bell. It is keyed to Kórol alone." He fastens a utility belt around his slim waist. "I must go to him. We will continue speaking when I return."

"I know where he is. I'm coming with you." I'm the one who left Kórol alone knowing some Eósy parasite sunk its fangs into his head. Tans looks like he wants to argue but ultimately sighs before grabbing a blue leather vest and taking off down the hall.

He's tied the vest by the time we arrive in the throne room, but we're not alone in the halls. Dozens of servants and residents of Ilsen push into the room. There's a din inside, the noise carrying into the hallway, as loud as when Kórol announced I was a Candidate. Tans and I elbow our way past the crowd and enter through the back door.

Kórol stands near the dais, his muscular frame engulfed by his fur cape, gaping at something in the corner. Tans blocks my view, but I shift to peek around him.

She cuts him off with a sharp wave of her manicured hands, her red fingernails shining in the light. The churning in my stomach curdles. The dragon huffs, steam leaving his nostrils as if annoyed someone caused her to stop petting it.

"There will be no tests, no Trials," she declares as her eyes narrow into slits. For a second, it looks as though she and the dragon shift as one; both their eyes squint and bore into Fílga's for questioning them.

"But tradition dictates—" His voice squeaks.

"I recognize you have *traditions*," her voice spits on the last word, "but I do not prove myself to you. You prove your fealty to me and that *you* are worthy of my presence."

She lets a soft smile play on her lips as she saunters to Kórol. He swallows audibly but doesn't blink.

"What a pity that a Candidate wasted your time, that the King's time was wasted. Those Trials were worthless, and I expect this mistake will be resolved promptly." When she reaches Kórol, she turns her smile to me, but the remorse in her words isn't present in her eyes. They are cold and emotionless like doll's eyes and look right through me.

Kórol nods, first slowly then more resolutely. "The Trials were worthless," he repeats.

"Now," she turns away from me, her gaze seeking Kórol's again. "I must speak with the King alone."

No. No. No no no no.

It's a repeated mental refrain as I rush back to my room, hand pressed to my mouth to keep from gagging. After a moment of indecision, Tans accompanies me instead of staying with Kórol, apparently content with the newcomer's announcement and the presence of his remaining officers. 'Accompany' is too mild a word, instead he chases after me while I sprint back to my spire, one hand pressing hard on my hip. Tans' limited healing earlier in the day (*God, was the Trial just this morning?*) wasn't enough and I limp the remaining distance from the stairs to my door.

The door slams into the stone wall after I heave it open and leap for the notes on my side table. I pull out the journal first and open it to the entries I read that morning before the last Trial, nearly dropping the book. With shaking hands, I scan them while Tans stands in the doorway, not breaching the threshold.

"Everything will be fine," he promises.

I don't answer. I find the entry from this morning, the one where the author said his Eósy enemy bewitched his father and took over his voice. I skim a dozen more entries until,

> I alone will speak against Her. This Sìnnách bewitched him but She will not bewitch me. She is no goddess, no beacon of hope for my people. She is an evil thing. I see the Sìnnách for her true self. To save my Father, to save my family, she must be eradicated.

The book falls to the floor. I grab my notes in its place, my smudged script scrawling the parchment. Questions on the Light and Dark Eósy, on Her and the significance of her red nails cover the margins. I brandish the pages in front of Tans' face, who stands with his arms out as if he thinks I might fall.

"It's her!" He stares back blankly. "Her, my Her, the Woman, the one who's going to destroy everything, She's the Sìnnách!"

He pales and the darkness behind my eyes and frothing in my gut ebbs for the first time since Kórol spouted Jane Eyre only an hour ago. According to the Voice, I still need Kórol, but I can overcome that hurdle with Tans by my side.

"Grace, think about what you're saying." He speaks more gently than he has before, gentler than when he held me by the lake after the dobhà, gentler than when he promised to be by my side in defeating Her. "You're exhausted and surely feeling confused and jealous about being displaced."

"I'm—I'm not jealous, Tans. Look, it's here." I wave the pages in front of him again, ducking down to snatch the journal. My hip aches and my knees buckle halfway to the ground. The pages fall to the floor, and I struggle to gather them back in order. "It's Her. She's—she's got red nails. And She bewitches people, like She did with Kórol. I told you that earlier. It's all in this book."

I'm kneeling on the ground, holding the proof of my conclusions for him but he doesn't reach for my offerings. There's pity in his amber eyes. "Don't look at me like that, Tans. I'm not jealous or—or crazy. The Voice—the Voice would agree too. They've been leading me. I don't—I don't think you can talk to them unless you ask, something about Sàrkany minds being closed off unless you invite them, but if you invite them, they'll tell you too!"

He kneels beside me, his silken hair covering his face as he takes the notes and journal. A relieved breath leaves me when he does, but it cuts off as he sticks the notes inside the journal and tosses the book behind him. The leather hits the stone wall with a soft thud. He closes his hands around my shaking fingers.

"Is it not possible that the Voice you hear is a Dark Eósy? They have veiled their reasons for helping you, convincing you that you have an enemy that my entire Kingdom *knows*, and has known for *centuries*, is good and Light."

I'm shaking my head before he finishes speaking. "No, but they said She would destroy me and everything I care for. They can't lie, you told me that. It—it *has* to be true, Tans."

"They cannot lie to you, but they can manipulate you and play with words. Perhaps the statement will *become* a truth, that she will destroy you but only once you attack the Sìnnách as they demand you do.”

“No,” I repeat. He tries to gather me in his arms, but I push him away. He looks hurt, but I can’t think about that now. If I look into those anguished eyes, I’ll start agreeing with him. He kisses my forehead, leaving a dull heat in its wake, before standing and abandoning me alone on the floor.

At the door, he falters. “It would be best if you remained somewhat inconspicuous. There will be questions about your completing the Trials. And—” he hesitates, but I can fill in the blanks. *And he can’t afford me doing something stupid like attacking the Sìnnách.* But he forgets that I need him and Kórol to succeed, something that seems less likely with every word from his mouth. There’s little I can do alone. “Goodnight, Butterfly.”

I crumple when the door closes, rolling into a ball on the cold stone floor. There’s a haze at the edge of my vision, like a mist undulating on the floor. I don’t feel the chill seeping through my gauzy gown because I’m in shock. “You better be here,” I say to the ceiling, sniffing.

“I am almost always here,” the Voice replies mildly.

“Why didn’t you tell me the Sìnnách was *Her*?”

“You never asked. You know my help has limitations.”

“It was implied when I asked if *I* was the Sìnnách, you ass!” Pain spikes in my head as I rest my cheek against the cool stone. “Okay. Direct questions because you can’t lie, correct?”

“Correct. Direct questions remove the uncertainty of our answers, meaning we cannot spin words in our favor.” There’s a brief silence before, “I am still limited in my influence when we are not in the same place, but with the conclusion already nigh guaranteed, there are questions I may be able to answer about what you should already know. I can’t have you giving up now, not when you’re so close.”

I scrape my fingers against the floor, thinking about which questions are most important. "Are you manipulating my thoughts, like the Sìnnách is with Kórol?"

"Of course not."

There's no 'of course' about it, not when dealing with Eósy. "Can you? Have you?"

They pause and I hold my breath. "No to both. The Eósy cannot enter your mind as they can a Sàrkany. Your human mind is different—manipulation spells don't latch, something in your makeup keeps you free from most internal magic, though I've no idea why that boy's healing works on you so well," they add.

"How are you getting into my mind then?"

"I am one of the Eósy most skilled in mind magics. I may enter the gaps in your mind as I can all beings, but I cannot manipulate your thoughts."

That eases more worries than I realized I had. I roll to my back and stare at the ceiling. "Okay, then. Is the Sìnnách the Her you've been talking about?"

"Yes."

"Is the Sìnnách bad?"

"Yes." The answers are bullet quick.

I stutter out a sigh of relief but there's still one worry pricking at my mind like a sharpened needle. "Are *you* a Dark Eósy?"

They giggle again. "What a question. Why does that matter?"

Fear trickles down my spine. "Answer the question. Are you a Dark Eósy?"

"No." Their baby-soft voice is almost bland. "Shall we return to your plan to destroy her?"

"You're still an ass," I say, unfolding from the floor and dragging myself to gather up my notes. I slump against the stone wall. "There is no plan. You've been saying since the beginning I need Tans and Kórol. I don't have them, *She* does. I just want to go home."

The Voice tsks and speaks in a sotto voice. "I should have expected someone who only lived between the pages of books to think literally." Louder, to me, they say, "You need no additional aid. Indeed, you are the best hope we have. You passed the Trials, did you not?"

I pull up my knees, wrapping my arms around them. I speak into the folds of my dress. "Barely." And they didn't matter anyway.

The Voice is unusually quiet and their childlike tone gentle. "Worthless though they may be, you showed you had some form of skills. And you still live. Both are facts to guide you towards Her defeat."

"When will you stop being so cryptic and just tell me what I need to do? I get it—you have limitations. But we're past all the stupid hints. I need actual, *solid* advice on what to do and who can do it, because there's no way I can do this alone." The words spill out of me like a dam breaking, the cracks starting small until the flood begins. "You started me on this stupid quest, maybe you should finish it while I go back home."

"I have provided you with all the help you need to finish this. I cannot intervene further," the Voice says.

"Go to hell," I snarl at the empty walls of my room.

They sigh. "Deception will be your armor, Grace. You will need fire and ice to succeed. And remember—everyone bleeds in the end."

CHAPTER 25

I wake exhausted, still slumped on the floor with my notes scattered around me. I force myself to rise and find Tans to convince him I'm right. As much as Tans seems to think differently, I'm not stupid; I don't have a death wish. I'm not going to approach the Sìnnách and attack her. She's a literal warrior with a dragon; I've got a subpar wit, a mindreading Eósy, and my main battle tactic is running away and getting others to do my dirty work.

But today, I'm armed with more information to get the help I need—proof that the Voice isn't a Dark Eósy and the Sìnnách is bad. Tans has to help me now. He's my last chance.

He doesn't answer when I bang on his door, meaning I must ignore his advice to lie low and seek him out somewhere more public.

Sleeping on the floor did my hip and sore muscles no good and I hobble to the throne room on the main floor. There are voices inside, muffled and rising in pitch. Swallowing my fear, I inch the wooden door open, which feels more like opening the doors to my prison cell.

"Our scouts and watchers report increased sightings of wildlife outside their usual hours." Tans is speaking, and I peer around the heavy door to see him standing in full leather armor to the side of the dais. A dozen well-dressed people stand in front of him. They all wear at least one glittering bead in their hair and kneel in front of Kórol as if sitting in church, though I suppose it's common when speaking with royalty in a room without chairs other than the throne. Behind the kneeling people stand several men wearing black leather armor, each with a hefty weapon strapped to their back or chest.

Kórol sits on his carved throne behind Tans, mimicking a multicolored statue. For the first time, I wonder who Kórol truly is, how much of the man I know is enchantment and how much is genuine.

Tans looks serious, meeting the eyes of every kneeling person with flattened lips and a dark expression. "We have had reports in these past months of strange happenings at the Gates and surrounding walls. Thus far, none have been more worrisome than several beasts breaking through unexpectedly. These 'holes' wouldn't normally concern us, except the breaches continue to occur. I fear we are bearing down on an invasion."

An older woman with a shock of white hair pinned up in a high bun stands and clears her throat. From the back, she looks familiar, like a recurring background actor showing up multiple times in the same movie. "Lord Commander Tansr of Gràmad," she starts.

Tans lowers his head. "Lady Rothàna of Làna, in this room, I am simply my King's General."

Now, I remember her. Her fun fact was that she was the first Council member to serve in the army before she took her seat. Lady Rothàna cocks her head in a facsimile of a bow. "Is this not something we should leave to the Sìnnách? It is my understanding that this connection with the Eósy is to *protect* us from these breaches."

"That's shortsighted, Rothy," a man only a few years older than me drawls. He stays seated while speaking. "We need not bother the Sìnnách with minutia. She is to be a beacon of light and loveliness, much like our Great Matron. These feminine Eósy should remain pure of these concerns."

Lady Rothàna cranes her neck to stare at the man unblinking until he shifts in place and ducks his head. "What is *shortsighted* is assuming that the Sìnnách's presence is not to *help* us, rather than simply behaving as a symbol. She is knowledgeable in ways none of us are."

They don't know the half of it.

At her compliment, Kórol loses the detachment he displays, and a loopy looking grin unfurls. Tans watches him with solemn eyes before addressing Lady Rothàna again. "We do not wish to appear idle by taking advantage of the gifts the Eósy give us without proving we are worthwhile supplicants." He motions to Fíl and Kórol's assistant, Sethen, who wait at the edge of the group. The two bring out a large map that they hold aloft. Tans points as he speaks. "The breaches have remained focused in an area surrounding the castle. The gravest of the breaches center in the largest Gate to the North, where our scouts feel a vast press of magic. It may be the epicenter of any attack to bring them down."

"Do you need something?" The ethereal voice emerges from directly beside me, and I jump, losing grip on the door. The Sìnnách looms over me, one sculpted brow raised and a smirk tilting her full red lips upward.

"I—I was looking for Tans," I stutter, praying She isn't a mind reader like the Voice.

She bares her teeth, though I imagine to others it parodies a smile. "You found him. Shall I pass on a message?"

"No!"

At the front of the room, Tans stops talking and his face turns bloodless.

"Regardless, I tire of the General's presentation. Let us have you tell us *all* now." She prowls towards Kórol and the others, whipping her long hair behind her and sparing no moment for me to keep up. I limp behind her, defeated before I've even begun.

"It's no trouble, just something I need to tell Tans," I explain when we arrive at the front of the room. The Councilmembers ogle me, with expressions ranging from disinterest to contempt.

The Sìnnách wrinkles her nose and dismisses my implied request with a wave of her hand. She sits on the arm of Kórol's throne. "I will be Queen of this Kingdom. Anything you wish to say to my General shall be reported to me."

The taste of something metallic rises on my tongue, I must have bitten it. "Tans and I were working on a project. I just—I had a few updates for him."

"A project. By the failed Candidate." Her stare almost burns me before she turns to Kórol, running a manicured finger down his cheek. He sighs in contentment as those red claws leave deep pink lines on Kórol's skin. "It is a wonder you were given leave to engage in *any* projects. Perhaps we need the Historian to remind us, but is there not a traditional outcome for failed Candidates?"

Snickers echo around the room. Tans aborts a step in my direction before bowing low. When he rises, he keeps his eyes on the floor. "My lady, let me remove Gr—the failed Candidate from your sight. She will remain in her room and you'll not need to gaze upon her."

"I should like that. Her visage bothers me." She pouts and half the people in attendance gasp or sigh.

"Her knowledge of the history and literature of her world may prove useful, my Lady. Perhaps my Lady is not content with guiding our Kingdom but also seeks to guide other realms."

"They would be lucky to have your direction," a kneeling man calls out.

"What an enterprising idea, Tansr. Remove her from my sight and we will speak of this later. Your King and Consort Queen will carry on this council meeting in your absence."

Tans grips my arm and pulls me outside.

"Is She planning on taking over Earth?" I hiss as we enter the hallway. I hadn't considered it, but the idea chills me. If I didn't already need to get rid of her, Tans gave me another reason.

"I doubt it," Tans says, dragging me into another room down the hallway. The room smells musty and assorted rusty weapons litter the floor. "But those in power always seek more of it. I'll provide some reason why the plan is infeasible in a few days and she'll bore of the idea. It is the way of the royals and Eósy. It was merely an easy excuse to keep you alive."

"I *told* you She was bad," I crow when the door shuts behind us. "She wants to destroy me!"

Tans drops my arm and runs his hands through his hair, almost forcefully yanking out several strands. When he looks back at me, cracks erupt in his expression. "No, she's an Eósy. Even the good ones are wily. You're a failed Candidate, and you *know* what our history does to those. It isn't personal."

"She wants to *kill* me. Death is always personal." My cheeks burn, and a sliver of wetness forms at the corners of my eyes.

He frowns. "That is a child's perspective on history. If you read something other than your little romances, you would understand that."

"Don't insult me, Tans. She is evil. I spoke to the Voice, and they confirmed it—She's bad and they're not a Dark Eósy."

"She's *not*, Grace." His voice is tired but firm. "She's an immortal being who has no time for the subtleties of humanity and morality. But if you keep sending dagger eyes to our Sìnnách while making pitiful doe eyes at Kórol, I don't know that I can protect you."

"I'm not making doe eyes, dagger eyes, whatever. I'm trying to help!" I blink the tears away and poke him in the chest as hard as I can. "I'm trying to warn you. *This* is what I'm supposed to do, to save you. And—and you said you'd help. Some friend," I spit, my voice breaking as I remember what I implied the day before, and how this is probably what I deserve. I clear my throat and start again. "You don't have to believe me. But I'm not sticking around until you do, until she attacks me."

I leave Tans in the storage room and stomp back the way I came, roughly wiping at my stinging eyes. The noise from the throne room is gone, meaning I don't need to avoid Her again. As I plan to retreat to my spire, voices sound around the corner.

"Certainly. We can kill her today," a muted voice says, while a bit of blond flashes in my periphery. I duck back behind the stone wall.

"I can poison her, t'would be easy. She trusts me," says a second soft voice.

"Good boys," a sensual female voice praises. It's the dulcet tones of the Sìnnách. "Although, I am unsure whether it would be more poetic to kill her now or wait until the Winter Solstice."

"You know best." That's Kórol's baritone. I inch around the wall and spy the Sìnnách and three figures next to her. I *know* those figures—know them well and consider them friends.

"What matters is the false Candidate dies," Fíl says blandly, like he's talking about the weather and not shooting an arrow into my back. I stuff my fist into my mouth to catch the gasp threatening to escape. The other two murmur their assent, before bowing and cowering in front of Her. My stomach clenches and I press against the wall out of view.

Footsteps sound and recede until I'm alone in the hall again. The hand over my mouth falls to my heart, and the gasp I stifled gurgles out sharply. My pulse races—it's starting, and she's using my friends to do it. With a nauseous stomach and blurred eyes, I tiptoe down the hall until I arrive at my spire.

I'm not equipped for this, I never was. I'll leave and find someone outside the castle who can handle this, the Great Matron perhaps. I'll convince her that the Sìnnách was a curse on the people, not the blessing she wanted for them and she'll send me home. If Fílga and Kórol's stories were true, she can fix it. At least my friends will still live.

I burst into my chambers and pack the few belongings I have. *You cannot leave*.

"Says you," I mutter. My canvas tote bag is worn through, but it's all I have, and I can't afford to bring much, or someone might notice I've left. I will only take what I need to survive until I find help. A wave of nausea arises at the reminder.

I do, and you know I can only speak the truth.

"Your version of the truth. As far as you know, I can't leave *Dalner*, I'm guessing. But there's nothing keeping me inside Ilsen. And you're not all-knowing, you already told me that. I'll find the Great Matron, or some other Light Eósy and *they'll* handle Her and send me home." Tears leak from my eyes as I shove a spare pair of clothes in the bag and toss in the knife Kórol gave me. I leave a few things so anyone who checks my room will think I'm around. Still, I grab the journal and my notes to hide the incriminating "Sìnnách=bad" scrawled at the top.

None of the them have the knowledge to return you to Earth.

"Another Dark Eósy then." It doesn't matter who, just someone who can save me while the Great Matron protects my friends.

All you need is here in the castle. Give yourself a moment and remain in your room. She will come to you, but you must remain in the castle.

"No!" I shout. "I'm not doing this anymore; I was never going to do this on my own, your own riddles confirmed that. I need to leave and find someone who can help, someone who knows what they're doing." The words tumble out faster than the tears spilling from my eyes.

No one else will help you.

I roughly wipe at my face to clear the wetness there. "Will, not can," I sniffle. "That's more wordplay. Tell me this—*can* the Great Matron kill the Sìnnách, and assuming she gets the knowledge, could she send me home?"

The Voice grunts, the word sounding pulled from them. **Yes**.

"Then that's that." I hoist my bag on my shoulder and head for the door.

A violent pressure builds in my head, sharp and pointed, like when I was directed to the journal, a more extreme sensation than when the Voice presses on my mind. I stumble into the doorway, dropping the bag and groaning against the wood.

You must stay.

"Go away," I rasp through the blinding tears that gathered from the mental spasms. "You can't make me." I say, the pain pressing harder and harder. I repeat it through clenched teeth. "You hear me? *No one* can make me."

The pressure vanishes, and all is quiet.

Not waiting for the Voice to make a second attempt, I peer out my door to confirm the hallway is empty. I shuffle down the stairs as calmly as I can, though my hands shake and my face must look manic. When I round the final corner towards the exist, I crash into another figure, taking in his blond hair before recognizing the rest of him. Fílga gazes down at me, his eyes murky and dull.

"Where are you going?" he asks. Even his voice is monotonal.

"I'm going to take a walk through the grounds." I struggle to breathe evenly and smile at him, fingers tugging on the edges of my borrowed tunic to keep them from shaking. My smile falters a little as his hollow eyes scan my face. Apparently satisfied with whatever he finds there, he steps out of my way.

As I brush past him, a wave of relief washes over me. It's short-lived as he calls out, "Sáven has prepared a special meal for you tonight. Meet us in the banquet hall after sunset for supper."

"Looking forward to it," I say faintly as I shuffle down the hallway. I hope the bolt of fear coursing through me doesn't reach my face.

I travel north toward one of the larger Gates. My plan it simple: get to a Gate and ask the Great Matron or another nearby Light Eósy to kill the Sìnnách. The histories in the library say the Light Eósy are helpful and beloved; it makes perfect sense that they'd want to keep Dalner from the clutches of a villainous Dark Eósy, no matter what the Voice implies.

By sunset, Ilsen is a speck behind me. I find nothing resembling a Gate, but exhaustion forces me to stop. As the moon rises above, I make a small campsite for myself, a poor replica of the ones the Pack made on our six-week journey. A lump grows in my throat at the memory.

I don't know how to make a fire. I've never needed to learn, not before on Earth, and not in Dalner with Tans available. I run my hands over my arms, feeling the gooseflesh under my fingers. I should have taken a coat, my ripped windbreaker at the very least, but there was no time to make plans. Curling into a ball, I pray I won't freeze to death overnight. If nothing else, it's a fitting end to my time in Dalner.

No matter how hard I try to convince myself and others, I'm nothing special. Even though I only attempted to fight Her to save the Pack, I'm not even a good friend to them. Everything I've done has been to save myself or to further my *own* goals. I tick them off like I'm counting sheep.

I refused to hunt when they asked me, taking advantage of their kindness and giving nothing back. I mocked their past King without thinking about how it would hurt them. I disrespected Tans by hitting on him more than once when it was clear he didn't feel the same. I—I assaulted him by kissing him in the Trial. I lied and manipulated Tans and Kórol's feelings to win the Trial of the Skill.

I take and take and take—take their food, take their friendship, take their clothes. The one thing I could do for them was defeating Her, and I spent half my time whining about it or acting wishy-washy. When it came time to stand, I ran away to find someone else and hide. *Of course* I'm not Dalner's heroine. I'm not the protagonist, I'm a side character that watches the actual heroes do the hard work.

I cry myself to sleep.

CHAPTER 26

S trong hands startle me awake. I slog upward, kneeing whoever touched me and crouching into a sloppy version of a
fighting stance Kórol taught me on the road. The cold dulls my
senses, and I can't feel my fingers or toes.

Darkness cloaks us but the assailant's amber eyes reflect against
the light of the stars. "Tans?"

He kneels on the ground next to a backpack and bow, one
hand holding his side where I kneed him. "I thought we agreed
you would stay in your rooms, for your safety. Traipsing about
in the bitter cold is *not* safe."

"Safer out here than waiting for Her to murder me," I growl,
flapping out a fist that misses him by a foot.

"That would be a better threat if you had your knife out,
Butterfly. I've seen your attempts at striking men, and pillows hit
harder."

I scowl and raise my fists again, useless though they may be.

He puts his palms out. "I apologize. That was a clumsy attempt to lessen the tension between us. I want to help you defeat
Her as I promised."

I stay in my ineffective fighting stance and shift towards
my tote bag, where I'll find the knife. This could be the last
twist—the Sìnnách sends someone to help me but he's bewitched too. "How do I know you're not spelled?"

He twitches like he wants to reach for me but holds himself
back. "If I was, why would I be here?"

"To kidnap me and kill me like the rest of them."

The blood fades from his cheeks. "I am sorry, love. I should have trusted you. I should have listened to your warning. But I saw what you described."

"You saw how Kórol was different?"

He rises but maintains his distance. "Not only Kórol. Fíl-ga, Sáv, my men, the staff. Everyone seems drunk or drugged. Worse—the same ailment nearly befell me."

I kick the tote bag to the side and plant my feet on either side of it, preparing to snatch the knife. "Prove it," I demand as I bend down. "Tell me what she did and why I should accept that you're not spelled."

"She called me into the throne room to speak with me. Kórol was there behaving as her lap dog while *She* sat on his throne." He glowers. "She commanded that he 'handle me.' I was unsure what she meant, but assumed Kórol couldn't harm me, just as I couldn't harm him. I was momentarily concerned when he brandished his dagger, but he cut into his own wrist instead of advancing on me. He pressed the open wound onto my forehead, failing to even *notice* the blood running down his fingers. He mumbled something in monotone, a mental rhyming spell. I can't recall the exact—"

"I do as I'm told, no thought do I hold. Driven to obey, never to betray."

"Yes! That is what he said."

My hands shake but I hide them by crossing my arms around my chest. "What happened next?"

"After he repeated it, the Sìnnách glared at me and told me to repeat something. I had enough sense to know I needed to repeat it, or I would not leave the throne room without harm befalling me. I did, and then I immediately searched for you."

"What did she ask you to repeat?"

"To find you." He creeps forward, until I flinch closer to the knife. At my nervous gesture, he shuffles backward. "It didn't work, love. I don't know why, but it didn't. It is only coincidence that She wanted me to do what I already planned. Pretending to listen to Her was the only way I could leave the castle without suspicion. When I couldn't find you, I assumed you deserted us. Rightfully so. We had not treated you well, least of all me."

"I didn't desert you. I left to get help and avoid being poisoned by the others." And leave Dalner, but that shameful admission will remain buried within me.

He clenches his eyes shut and exhales. "Do you trust what I have told you? Do you trust she didn't enchant me?"

I study him again while I tuck the knife away and stand. He doesn't look drugged, or drunk. His voice is the same. He's missing his usual confident swagger, but that vanished before the Trial of the Will. "Come here."

He trembles as he cautiously approaches me. I cup his smooth cheeks in my hands and stare deeply into his eyes. They're the same brilliant brown, swirling from amber to chocolate. "Every atom of your flesh is as dear to me as my own," I whisper.

The muscles in his jaw tick under my stiff fingers. "What?"

"Does that seem familiar?"

He blinks and wets his lips. "What's an atom?"

I laugh, but it's shaky, and release him. "I trust you."

He touches his cheeks, stroking the spots I held. "Do you know why I was immune from the spell when She could ensnare the others?"

"I'm not sure. But it didn't work on me either."

"She tried it on you as well? I should have listened to you earlier."

It's a testament to my patience and panic that I don't respond with a sarcastic *no kidding*. "She didn't, but one of Her minions, I guess. In the low hills with Kórol, someone kidnapped me and did exactly what you described, including the same rhyme, and told me to go to *Her* keep."

We're quiet for several minutes. An animal brays in the distance, the only sound besides our breaths in the dark. Tans winces. "Tomorrow's problem," he mumbles before plastering a falsely bright smile on his face. "What is your plan now?"

"I'm heading to the wall to convince one of the Light Eósy to get rid of Her."

No longer resisting reaching for me, he grabs my hand and runs his thumb across the back in small circles. It's unnecessarily distracting. "That's the land of the divine, Butterfly. You cannot go there."

I try to shake out of his grip, but he tightens it. "I have to do something, Tans. I said I would and getting help is the only way to defeat Her."

"No, love. I mean you are physically incapable of breaching the Gate. Only significant magic would open the Gates beyond the rifts. But even those wouldn't allow anything other than animals though, not without the application of additional magic, I assume. It's purposeful that we cannot cross into Dànna much as they cannot cross here. "

"But—the Sìnnách came here. The Great Matron comes here."

"At our invitation, expressly or impliedly, much as how they can slip into our minds by invitation," he explains. "The same circumstances are necessary for us. With the walls intact, unless they invite us to cross through a Gate, we cannot traverse their land."

"But—the breaches—"

"Are because the Dark Eósy are poking holes, a great number of them conjoining their magic to create rifts. We'll find no allies in Dànna, love. You'd be better off tossing yourself into the sea."

Wrenching my hand free, I collapse to the ground to cover my eyes. "So, I can't do anything." No way to defeat the Sìnnách; no way to get home. I'm dueling against a double-edged sword with only a spoon to protect myself.

He sits beside me and places a warm hand on my knee. "That's not true. You told me it was your purpose here, after all. Have you discovered anything from those riddles or your Voice? I recall you confirming they weren't Dark, that's a benefit."

"And that's what I'm talking about. I have *riddles* and a voice in my head. She has a dragon and a mindless army. I don't like those odds."

"You have more than that, Grace," he murmurs. "You have me."

Relief and the innate human need for comfort has me throw my arms around him. He tentatively wraps his arms around me and hugs back, exhaling deeply. "This has been a strenuous day for us both, Butterfly. The sun will be upon us in a few hours. Let us rest and plan our next steps tomorrow."

He joins me in my shoddily made camp, adding his pallet to mine and suggesting we share. I unsuccessfully attempt to convince him to build a fire, but he explains that the fire might lead anyone the Sìnnách sent after me directly to us.

Which means I'm still facing down a frozen night. I lay down on my half of Tans' pallet, Tans remaining behind me back-to-back with several inches between us. I shiver, a quiver born from both chill and nerves. I can't blame it entirely on the cold, but on the bone deep anxiety and dread from both Tans' proximity and the knowledge that I'm still at risk to be killed by an immortal assassin soon. Tans turns, his chest inches from my back. Multiple unwelcome flashbacks to the cave with Kórol run through my memory.

"I can help with that," he offers.

"Go for it," I say lightly, too cold to say more, lest my chattering teeth overtake the words.

"It doesn't work if I'm not touching you," he whispers. I crane my neck to see his face but only his outline reflects in the moonlight. "It does not work if my body is not touching yours. Unless you desire actual flames coming from my fingers, which I would advise against for many, many reasons."

I scoot backward, my body assenting rather than my voice, as I forcibly remove the Kórol-related memories that bloom. But this awkward male encounter is nothing like my experience with Kórol. This time, Tans wants nothing to do with *me* that way and *I'm* the one with the uncomfortable crush, except mine isn't magic made but true. This time, there's not a contrived romance plotline forcing Kórol and I together. There's no otherworldly trope to explain tension and attraction chasing through me. Still, his arms open, and I turn to press into his chest. His arms wrap around me and my head falls into the crook of his neck, right above his shoulder. It's like snuggling with a heated blanket.

"You're a furnace."

His body shakes against mine, chuckling. "That is the point, love."

The rhythmic rise and fall of his breath and his tightening arms lull me to sleep.

We have one full day before the Solstice. After we eat the snacks Tans brought, I halfheartedly suggest we let the Great Matron handle it when she arrives. Although we can't go to her, she could still be an asset. The riddles are worthless without Kórol anyway. Tans considers this plan when a niggling thought hits me—the Voice was clear that she *wouldn't* help, not that she couldn't. Maybe—

"Do you think the Great Matron knows the Sìnnách is evil?"

Tans' eyebrows rise in alarm. "Of course not. Something must have corrupted the Sìnnách over the centuries. Perhaps one of the Dark Eósy twisted her when she ascended the wall."

"We don't know though, since there's no way to tell Light from Dark."

Tans shakes his head sharply. "We know the Great Matron. You've seen her image; she is goodness and light."

"You thought the same of the Sìnnách."

Tans ignores me and begins unbraiding his hair. "The Great Matron isn't a viable option. Let us focus on those riddles. We know you must use some deception, perhaps you lie to the Sìnnách and can defeat her. And myself and—ah, it slipped my mind to tell you before, I believe Kórol and I are the 'fire and ice' in that hint."

My face flushes uncomfortably at the reminder of *how* I realized that, and I can't meet his eyes. "No, I know." I change the subject. "But he won't be much help now unless we break the enchantment. The Voice said it would end when She died, but maybe there's another way?"

"That I don't know. Obviously, our usual practices of guarding our minds, watching our words, and rejecting outside influence does no good if they have been invited in."

"Which still leaves us not knowing how to kill Her."

"Your Voice implies she bleeds like anyone else," Tans says in what he must think is a reassuring tone. It isn't. "Eósy can die, history tells us that, else the separation wouldn't have occurred. I've no idea if the Sìnnách is a corrupted Eósy or something worse. Only Raddare the Eleventh may know, when he banished the Sìnnách the first time." He re-braids the silken stands and stares back behind us. Ilsen looks like a miniature figurine of itself. "Except for you, he was the only one to notice the Sìnnách for what it was."

"Well, maybe not only the two of us."

"What do you mean?"

I pull out the journal from my tote bag and hesitantly hold it out to him. If he throws it again, I'll punch him. "The Voice led me to this book, and the author figured it out."

He takes the book and skims the first few pages. His eyes widen with each page. "No wonder you learned the truth. This was written by the Eleventh Raddare. Your teacher was the only man to see it previously." He flips towards the end of the book. "Did he say how he defeated her before?"

"I haven't finished it yet."

He scowls and waves it. "Do you mean to tell me that this book told you of the Sìnnách's schemes, but you never *read* ahead to see how he handled Her? You, whose *only* Earth pastime was reading, couldn't finish the most important book of your time?"

I strain to grab it, almost falling in his lap, but he holds it out of my reach. "I've been a little busy! And I didn't know it was his journal. I didn't even *get* to the Sìnnách part until right after the last Trial."

"What could have been more important than this?" he demands, glowering.

I elbow him in the gut and snatch the journal when he flinches. "Maybe completing all the Trials to stay alive and trying to figure out the riddles. I tried to show it to you two days ago, and you threw it at the wall!"

Tans seems chastened and slumps. "I have many regrets, Butterfly. Not believing you is one in a lengthy line. Perhaps between the two of us, you have the time to read the *correct* passage?"

I thrust the book back into his hands with narrowed eyes. We skip through months of the author's life, our shoulders bumping. The sun is high above when we finally find it.

> I can scarcely write this entry. I found Father kneeling (him kneeling! a King!) in an abandoned solar. She sat with closed eyes, although I knew she was aware of my proximity as I sensed her vileness brushing against me. I approached her cautiously, but she still did not greet me. Neither did Father, though I assume he was not aware enough

to recognize my presence. I praised her and while she basked in my fealty, I took a cold iron dagger from my breeches and, with a speed I will never repeat, sliced clean through her pale neck. Thick, oozing blood, dark enough to weep black, ran in rivulets into the bodice of her corset. It appears that everyone, even the Sìnnách, bleeds in the end.

I read it again. *Everyone bleeds in the end.* That's *literally* what the Voice said, meaning I may owe them an apology. I stifle a frustrated huff.

Tans peers over my shoulder. "He makes it seem quite simple."

"No kidding. Do we have any cold iron though?

He digs into my tote bag, squawking once, which means he touched my phone again, before pulling out Kórol's knife and handing it to me hilt first. Smoke billows off his pinky finger. "Your blade should suffice. Though perhaps we throw your Earth device at Her and see if She lights on fire."

I ignore the joke. "I thought that knife was steel."

"Steel is formed by smelting iron," he replies patiently, though one corner of his lips tilt upward.

"But doesn't that make it hot iron?"

His face splits wide into a grin as he tosses the knife back into my bag. It connects with my phone and his grin turns spiteful. "Cold iron simply means a weapon."

"All this wordplay is going to cause accidents," I grumble. It reinforces my reasons for disliking subtext—text only, where everyone says what they mean. "Why wouldn't he just *say* a weapon?"

He stands and hoists my tote bag over his shoulders, holding out a hand for me. "Perhaps we should ask him. We can open his tomb and invite him to a feast. But let us wait until we have dispatched the harpy who has bewitched my King."

I let him pull me to stand and wipe the dust off my wrinkled dress. "I wonder how She managed to respawn when no one else seems to have that skill."

"You'll have to explain your nonsense talk later."

I roll my eyes good naturedly. "Fine, so let's find one of those bandits that hang out in the woods and get him to stab the Sìnnách in the stomach."

His dark eyes fix on me. "There is no time to proposition an assassin. We must stab her ourselves."

"*Us* do it? Speak for yourself. No way am I getting close enough to stab her, Tans. I'm here to provide the hints, then aim and point someone in the right direction." I know my limitations, more so after crying myself to sleep the night before.

"You must try, Grace. I'll be with you, but it is *your* purpose. The Eósy must have brought you here, gave you this quest, you who the Voice and journal spoke to, you who recognized Her for what She was. You surely don't plan to give up."

"No, of course not," I growl. "I'm just taking an... administrative position in the assassination. But it means you or someone else does it. Seriously, Tans, you're the warrior. I'm a nobody."

He's in front of me in an instant, eyes burning with sincerity. "I don't understand how you cannot see your worth in this. You proved yourself in the Trials. You recognized the Sìnnách for what it was. You kept yourself safe as an outsider in our world. You tamed Kórol, you captured—" His voice catches. "You captured the hearts of our people. There is no end to what you can do, including defeating Her."

"I'm not the hero here, Tans," I whisper, leaning into his chest for comfort. He drops my tote bag and embraces me. "For a minute there, I—I thought I might be. God, I—I was so *stupid*—"

"We were all duped, love," he murmurs into my hair. "But your purpose remains, and I vow to stand with you as long as you will have me."

"Okay," I sniffle. "Okay. Then we go back. We do it together, and whoever gets closest can stab her, whether it be the unskilled Earth girl or the extremely competent and veteran army general."

"You cannot wiggle your way out of it with compliments," he teases, picking up my bag again. "Now, Sìnnách-killer, what do we do first?"

I drop my head to my chest in thought. "We need to get close to her, right?" My head lifts. "Which means we have to avoid her mindless army and the dragon. So, we figure out how to do that."

He straightens and throws his pack and bow over the opposite arm before walking in the direction we came from.

"Where are you going?"

"We must fight fire with fire. I'm seeking our fire," he calls behind him.

I scamper to catch up to him. "Is that a magic joke?"

"No. It's a Sìnnách joke."

CHAPTER 27

He meant a dragon. It wasn't funny, which I told him. Repeatedly.

Joking or not, the plan is to catch one, sneak all three of us into the castle, let our dragon distract the Sìnnách's dragon while Tans fights Her, and I slip behind Her and stab Her in the back. It isn't the worst plan.

Dragons, Tans explained once he remembered that Sáv and the others kept me in the dark about them, are found around bodies of water, which is why I saw one at the small stream on my first day in Dalner. Tans leads us to a nearby stream only a few hours away, where we'll arrive before sunset. We head west, out of the mountains and towards the sea that greeted me when I hunted the sprites.

We travel in weighted silence, as he apparently remembered that our friendship was strained. I don't call him on it or attempt to fix it, refusing to do anything that might make him bolt, like Sáv says is his custom and something I've experienced already. I'm not sure what he's thinking, but he sends me pouting glances every few minutes.

Near midafternoon, we arrive at the stream prepared to wait until sunset. Though the sun is still overhead, several dragons descend, splashing in the water and lifting off with wriggling fish in their jaws, imitating vicious and oversized herons. We sink to our bellies and watch them from ten yards away.

"I thought it was too early for dragons," I whisper.

"They should not be here yet. But that is a problem for after. We must focus on the now. What's your plan for the dragon?"

I gawk at him, but he seems sincere in waiting for my instruction. "Are you kidding? As we've already established, I'm not a Sìnnách so there's no way in hell I can 'tame' that thing."

"I saw how the beast at the Trial let you touch its snout. I also saw that you did not flee in fear."

"Only because I was imitating a kid's movie," I hiss. He cocks his head. "I don't have time to explain it to you. Suffice to say, these dragons are not like big scaly cats."

"Well, we must think of something. Their presence in the daylight may mean they will fly away early, and we'll miss our chance."

I thump my forehead on the mossy ground and groan as quietly as I can. "Fine," I say to the dirt. "Just do as I say."

I explain my (stupid, reckless, cruel, and will *rightfully* get me burned alive) plan to Tans. We wait until a single dragon lands near the stream to drink while the others coast in lazy circles above it. On my signal, Tans notches an arrow into its bow. As the sun dips below the horizon, the beast finishes its sip and preens itself before preparing to take off. As it opens its wings, Tans lets the arrow fly.

It squawks and falls to its side with a thud. The remaining dragons roar and abandon it to its fate alone by the stream. When the last dragon flies away, we scurry toward the one we injured. Tans' arrow nicked the base of its neck and a dark pool of blood dribbles down its large leathery body. It doesn't rise or fight back, instead hazily watching us with slitted red eyes.

"Hello, dragon." It offers no sense of understanding me. I whisper to Tans, "Do you think it knows human and Sàrkany speech?"

"How would I know? I'm not Sáven. I have no animal proclivities."

I nudge him in the stomach. "Real helpful," I grumble. Holding out my hands protectively, I stand in front of the dragon's fiery eyes.

"My name is Grace. I don't know if you can understand me, but we can help you. My friend," I motion to Tans, "can heal your wound. I'm sorry this was the best idea I had and you can rightfully burn me alive later, but we needed to get your attention." Its gaze rests on my face. I kneel in front of it, my heart stuttering out a staccato beat loud enough for even the departed dragons to hear.

"There is a Dark Eósy here," I continue. "She bewitched our King. She rides on a dragon herself, and she may have bewitched it as well. We need you to take us to our castle," I point to the direction of Ilsen. "Distract the other dragon, while we kill its master. Then you *and* your comrade will be free, and you can light me on fire if you want."

The dragon blinks and puffs labored breaths of air. It doesn't react to what I've said or show me any comprehension beyond the pain it must feel. I stand and back up haltingly, letting Tans support me. "You should heal it."

"How do we know if it is going to help us?"

"We don't. But we can't let it die." I won't have another unwarranted death on my conscience.

He appears to disagree but approaches the dragon anyway. He whispers to it soothingly as he digs the arrow out. A considerable smattering of blood follows, buckets falling on the dirt and I blink away the guilt-shaped tears forming in my eyes. Tans spits on his hands and places them over the wound, his hands sticky and slipping. Seconds later, the split skin closes, and the spurting injury vanishes, leaving only a small, puckered mark where the arrow entered. The dragon flutters its wings, as if testing that it can still fly. Tans backs away to my side while the dragon's eyes widen, and it bares its teeth.

But instead of clipping us or burning us alive, the dragon stretches its wings and bursts upward, creating wide waves in its wake. We watch until it vanishes, its dark form barely recognizable in the night sky.

"It was a worthwhile attempt," Tans says, rinsing his hands in the stream and wiping them dry on his undershirt. "Now what?"

I wish he'd stop asking that, but I try to act brave. "First, sleep. Then, we—we try to kill Her and hope our friends don't kill us first."

Tans holds me snuggly against his chest that night, the weight of tomorrow pressing on us both.

"I wish I were back home," I whisper it into the skin of his neck.

He stiffens. "You would want to leave us?"

"I'd take you with me. All of you. But I can't—I can't do this, Tans."

He stirs against me, his breath on the space just behind my ear. "I believe it is time for another discussion about caterpillars."

I roll my eyes, but a smile blossoms before I can stop it. "I thought you gave up on that analogy which, *seriously*, was a fantastic decision."

He ignores me and cuddles closer. "And when the caterpillar thinks its life is over, it suddenly becomes a butterfly. You're in the middle of your metamorphosis. You've shed your caterpillar skin and closed your surrounding cocoon. You simply need to emerge."

I laugh wetly. "When we get through this, remind me to tell you some other aphorisms. I've got loads from all those Earth books."

He nestles into me. "I like that you say when."

"Well, if or when *I* fail, I expect you to keep us both alive by lighting everyone on fire."

The warmth of his arms smothers me. "With my last breath, I will keep you safe. This I promise you. I can do nothing else because having met you, I know the days spent without you was not a life and the life I have lived since knowing you have made up for the days I may lose tomorrow."

I almost can't breathe; my heart flutters and cheeks redden without my permission. Move over, literary love interests, Tans has them all beat. "Tans, I—"

He covers my lips with his fingers of one hand, the other wrapped around my back. "I know what you will say. But my heart cannot bear it, not when the end is near. Please don't make this more difficult than it is."

My lips move against the pads of his fingers. "I *have* to say something when you talk like that, especially now."

He releases a trembling breath and runs his index finger over the curves of my lips before dragging it down to my neck and letting his hand join the other, enveloping me in his arms. "Now is exactly why I *cannot* hear it. It has been exhausting, Grace. Trying not to betray Kórol, remaining your friend—but my feelings are overwhelming and to hear the continued confirmation that you feel differently when we approach the end—" His eyes pinch shut. "Call me cowardly, call me childish, but I want to face our fate without being reminded of the truth. I know you have made your choice. And I will follow you tomorrow and the next day and the next as your very best friend, but please allow my heart a night's reprieve."

Wide eyed at his confession, I can't help myself—I lean forward and mash my lips against his. Like the last time, he opens against me immediately, his tongue dipping into my mouth as though he can't help it before he breaks the kiss. He leans his forehead against mine and closes his eyes, the breath caressing my cheek sounding distressed and uneven.

"Don't do this, Grace. I don't need your pity."

"It's not pity, I want this, Tans." I try to kiss him again but he ducks his head into my neck.

"I cannot simply be a notch in your belt, your last comfort before tomorrow, because you don't have Kórol," he growls, voice helpless and rough. "Neither Kórol nor I deserve that."

A disbelieving laugh erupts from my throat, one that bubbles and threatens to turn manic. "I never wanted—I was never *with* Kórol!"

He shakes his head, eyes meeting mine again. "How can I believe that? I saw you on the trek, and how he behaved towards you when we arrived here. You told me he wanted to marry you, and you loved our friendship the way it was. Kissing me was *betraying* him for the Trial, for Fates' sake."

I barely keep from pinching him, settling on kissing him again. "He was bewitched to want me," I say when I withdraw. "I told you that. Any time I tried to tell someone I didn't feel the same way, they were spelled to change the subject. And I was trying to tell *you* I wanted you, and *you* rejected *me*, saying you cherished our friendship. I do too, which is why I didn't subject you to a confession that would have ruined it!"

His eyes blaze; before I can blink, his hands snake up my back to plunge into my hair and yank me towards him. He presses desperate lips to mine over and over, as though he can't keep still. We finally fuse together, unable to be torn apart, as his hands trace over any piece of skin he can reach, each stroke of his fingers like the strike of a match. He kisses me like we could move the very mountains themselves.

All those flowery words from books suddenly make sense, and a mindless pleasure spreads within me—it's wonderful and scary and overwhelming and amazing. He drags his hips on top of mine, pressing me into the thin pallet. A blaze burns from within me, as the kiss goes on and on. With a breathless gasp, I pull away.

Tans lips are puffy and wet, his fiery eyes dazed. "Why did we stop?"

The dark hides my blush. For all the pseudo-erotica I've read, facing an opportunity to recreate it is something I didn't expect. "It's—I've never—"

He falls to the side, pressing a kiss to the corner of my lips. "I understand. Those are decisions better made when the threat of death is not so present." His voice is whisper soft, tickling against my skin. He wraps me back in his arms, stroking his fingers down my back. Disappointment and relief chase through me.

"We'll pack the condoms next time, tomorrow, maybe." I'm only partly joking.

He huffs, which turns into a half-hysterical snicker. "I'll use an Earth one for you."

We both fall asleep smiling.

I wake after Tans again, his breath tickling my ear and his arms crushing me. It's still dark, and I wiggle to get out from the cage of his arms, but he won't let go.

"Butterfly, stop. Stay still," he demands, his gaze focused beyond our feet. There, a few yards away, a dragon sits on its haunches. An elbow to the chest frees me and I rise quickly to stare at the bestial intruder. On its chest is a trail of dried blood leading up to a small, puckered mark. The dragon huffs and lies on its stomach, as if beckoning us to straddle its back.

CHAPTER 28

The weightlessness of flying through the open sky is both terrifying and awe-inspiring. Seated astride the dragon, we can watch the first rays of sunlight rise above the horizon. But the actual act is nauseating because there's nothing between us and the ground. I almost fall once, slipping off when we were only a few feet aloft, and Tans keeps an iron grip around my waist for the remainder of the trip. If I needed another sign that I wasn't a dragon-rider, I have it.

The dragon flies us back to Ilsen in under an hour. Tans suggested we head straight back because it's the Solstice, meaning everyone will be preparing for the evening and we can catch the Sìnnách alone.

The dragon drops us to the ground right in front of the gates. The castle grounds are still, allowing us to sneak in undetected, which isn't something I expected to do with a dragon in tow. Tans leads us through a half dozen winding passages, the same they apparently took for the Trial of the Beast. He outfitted me in an extra pair of armor he took on his original flight from the castle, blue like his with a red embroidered dragon spanning my chest. Black greaves and bracers and my borrowed dagger finish the look, the entire guise making me appear more competent and heroic than I feel.

We pop out in the hall nearest the throne room, where I anticipate meeting our demonic foe. Gulping in a breath that I hope will give me courage, I throw open the doors, exuding a confidence that's only skin deep. Tans and the dragon trail only steps behind.

The Sìnnách sits at the throne and inspects her nails while two figures kneel at her feet and her dragon rests in the corner. At a closer glance, I recognize Kórol and my opponent from the last Trial. I hadn't realized they didn't return the Brute to his burrow, though the Sìnnách's arrival that night may have changed things. But it means our half-cocked plan where Tans distracts Her with a brawl while I stab Her in the back is now *un*cocked. Now, we must fight through Kórol and the Brute first. I muster up all the heroism Tans, the Pack, and the Voice think I have and confront her.

"You've overstepped, harpy," I call, my voice echoing around the nearly empty stone room. I thought about what to say on the ride, better to focus on than my impending death, deciding on a powerful and poetic screed to carry my legacy *after* said impending death. "I, like the King before me, will eradicate you. This time for good."

I swallow a wince when I finish; my expectations of my wit are too high.

Without looking up from her nails, she tilts her head towards her dragon, which roars and rears on its hind legs. It opens its wide black wings and rushes towards us, skimming the stone floor with its claws poised to catch and scratch. But I brought fire to this firefight, and my borrowed dragon mimics its foe, flying into the air to strike its brother. The beasts lock claws, their necks wrapping around each other like embracing swans as they slam into the wall behind me. The two continue their fight as if the humans aren't present.

My attention returns to the Sìnnách and I clear my throat. "Like I said, I'm going to eradicate you."

After my repeated declaration, I run towards her, Tans on my heels. But the men at her feet are nimbler, bounding forward before either of us take our first steps onto the dais. Tans latches onto my former adversary.

That leaves Kórol for me. Luckily, the enchantment that dulled his mind makes him slightly less agile as I duck while he trips over my body. The edge I have over Kórol is short-lived; whatever allowed me to trip him doesn't keep him from catching me before I reach the Sìnnách. He knocks me hard to the ground, my squawk of pain muffling against the stone. My hands and feet are slick with sweat and my hip screams as I crawl away. But even with dulled senses, he's quicker and stronger than me. He grabs my ankle and pulls me backward as my fingers claw uselessly at the stone ground, flipping me onto my back as he yanks me towards him. His eyes flash in time with the glint of the blade he slashes into my flesh, nicking the bone above my ankle.

I scream while Tans extricates himself from the other warrior, the Brute's crumpled form laying on the floor halfway up the dais. Tans leaps onto Kórol's back, wrapping his arms around Kórol's throat and squeezing. "Go, Grace," he yells.

Kórol releases my ankles to grasp Tans' fingers on his throat, his knife clattering to the ground. I hobble on to my feet, slipping on the blood that runs down my right foot, and dart my eyes around the room. I'm no longer thinking of the Sìnnách but of keeping Tans safe from Kórol's mania. The Sìnnách's eyes flick disinterestedly between the din before her and the dragons battling above.

Before I can dive for the knife, Kórol elbows Tans in the stomach with his free arm and bashes his heel on Tans' foot, mimicking what he showed me months prior, shattering the bones in Tans' foot with a sickening crack. Tans loosens his grip on Kórol's neck as pain blooms over his face. It's only for a second, but long enough for Kórol to break free and throw Tans across the room. He lands with a thud against the hard-stone walls. I can't tell from the distance whether he's still breathing.

But there's no time to think, no time to run to the knife *or* get to Tans' side as Kórol charges me, his hands gripping my forearms and forcing me backward. My feet kick outward as I slip in blood trying to scramble away. He shoves until I hit the wall, the stained-glass window above me reflecting red light onto his cruel face I wriggle and squirm, trying to maneuver out of his grip in any way possible. I slam my knee upward, hoping to gain an opening to writhe away from him. But he parries and a vile predatory grin crawls over his lips. He pushes me harder into the wall, cracking my skull hard against the stone, and slips his leg between mine, pinning himself against me.

"Kórol. Please," I croak. I'm woozy from the body blow and blood soaking into my shoe. He says nothing, only widening that unnerving smile as his eyes rake over my face, my throat, my chest. He brings one hand to my neck, letting his finger trace a small circle right above my collarbone, outlining the polished scar I earned from the first kidnapping. The skin sears against the ice streaming from the pad of his index finger before he lunges, biting almost directly over scar. I howl as his teeth rip through my skin and beat my arms against his back. He laughs as I do, licking his lips and lunges for me again, but aborts the motion before his teeth make contact a second time. He releases me jerkily, face shifting from ferocious to confused. His eyes lose the milky haze, and a brilliant ice blue peers at me.

"Miss Grace," he murmurs. "What?" He brings his hand to his lips and wipes the blood on his lips and beard, horror crawling over his face when he sees the bloody bite on my neck.

"No time," I rasp. There's no time to question how the enchantment broke either. "Get your knife and follow my lead." The Sìnnách strains in her chair, watching Kórol. He grabs the blade by our feet and presses it into my hand before I push off from the wall.

I bolt to the dais, Kórol chasing close behind, when realization hits the Sìnnách.

"Obey," she snarls to Kórol. "Kill her." When Kórol doesn't immediately comply, she rises, her fingers reaching out toward Kórol and her dragon.

She's too slow, losing precious seconds to her confusion, allowing me to rush to her side and bury the knife in her stomach. Something black and oily pours out as I yank the knife free and the Sìnnách's eyes roll backward before she falls to the ground. Her porcelain body tumbles over the dais as she jerkily grasps the wound, the blackness spilling from beneath her clenched hands. Her mouth widens in a snarl, and she screams invectives at the dragon, at Kórol, at all the Sàrkany. Behind me, Kórol grabs my shoulders to pull me away, but I jerk free, almost falling. Panting, I lean down, holding back the vomit threatening to rise from the scent and look of the black blood pooling around her body. Her dark marble eyes focus on me, and she gurgles, blackness running from her mouth as she attempts to speak. The words never form as the last breath gasps from her mouth.

Like a switch flips, the dragons stop fighting and clamber towards the ground. With a sudden roar, the Sìnnách's dragon soars into one of the remaining stained-glass windows, showering the throne room with flecks of glass as the two-winged beasts flee from the room. As the last piece of glass falls to the ground, the room stills.

With a jolt, I tumble over Kórol, scrambling to Tans' body. Kórol races at my heels, both of us arriving at Tans' side simultaneously. I tap his cheeks as Kórol checks his chest, but his eyes stay closed. I grip the folds of his tunic and shake him hard until he makes a wobbly noise, breathing out staccato puffs of air. His eyes flutter open, seeking mine and murmuring my name, then Kórol's. I cradle his face while Kórol sniffles beside me when as an icy breeze billows over us. Kórol jumps to stand, and the three of us stare at the open window.

"Hello, children," a woman standing atop the broken glass croons. Kórol and Tans gasp at the vision there. Encased in a gown of white, and a crown of flowers sits atop her head as her silver-blonde hair cascades down her back until it curls right below the curve of her breasts. Her skin resembles cold and polished marble as she looms over us imperiously. She's beautiful.

No, she isn't. She's terrible.

No, that's wrong again. She's horrendously beautiful, a too-perfect flower, a poisonous one that begs to be touched.

She makes my skin crawl.

Her eyes are black but rimmed with an unearthly violet glow and they watch me with derision. But there's something else swimming in the purple depths, something that seems out of place. Grudging respect, maybe, but I'm probably delirious. She clicks her tongue before smiling wide, looking like a predator eyeing its prey. Her dangerous aura steals my ability to speak and think. The men by my side seem to have the same problem, as they remain slack jawed.

"My Lady, you're early," Kórol stutters out. She ignores him, her stare on me alone.

"Little Grace, we meet at last." She saunters to the throne oozing sex and sensuality, not even offering a consolatory look at the crumbled Sìnnách beneath her feet. The Sìnnách's oily blackness, her blood that pooled on the ground, licks at the edge of the woman's gown, tendrils soaking upward before the woman in white flounces onto the dais and melts onto the throne. Her red manicured nails rap the side of it as if in anticipation. "I know you were expecting me, but I had hoped you would leave my golem alone until I could play with you too."

My eyes flit to the single undamaged stained-glass window a few feet away and I understand what Kórol meant. "*You're the Great Matron?*" I ask under my breath, mind coming to a troubling realization, one I scarcely considered with Tans the day before.

Her eyes harden, and she scoffs. "The insects chose that name, believing I was the Mother behind the wall. But Lady of All Who Once Opposed Her was too unwieldly and tended to give away the game."

At her declaration, Kórol and Tans seem to arrive at the same conclusion I did—that she isn't the embodiment of goodness they think. Tans snakes a hand around my ankle and sends jolts of heat up my leg, soothing the burbling wound slightly.

She slants her gaze over us. "Will you not bow? So many years and yet you still have trouble with the few demands I make." The three of us don't budge. She flicks a finger at me, displaying a single scar on her porcelain skin, a jagged line running down her forearm. "Do not make me cut out Little Grace's pretty doe eyes." I gulp, and she catches the movement, her lips curling upward. With a bit of effort, Kórol kneels. Tans, still on the ground, shifts to his knees.

"What good boys you are," she coos. "Terribly naughty for you to break my spell, but your immediate fealty warms my heart. Punishment will, of course, still be forthcoming, but only after I spell you again. The years have taught me it is always more satisfying to make a man scream when he's asking for it." She licks her lips before turning her gaze on me. The shock of her words hits me all at once, the conclusion as nauseating as I imagined. *Her* spell, *her* Sìnnách. Her.

"Yes, let the gears turn in your simple brain, stupid girl. That thing," her eyes flick to the body of the Sìnnách before her, "was a creation of mine, a conduit until the Thirteenth Raddare let me through the Gates each Solstice. And after a millennia of deception, after centuries of planning, you managed to ruin it in a month and a half," she says, wrinkling her nose at me.

I manage to stammer. "I don't understand. You're supposed to be a benevolent being. Giving them blessings, giving them—"

"Giving them the Sìnnách, this great savior?" She laughs, so crisp and clear a sound that I worry my ears will bleed. "That was quite a diversion. No one ever considered that someone who rides dragons, must command them, *subjugate* them." She slides her gaze to Kórol. "The dragon people of the Raddares. And my revenge plan against them and their wall was *finally* complete when Leda's stupid child, the child that should have been mine, opened his mind to me. He didn't let me through, but my golem was an adequate substitute, giving me power and worship. Of course, I didn't know then what I do now, that only spelling the King meant there were prying eyes to stop me. Little did *I* know Raddare the Eleventh would be one to do so, destroying my golem." She glares at the remaining stained glass window, at the image that looks so like her. "Little did *he* know he would bring them closer to me, his own descendant begging me to return."

The violet in her eyes gleam as she stares at Kórol. "Do you know how long I waited to bring agony to your line, how long I planned and studied?" She frowns and claws her fingers against the wooden throne until it slivers crack from it. "And the Raddares accepted a shoddy substitute, again."

While she speaks, I try to think of a plan. The Voice's riddles are still in play—I've got Tans *and* Kórol now, they can over-power her, while deception is my armor. "What do you mean? I wasn't the Sìnnách," I say, praying she can't hear my thoughts. I imagine a brick wall between us, refusing to invite her in, like Tans said.

"Exactly." Her calculating stare drags over my body. "But they *thought* you were, the Fates only know why. With you present, they would no longer need me, love me. I did not accomplish all of this to allow someone to take my place."

"But you're a god—"

She sighs and dislodges her nails from the splintered wood. "Only when you worship me. We're magic, not divine." She looks back at Kórol. "The wall your ancestors demanded is the only thing keeping the worst of us from taking our vengeance against the Raddares. You've been protected with me as the only one you invite in, you ungrateful things, but I've half a mind to let them tear the barriers down."

My heart threatens to beat out of my chest, and I cast my eyes around the room, working to buy us more time. I can't focus. I think of the books I read, even in romance does the villain monologue about their plans. I need her to keep talking. "So, you brought back the Sìnnách to keep people worshiping you when I showed up."

She nods, tossing silky strands of her hair over her shoulder. "And I learned I couldn't risk simply spelling the King alone. I needed the entire Kingdom." Then she smiles and the venom behind her eyes sparks. "You must tell me how you broke my spell."

"Never." My confidence is short-lived, and a lie, but it can tell me whether outright lying is the 'deception' I need.

She shrugs elegantly, her expression placid. "I can dream up any *number* of ways to force it from you, even if you evaded death at the hands of my captors. You have given me so many chances to play with you already."

She only confirms what I already guessed. Though I didn't realize *she* was Her, I knew the bandits and the spelled man in the low hills were not coincidences. She continues, "The Trials were wonderful, by the way. It gave me more entertainment than I anticipated."

I let out a small gasp at that continued confirmation of how deep her influence went. Whether she notices, I can't tell, but her mouth forms a Cheshire-cat like grin.

"You surprised me, how you managed to drag yourself forward. I assumed the dragon would kill you. When it didn't, I was intrigued at how far I could push you. If I couldn't break your body, perhaps I'd break your spirit—forcing you to kill something precious. But still you persevered, like a cockroach. And then, the Trial of the Will." Kórol and Tans both tense, and she flicks her attention to them for the briefest of seconds. "I've learned to appreciate emotional anguish, but I had hoped you would die."

She stands, stepping over the Sìnnách's corpse and slinking down towards Kórol and Tans. In tandem, three of us slide our gaze to the dagger by the Sìnnách's body. She hasn't secured it. Perhaps she thinks we won't live to need it.

She scratches a manicured nail down Kórol's cheek, turning back to me as her hand slithers down Kórol's chest. "The Trials should have killed you, either by your own despair or by the tests themselves. I do not know how you bested them and kept these two devoted to you."

She pauses, her fingers contorting into claws over Kórol's heart. "I watched as they desired you, although Fates knows why. One wanting you is shocking given your grooming regimen, both *alarming*, and I saw how irrational they became. Your insecurity fed their desire, their jealousy." She grabs Kórol's chin and clenches until a drop of blood runs from his beard down her fingers. "Preposterous or not, it was glorious, a fitting torment to the Raddare line."

She wipes her palms on her dress, leaving dark blotches of blood and oil on that delicate white lace. "And yet, it still isn't enough."

She places her palms on Kórol and Tansr's foreheads as I slowly slide closer to the dagger, pressing one hand to my hip to keep me steady. The wound on my leg clotted, but more blood trickles out as I limp towards my goal. She angles herself in my direction and absently addresses me. "You'll note there is no blood this time. That is only necessary there's no ability to touch." She frowns while I freeze in place. "I tell you this should you have it in your miniscule brain to interfere. You'll find my power is more potent than you've experienced previously."

She twists back to my friends. In a bored tone, she drawls, "I do as I'm told, no thought do I hold. Driven to obey, never to betray." Kórol and Tans open their mouths and shudder violently. Based only on the intensity of the trembling, I doubt they'll remain standing. They do but it looks to be a near thing as both hold each other for support. Her mouth offers a razor's edge smile, and she delicately taps both men on the cheeks. "Crude rhymes but still effective. Boys—you are mine. Repeat."

"I am yours," they say in unison, their voices foggy.

She sighs. "I do love when they say that." She turns to me and drags her eyes between me and the knife. The Cheshire-cat grin reappears. "Kill her."

I leap for the knife as both men lumber towards me. Even spelled, somehow this time they're much quicker than me, reaching the knife before I do. In the scuffle for it, I ended up splayed on the ground as Tans grabs my hair. Grunting, he pulls me upward by the scruff of my shirt, one hand lightly holding onto my gathered mane. It doesn't hurt as much as it should. Kórol seizes the hilt of the dagger while I squirm and struggle against Tans until I elbow him in the nose. His grip on me doesn't loosen, and he snakes his arms around me, pinning mine down as my back presses into his chest. His chin is next to my ear and the warm blood from his broken nose drops down his face onto my neck. The Great Matron watches idly as if the entire fight bores her.

Tans drags me in a circle until she can only see our backs. Kórol shuffles towards me, the knife pointed straight at my abdomen. I struggle again and lean forward, prepared to crack my skull into Tans' face.

"Butterfly," he says. I stop struggling, wondering if I dreamt it. Tans' breath is hot on my neck as he whispers again. "Keep fighting. She can't know."

I wiggle, straining my neck to study his expression but his head stays pushed up against mine, forcing my eyeline on Kórol's advancing form. When Kórol is a foot from me and presses the tip of the blade into my stomach, I look at him, expecting to see the drugged and cloudy eyes of a bewitched man. But the eyes staring back at me are clear, the same kaleidoscope of silvers and blues shifting in the light like a snowbank during a sunrise. *Deception would be my armor.*

"Now!" Kórol yells.

In what feels like hours but is only an instant, Tans releases me while Kórol shoves the knife into my hands. Both men spin to face the Great Matron while she buffs her nails. They both unleash their magic before she notices something is amiss, strings of ice and fire flowing towards her. *You must have fire and ice to succeed.* When the flames and ice hit her, she roars.

"Betrayal," she screams at the air, not watching me but gawking at the burns forming on her previously pale arms. "You will regret this," she snarls as she focuses her rage on me.

Before she unleashes whatever manner of pain she has planned, I jump forward, half tripping until I slam the blade into her chest. She sputters, her face the perfect mask of confusion, before she falls to the ground, landing parallel to the corpse of her creation.

Everyone bleeds in the end.

CHAPTER 29

T he three of us tumble together into a hug, almost sprawl-ing on the ground.

"Please tell me there's no other Dark Lady flying through the window," I say with my face muffled into Tans' neck.

He releases a breathless laugh. "I should hope not. Kórol, did you understand her when she spoke of Leda and revenge?"

"I know of my ancestor Leda, but how she connects to the Great—to that woman, I've no idea," Kórol says.

I lean back and look at the two men, both of their arms still around my waist. Better to focus on her motives than how close we all came to death or worse. "She sounded like a spurned lover. Saying Leda's kid should have been hers and all that anger about being replaced."

Kórol instantly removes his hands from my body and steps away, as if wanting to distance himself from the memory.

But Tans keeps me in the circle of his arms and smiles. The blood caking his face makes it a horrific image. "I suppose it matters not, so long as she remains dead."

"What happened?" I ask, wiping my sleeve across his chin to wipe away the rusty red. "When she spelled you again, I thought I was doomed."

"Her trick did not work the second time. She could not force my devotion again," Kórol says.

"Your blood," says Tans. He gestures to the wet stains on my sleeve and the wound on my collarbone. "

I use the cuff to remove the rest of the blood from his face. "The Voice did say my blood made it hard for manipulation spells 'to latch.' But I didn't realize it was contagious."

"We've tasted it," he says. "She couldn't enchant me, but I ingested tiny amounts of your blood when I healed you before. When Kórol's mouth split the skin on your neck, the charm broke."

I shiver and press more firmly in his lap. "God, that's unsanitary."

Someone throws open the door to the throne room and people rush inside. I bury my head in Tans' slim chest, and Kórol slides behind me, the two imitating a human shield. Seconds later another two bodies collide into us, blond and red hair intermingling in front of my face. When we pull apart, their eyes glimmer with tears, but none try to rub them away. Tans keeps his hand on my low back and lets soothing sparks of heat slide over my spine. Kórol still looks shocked, but blinks away the panic, leaving a somber mask in place.

"We know what you did," Fílga exclaims, hands shaking as he rubs my shoulders. "It must have happened with Her death. The enchantment broke, and we remembered what she told us to do and how she mesmerized us." He scowls darkly. "I cannot believe I didn't see her for what she was, after all my...studies. Or that she was able to spell *me*."

"Can't thank you enough or apologize enough," Sáven says. "Who killed them?" he asks with a predatory gleam in his jewel bright eyes, gesturing towards the corpses.

"Our Butterfly," Tans says, sounding proud.

More people propel into the room, taking in the scene—the corpses, Tans and my wounded bodies, Kórol standing behind me like an honor guard.

When a dozen or more men and women stand in front of Kórol and ask questions en masse ("what happened?" "the Sìn-nách was evil?" "what do we do now?"), Kórol stalks to the throne, standing between the two still bodies. More castle inhabitants enter the room, seeking their King after coming out of the spell they were under.

"As you can see, the Eósy tricked us long ago," Kórol says. "She presented herself as a leader of the Light, but planned to remove our free will, after keeping us under her control over centuries through false hope and devotion. With the help of Miss Grace, we were able to thwart her plan."

Tans squeezes my shoulders and Fíl offers me a proud smile.

"We have learned many things from this trickster," Kórol continues soberly. "Including a threat that the wall between us may fall. Given how an Eósy we believed was good and right for centuries deceived us, we must be circumspect in any encounters with the Eósy and diligent in keeping the threat from breaching our walls."

He glares at the only remaining stained-glass window, the one depicting the Eósy family—the woman in white, the man at her side, and the angry child at their feet. "Tomorrow we will hold an open Council meeting and prepare our armies for an attempted invasion." He dips his head. "Tonight, we celebrate that we have overcome the centuries of deception. But for now, leave us to heal."

Several men in leather armor direct the citizens from the room as the Pack drag themselves and me into a small annex room next door. The door is unobtrusive and located right behind the throne, half covered by a tapestry. The room is empty except for a half dozen chairs, pieces of what look like broken thrones, and a few candles. There's a solitary window on one wall, the same six-inch wide and wall length kind in all the other spire rooms. Tans carefully deposits me into a chair and heals the damage to my leg, before healing Kórol then himself.

Without warning, Kórol drops to his knees and groans. The mask falls with it, his eyes panicked and breath stuttering. Tans reaches for his face and cups it in his hands, staring at Kórol's agonized expression.

"What's wrong?" I ask. Fíl rushes to his side and kneels a foot away while Sáv stands next to me, and we both watch torment run over Kórol's pinched face. Tears escape and he squeezes Tans' wrists.

"Is it the swell?" Sáv asks, mouth pursed in concern.

"The echo, perhaps, as Miss Grace defeated the enemies," Fíl suggests.

"He was no more than a weapon, a tool for those deaths; that wouldn't cause the echo of defeat. And, though I was indisposed, Grace and Kórol's fight ended in a stalemate," Tans says. Kórol still holds tight to his wrists while Tans rubs circles on Kórol's temples. "This is something else."

Kórol's gaze darts to me as he releases Tans and dry heaves. Tans brushes Kórol's back soothingly. "It is—" Kórol heaves again, "it is not the mind magic, but the memory of the enchantment. I couldn't show my weakness in front of my subjects, but I..." He looks back at me. "I was out of control with need for you," he whispers. "I—my mind was not my own. My thoughts were not my own. I *touched* you in that way, wanted you fiercely and I..." His eyes shutter, and the room chills.

I don't move, except to cover my mouth with my hands. I hadn't considered how enchanting Kórol to desire me might feel to him. "She violated you. *I* viol—"

"Don't," Tans interjects sharply. Kórol and I both flinch. "Don't place blame on yourself. Anything that happened is because of the machinations of the Great Matron and her puppet."

Kórol looks at my seated form, eyes red rimmed. "I know you are blameless. I seem to recall you tried to convince me otherwise during the worst of it. I—I simply do not know how react to what my mind and body demanded."

"Perhaps we ought to retreat to heal, physically and emotionally, privately," Fíl says. "You committed yourself to a Council meeting tomorrow morning, Kórol. Will you be up for it?"

As if those are magic words, Kórol straightens, and the mask reappears over his expression. "I am the King, Fílga. I can divorce my personal and public roles, as you well know."

Tans scowls. "Until we know more of the potential invasion and can put this behind us, we may hide our concerns for quite some time."

"Take the night," says Sáv. "Threat'll still be there tomorrow. But the relief might not."

Tans' mouth ticks upward. "Since when are you the voice of reason?"

"I'll tell you when you're older," Sáv says as he grabs Fíl's hand.

Nervous laughs tinged with relief ring around the small room.

Adrenaline chases Tans and I until we're alone in my chambers. Both newly healed and in shock, we sit on my bed side by side. We've changed clothes, separately though I can't remember it, and someone dropped off a platter of meats that lays empty outside the door to my room, but I have no memory of eating anything. It doesn't feel real, that the month of buildup ended like it did—with no real bloodshed from my side, with my enemies almost *letting* me execute them. The residue of the deaths I caused may taint me later, the effects on Kórol and everyone something that may take long to heal. But I'm safe; we're all safe.

"I'm not courting anyone," Tans says. The words are soft against the emptiness of my room. I blanch, the thought of him already dating someone not even crossing my mind, especially after last night's confessions. He sees my expression and intertwines our hands. "Seeking introductions was a misguided attempt to remain respectful of my friend's feelings, my understanding of your own, and to guard myself from further hurt. But I wanted you to know."

I lean into him. "I'd hope you weren't. And don't worry—tomorrow, I'll remember you made us go through all that based on simple miscommunication and will yell accordingly. And you can yell at me for my part. But right now, I'm thrilled we're alive and together. I can't even believe it."

"I deserve every bit of your ire." But his tone is teasing, as if he knows it doesn't matter how upset we might be in the future, since we have each other now. "I cannot believe I was willing to give this up," he says, wrapping his arms around my waist and pulling up to lie down next to him. "My heart was riven without you, and I had no hope it would be whole. And yet, here you are."

"Flowery words won't stop tomorrow's yelling."

He rubs his hand soothingly over my back and I inhale the cinnamon and smoke smell of him. "Then I will have to try harder, Butterfly. Do you—are you still wanting to go home?"

I trace small circles over his trim stomach, which tenses with each second I don't respond. "No, that—that was about me running away. I don't have anything like you all there. Especially you."

He smiles and I inwardly congratulate myself for causing it. After a few minutes of snuggling, he sits us back upright. While he keeps one hand twined with mine, the radiant smile falters. "I should have realized something was wrong earlier. Kórol has always been a serious sort, but his behavior the last month was very out of character. I stupidly accepted it as consequence of his belief that he found the Sìnnách." He says the word venomously before wincing in my direction.

I clench his hand to show there's no offense. "Should we help him somehow? I didn't even think of it before he mentioned it, but it's assault."

He looks pensive as he twists a braid between the fingers of his free hand. "Everyone handles trauma differently, and it is a personal form of healing. I will stay by his side as I have always done, and hope he lets me know what he needs."

"I hope to get to know the real him," I say. "Maybe we can do some matchmaking and find him a partner that he wants."

Tans shakes his head. "His attraction to you was only part of his oddness. That he was physically attracted to anyone should have been the first sign that something was amiss. As I said, I misjudged it. I have always been the more open of us, the one willing to play the fool and announce my thoughts loudly. The joke was that I flirted enough for the both of us. I assumed love might have changed that for him." He huffs bitterly and closes his eyes. "Truly, I should have realized. At his most open, he is not demonstrative. Even this afternoon, when he relived those memories—I've never seen him so anguished," he finishes quietly, eyes heavy.

He lays us back down and I try to comfort him as best as I can with his body warmly blanketing mine. "It makes little sense," he continues after another few minutes of silence. "Why would the Gre—that woman enchant Kórol in that way? Surely, it happened early on when we met you, that is when his temperament first changed."

"To mess with me by getting Kórol to put me through the Trials? To punish me for attempting to replace her with the bonus of psychological torment? And she seemed like she preferred other people getting their hands dirty. The Trials killed false Candidates in the past, meaning she could get rid of me and hurt me. That was the point of the Trials, she said."

"She also claimed that your introduction as the Sìnnách way-laid centuries worth of plans. It *surprised* her that Kórol desired you. Why would she be surprised if she, or her creation, enacted the spell? As you said, his feelings convinced us of your Candidacy at the start. No offense, love, you're capable but—"

I reach behind to pat him on the cheek. "You don't need to convince me. It was farfetched anyway. Do you think there's something else going on? I was joking before, but I really don't think I can handle another Dark Lady today."

"I am simply thinking. The warrior in me puzzles out strategy and tactics." He speaks into the skin of my spine. "Or weren't you aware that *I'm* the smart one?"

I wriggle against him, but that 'unreal' feeling sinks into my stomach. I have no head for strategy, but I know stories, predictable ones at least. Nothing about my time in Dalner is predictable, but it still follows the tropes. I'm not the fated hero but end up a savior anyway. But in real life, no one's born a hero, they must earn it. No one is that lucky, meaning we're missing something.

"Did you get any memories from the Brute?" I turn to lean over him as he stares back blankly. "The dobdehìà. Did you get any memories from it?"

"A few, all focused on the woman as he was her tool, but I couldn't appreciate them given her sudden appearance," he answers slowly, his expression turning confused. "Why?"

"I didn't."

He pets my sides and squeezes my waist reassuringly. "Well, that's not unexpected. You are not born of magic; you'd not experience it."

I bat his hands away in agitation. "But I defeated Her. I should have gotten *something*. I've felt it before—and if you say it was only the echo, I will kick you, healing leg wound or not. I should have gotten *some* memories from Her at the end."

"Perhaps it only works on Sàrkany, and not beings of magic like the Eósy."

"Is a dobdehìà a being of magic?" He nods. "Well, I got memories from it after the Trial. I got memories from the two men who kidnapped me too even when they were just tools, and the hint of Her. I dreamed memories after the eel. The only time I didn't was with the sprite, who gave me its life, and Kórol. Something's different now, since I didn't get those memories."

"Which means—" He pauses, giving me a pitying look as dread seeps into my skin. "You might have been merely a tool for another impending threat."

CHAPTER 30

Tans suggests we congregate with the others immediately. I hesitate, not wanting to foist my presence on Kórol but he disagrees, repeating what Fíl said, that Kórol can separate his roles and desires. Since he knows Kórol best, I trust his insight.

We meet in the throne room, which was cleaned in our too-brief absence. The only remaining evidence of what happened are the broken windows.

We perch by the dais where I drop onto the floor next to the stone platform and absently thumb the journal and notes in the pocket of my dress. I brought them out of habit more than anything, a reminder of what I've learned, and what I might be missing. Tans sits on the platform and nudges me to lean into his side. My head lolls upward to look at him as the light from the remaining stained-glass windows beams onto us, the glare focusing my gaze. I stare at the glass Great Matron and her consort, and the sullen child at her feet.

"I don't know who the bad 'Her' *is*, if not the Great Matron. The Great Matron made sense as the villain—a spurned lover who had history with the Raddares. Who else cares enough to attack?"

Tans tracks my gaze. "If we take Her ravings as representative of the entire race, any of them might seek to claw their way through the wall. And we cannot discount that the threat may not be a woman."

"But the Voice—"

"Is still an Eósy and everything that implies." He pulls on a braid, but I snatch his hand and interlace it with mine.

Fílga and Kórol arrive soon after we do. Kórol's step hitches imperceptibly as he stomps through the side door and approaches the dais. "You have concerns?" Kórol asks, bypassing the niceties.

"Grace didn't experience the swell of mind magic after defeating the Great—the Woman," Tans explains. "She believes this was in error, as she has experienced it many times before. It's possible she was a tool for some other scheme, either, as she thinks, because the real Her has yet to arrive, or as I'm beginning to believe, because the Woman's death created a power void and another, worse Eósy will rise, who may have used Grace to create the dissention and will attempt to breach the walls."

That leads to another long discussion about Her, and how I learned about Her.

While Kórol and Tans hash out the possibilities, I stare at the window. "Where did that image come from?" I direct my question to Fílga. "Did someone make it up or are all three figures real Eósy?"

Fílga clicks his teeth in thought.

"They are real," Kórol says in his stead. "My Father explained they are the three central figures of the last known Eósy royal family. Do they have some meaning to you?"

"If the lady in white is the Great Matron, the little one is the Voice, maybe. They could have been the one leading me to defeat the Great Matron, and may know what's coming next, the real Her I need to defeat. Or maybe her consort."

"Or the Voice mimicked a child to lure you in, and they are the true enemy, and that image shows nothing more than a story," Tans says.

Fíl frowns. "If that is not who we know as the Great Matron, then it is someone else. I assumed it was the original ruling Raddares, not the leaders of the Light across the wall. They were all heirs to the winning families."

But he's ignored. "Where is your Voice now?" Kórol asks.

"They're gone. We got into a fight and I think I kicked them out."

"Could you invite them back?"

Tans squawks and I drop his hand to avoid the inadvertent lick of flame he lets loose. He winces apologetically in my direction. "Kórol, if her Voice is the enemy, I cannot in good conscience let them create chaos in Grace's mind."

I roll my eyes. "They wouldn't 'create chaos' in my mind."

"You can, Tansr," Kórol says through clenched teeth. "Remember—we divorce ourselves from our personal wants and the needs of the Kingdom. I am doing my duty for my Kingdom, just as you must. If this Voice knows or can give us more information about the threat still outstanding, I urge Miss Grace to contact them." Kórol addresses me directly. "Do you believe you can eject them from your mind if the need arises?"

I wet my lips and nod. Tans pinches his eyes shut tight. When he opens them, the amber faded, and only muted mahogany remains.

"Every arrow in the quiver," Tans grumbles. "Fine. We ask them."

Kórol calls an emergency meeting of the Council, moving it up from the next morning. He hopes for a miracle and the key to keeping the walls up and avoiding bloodshed. Knowing how the Voice operates, I'm hoping for a *little* more information than we currently have, or proof that I finished my purpose here. I did my part, as shocking as it seems—I got rid of *two* enemies of Dalner.

Tans clasps my hands as we wait, standing next to the stone platform where Kórol would sit in his throne. When the heat gets to an uncomfortable level, I pull away.

"What do we have to lose? The Voice can't interfere, and they can't come physically here without us asking them. Best case scenario, they know the real threat and will tell me." I pause. "No, *best* case scenario, there's no threat, and I didn't get the swell for some other random reason. But the *absolute* worst case is that we learn something new."

"I simply worry."

"It may not be a brilliant plan, but even my worst ones have worked out so far."

He groans as several people file into the room. "True, although that your foolhardy plans haven't somehow ended horribly *yet* is not as reassuring a thought as you may think."

"I'm a butterfly, remember? Metamorphized and ready to fly."

"Butterflies also have an incredibly short lifespan," he says under his breath.

I lean up and swiftly kiss on the lips. "Then you should have used another metaphor."

He can't respond as Kórol sits on the throne and starts the meeting. The congregated group are the same people who were present two days ago when I barged in on Tans' presentation. The Council members kneel on the floor, and Tans' armored troops stand behind them. Fíl waits off to the side with his notebook with Sethen standing beside him. It's a perfect simulacrum to the last group meeting, but without the murderous she-devil in the corner.

"Thank you for being available on such short notice. I appreciate that there are many uncomfortable revelations over the past day, and there are more to come, including those of the possibility of war," Kórol says.

The Council members babble at Kórol's declaration while the soldiers straighten.

"Not two days ago, if memory serves, we sat in this room and listened to Lord Commander Tansr of Gràmad explain a threat against us. At that time, we were all under the spell, some of us literally, of the conduit acting under the orders of the being formally known as the Great Matron. Lord Commander Tansr noted we would be prepared for a potential invasion within the month. But, pending further information, they may strike earlier."

Another buzz goes through the group and Lady Rothàna stands. Her hair cascades down her back, the bright color in contrast to the skin displayed at her neck, and she juts out her chin. "I want more information about the Great Matron," she demands.

Kórol minutely inclines his head. "Lady Rothàna of Làna, the Crown recognizes your query but declines it at this time. We must focus on the possibility of an imminent assault by the Eósy and the consequences thereof. A more detailed explanation will be provided when we handle the current threat at our gates."

"No pun intended," I whisper to Tans, who smiles faintly.

"Point of order," Lady Rothàna says. "The deception by the Great Matron could prove helpful in discerning who is leading this current charge and when to expect it, or if it is even as imminent as you claim."

"I do not disagree with you, Lady Rothàna. Indeed, that is why I have interrupted your suppers. Miss Grace, whom you all should know of at least by reputation, has a link to the Eósy and a plan to obtain the very information we seek. She will allow that rift for us now."

All eyes turn to me expectantly.

The Council members remain kneeling while I stand on the dais with Tans and direct my attention to the high stone ceiling. I imagine opening a door and beckoning in the Voice, assuming I kept them out at all. "Good evening," I say respectfully, aware of all eyes on me. "I wanted to thank you for your help in handling the Sìnnách and the Great Matron."

There's no response. The expressions on the onlookers' faces vary from suspicion to concern. I try again, closing my eyes.

"Not to seem ungrateful, but I'm hoping you can help me again. I got the impression—"

"Grace, Grace, Grace." The childlike singsong voice echoes against the walls, no longer a speaker only I can hear but something surround sound. My eyes snap open and Tans clutches my shoulders. Everyone looks to the ceiling and windows, but nobody appears, only an oozing wet mist at our feet.

"It is I who should thank you," the Voice continues, their tone deepening. "You did exactly as I had hoped."

"That's—that's good to hear. But maybe you can confirm—was the Great Matron the Woman I needed to defeat, or is there someone else coming?"

A pressure pulses into my head, like someone batters my skull with a rock. Tans' grip is the only thing that keeps me upright. "Both, Little Grace."

A panicked murmur goes through the assembled crowd. I reach behind me to move Tan's hand before it burns a hole in the fabric covering my shoulder. "Can you give me a little more information?"

"About you playing into my hands or my intent to breach the Gate? Because the answers will be the same."

Nerves lick up my spine as I sink to the floor, landing heavily in the chilled mist. Tans stares down at me, his face confused and bloodless. I swallow the bile threatening to spill out of me and attempt to focus on *why* I thought this was a good idea. But I can't help knowing— "Both?"

"Let me indulge you, if not because it will be meaningless, but because *I* was forced to listen to your thoughts. And after all my planning, I find myself wanting to brag. The Eósy you so quaintly refer to as the 'Great Matron' held all the power. She was the only one for whom the Sàrkany ever invited to pass from our realm to yours, making her the gatekeeper of Dalner, pardon the pun. Her followers kept the rest of us from applying the magic needed to bring down the walls. I needed Her out of my way."

"But She was going to destroy me, us. You can't lie—that *had* to be true."

"It was true, dearest," they say in a crooning tone, the nickname Tans' uses sounding vile. "You because you were a threat to her plans. The Sàrkany—I extrapolated. Her game had an end, though not for centuries, and she would slake her desires in more bloodthirsty ways. You did us all a favor." They laugh shrilly until the noise deepens into the rough rasp of a grown man. "Me most of all."

"No—no, that doesn't make sense! You said you weren't a Dark Eósy."

"Silly Little Grace, thinking in terms of good and bad, light and dark. Real life isn't as simple as those books you hide in. Those factions existed at when the walls were erected, but time changes all things. And with your Great Matron gone, our power structure is in flux and I spent the last few hours *finally* convincing my brethren to tear down the already weakening Gates."

"Are you hearing this?" I hiss to the surrounding crowd, but no one stirs or looks at me with any sense of understanding. I look back to the ceiling. "When are you coming?"

"Do you truly imagine you hold any power?" The Voice guffaws. "Who do you think brought you here? Who do you think allowed you to understand the language? What would you do if I took it all away?"

I stare back at Tans, whose expression is distraught. My shock gives way to anger; I must get something useful from this. I'll let this villain monologue until we can ram the words down their throat. "Why did you do it then? Please—feel free to explain in detail, including the inevitable finale you planned. It is your turn to talk, don't forget."

I can feel the Voice's delight echo around the large room. "There's the fire I inspired." I scoff as they continue, "In another world, we might have been friends. More, perhaps. Your weaknesses aside, we're the same, you and I. Resilient, self-interested, and seeking something more."

"We are *nothing* alike," I snarl.

"Perhaps not. After all, I earned my successes alone. You were handed your accomplishments by me—each test, each trial, each altercation was delicately planned. Similarities or no, you weren't special, merely a warm body to act in my stead. I chose a human because they have no magic in their blood, keeping your mind clear, but I chose *you* because no one would miss you on Earth and you wouldn't search for a method to return. You were so intent on 'belonging' that you snatched onto any idea of your so-called importance I slipped into your head. Manipulating the King to want you and the others to accept you were the fake Sìnnách was the only bait She needed. I created you and pointed you at an unmoving target, one whose own hubris caused her downfall."

I reach out for Tans' hand, who gives it to me instantly. I clench it to keep from trembling. "We'll still stop you; we've come this far." I'm proud my voice remains steady.

They hum. "That seems unlikely. When we breach the walls at sunrise, I anticipate you'll be *far* away, cloistered in cotton. And even if you did join us, you are no match for the desperation of my brethren."

The mist begins to dissipate before the Voice sounds in my head. ***Oh, and Grace? Thank you again. Truly, I couldn't have done it without you.***

The mist vanishes and I vault into Tans arms, shaking as I embrace him. "You caught all that? Not the manipulation part, because I'm *not* dealing with right now, but the part about sunrise. No one needs to say 'I told you so' since we still got something useful."

But no one says anything. I look around at the many faces in the room, each a picture of confusion. "Someone say *something*, please. The plan? Keeping the Voice from breaching the Gates?"

Kórol watches me with an odd expression. "Yd leyms, Tan-sr??"

I shift away from Tans to stare at Kórol. "What are you saying?"

Tans tucks my hair behind my ears, his expression blank as he looks around me to the others. "El sáche club. Fílga, sam reyth atla cyl tlamch?"

"You—you can't understand me anymore?"

They watch me and talk amongst themselves before Kórol makes announcements to the assembled group, but I don't understand a word.

I can't warn them.

CHAPTER 31

The room empties before I react. Kórol, Tans, and Fíl speak quietly as the last of the Council members leave. Their eyes dart furtively to me, ironic since I can't understand them anyway. Kórol and Fíl finally exit while Tans watches me where I remain slumped by the dais. His jaw works behind his lips, but he stays silent, his expression a mix between furious, exhausted, and mournful.

I press my fingers hard against my closed eyelids. Not two hours ago, I'd *almost* accepted that I was "special," finally listening to that that tiny spark that said '*yes, I was chosen, I'm here for a reason.*' I choke out a bitter laugh. And worse—I did this to Dalner. If I'd tried to go home, if I hadn't bought into the Sìnnách lie—the Great Matron would have been the only threat, and all she wanted was attention for the next century or more, not bloodshed.

With a growl, I snatch the journal and notes from my pocket and hurl it at the throne as hard as I can. The loose parchment flutters like butterflies with broken wings, like me, and cascade around the dais. The journal loses a few inner pages from the force as it hits the wood and falls onto the seat.

"You'll regret this!" I scream at the high stone ceiling. Gone are the feelings of sadness, gone are the feelings of hysteria. I've hyperventilated and panicked too often in Dalner. All I have left is rage.

The Voice made a mistake by confirming I won't be missed on Earth. Now I know that my home is here; there's no going back to a place where I have no one. In Dalner, I found friends and a family. The Voice hurt those friends. They assaulted Kórol, nearly killed him and Tans, who only tried to protect me. It's my turn to protect them now. I may not be the heroine, but I can do *something*.

"You—you think you're *so* smart," I hiss. "That I'll just sit back and let you hurt my friends, *my family*. I don't need to talk to them, I'll—I'll do *charades* if I need to. You'll never see me coming!" There's no answer, not that I expect one. "And you're *never* getting inside my head again," I finish as I roughly wipe the tears of fury from my face.

I've sat by too long. The Voice was right: I've *let* things happen to me and let others handle things for me. But the Voice is my mistake, mine to rectify. I may just be a non-magical human with stupid non-magical blood but—all thoughts stop, everything spinning within me focuses on that single detail: my blood can counter magic. The hissed fury transforms into a gasp.

The inkling of a plan forms. A stupid one for sure, one that if Tans could understand would make him light something on fire. I hide the possibility behind my eyes, not that I expect he'll figure it out.

Tans gathers up the evidence of my tantrum before sitting down, the long lines of his body hunching awkwardly next to me. His hands shake as he drops the bundle of crinkled paper at our feet.

"El khàru cet brogan tellàch e a mychtak Sìnnách. Cel ktòsu et," he says, earnest enough that I can almost guess what he's saying. *It didn't stop us when we learned you weren't the Sìnnách. I'll be here for you, regardless.*

I lean into him and he sighs as if relieved, pressing my face into his neck. It's uncomfortable and too hot, but the feeling only fuels the burning need within me to return what he and the others have given unconditionally to me.

"Cel kcurad et," he whispers into the skin behind my ear.

"I'll fix this," I seethe into his neck, letting anger control me to avoid drowning in guilt.

He pulls back and his eyes soften, his lips part and kisses me delicately, gentler than I deserve and softer than I want when I'm trying to keep anger stoked within me. "El relág el ktág-che atla ruth-il," he murmurs against my lips. I tamp down the frisson of desire those unknown words inspire. There's no time for that now, not until I warn them of what's to come.

He makes protesting noises when I wriggle out of his arms, but I ignore him. I wasn't joking when I threatened to use charades. It can't be that hard. All I need is to communicate a single phrase. *Hey Tans, the Eósy army's breaching a Gate at sunrise.* Or maybe, four or five words—*gate, Eósy army, sunrise.* Tans is brilliant, a strategist; he figured out the Voice immediately. He can figure this out easily. I turn to face him, sitting cross legged and letting my skirt drape over my legs. Tans shuffles closer, pressing his thigh to my knees, like he can't help the contact.

"Eósy," I say, staring expectantly at him.

"Eósy," he repeats with a glower, turning and resting his hands on my covered thighs.

"Gate, how do I act out a gate," I mutter. I hold up my hands parallel, the sides of my palms and pinkies resting next to each other. I turn one outward, like a gate opening. "Gate," I say while Tans watches the movements with a furrowed brow. He reaches out to caress my cheek, trailing one finger down the side of my face and cupping it in his warm hands.

"Yl by chàkres, rittak."

I gently remove his hands and put them back on my thighs. "Okay. That probably looked like a door. Gate," I repeat more forcefully, trying again. Still keeping my hands flat, I turn them and touch the tips of my middle finger together, then bend the fingers of one hand up to my knuckles. I'm almost proud of that attempt as I simulate a gate attached to a fence that pens animals. Tans covers my fingers and I frown up at him.

"Mótceltu by hág ráspunalln. Fyanmótcel by celg preleg bylh láol iánt a dom veldàch tráfum." He leans in for a kiss, but I stop him before he deepens it.

"We don't have time for this." I clench my teeth. "*Tomorrow*, all you want, but right now you have to work with me."

He's frowning now too and slips his hands up to my hips. "Od sáil nespengà elf? Cel kcurad et, stòrnameg ilg chàkres tlótak."

"I'm trying to warn you, Tans. What happened to divorcing personal wants from the needs of the Sàrkany? Seriously—and I'm still talking to you like you understand me," I finish with a groan. "Eósy, Tans. We need Kórol—get me to Kórol. He'll pay attention and not try to make out with me. He can barely stand to be around me. Kórol Kórol Kórol."

Tans runs his hands through his hair. "Kórol?" he asks, and I nod. "Cel kveldà Koról, àin yl kgenches là el stare." He waggles his brows, but still looks pained, and helps me up with an outstretched hand.

The slightest relief pools into my stomach at his immediate obedience but I remain wary. "I'm going to assume that means, 'yes, dearest, to Kórol we go,' and not something about ignoring Kórol to cuddle."

"Kórol," he repeats, rolling his eyes. He uses his index and middle finger to mime someone walking.

"*Now* you want to play charades," I sniff, but a smile leaks onto my face against my will. "We'll have a group field trip to the gardens, and I can show you an actual gate since you're going to take it seriously," I suggest as he leads me to the side door.

Before he opens it, I turn back for the journal and my notes sitting haphazardly on the floor. Neither will be helpful now; one, I can't read and the other, I can't explain because of the language barrier. But they're still mine and were important once.

When I shuffle back towards Tans, one page with my notes scrawled all over it falls to the floor. Huffing, I grab it and shove it back inside the journal, but something stops me before I shut the book and hide them away in my pocket. The words—the pages with my notes—I let out a whoop that causes Tans to startle and fly to my side in concern.

"No, no," I tell him needlessly. "I'm okay. But look." I point to the parchment tucked between the bound pages. He reads over it and stares back at me with a confused expression on his face. "I've been writing in your language the whole time! And I remember some of what I said." I link his arm with mine. "No field trip needed. Come on—Kórol Kórol Kórol."

As his expression goes from panicked concern back to pained reassurance, he pulls me from the room.

Tans takes us to a part of the castle I haven't explored before, in a spire past the kitchen up a winding set of steps to a windowless room. The walls are wood, not stone, and covered with maps and large charts. Kórol stands at the head of a rickety looking table while several armored men surround him, leaving a hands' breath between them and Kórol, though they squish together themselves. The group studies a vellum map flattened with small stones in the corners. Fílga writes frantically at a small desk near the back wall, a dozen or more ancient books sitting at his feet.

Kórol furrows his brow when we enter and addresses Tansr, I think. "Il cuno trá mótfummer iánt el nevo il." His tone seems concerned. When he looks at me, he flinches before grimacing out a smile. "Byr il ánó, Grace?"

"Still gibberish to me, sorry. But I think I can help." I motion to the papers in my arm.

"El sócad cel tolerh ylg," Tans says. "Yl sàlipms tlóh de a Eósy."

Kórol confers with Tans for a moment before he gestures for the others to back away. In the space, I lay out my notes on the vellum map. Up close, it mirrors the map Fíl showed me when we first met.

"Okay, this is a cheater's version of charades," I explain for my sake, and to avoid the utter silence around me. It will certainly stop the guilt from clawing at the edges of my mind. "I've got four words. Something's up with the Eósy, you know." I look up at Tans.

"Eósy," he repeats.

"Right. First one down. So, I remember reading a book on the difference between Dark Eósy and Light Eósy and how one helps the Gate and one hurts the Gate." I tap my finger on two lines of text written in my messy script.

Tróm Eósy=rut gósca
Mórt Eósy=gult gósca

"I don't know which is which, but the last word, gósca, means gate." I exhale heavily. "Which is the second easiest one since you should have guessed something was up with the Gate anyway. Whatever, take the wins where you can, Grace. Gósca."

The men look at each other and then me and gesture for me to continue.

"Great. Next word—break." I mime holding something between my two fists and snapping them in half, but I get the same uncomprehending expression Tans had in the throne room. "Break." I repeat the motion without success. With a growl, I grab a writing nib to draw the word, muddling out a broken board that looks like the arms of two puppets shaking hands. "Break."

Kórol purses his lips but still no one catches on. Groaning, I try again, making a broken vase, but it looks like abstract art, then a broken heart. None of them understand and I exhale shakily at the reminder of how much I took for granted when I arrived in Dalner. Maybe if I'd read any fantasy before arriving, I might have realized how ludicrous it was to not further question how they spoke English.

But I can't give up. I try again, feeling a burning behind my eyes and press hard enough on the parchment that I snap the nib in half. I look up at Kórol, whose face is still blank. I grab another nib from in front of a bearded man with black and red leather armor and snap it, and another out of the hands of a man in blue leather, and another. "Break, break, break, break," I snarl with each snap.

"Cet byrche chapragstak, kave," someone I don't know says.

"Il hor ilgad." Tans' response is harsh. Clearly, the other guy isn't praising my ingenuity.

Kórol ignores the byplay and repeats my mime. "Sás teykh ráolh?" He does it again and then takes yet another ink nib and snaps it in half. "Ráol?"

I mimic him and nod. "Rah-ole. Yes! Okay. God, this will actually work!" I don't dance in place, but it's a near thing. "Eósy ráol gósca," I say. The others straighten.

"Now—Eósy army." I slash a dozen tick marks on my paper to signify the amount of potential Eósy soldiers. I motion to all of them and mime a battle by bashing my fists together and aiming fake weapons around the room. They stare at me blankly, probably because the battle I enacted had guns. I add two stick figures with poorly drawn knives and point to the hilt on Kórol's belt.

"Noatrá," Tans says. He pulls out a knife from his boot and points it at the other men in the room in a defensive motion.

I don't know if he is saying "battle" or "fight" or "army," but the exact word doesn't matter, as long as they understand *something* is happening or coming and that it isn't the single Eósy we thought it might be this morning. "No-uh-trah," I repeat.

The others whisper amongst themselves, and Tans makes a few gestures that causes one man to run down the stairs behind us. Fíl continues to write furiously in the corner while Kórol shouts over at him. The din increases, and I lose their attention. But there's only one word to go, and the most important, the one I should have started with.

I slam my hand on the wooden table. The sweat smudges the beautifully drawn map, though I don't know when I started sweating. All eyes are back on me. "I'm not finished," I snap. Kórol gestures to the half-filled parchment.

Instead of drawing, I hold up the journal and point to the embossed sun on the cover.

"Mót," someone says.

"Sunrise." I point at the sun again. Tans leans against Kórol and they both watch me with expectant eyes. I search the room, looking for something that might help me explain it, but nothing stands out in the windowless room. I hiss through my teeth and draw a sun cresting over a mountain.

"Là yl teykh mótnàltgge mótceltu?" a man in blue asks.

My problem, aside from a complete lack of artistic ability, the language barrier, and my utter uselessness without both, is that sunset and a sunrise look the same. With another frustrated growl, I draw a second sunset and a full sun. I cross out the second and third sun, finally pointing at the first one, until the last nib breaks from the pressure.

"Sunrise, today." I smash my hands together and pretend they are a pillow by my face and then fake-snore and wake up pretending to be alarmed.

"Mótsu," Kórol announces. He looks at me with a clenched jaw and the temperature in the room drops. He points to the floor, then the picture and repeats my mimed pillow. "Mótsu."

Hoping I understand, I point to the floor. "Today. Sunrise, mótsu." Like 'army,' whether 'mótsu' means sunrise, tomorrow, or even *morning* doesn't matter. What matters is that they knew something is coming now and we have no time to waste.

Fíl stands between Kórol and Tans, papers in hand. "Yl by met á Mótcel Luggesu, ed a gósca by láigge. Mótsu by a cus lucrugge reum hág hátselltak," he says. Kórol heaves once before spitting and barking short phrases to the group. All but my three friends leave the room and my knees almost give out.

I did it. I warned them. The guilt ebbs enough to allow me a single relieved breath. It isn't enough, but it's a start.

Kórol utters something under his breath as Fíl directs his attention back to the map, which now has rows of squiggles crossing it, slick and oily lines over the smudges I created. The two peer down at them while Tans draws me into a hug. When he finishes squeezing the breath out of me, he releases me but keeps me caged in his arms. His eyes flash amber and he tries to kiss me around his beaming smile. Even under these *awful* circumstances, I can't help but grin back at him.

"Ilg vek pràp sesàrms tráfum! Il byr rurepry. El rit il." His smile slips and he looks shocked as all the blood leaches from his face.

"Sá il?" Fíl has a question in his tone. Kórol's lips upturn slightly.

"Pífcheág," Kórol says solemnly, which clashes with his amused expression. "Yl by a sol kav yt dezlás ylg."

Tans looks at me like I hold the answers to every question, ironic since we can't understand each other. I've missed something world-shattering. "Feeling out of the loop here guys. Gósca ráol? Eósy noatrá today at mótsu?"

All the tension that released at their secret conversation rolls back into the room, and I almost regret causing it.

"Sol mótfummer," Kórol says. "Grace cládys mu."

Tans tilts his head before glancing in my direction. "Pífmergge. El kcler il sol mótfummer."

CHAPTER 32

With limited time, both of us head back to our spire. There's a weight in the halls that wasn't present earlier, one of dismal expectations and doubt. Though, I may be projecting.

I end up limping after Tans, who doesn't stop at his floor but sprints the extra fifteen stairs up to mine.

"Cel cuno sol mótfummer, rittak. El sàlip nochh benevà," he says, slamming the door. His words are gentle but his eyes blaze. He backs me up to the bed, knocking me down before covering my body with his and kissing me fiercely.

"What—what did I miss in that meeting?" I stutter nervously from the amorous attack while his lips shift to my neck. "We don't have time for—actually, do we have time? You'd know better than me. God, only a few hours, and the internal monologue's an external one. If we don't fix this soon, I'll—"

He silences my babbling with another kiss.

Twenty minutes, an hour, a day later, we pull apart. His chest heaves like he's run a marathon and I'm no better. Tans' braids are fingered free, and he's missing his top. A small smattering of black hair dusts his chest, and a dark line of it trails from his navel before it disappears under the waistband of his pants. My lips buzz with sensitivity and the first few buttons on the neckline of my dress are open. Tans looks at the extra skin and licks my collarbone.

"I know I stopped us last time," I start, eyes closed as he braces half above me, still littering kisses on my bared skin. "And having sex before we die is *incredibly* cliched but—I think we should. Just in case. Now, that is."

As expected, Tans doesn't react to my statement. With flushed cheeks, I risk one last bout of charades. He understands *that* mime immediately, an anticipatory expression blooming. He leaves immediately, shirtless and barefoot.

I wrap my arms around my stomach protectively while I wait. I can't explain *why* 'now' feels like the right time for this when it didn't feel right twenty-four hours earlier. Maybe because, no matter how I appreciate the trope, having sex outside doesn't sound comfortable. Or maybe because the stakes changed. Yesterday, no matter how unsure I was, I assumed I was brought here for a greater purpose, and the five of us *together* would defeat Her. That's gone now. I may die tomorrow; there's no supernatural force nudging obstacles out of my way anymore. There's no waking up on Earth when this is over. I need to live while I can.

Tans returns, gracing me with a coy smile, while he holds out one of the fluorescent condoms I brought from Earth, the sight of it inspiring giggling tears. I reach for him the minute he comes within grabbing distance, prepared to bury any feelings of uncertainly or fear or the reminder that this could be my last chance for this. The narrow planes of his body and his growing interest press against me as my eyes flutter shut, savoring the feel of him against me for the first, and possibly last, time.

He whines when I push him away but understanding dawns as I open more buttons. With an urgency that our limited time is only partially responsible for, we quickly undress. I rip a seam near my stomach; Tans trips over his pants when he wrangles out of them. When we're both laying bare on my bed, he braces over me again. The embarrassment I didn't feel when he healed me after the last Trial appears, only vanishing when his hooded gaze drags over me. He settles it on my face, revealing immeasurable desire and anticipation. The wonder in his eyes removes the rest of my nerves and I pull him down, reveling in the groan he makes when our bodies connect.

He brushes his lips on my cheeks, leaving a trail of light kisses down my jaw, moving to my collarbones, and right above the swell of my breasts. He finally pulls his lips from me, breathing ragged, to stare down with an expression of awe and need. "El rit el," he whispers before guiding us together.

It hurts less than I expect, and I imagined more foreplay than a few kisses and questing touches, but we have so little time. He's unnaturally warm on top of me, kissing my mouth and nuzzling into my neck as he slides against me. His slim hips press hard against my inner thighs as my hands caress his wiry back. Tendrils of his wavy hair cling to his lips as he shudders with each thrust. Only twice do his hands roam to my chest, and I shiver when they do, feeling a glimpse of the pleasure the books promised. But Tans is lost chasing his own bliss and soon he trembles above me, choking out "el rit il" again, amber eyes pinching shut.

He lands to the side of me with a thud, as if he can't brace himself any longer. A film of appreciation and satisfaction grows in his eyes as they fix onto me. They immediately turn apologetic, because of my lack of shown enjoyment at the act or because we're out of time.

I offer what I hope is an encouraging expression, weak though it may be. It isn't how I imagined my first time—while his spear may have 'plundered the damp petals at the juncture of my thighs,' I didn't 'fall off the precipice of need in tandem with him' or 'writhe as he abandoned all control until my blinding moment of release.' But as I'm intimately aware, life doesn't imitate the books. I was probably asking for too much to have an orgasm with my boyfriend before I die.

"Now *we* have to live because we need to try that again," I joke faintly.

Unsurprisingly, he doesn't answer, tossing the spent condom away. But before he leaves the bed to dress, he leans back over me. His long hair tickles my neck and his eyes trail back down my body. He doesn't speak as his lips press against my neck. Leaning on one elbow, he drags the other over my chest until I shiver. A smirk graces his lips, and he lets his mouth replace his fingers.

The breath whooshes out of me at the sensation, so distracting I don't notice his hand slide down past my hips to the space between my thighs. Everything goes white, his subtle movements feeling better than anything I've furtively done in my empty dorm room. I bite my lips and squirm as the feeling rises, peering down at Tans' dark head. His eyes watch me unblinking, full of desire and something else, something I think I feel and think he's confessed. Any worry that I'm taking too long, that I'm not doing it right, even by letting him touch me, disappears at that look.

There are moments where it doesn't work, where his fingers miss what I need or his teeth graze uncomfortably against my skin. But still, the pleasure builds, good and better than the books described. Better because it's with Tans and real. Better because it isn't perfect, but because it's us.

Finally, I'm at the cliff of sensation and I tense all my muscles as I let it crescendo. Tans' lips suck almost too hard as his fingers press in the right spot once, twice. I stop counting as it comes, and I smother a high-pitched sound between my pursed lips. It—my brain—the thoughts are gone. It's quiet, just for a minute.

Tans surges forward to kiss me, the fingers of one hand wet against my cheek. His grin is loopy, as if he just reexperienced his release. With a laugh, I kiss him back until we lose ourselves together again.

Tans must be keeping track of time as he finally pulls away and begins dressing. As he rummages through the rumpled bedsheets for his tunic, I grab in the sole pair of pants in my room, topping it off with my stained t-shirt and ripped windbreaker. It feels symbolic, to meet the Voice wearing what remains of my Earth clothes. I grab Kórol's knife and tuck it into the back of my pants.

The idea I planted only hours ago grows small seedlings that claw out of the dirt. I've been taking notes in Dalner and listening—to the Voice, to Tans, to Kórol and Fíl. I pocket my cell phone.

While I work through the pieces of my plan, Tans sits on the bed and braids his hair, watching me warily. When he finishes, he drags me closer by the hips, a somber expression replacing the pleasure that was recently there. "Yd byr il sámed?"

I cradle his head into my stomach for a few heartbeats. He can't have figured out my plan, not when the roots are shallow. "When do we leave?" I point to the two of us, then the door, and mime marching.

His forlorn expression turns confused. "Il byr che esymed." He points to me and shakes his head while walking me backward towards the bed. He tries to remove my windbreaker but can't get it over my arms without my help. Undeterred, he reaches for my phone until it sparks, and he drops it with a yelp. He sticks his smoking hand in his mouth and attempts to scowl around it. His hand smells of burned flesh. I wince, but—the roots of my plan grow, and sprouts branch off the seedlings.

When the smoke clears, he pushes me to the bed. "Il byr cládymed mu, ritak." I shove the phone back in my pocket while he mimes, holding out a hand like a stop sign. "Il byr cládymed." He then points to himself and mimes walking out the door, saying, "el byl esymed."

I think get the gist, if not the actual translation—I stay and he goes. I chance repeating what he says phonetically, and I hope he said, 'I'm going or 'I'm leaving' and not 'wait here, my love, while I go to the restroom after our masterful sexual escapade.'

"I'm going. El by-el eh-see-med," I counter, standing and shuffling towards the door.

He shakes his head sharply and his amber eyes darken, which tells me that my assumed meaning was right. He points to me and the bed again. "Il byr cládymed." He points to himself and the door. "El byl esymed."

I'm getting the hang of pronouns now, and my mind replays his twice repeated '*el rit il*' and what word could be sandwiched between 'I' and 'you.' I duck my head to hide the smile threatening to spread over my lips. *There's no time for that*, I remind myself.

I plant my feet in the threshold, meaning the only way he can leave is to reposition me. "This is *my* turn. I've been riding on the backs of you guys for too long. We're *both* going. Il and el by-el eh-see-med."

"Il e el byr esymed," he says with a roll of his eyes.

"Close enough." I throw open the door. "Glad we agree. Il and el by-el eh-see-med."

"Il clágrádmer elf. Met el rit il." He gestures to the open door and growls. "El sprun et vek pràp sesàrs tráfum."

The smile breaks through against my will. *El rit il to you too.*

Kórol and Tans argue when we arrive in the throne room. Fíl splits his attention from watching them and making check marks on some parchment with Sethen. His jaw tightens with each word, the crease on his forehead nearly splitting his face in two. Kórol repeatedly echoes the "Il byr cládymed" phrase Tans said back in my room, which confirms it was a command for me to remain behind, but he can't convince me to stay in my room either.

"If I didn't listen to you when we could speak the same language, there's no way I'll do it now," I tell him when he ventures near, though he keeps a more-than-respectable distance between us and can't look in my eyes for longer than a heartbeat. The disagreement ends with me firmly repeating "El by-el eh-see-med" several times before Kórol balls his fists and stomps back to the maps, jerking his head to Tans and then the stone dais.

With no other naysayers, I shadow Tans to the dais where we wait to embark, and observe men entering and exiting as if a turnstile was installed on the heavy door. There's an urgency to each of them as they circle the room, going from a corner stacked with leather vests woven tightly together like chain mail, to the next piled with small satchels, and the next where young children in red tunics hand out swords and longbows, before finally reporting to Sethen, who inspects each one and directs Fíl to make more markings on his parchment.

One look at Tans, General and Lord Commander, explains why he doesn't do more to prepare—he's as taut as the strings of a bow and almost yanks his braids out of his head. I run my hands gently down his arms until he slumps next to me. But he still snatches my fingers and holds on as if he worries that I'll float away if he lets go. Knowing what I intend to do, it isn't an unreasonable reaction.

Sáv arrives carrying a substantial cloth satchel covered in grease stains. From the smell, it holds more snacks he drops in one corner, bypassing Fíl's corner completely and narrowing his eyes. Fíl twitches and pulls his parchment closer to his face. I clearly missed something again.

Before Sáv leaves, he brings us a folded handkerchief filled with pieces of dried meat identical to what he offered when we first met. Because Tans keeps his iron grip on my hands, Sáv sticks it in my pocket himself. He must graze the cell phone as he jolts backward with a wince and sticks his fingers in his mouth. They aren't sparking, but they're burned red.

The sprouts of my plan grow floral buds.

"Met celg sàrcestorták," Sáv murmurs. Tans' answering chuckle sounds pained.

With a lot of hesitation and a stern look from Kórol, Tans leaves a few minutes later, following Sáv from the room. Alone with my thoughts, I stare up at that damned stained-glass window. *Are all of you bad?* I ask mentally. I'm relieved when no one answers.

Fíl and Sethen direct a swath of newcomers to different corners. Guilt rises in my throat like a sickness. These men will risk their lives for something that is technically my fault. Had the Voice not chosen me, had I not killed the Great Matron, had I tried to go home instead of playing 'Grace is the chosen one,' the Gates wouldn't be breaking open and the walls coming down. I owe it to them, owe it to myself, to keep that from happening. A weight settles in my stomach, uncomfortable but necessary.

The plan blooms into something ugly and poisonous.

Tans returns wearing his blue leather, magnetized to take me in his arms. I burrow face into his narrow chest and speak into the soft cloth.

"You'd think with all the romance novels I read, I could think of a good monologue for us right now. Since you can't understand me, let's pretend that's what I'm saying instead of doing my absolute best to keep from thinking that this could be the last time we're together like this." I peer back up at him, eyes stinging. "You're going to hate what I've got planned; you'd try to talk me out of it if you knew but—I have to. I'm—I'm not a butterfly, not yet. I haven't changed, grown, *whatever*, yet. I'm still a stupid caterpillar, and I always will be unless—unless I do this for you all." I kiss him hard on the lips. "Try to remember that, please."

He cups my cheeks in his hands. "El rit il."

"Tansr, Grace," Kórol's voice calls from the far side of the throne room, interrupting our quiet moment. "A braigrad tors. Yl by fum."

It's time.

CHAPTER 33

We head north, the pale moon lighting our way. The night is still, the ride as somber as the darkness surrounding us. All the men from the annex room that evening sit on antlered horses riding behind a hundred marching soldiers and dozens of healers. Kórol and Tans put me on a horse too, and box me between them. As Tans hoists me onto the animal, Kórol hands me a deep blue woven leather vest, similar in design to the other soldiers but much lighter. I finger it idly as the horses trot forward and the two men talk over my head. I doubt it will stop magical attacks or knife wounds, but I don't want to risk it. I shove it in a saddlebag.

We advance through the squat hills and valleys, the healers constantly giving aid to the walking soldiers so they can keep marching without rest. Magic must be with us, as we travel the countryside faster than what seems physically possible. Trees emerge in small pockets, dotting the expansive landscape. It reminds me of the pilgrimage; fitting that the fields of Dalner will be where I make my one and only stand.

After several hours, Tans bellows something, causing all the riders to slow near one of those small masses of trees. The marchers continue forward without interruption, descending into another valley.

Tans helps me off my horse while the riders tie them to the trees. I lean against the broad animal and squint at the vast space in front of the marching soldiers. At the edge of my vision, however many miles away, there's a rolling shimmer. It reminds me of that trick of the eye where a concrete road looks wet and sparkly from afar but there's never anything there. That must be the wall.

Suddenly, there's a pressure on my waist, but it's only Tans who slakes his arm around my stomach. He twists me to face him, staring at me with undisguised misery, gaze darting over me as if memorizing my features. "Mándy pà elf mótceltu," he says fiercely before kissing me hard on the lips.

With a final grimace, he releases me and sprints towards Kórol, who stands with the remaining riders. Confused, I try to follow when something rips me backward toward the trees. I was wrong—Tans held me to hide the pressure of a rope tying me to the trees with the horses.

"Tansr! Are you really doing this to me right now?" I screech as the other men turn away.

"El rit il," Tansr shouts back. "El kdurhaleg il, stòrnanmed hek ilg leídysly." Then he, Kórol, and the dozen men with him, trail the marching soldiers as the first light of the morning peeks out of the horizon.

If 'el rit il' means what I *think* it means, Tans has a frustrating way of showing it. Though—to give him credit, if he *does* know what I'm planning, shackling me to a tree is a rational thought. But to my knowledge, he doesn't, and the consequences of my plan are mine to make. After all that's happened here in Dalner, I'm owed free will and my own choices.

If this were one of the books I read, my secret ninja skills would emerge, or I'd reveal a background in gymnastics that allows me to shimmy out of the rope. But, like every other moment since arriving in Dalner, this isn't a book, and my two years of toddler gymnastics won't help me here. I'm not inherently special; I must earn my successes now.

It takes seven minutes of wriggling to realize I can't slip out of the loop. It takes ten more minutes to stop complaining to the horses about how unfair and disrespectful Tans is, and another five to remember that my audience is animals who don't understand me in *either* language, and who wouldn't care anyway. Then it takes *another* ten minutes to stop pouting and realize I still have Kórol's knife tucked in the waistband of my pants. I blame the idiocy on the fact that I'm closing out an *exceedingly* difficult seventy-two hours. After another twenty minutes, because Sàrkany ropes could pass for thick ship docking lines, I free myself.

By that point, the sun is a wide crescent in front of me. The distant shimmer undulates quicker now, and I break into a run, barreling through the field with its many dips and hills. But even with the slightly fitter physique thanks to Kórol's exhaustive pace on the pilgrimage, I can't run multiple miles without stopping, not with my hip. I slow after ten minutes and limp to the shimmer. My destiny in Dalner must be to do everything in the most unskilled and nonsensical way possible—limping, stabbing unmoving targets. My current plan is another in that long line.

Before I can delve too deeply into those thoughts and fearfully repeat my *most* common activity in Dalner (running away), the thunder of war reaches me. When I crest another small hill, the clang of steel and grunts of pain come in view as Kórol's men engage in full combat. From that distance, the only thing that distinguishes my side from the enemies are the blue and black leather Kórol's army wears.

I can finally see the shimmering Gate. It's a massive force field that pops into existence with nothing around it, more like a portal than a swinging gate or opening in a hedge. It looks as though I could walk completely around it, as if there's no fence around the opening, but perhaps I'll be like to a bird slamming into a clean glass window. There's a handful of openings, slim patches in a row along what must be the wall, exposing a reflection that looks identical to Dalner except for the bleaker color scheme, with dead grass and yellowed trees on the other side. Eósy stream through the holes into Dalner and immediately sweep into battle.

So far, Kórol's army outnumbers the Eósy three-to-one, but the bottleneck of Eósy bursting through the holes doesn't reveal how many are waiting on the other size. The patches in the walls widen as the sun brightens, but I can't tell how or why. With a fortifying breath of air and a reminder of why I'm doing this, I leap into the fray.

Up close, I'm shocked I thought the two armies were the same, when the Eósy are carnival mirror versions of the Sàrkany. Most of the fighters are human-shaped, the rest an exhibition of creatures and colors. The distraction of seeing Eósys momentarily stops my search, until two wolflike creatures, one black and one tepid green, lock jaws directly above me as each try to overpower the other.

Scarcely sidestepping a kick to the head, I stumble through the field, looking for the horror that must match with the Voice. Blood and screams assault me from all sides. A tall man with canine teeth and mottled gray skin tries to snatch at my wind breaker one-handed, the rest of his attention on fighting with a boy in black. Almost effortlessly, the Eósy slices through the boy's neck before prowling in my direction.

Blanching, I scuttle away, narrowly dodging another raised sword coming down between a man I absently recognize as someone who met with Tans and a pale green skinned Eósy. The two grapple around me as I surge to the side. I must live long enough to make it to the Gate, but the precious time I spend avoiding joining in *that* conflict means the gray Eósy catches me.

His clawed hands grab a chunk of my sweat slick hair and wrench me towards him. I jerk my head forward, hoping to sacrifice a few locks instead of fighting the monster above me. My hair skims my shoulders now, meaning he shouldn't be able to keep a solid grip on me unless he presses up against my back. Maybe there's magic in it, or he's much stronger than I expect because I remain in his clutches, now with an agonizing headache.

Only his grip keeps me from hitting the ground, as his nails prick at my scalp. He drags me up and backward until my feet dangle off the ground and I inhale a scream at the pain. My hands clench onto his; I try to peel his hands off my scalp, scratching at his fingers. He snorts as he spins me to face him, baring his crooked teeth. The gray skin on his face looks sickly and his eyes are tinged yellow. A scent of decay rolls off him as his gaping mouth shifts closer to me. Shivers of fear lance through me at the possibility of having *another* set of teeth-shaped scars and I redouble my efforts clawing his hands, kicking my legs towards his abdomen. The feeling of my feet digging into his ribcage does nothing to deter him as his teeth skim the skin on my neck. With an anguished sob, I drag my nails over his face and slash at his eye. He snarls then and drops me to the ground, one hand covering his face while the other reaches behind him for his sword.

I hit the grass with a thump as the breath knocks out of me. The roar of battle swells around us while I quickly consider on my options, only one which *might* let me finish my plan—either crawl away or try to grab the small knife sitting snuggly against my back. Remembering the gleam in his eye as he lowered his mouth to my dangling body makes the choice easy. I clutch at the grass and scramble away, pulling up clumps of earth in my wake. He takes that choice away as he snatches my foot and flips me over, dragging me back to him. His eyes narrow and spurt hatred, the yellow iris of one eye tinted red. Kicking wildly, I scramble to release the knife from its place at the small of my back. It's red with blood and my skin stings, but no more than the rest of me. I swipe outward before he roars and knocks it from my hand. He wretches me upward, one long arm suspending me upside down while the other holds a curved sword. The snarl is fixed on his face as he jabs his weapon forward. White bursts from the corners of my vision from the pain. Before I can do more than scream, he drops me again, howling and clutching his own abdomen.

Luck keeps me from landing on my head and fracturing my neck, but I still feel the twinge from my shoulders crashing into the dirt. Both hips bite, the original scar and the new twin wound bleeding red. I roll to the side with a groan and spin to watch the gray Eósy. Burgundy blooms from his chest, surrounding a blade that sprouted from behind him. He presses one clawed hand to his stomach while the other still holds the sword he stabbed me with, and he thrusts it at the fighter who injured him. Too pained to do much else, I curl into a fetal position and watch my savior battle the gray Eósy. Fire crawls to life on his hands and springs out from his blue leather form, stronger and brighter than I've seen before. The gray Eósy howls again as he takes the flames directly into his grotesque face. The Eósy swings the knife and the soldier parries, blood and noise arcing through the air as their weapons connect and the man's long hair sways backward to show me his face.

I recognize that soldier—I know his magic and his face and his touch. The two struggle until Tans' speed overpowers the Eósy, and he goes down, his long limbs gangly and scraping into the blood stained grass. Tans thrusts his weapon into the Eósy's stomach again, who gurgles before going silent, the sneer forever etched onto his lifeless face.

Tans pulls his sword from the Eósy's rib cage with a slurp, crimson blood dripping down the tip, and runs to my side. He yanks me to him roughly, murmuring words I will never understand and sending a wave of heat down my back that reduces the agony I felt from being dropped twice. It does nothing for the stab wound. I almost giggle, the combination of adrenaline, exhaustion, and probable blood loss making me loopy. It isn't how I envisioned the first step of my plan happening, but I'll take success where I can.

The desire to giggle increases until the sound involuntarily bubbles from my throat. Tans stares down at me, keeping one arm around my back and the other on his weapon. His face is questioning and angry.

I shove my hands in the pockets of my windbreaker, wincing as I wrap the sides together to keep him from noticing that some of the russet patterns on my shirt are home-made. He can't heal what he can't see. And my bravery, my desire to prove myself, isn't limitless and multiple stab wounds aren't ideal. My arms around my waist doubly benefit in keeping pressure on the wound, as I'm getting woozy.

Limping slightly, I shuffle towards the Gate and the mirrored wall around it. Tans grabs my arm and hauls me backward but stops when I shriek in pain, the sound barely audible over the din of the surrounding battle. His expression is uneasy, and he tries again with a gentler touch, but I rip my arm away and stumble to my goal. Tans tries a third time until his luck runs out, or mine continues, when another Eósy leaps between us. His focus switches from evacuating me to keeping us both alive. I take advantage of his distraction and hobble towards the shimmering force field, zipping up my windbreaker to better cover the bloody mess on my shirt.

There are half a dozen openings now, spanning across a fifty-foot distance, while streams of Eósy pour from them as men in blue and black leather struggle to drive them back through the holes. My plan feels even more reckless now, as I don't know if the opening in the wall matters, which Gate, if it will even work. But I have to try. With a suppressed groan, I stagger towards the closest one when something catches my eye.

Leaning against the side of the largest opening stands a golden-skinned man with short blond hair. I do a quick double-take, as the portal appearance of the Gate gives the impression that the air itself props him up. He is stunning and terrible, just like the Great Matron. From afar, his blond hair looks white, and the golden skin shimmers, like thick glittering paint was slapped on a human-shaped canvas. He's lanky but muscular, slender with bright eyes, an inverse toned Tans. Something about him seems familiar and I spend precious seconds holding myself steady and watching him while Tans battles behind me, the zinging and clanging of swords nearly clipping my back.

The blond Eósy's arms are crossed, and he surveys the battle with a detached disinterest, which is only belied by his mouth rapidly moving. Every so often the muttering stops and one of the holes widen. When it does, he sways but still manages to tick his mouth up into a grin. That *must* be the Voice, no longer only an amorphous and genderless voice but a man who could stand shoulder-to-shoulder with the Great Matron in glass.

Renewed determination forces me in his direction, and I escape another stab wound by luck alone. Tans takes down three Eósy whose path I wander through on my way to the Voice. He's stopped trying, or is too distracted, to drag me off the field. Instead, he acts like a warrior guardian angel, my own Gabriel or Michael, protecting me from the dangers I voluntarily cross. His immediate willingness to protect me is another reason I'm lucky to have him in my corner, and why I must go forward with my plan. I can only hope, if I survive, he'll forgive me.

"Hey!" Blood loss makes me groggy, which shows in the breathy and ragged quality of my voice. I stop ten feet away from the opening and Tans grabs hold of my arm again. He yells something behind me, but the rush in my ears is too loud for me to hear it, and the deafening drumbeat of my nervous heart makes me not want to try. The blond Eósy notices, uncrossing his arms and flashing his teeth in a simulacrum of a smile.

"You decided to join us," he says, finishing the exclamation with a hysterical sounding laugh. It's him, alright. "Your vision of yourself doesn't do you justice. What say you, Daryt? Is she as I described?"

The Eósy nearby pause in their individual fights to appraise me before all of them deem I'm not worth the time and reengage the blue-armored men charging them. Only one of them, just as attractive as the Voice but with silver-pale glittering skin and black hair, saunters towards him. He stops a few feet away from the Voice, baring his teeth and snapping them in my direction. Tans stiffens at my back, moving his sword out in front of us. Hidden by his movement, I press my forearm harder into my wound and confirm the windbreaker still covers the blood seeping into my tattered t-shirt.

"Duller and worthless," the same Eósy says, his voice slithering towards me and finishing with a smirk. A sting of shock runs through me when I realize he speaks English too.

"Now, now, she made today happen. This is how I differ from our predecessor. We must acknowledge the work of others."

"Not the only way you differ," Daryt says with a grunt. The Voice scowls and counters back with a comment in Sàrkany that I don't understand. The benefit to the Voice's teasing conversation is that the wall's openings don't widen, but the byplay between them distresses Tans, as with each nonsensical word, he tightens his arm around my waist. Any tighter and I'll pass out.

"It's good to know you're even more annoying in person," I yell, leaning towards them and forcing Tans to step forward to keep our balance. We're five feet from the wide Gate opening now. Daryt snaps his teeth menacingly again, but the Voice holds up a hand to stop him.

"We all have flaws." His shrug is graceful, and he follows it up with another completely human behavior of running a long-fingered hand through his short white-blond hair. "I find myself too grateful for what today means to counter your tantrums yet again."

"Then how about you take that gratefulness and head on back to Dànna?" I counter, struggling to inch forward again but Tans' vicelike grip thwarts me. "Consider it payback for my helping you. I'll even escort you back."

"What you claim as wit is taxing. Had you not learned to block me, I might have closed the connection more often." He laughs again, and the other Eósy echo him. "Your internal monologue was quite tiring at times."

"Imagine being me," I mutter. Louder, I shout, "Why don't I come over there and let you say that to my face?"

"I intended to spare you, dearest, as a gift for your unwilling service. I didn't lie when I said I liked you." The Voice trails a slow and appraising look up Tans. "But I know you and *your* flaws. I imagine in a moment you'll run and let that handsome boy behind you fight in your stead?"

"Never!" The word falls out of my mouth involuntarily, but I've never meant anything more.

"Oh, *I* understand. Do you believe engaging me will make you *special*? That this will make your reason for being here have worth other than as a receptacle for my goals?" He smiles ruthlessly and lopes towards the center of the Gate. "Poor Grace—clever but not brilliant; pretty but not beautiful; persistent but not heroic; on the edge of being important and crashing to the ground instead. Recognize that we are what we are; that will not change. Go home before someone here proves your inadequacy."

One hand presses hard into my abdomen, staunching the blood as I stumble another foot forward. That he's right is of no consequence now. "Do all Eósy just love to hear their own voices, or am I so unlucky as to have met the worst ones? Just quit with the games. I'll meet you in the Gate and we'll do this one on one."

"This is a waste, dearest, but I will claim you, not for my pleasure but for my own service."

I hobble another foot forward, only half my attention on what the Voice spews towards me. I could jump and make it to the Gate at this point. "Another bastardized Jane Eyre quote? It doesn't even make sense in this context." Bravado rings falsely from my wavering voice.

"Semantics," he replies, pulling a long and thin blade from behind him. I can't even imagine where he kept it. "I tell you this to remind you that I've been in your head. I know your weaknesses and your strengths. I know every angle of your thoughts, including how that trite piece of Earth literature disconcerts you. With your 'Great Matron's' memories, I even know exactly how your last battles ended. As I told you before, I *made* you."

"Then this should be easy." I hobble another foot; I'm so close. Blood soaks my shirt, but I don't look down. *Deception will be my armor.*

Tans screams behind me along with an echoing roar from Kórol. The blade flashes in the light as the Voice whips it above his head. "Thankful or not, Grace, I will not simply stand there like your last two foes and let you stab me. I will fight back. And I will kill you if I must."

I look back at Tans, whose eyes are filled with horror as his fingers claw onto Kórol's arms, who keeps hold on him and nods to me. In Kórol's ice-bright eyes, I think I see understanding. *I need fire and ice to survive.* Without them, I'd never attempt this. I do this for them, and the two men back home. My friends, my family.

I dip my head to him and smile wetly at Tans. This is the perfect end to my accidental heroism, to the coincidences, luck, and manipulation that allowed me to succeed. "I'm counting on it," I whisper. And I propel myself towards the opening.

Because the Voice was right: everyone bleeds in the end.

CHAPTER 34

I sleep, and I dream—my first sleeping dream since the battle with the dobhà. I'm wading through memories now, ones that claw into my brain without warning or order.

Hundreds of years ago, too far back to relate to me, the Voice—his memories tell me his name is Leyden—bites back a growl while listening to the Great Ma—the Woma—Bittálli. His skin isn't golden, but as pale as Bittálli's. She looks as she did when she leapt through the window.

She rests on a plum chaise lounge and idly inspects her blood red nails. "I cannot comprehend why I would use the Sàrkany's gullibility to breach the Gates." Her voice is both melodic and shrill, like the discordant notes of a bird before sunrise. At one point, he'd cherished her attention, when he was growing and she was amassing her followers.

"You wouldn't," he mumbles, leaning against the wall of her tower and staring out the mirrored window at the Sàrkany she watches.

"This is my retribution," she continues as if he hadn't spoken. Knowing Bittálli, she failed to hear him, given she's ignored anything other than the sound of her voice for the last century. "I will not sacrifice the pain I seek from the Raddares for them."

"This is our—your—opportunity to increase your power. Imagine the fealty you'd inspire if you—"

"No." She snarls in his direction. "Do not question me unless you desire your own punishment."

The scene shifts. Hundreds of years ago, still too far for me to comprehend, the Voi—Leyden slams the door to his own tower. His skin is tinged gray, only noticeable in contrast to the bright candlelight. Dozens of plans blanket the stone walls, his looping scrawl splattering the pages without pattern or purpose.

Bittállí focuses only on Herself and her long-broken heart, not the benefits breaching the Gate will provide. That golden parchment of hers, her deluded revenge plot, taunts him each time he visits her tower. She's forgotten where she came from and the Eósy that put her in power, and why. She remains too shortsighted, ignoring the needs of others for her own scarred organ.

Leyden stares out his own mirrored window. If Bittállí was removed—but no. It's his fault that she remains too powerful for that. Magic will never be her bane. Perhaps there's another path.

He rips a clean strip of parchment and begins planning anew. It may take centuries, but time is something he has in abundance. At least, he hopes.

The scene shifts. A hundred years ago, when my Grandma's mother was a girl, Leyden speaks to his bait. He took her from a tenement in some Earth city, he didn't concern himself with the name. She was stunning, her skin buttery smooth and eyes the color of the morning sky. The Twenty-Second Raddare will be unable to resist her beauty, turning his attention from his devotion to the so-called Great Matron. Bittállí will suffer an apoplexy when She sees the human substitute for her Sìnnách story and realizes the Raddares have moved on from her again. Then she'll have no choice but to raze the walls or die before them. Either way, the walls will fall.

Except, the human won't stop screaming, braying for her mother and sister, screeching about the demon speaking in her head.

Leyden kills her quickly, not out of mercy but to end the noise.

The scene shifts. Decades ago, when Mom was barely an adult, Leyden scratches his graying skin, pulling out a pot of golden power and bathing his cheeks with it. There are less sprites now, so he must be circumspect with how often he hides the weakness displayed on his skin. With luck, it won't matter soon. He gazes at a different woman. She's lithe and graceful, spending her free time practicing choreography around her empty apartment. She lives alone, estranged from family, and can't support herself as a dancer. She lost her day job because she overslept one too many times. Her beauty will overcome any other limitations she might have.

With no family or occupation to anchor her to Earth, surely this one's mind won't fracture like the last. And if her feminine wiles don't entice the Twenty-Third Raddare, Leyden will exert a little outside pressure on the man.

The scene shifts. Before Mom died and I'm learning to read on my own, Leyden observes a young girl. She's an orphan, one who lives in her head and avoids the other foster children. With each failed human pawn, he's learned. This one has no dreams of professional fulfillment—she won't refuse to attach to the reality he presents because she believes she'll 'become a prima ballerina,' whatever that means. This one will befriend the lonely Twenty-Fourth Raddare and, with Leyden's manipulation, cultivate her status as a Sinnách until Bittállí is forced to show her true self, leaving the Raddares no choice but to destroy her. Then the walls will be his to tear down.

Leyden prepares to pull the child into Dalner, gathering the magic within him and from the earth, a blue ring burning around his irises and pale skin graying underneath the golden salve. As he rips a hole into the room and reaches forward, a man enters. The girls sees him and starts crying, before running into his arms.

The pot of salve shatters against Leyden's parchment-covered walls. This one won't work either.

The scene shifts. The year my father marries his second wife, Leyden watches me exclusively. He follows my life for five years, learning everything he can about me. He can't afford any more false starts.

The scene shifts. While I huddle in a cave with the King, he lounges on Bittálli's chaise. "You could best her," he says, stretching out his full length and staring at the roof of the turret high above them.

Bittálli stands at her desk, her fingers digging into the wood and no doubt leaving hand-shaped indentations. The golden parchment rests atop the surface, altered from his first glance at it centuries ago. Her anger comes quicker than any other emotion, though he can remember a time in his childhood when she used to smile.

"Of course, I will best her," she snarls. "I have destroyed beings more important and powerful than her. The spell should force open her mind and do my bidding, but these worthless vassals can do nothing right."

The latest failed-kidnapper was not long for this world, either because Bittálli convinced him to kill himself or the split wrist would take him. She mastered manipulation spells, but not much else, content to use her charm and looks to gain attention and use the distraction to tunnel through the minds of her thralls. She refused to do any of the work herself, but never explained why. It was a snag in Leyden's otherwise perfect plan.

"Your fondness for overcomplicated plots aside, you must go to her, then you may do the deed yourself. Vassals, even spelled ones, will never give you the satisfaction that killing someone yourself does," he says. The manipulations are unending. But he's primed me so completely that Bittálli is more likely to run into my blade in her hubris than believe a non-magical human is a threat.

She crosses the room and drops next to him with a supernatural fluidity. "I don't enjoy getting my hands dirty," she says, pouting and leaning her head onto his shoulders. Only his centuries of control keep him from stiffening.

"Fine. Bring her to you and then have a vassal kill her. It would take divine interference for her to defeat you now."

Bittállí smiles viciously. "What do you think about delaying her death a bit longer?"

The scene shifts. While I remain ensconced in the castle after learning the truth about my arrival in Dalner and his scheme, Leyden laces up his breeches. He's not one for regrets, but the inkling that he should not have given the exact time of his invasion scratches his skin like one of Bittállí's red nails. After saying it aloud, he cannot change it, the words now a truth. Making it a lie would burn him from within.

Grandiose speeches aside, he can't deny some luck brought him to this place. Yes, he created me and aimed me just so, but at any time something could have gone wrong. Had Bittállí not been bound by vows to never engage an opponent one-on-one, something Leyden only learned with her memories, she could have burned me to ash. I could have died at that lake, or perished from infection if healing magic didn't work, or lost my mind like the half dozen other girls he attempted to use in this plot. And I could have simply refused him and chosen to do nothing.

He cannot risk failure now. Leyden stalks to the chaise he stole from Bittállí's tower, where he's left the remains of his plans. He jots down a quick note suggesting they bring weapons in addition to magic when they meet at the wall. He can only hope his luck holds, and that even if I warn them, tomorrow the walls will fall. And finally, he will be able to breathe.

Dozens of other scenes slide through my sleeping mind—of Leyden, of Bittállí, of two somber Eósys whose tar black eyes are ringed in green and silver, of Leyden's manipulations that began the moment I arrived in Dalner.

The memories end with the skirmish in the Gate.

Leyden stands above me, his sword held aloft. He can't let anything stop him now. I'll become one more sacrifice in the long line trailing behind him.

The blade slices through the air with a hum but before it can connect with my neck, I breach the seam of the Gate. A flash of light coils from my pocket, lighting the windbreaker on fire. I fall to my knees as blood pools to the ground, igniting with the flash from the cell phone and blinding us. Leyden can only feel horror at the sight. I'm propelled backward as Leyden slams back into Dànna and the openings close.

I sleep without dreaming.

I wake up, face up and prone, not outside but in a bed with a white sheetrock ceiling above me. It isn't the pain clogging my head or the feel of the scratchy sheets below me that tells me something is amiss, but the smells. My eyes pinch shut. It doesn't smell like my room at Ilsen or the ground where we slept on the trek. Instead, it's acrid, like sweat or grimy clothes, like the kind Julie and I tossed in the corner instead of doing laundry. The scent of spearmint wafts from directly beside me, almost indistinguishable from her boyfriend's favored cologne.

My fingers clutch the bed, pulling at the worn cotton sheets under me, just like the sheets in my dorm room.

I refuse to open my eyes. If I do—I'll be back in my dorm. If I'm back home in my dorm—if the last few months *were* a dream.

If, after everything I've done, everything I've learned, everyone I've... loved.

No.

I struggle to my side as I refuse to let myself cower from the possibilities. My breath bursts from me as the rest of the room is exposed—I'm not in my dorm, but in a small, curtained enclosure. What I thought was a white sheetrock ceiling is a whitewashed stone ceiling instead. It appears to be a medical bay, with an aged single bed under me and frayed white curtains offering privacy from the larger room. Through the lightweight hospital gown, or Dalner's long tunic nightgown version of it, I feel the scar tissue on my abdomen, almost directly mirroring the scar on my hip. It's slightly raised and puckered, and there's a large leathery burn around it as if it was quickly cauterized. My arms are another mass of skinny scars trailing up into the sleeves of my tunic.

Kórol sits next to me, explaining the spearmint smell. His eyes are closed, his hair musky and clothes covered in dried blood. I release a sob of relief tinged with grief and Kórol jolts upward at the sound.

Eyes wide, he swings on his feet, reaching out before aborting the gesture when his trembling hand is inches from my cotton covered shoulder.

"Il byr," he says before shaking his head. He closes his eyes tightly and reaches out again, gently placing his palm on my shoulder as a half-smile forces its way onto his lips. After a few heartbeats, he shakily removes his hand and fists it over his heart.

"Yl by dusigall," he bellows, voice echoing over the closed curtains. The pain in my head momentarily rings at the sound before the fog dissipates. In an instant, the curtains flutter open and two men barrel into me, displacing Kórol at my side. I squeak at the onslaught of affection, more out of surprise than increased pain. I'm a giant bruise; their embrace can't make it any worse.

Fíl and Sáv make apologetic sounds as they shuffle back towards the sides of the enclosure. Fílga pulls out a small bundle from the band of his pants and drops it on my lap, the fabric covering unfurling to show a hunk of burned and melted plastic. From the battle memories I dreamed and the lack of Eósy overlords in the medical bay, I know the plan worked. The cell phone combined the heavy magic the Voice—Leyden—pushed onto the Gate to like a flint. Once I added my non-magical blood, the magic dissolved. I didn't anticipate the Gate, and the walls surrounding them pockmarked with Leyden's holes, to seal too. I lean back onto my scratchy pillows. I got lucky, lucky that my blood did more than stop mental manipulations, lucky Leyden didn't kill me first.

"Tans?" I ask the other three, my voice croaky as my stomach lurches uncomfortably. He'd been right there when I flung myself into the Gate, with Kórol and surrounded by dozens of Eósy warriors near the gate. Kórol looks physically fine, but Tans' absence forces a rock into the pit of my stomach. Fílga hands me a metal cup of water but I can't drink it, not yet. Even though I know they can't answer, I ask my panicked question. "Did—did he survive?"

There's a scraping sound on the other side of the curtain, and a knotted stick appears between the folds before Tans hobbles inside. The tears reappear, my sob now more joyful than any other feeling. He slides into bed beside me, hissing in pain. I gingerly drape my arms around him as he buries his head in my neck.

"Il trebi penathall hág mándymed hy cel lag, rittak," he murmurs while the others leave the enclosure. His eyes are dark like scalding espresso and his skin tinted gray. I brush my fingers through his matted hair as those dark eyes fix on me. I kiss him once, twice, a third time, both of us trembling. He rests his forehead against mine, his breath skimming across my face, warm and sweet, enveloping me in his cinnamon smoke scent. He kisses the tears on my cheeks as his own leak from his eyes. His breath stutters as he shakes his head. "Od salol yl? Od salol ilgad?" he whispers.

I don't need to speak the language to understand what Tans asks—why I did it.

Because real life is about making hard choices and taking chances even when you don't feel like a hero.

But that is only part of the answer, part of what I found and need to keep. And no matter what, this *is* my story, my romance novel come to life.

"Because I love you," I confess. "El rit il."

His answering smile blinds like firelight.

GLOSSARY OF SÀRKANY SPEECH

Chapter 1

- Don't speak nonsense: *Sásche tlóh chàkres*

- I said don't speak nonsense: *El tla il sás-che tlóh chà-kres*

Chapter 8

- Stag and Hawker: *Dobra e Kàdora*

- Dragon people: *Sàrkàny*

Chapter 19

- What happened to her, Tansr?: *Yd leyms, Tansr?*

- I don't know. Fíl - did you understand anything they said: *El sáche club. Fíl- sam reyth atla cyl tlamch?*

Chapter 20

- We will overcome this: *Cel ktòsu et*

- You defeated those awful trials and the pretender Sin-nach: *El tòsu cet brogan tellàch e a mychtak Sinnach*

- We will fix this: *Cel kcurad et*

- I promise I will not let anything hurt you: *El ktág-che atla ruth-il*

- It's nonsense: *Yl by chàkres, rittak*

- Tomorrow is for responsibilities. Today is our oppor-tunity to be together before the world finds us again: *Mótceltu by hág ráspunalln. Fyanmótcel by celg preleg bylh láol iánt a dom veldàch tráfum*

- Why do you deny me? We will fix this, including your nonsense speech: *Od sáil nespengà elf? Cel kcurad et, stòrnanak ilg chàkres tlótak*

- We'll find Kórol, though he'll not kiss you like I can: *Cel kveldà Kórol, àin yl kgenches là el stare*

- You have many hours before I need you: *Il cuno trá mótfummer iánt el nevo il*

- Are you well, Grace?: *Byr il ánó, Grace?*

- I believe we should indulge her: *El sócad cel tolerh ylg*

- She wanted to speak of the Eósy: *Yl sàlipms tlóh de a*

Eósy

- Dark Eósy=hurts gate: *Tróm Eosy=rut gósca* | Light Eósy=helps gate: *Mórt Eosy=gult gósca*

- Those aren't unlimited, girl: *Cet byrche chapragstak, kave*

- Watch yourself: *Il hor ilgad*

- Do you mean break?: *Sás teykh ráolh?*

- Could she mean noon tomorrow?: *Là yl teykh mótnàltgge mótceltu?*

- Sunrise: *Mótsu*

- It is still the Winter Solstice, when the gate is at its weakest: *Yl by met a Mótcel Luggesu, ed a gósca by láigge*

- Sunrise is the next best choice for attack: *Mótsu by a cus lucrugge reum hág hátselltak*

- Your bad plan worked again: *Ilg vek pràp sesàrms tráfum*

- You are incredible: *Il byr rurepry*

- I love you: *El rit il*

- Do you?: *Sá Il?*

- Of course: *pífcheág*

- It is obvious: *Yl by cheág*

- She's the one woman who teases him: *Yl by a sol kav yt dezlás ylg*

- Absolutely: *Pífmergge*

- Grace remains here: *Grace cládys mu*

- One hour: *Sol mótfummer*

- I will see you in one hour: *El kcler il sol mótfummer*

- We have one hour, love. I want to take advantage of it: *Cel cuno sol mótfummer, rittak. El sàlip nochh benevà*

- What are you doing: *Yd byr il sámed*

- You are not going: *Il byr che esymed*

- You are staying here, love: *Il byr cládymed mu, ritak*

- I am going: *El byl esymed*

- You infuriate me. But I love you: *Il clágrádmer elf. Met el rit il*

- I hope this bad plan works again: *El sprun ilgo vek pràp sesàrs tráfum*

Chapter 21

- Still our firestarter: *Met celg sàrcestorták*

- The battle comes. It is time: *A braigrád tors. Yl by fum*

- Yell at me tomorrow: *Mándy pà elf mótceltu*

- So I will protect you, even from your own brashness: *El kdurhaleg il, stòrnanmed hek ilg leídysly*

Chapter 22

- You are: *Il byr*

- She is awake: *Yl by dusigall*

- You should be prepared for yelling by both of us, love: *Il trebi penathall hág mándymed hy cel lag, rittak*

- Why risk it? Why risk yourself?: *Od salol yl? Od salol ilgad?*

AUTHOR'S NOTE + BONUS SCENES

Thank you for reading *If the Walls Fall*! Grace's story has been a labor of love and I hope you enjoyed reading her tale as much as I enjoyed writing it.

If you're interested in more expanded and bonus content, check out my website (**kmalady.com**). You can find other fun information there, including a **free prequel novella** told from the point of view of the Great Matron (when she was known only as Bittállí), focusing on her reason for revenge, and **extended scenes** in the Great Matron and the Voice's points of views (taken from chapter 34), along with a look at where the Voice is now (who will return in book two).

I've also got several other books upcoming, including book two of The Ascend Trials, and more fantasy romance and romantic fantasy stories.

SNEAK PEEK OF BOOK TWO

G race and her friends will return for Book Two. Check out a short sneak peek below.

It's dark; a single window lights a small circular room. Wet tracks run down stone walls like sweat and the scent of sea salt tinges the air. There's a hazy quality to everything, more real than the many dreams I've had since defeating the Eósy and sealing the Gates, similar to how it felt when I experienced the swell of opponents' memories. But since that day, I've had no confrontations that would bring about memory magic, assuming it even still works with the wall as it is. And never was I able to move around without the dream's maker controlling me.

Something tinkles under my feet when I spin a half circle to better inspect the not-dreamscape. Glass litters the floor and I skitter backward to avoid piercing my bare feet. The back of my knees hit something hard, and I slip down with a thump, knocking a candle to the ground as my backside connects with a wooden bench behind me.

A thin sleeping bag sits beside the bench, with a person-shaped lump resting on it. The body slinks into a sitting position and turns to face me, revealing stark blond hair glinting in the moonlight and a familiar, but pale, face. The Voice's, no, Leyden's bright eyes widen in surprise.

"Grace?"

I wake with a gasp, a heaviness on my torso holding me down and unable to surge out of bed. I wriggle until the prison releases me.

Tans groans into my neck and snakes his arms around me again, pulling me to him and locking me back into the cage of his body. His fingers trail over the scars on my hips under my nightshirt.

"Was it the dragon or the sprite?" Even in almost-sleep, he speaks slowly and clearly, allowing me to understand his words in the language I've spent the last six months learning.

I inhale and release the fear the nightmare left behind. Unlike the memory of my past sins, this dream didn't leave me feeling nauseous and guilty.

"Neither," I whisper into the dark of our shared bedroom, my voice shaky and broken. "Something different."

www.ingramcontent.com/pod-product-compliance
Lightning Source LLC
Chambersburg PA
CBHW061046190726
48286CB00006B/1636